Red Solstice

An MIA's Hell, Lust, and Life

Copyright © 2012 by Franz X. Beisser III

First Printing March 2012
Second Printing April 2013

http://www.fxbiii.com

All rights reserved. No part of this book may be reproduced in any form by any electronic or mechanical means, including information storage and retrieval systems, without permission in writing from the author and publisher, except by a reviewer who may quote brief passages in a review.

Published by FE LLC
1467 Joppa Mill Road
Bedford, VA 24523
All rights reserved.

ISBN: 0985763302

ISBN-13: 978-0-9857633-0-5

Also by Franz X. Beisser:

A Time & Place: The Making of an Immigrant

Come to a time and place few ever see. Over 100 autobiographical short stories and anecdotes that paint a picture of how an immigrant family was made in post-war Germany.

Remembering Emily

Intimate and poignant memoir about the life and passing of the author's first wife Emily.

I never knew my father.
He left before I was four years old.
He went to war and never returned.
Missing in action, they say.

For more than sixty years
I've wondered what might have been.

I had to write this book,
To cross the troubled waters,
To feel his struggles, as they may have been,
To rest my mind.

How could I find his words?
How could I portray his pain?
How could I calm my own nagging heart?

I myself needed to put on his shoes;
Step into a time that I never knew.
Yes, it is he I needed to become—
To at last get to know him.

AUTHOR'S NOTE

My father, Franz X. Beisser, was born in Munich Germany on February 29, 1908. He married my mother, Friedl, in 1935. I was born in 1940, my sister in 1943. My parents, sister, and I lived in Munich when World War II raged.

My father, a master precision tool and die-maker, worked at a firm that specialized in camera shutters and other instruments for the medical field. To keep up with Hitler's war effort, the company switched to engineering and perfecting military parts and mechanisms. One highly classified and revolutionary project kept my father from being drafted into action. He never mentioned nor talked about the project's purpose, not even to his wife. Only in the days before his departure, to fight on the German front in Russia, did he confide to my mother about the secret project.

At the age of thirty-five, after the project's perfection in early 1943, my father was conscripted into the army. He received his basic combat training in France. My mother, my sister, and I stayed behind in an apartment in Munich. Soon the bombings by the Allied Forces became so fierce, our window curtains were singed from the explosions. Air raids, seeking shelter in the basement, and bombings became our frequent routine.

While my father trained in France, women and children were encouraged to evacuate to the country. We settled in Griesbach, a small town in Lower Bavaria. After France, my father spent a few weeks with his family, at which time—unbeknownst to him—my mother conceived.

He entered combat as part of the 2000-kilometer-long Russian front. At first his letters from the front were frequent. Soon they became sparse. Finally they halted. My father, a World War II German infantry soldier, is listed as missing in action. His last letter, in mid-1944, came from the battlefield near the Crimean Peninsula, on the Black Sea.

In 1950 my father was declared dead by the German authorities. My mother remarried in December of that year. In March 1955, the family immigrated to the United States.

This book is a fictional account of what might have happened to my father. All accounts of family and its activities in Germany are true. Some family names were changed. Characters other than immediate family are fictitious. The locations are real, but the cities, terrain, and towns outside Germany are described fictitiously. Dates and events, though placed in a proper historical sequence, are not necessarily accurate. The historical accounts and geographical locations, however, are based on facts.

My father would be over 100 years old now. The hope of him coming home, or his family learning of his whereabouts, is practically nil.

I wrote this novel from my father's viewpoint. To find his heart and soul, I offered my own experiences of those early years and my lifelong yearning to finally meet my father as a man of valor and integrity.

Franz X. Beisser, III

BOOK ONE

1

Steel crashed against steel. I shuddered at its finality. Blindfolded and prostrate, I lay limp on the floor, beaten—inhaling the filth under my chin. I heard the trucks roar away. The pounding stopped.

"Deutschland Über Alles—Ha! . . . Deutschland Über Nichts! . . . Franz Brunner, a prisoner of the Russians—the Russians! Hitler, do you hear?"

I discerned raspy breathing and blubbering moans from my fellow captive Germans—my battle buddies. My heart thumped. Flies buzzed. Odors of fright, sweat, and waste mixed with the searing heat. At a distance someone barked orders; someone laughed. Nearby I sensed no hostility—no footsteps—no brutes.

I fumbled with my blindfold. . . . *Is someone watching? Maybe?* I yanked off the rag. My eyes, forced shut for nearly two days, slowly adjusted to the sun's glare. We were on a train, locked in a stinking cage—a cattle car!

"Hey, nobody is watching," I said. "Take those blindfolds off."

My listless brothers lay piled on the plank floor of the cattle car, wilted and exposed to the searing sun. One by one they slowly untangled, as would a handful of balled earthworms, then crawled toward the nearest steel bars to lean against.

No roof for shade. *Scheisse* stuck everywhere. I grasped the steel bars and pulled myself to a half-sitting position. Thirst became the new torture. My cracked lips burned in the sun.

Loose straw had gathered into the corners except where grungy animal dung plastered it elsewhere. A watering trough, hooked to the bars on one side, showed a thick coating of dried filth. Under it was packed a crust of grain, straw, and manure. Thousands of flies swarmed—aggravated—determined to suck us dry.

Beyond the men, the last of Company C, I saw our car formed the tail end of a long train. The men sat slumped. Vacant and hollow eyes spoke in silence. Some showed anger, some bewilderment. A dejected lot, stunned to see how quickly the unity and determination of a fighting force had degenerated.

Having seen enough, I covered my face with the blindfold rag. Time stopped. Only the mind whirred on. We waited . . . waited. *For what?* A disturbing thought.

Karl broke the static quiet.

"Franz, what's next?" His hopeful tone moved me. As the eldest of the group, I suppose he considered me a leader. I took my time to respond.

"Don't know, Karl," I said, "we're beaten. They gonna aim at our minds next."

Karl and a few others nodded.

Again silence. The sun continued to cook the last bit of sanity out of my brain. I found my canteen, shook it . . . empty.

"It happened fast. Huh?" muttered Otto. "Only sixty-two of us when all hell broke loose." Every man digested the words.

"Not counting the wounded on stretchers behind the kitchen," volunteered Dietrich.

"Twenty-six right here, I think," said Sepperl.

"Hell," Walter snarled as he slammed his empty canteen on the floor. "If they hadn't stripped me of my last grenade, a handful of them bastards would tend the fires of hell right now."

The comment took a few moments to settle.

Then Werner said, "Damn, this tank headed straight for me, wanted to grind me into the dirt." After he gathered a shallow breath he added, "Poor Oskar got buried that way."

Only groans and grunts followed. The men tentatively stretched their bodies, testing their pounded ribs. I too winced as

I attempted to take a deep breath. To stay lucid, we instinctively muttered and questioned each other.

Still trying to adjust to the light, I looked for the sergeant. "Hey, Sarge," I called. No answer.

A young soldier spoke. "I saw him scoot on elbows and knees over the hill before hell broke loose. . . . I guess he smelled something wasn't right."

"Poor guy. Took care of us right to the end, his end."

More silence.

"I almost puked back there," said Dietrich. "Four barbarians opened fire at the wounded boys on their cots." Shifting on his elbows he added, "They massacred all eight. Rifles on hips, like shooting rats. I saw the devil in their eyes."

"Didn't our men have weapons?" I asked.

"No."

"Too damn bad," said one of the men. "They could've gotten a few shots off before being stitched to their cots."

"Yeah . . . too bad they didn't."

The men slumped a little lower. No one spoke for hours.

Sixteen-year-old Konrad broke the silence. He kneeled and stuck his face between the steel bars. "I want to go home now," he sobbed. His chest heaved as he cried for his mother. His knuckles turned white gripping the bars.

I am sure most of the men wanted to sob then. Tears would overwhelm later—each man—in his own time.

It was late summer—1944. *What do they want with me? Why didn't they shoot me?*

Finally, the train started to roll. The stirring air forced the flies to lay low. Only a few pestered my mouth and neck in search for a little moisture. The breeze whipped straw. Dust swirled. Into vastness and distance the train rumbled.

I lay beaten. My head rested on a hardened crust of manure and straw. I slowly summarized the past brutal events.

2

Weeks earlier, while we maneuvered into position to take our stand, I saw to our right a vast body of water and to our left a swamp that stretched for many kilometers. I wondered then what brainwashed officer, infatuated with the superior race madness, led us into such a fix. I had the distinct feeling of being herded, like a pack of rats, into a sack.

When the ground attack came, I took cover behind my mortar piece. For days we had lobbed shells at the Russians. Then the pot boiled over. The Russians countered. The hordes came in waves. Enemy foot soldiers oozed out of the woods in the manner of brown lava. Werner, our lone machine gunner, mowed down as many as he could. They kept coming. The new wave of men grabbed the weapons from their wounded and dying comrades. The hordes crept within a stone's throw. The final barrage from enemy artillery, mortar, hand grenades, and machine gun fire heaved the ground. The shockwaves pummeled eardrums. Explosions flung clods of dirt and rocks. I lost all sense of my whereabouts. The world caved in. My last thoughts were, *No more letters from home.*

When my head cleared, the hiss of scorched equipment, the smell of gunpowder, the stench of sizzling rubber and searing flesh insulted my very soul. Looking up, a sputtering tire being eaten by little flaming demons stared at me. The melting rubber dripped and slithered to the ground as it searched to devour one last morsel. The wounded screamed in agony and were silenced with a shot, rescued from madness.

A Red Army soldier hovered and blocked the sun. He grabbed and yanked my shirt to have me stand. His steel-blue eyes cut me into fork-sized bites. The heavy base of my mortar piece pinned my left foot to the ground. While I scrambled to free myself, he disarmed me of weapons and battle pack. He slipped my pocket watch and wedding ring into his breast pocket and added my pocketknife to the bulge in his trousers.

Increasingly, more Russian soldiers took part in the mop-up, stripping the dead and dying of their belongings. More single shots reverberated among the melee. None from our weapons. They herded the able men to a guarded group. . . . my foot stabbed with pain. I thought of *Sieg Heil!* Out loud I said, "*Scheisse!*" One menacing brute, his eyebrows furled, chin stuck to one side, prodded my backside with his rifle, goading me toward the small group. I heard more orders barked and saw mad men responding. Their demeanor showed they would rather have killed us than fool with rounding us up. In the huddle of frightened Germans, I felt even God had forsaken me.

When the last dying man gurgled his final breath and lay sprawled, hugging the dirt, the captors turned to us in the group. Our hands tied behind our backs, they yelled, cursed, and prodded us to walk, and walk. . . .The knoll behind us, our last stand, oozed a ghostly quiet. The funeral over.

For hours, laboring breaths and boots trudged through tall grass and brush. *"What do they want from me? Did they save the few of us to be delivered to some deranged sadist so he can kill us one at a time and thus get his jollies?"*

The pain in my foot pounded. I lagged behind.

"Are you all right?" One of my buddies hollered, noticing my hobbling.

"I'm good," I managed to say before a vicious rifle jab in the ribs jarred me erect to move faster. More than once the brutes kicked and poked to keep the men in a tight bunch.

Finally, as dark settled in, we stumbled into a clearing. Trucks of all sizes were in line ready to roll. Soldiers milled among the diesel fumes and dust, resembling a disturbed nest of ants. The commanding officer slowly made his way down our lineup and held the gaze of every prisoner, his stare fixed, cold and unflinching. Pure hatred. I smelled his breath. A slight snarl revealed his eyeteeth. Finally, he gave his orders.

Systematically, they blindfolded us. I'm sure all the men thought we were being readied for execution. "Jesus save us!"

one cried out. A swift backhand struck his face. A different silence seeped in. A silence of loneliness, of nakedness, of darkness. Every fiber and muscle in me tensed. I twitched and trembled and could hardly draw a breath. Through the blindfold I sensed pointed rifles and the watchful eyes of guards.

Headlights glared, exposing our dejected group. Nothing of us was hidden. In their eyes we were all Nazis, despised, the symbol of evil. Whatever they planned doing to us, they would feel no remorse.

Suddenly, strong hands and arms pushed and manhandled me until I landed on a pile of human beings. The bodies were piled two layers deep, like cordwood, face down, in the back of a small flatbed truck. The bottom layer of men with heads forward. The top layer with heads toward the rear. I could feel the engine idling. I considered myself fortunate being among the top layer. However, when the captors ratcheted straps down on me, I wasn't so sure, my face mashed against someone's boot. My right hip rested on the canteen hanging on the man's belt below me.

Soon the truck jerked forward, and others followed. Tree limbs and bushes smacked against the vehicle. Every hole and rock sent punishing jolts through our bodies. The men on the bottom gasped in unison when the truck dropped into a rut. Likewise, men on top groaned when the truck bounced back. The straps did their job, cutting deep into ribs and muscles. Steady breathing became impossible. My lungs held little air; the relentless pounding made sure of that. Pain stabbed from spine to chest.

How much more? How much longer? I could no longer brace against the jolts. The man under me became as a sack of wheat. Some men soiled themselves. The stench added a new insult.

Finally on a gravel road, the driver revved the engine. However, the frequent ruts and potholes sent vicious stabs of pain through every muscle. I imagined being tenderized, as the Huns did their meat under saddles while riding.

I endured the torture all the while despising the Führer, determined not to succumb for him or his vision.

—

At last, a lone train whistle wailed in the distance. It sighed, "Good-bye." My tortured mind saw my wife and children waving for the last time while a whistle wailed. I wept then, but not now.

Coal smoke invaded my nostrils. The hiss of a steam engine breathed like a resting dragon. The truck backed until it met hard resistance. My head smashed against the tailgate. Voices, gruff and jabbering, strangely foreign, invaded my ears. Someone loosed the straps and untied our hands. Two pulled me unto the tailgate, then, still face down, they grabbed sleeves and pant legs and pitched me into a larger container. Like a sack of potatoes I slid and crashed against something hard. Grunts and moans spewed from every man as they bounced and bumped against the others. Still blindfolded, I struggled to scoot out of the way, then slumped and waited for the next insult. It soon came. Something heavy slid across metal, and with a shattering metallic reverberation, it slammed shut. Steel against steel, its finality absolute.

—

Now, the train rocked on. Amber fields, thatched huts, and hunched-over peasants, flickered by. The rocking and clacking should have lulled me to sleep, but pulsating pain in my foot smothered all other awareness. I looked and noticed that my gashed boot oozed blood from its split. One by one, I loosened the taut laces. With each release I felt the foot swell as a lump of yeast dough. I held my breath. The bloody heel emerged first. The still-soft blood helped peel off the sock. I gaped at my smashed toes. The big toe's nail stood erect, its flesh flattened to one side, the bone crushed and separated. *If the brute had realized this, he would have shot me on the spot.* I also knew all too well, the next man in charge, wherever the destination, would surely arrive at the same conclusion. My hope of a future quickly faded.

With the canteen dry and the medical kit confiscated, I couldn't clean the wound. The swollen foot, dark red with blood, stared at me. I covered it with my blindfold and hoped to keep the swirling dirt and green flies from the raw tissue.

The sun baked. We rocked on. Two men tried vomiting through the bars, their heads banged against the steel in rhythm with the train. Too weak to hold on, they slid down and sagged to the floor. Their bile mixed with the loose straw. Vacant eyes in other men revealed a wish to die. This, the second day since the men in brown took us prisoner.

—

Before dusk, more German soldiers piled on. Again, the steel door rammed shut. A spindly old truck with solid rubber tires, pulled alongside the cattle car. The driver filled our trough with water from a rusty barrel. Company C scrambled, canteens in hand, to the trough. Crud, straw, and bits of manure swirled in the water as we submerged our canteens. We drank and dipped again. The mixture thickened toward the bottom, but still wet. The new men, confused and bewildered, sat and stared.

Forty-six men now on board, an impersonal and sullen bunch. Some, who had caps, pulled them down until their ears stuck out. No one talked. Not everyone could find a wall to lean against. Dejected, they sat back to back in the middle of the cattle car; we stared. No introductions. No questions, like, "Hey, what happened?" Or, "How are you men?" Our own misery offered enough to deal with. I waited for the muck in my canteen to settle before I took another swig.

To my right, the sun set in a sliver of fire. I took notice of our direction: northeast. The air cooled. The flies hunkered down. The smell eased as uniforms dried. With dark approaching, men collapsed into whatever space the bars or the fellow next to them provided. Soon the night draped a welcoming death cloak over the group. We rolled on.

I felt chilled. *A fever? No hesitation with a quick bullet.*

Stretched out on the filth-encrusted plank floor, my head propped by the hardened crust at its edge, I rested. Not long after teetering into sleep a strange sensation aroused me. Along with the throbbing of my foot came a tingling sensation. Not a tingle of nerves, but a tingle of being touched. The sickle moon offered a little light. I strained to focus on the gray-colored rag that covered my foot. The tingling continued. Fully awake and curious, I noticed the rag slightly moving. Something dark scurried across its corner only to disappear into the shadows. *Rats! Rats are chewing on me!* Desperate, I loosened my belt and slid my pants down enough to tuck the injured toes out of reach of the ravenous critters. The rest of the night I stayed on rat alert. My mind saw tiny beady eyes, fast moving little razor teeth. I imagined my foot being chewed off by morning.

—

Day three. My foot now noticeably redder, showed infection extending to my ankle. My toenail and bone still stuck out. Instead of dark red and bloody, it looked an ashen gray. Only a thin edge of congealed blood ringed the area where bone met flesh. I looked for my sock to slip over the exposed toes, but it wasn't where I thought I dropped it. I spotted a semblance of it among the men near the latrine corner.

Not wanting to stir the others, I whispered, "Hey Max, would you pitch that sock to me?" He made the effort.

In my hand I held only the stretch part above the ankles. The blood soaked portion, along with the wool, satisfied the rats—gone, devoured. I shuddered to think them still hiding among the limp men, or tightly packed inside the mixture of grain and manure under the trough.

Max motioned to me, "Check out Wolfgang."

Wolfgang's legs stuck straight out, his head hung sharply forward. This alone not unusual, but he sat erect hovering off the floor. Herbert scooted over and knelt beside the man.

"He's hanged himself!" he said loud enough for all to hear.

I too crawled over and gasped, "He's cold."

I shuddered to see the blue tongue and bulging half-closed eyes. We slid back to our spots and stared into distance. I wanted revenge. The train rocked on.

A time later I spoke to anyone who may have wanted to listen, "This wretched train isn't the end. If they wanted us dead, they had their chance." Some nodded, some never changed their expression, and some, I'm sure, never heard a word.

Wolfgang killed himself. We saw exactly the method and the result. He stood up, took off his belt, looped it around his neck and a steel bar and buckled it. Since the belt was twisted behind his head, he must have turned his body until little slack remained. To generate sufficient force to snap his neck and choke, Wolfgang likely kicked his legs straight out to create the sharp fall. The head and belt slid down the steel bar until it suddenly stopped at the cross bracing about a meter off the floor. I pondered. *Clean, sudden—no more thirst. No salt mines.*

We placed the dead man along the north wall, facing out, his head covered with a blindfold rag. One of the men found the strength to say a short prayer. To me, at that point a waste. Prayer and hatred don't mix.

The train pushed on. *Water! Water,* screamed my brain. My swollen tongue made speaking and swallowing difficult. We all gaped and stretched our jaws, trying to lose the gagged feeling. I had difficulty focusing. Hallucinations, in sync with the pounding heartbeat, flickered and danced before me. My burdened mind could not vanquish the dead man hanging. The stifling heat wilted even the strong, reducing words spoken to a few. *Did the flies get their fill? Or did they check out the dead man before the rats got there.* I shuddered.

Late in the afternoon the sky darkened, the wind whipped, then vanished. One man cried out, "God, send us rain!"

Moments later, all heads turned toward the distant peals of thunder. I imagined a taste of rain on parched lips. The sky churned. Dark clouds wrestled and rolled ever closer. Emboldened gusts carried the smell of rain. My brain burned with fever. I tried to devise a way to catch the precious rain, should it come. Then the wind died; my heart died with it. Moments later it roared again.

"It's coming now," one man gasped. "Come, rain, come!" It did. We all faced heavenward. Some stood holding to the bars, some knelt with heads back and mouths wide open. Others cupped their hands. Still others diverted the rain running down the bars with fingers into their canteens. I did the same. When I realized it would pour a little longer, I also directed the flow into my boot with the other hand. One last lightning strike. Enough! . . . As quickly as the storm hit, it abated. The men slumped. Some sucked and chewed on their wet sleeves. We tasted water, but not nearly enough. I gulped down the one good swallow out of my boot. After it hit my belly, I remembered the dried blood.

Hours and distance became an empty blur as the train pushed toward an unknown. It continued to wring from us all self-esteem and human dignity. We would have sold our souls for a long drink of water. My eyes burned as if rolled in a puddle of salt water. The night, or death, encroached again. I loosened my shirt and covered my face.

—

At daybreak of day four, the temperature felt noticeably cooler. When the smoke from the engine didn't waft into our car, I could smell the freshness of a forest. Squinting, I saw trees wave as our cage passed.

"No!" I gasped out loud. Two men precariously hung, dead, swinging from their necks in rhythm with the train. I balled my fists and remained silent. Later, we strained and dragged, with energy drawn only from one's inner spirit, to give the two a resting place—in the corner. Lying on their sides, one man's arm laid draped over the one already there, the third man's did the same over the second; brothers in death, all facing the Russian vastness.

The steam whistle blasted. Our train slowed and rolled into a fairly large town. A few men perked up, hopeful. At first, the town stayed hidden as we pulled between two other trains. Soon after, we eased over to the outside track and came to a gradual halt. The locomotive belched one more exhausted puff and then followed with a lengthy hiss. The sun hung overhead, humming with a high-pitched sting. At the head of the train men shouted, gave orders. To let us know we weren't forgotten, a yard worker climbed between our car and the one in front and flipped two heavy levers. Stepping to the side, he waved his arms. With a jerk the front of the train slowly pulled away and left us sitting on the track, bewildered and exposed. One lone cage.

We lay, waiting . . . waiting.

This is my last sunset, I thought. My left arm hung from between the bars. *I'm going to meet my brother.* A warm sense of peace washed over me. Suddenly, a touch on my hand flashed me back to life. I did not want to come back from the warmth of everlasting peace. I turned to look. There, quiet and still, stood a woman. *An angel!* She looked straight into my eyes. The setting sun had moved behind the cattle car. Her face however, illuminated by one last golden ray, showed a lovely, broad face with wide-set green eyes. Her pale, pinned-back hair revealed defined cheekbones. I stared in disbelief. Again I felt her touch on my hanging arm. This time she placed a tin mug in my hand. With both of her hands she held mine and the mug. Steady and sure, she reached through the bars and gently guided me to drink. Her eyes never left mine as the mug found my lips. Cool water! My hands trembled; I struggled to drink. Determined, holding steady to the mug and my hand, she continued to aid my feeble efforts. Sip after tiny sip, controlling my drooling and difficulty of swallowing, she stood there until the mug slowly emptied. An amazing calm washed over me. She did not smile, but had an expression of pity. Her lips slightly parted, wanting to speak, said nothing. *An angel for sure.*

After easing back to rest I turned to steal one last glimpse of the woman—she had vanished. My eyes fell shut, but there, burned into soul and mind, I saw her face. I feasted on that memory, recalling also a telling scar on her cheekbone.

"Thank you, thank you," I whispered. "I wish I knew your name." I drifted off to sleep.

During the night, the jolt of being hitched to a new train, jarred me awake. Our car was now much closer to the locomotive. A bright light bounced toward us. *Yes, the angel sent a water truck!* Amazingly, the driver pulled a hose from the truck, unhooked the trough, and rinsed it before he filled it. I, the only one awake and able, scooted to the trough. I wanted to lay my head into the water. *This water is not yours alone,* my conscience warned. *Share this water with the men before the train starts and sloshes it from the trough.* I dipped a few swallows into my canteen, rinsed the sediment loose, then dumped the murky soup through the bars. Systematically and with honor, I repeatedly filled my canteen and dragged myself to each man. The angel gave me the strength. Some at first could not swallow. Some, their eyes had rolled back. Some heaved and some burned with fever. I persisted through the night and gave every man a drink. My foot screamed, my head pounded, I collapsed into sleep.

—

When night relinquished its chill to day five, the new whistle sighed. Through weary slits I glanced at my dying world. Stalin, his fading portrait painted on boards of a defunct water tower at the edge of town, stared at me. One eye, strangely hollow, caused by a missing board, seemed to bore at my brain.

Soon, the weary chug of a new black machine dominated . . . moving on toward the east. The rhythm of track and wheels slowed. Our car responded to being slung from side to side, by always finding both rails of the track. A few men, on hands and knees, inched their way to the trough to fill their canteens. Soon, as before, it supplied no more. Our thirst remained. The constant ache in my middle back, the rapid heartbeat, and shortness of breath combined to send a signal of my own body's poisoning. The dead men blended with the floor as swirling straw piled around their necks and ears.

The train's whistle howled and whined, echoing off woods and canyons—imitating lonesome wails of hungry wolves.

3

Groaning on, ever eastward, the valleys narrowed to ravines. The rail tracks wrestled streams for space through narrow gorges. Rugged peaks replaced the hills. I imagined being inhaled by a dragon with one intent—to swallow forever. I lay flat on my back, eyes blurred, and recalled blips of days long ago when a train built to be enjoyed by humans carried Friedl and me to the mountains—the days of youth, days of life and joy. Now, as the locomotive pushed ever deeper into the raw and cold of strange mountains, I questioned my resolve. *Do I want to face what lay ahead?*

Sleep, deep sleep, eluded me again. I shivered all night from fever. The raw wrap of a new cold added to my despair. Convinced all things beautiful and good had vanished, I lay motionless, eyes half open. Death now only a matter of how long I stayed sane. The toxins in me cramped my body. I welcomed the frequent spells of warmth and the bliss delirium brought.

—

At daybreak of day six, a gripping mist blanketed the world. The engine's whistle signaled to a town ahead. Silence. The death train rolled to a stop. Not a breeze stirred. A new odor affronted my nostrils—one not from the living.

I discerned a long loading dock. Ghostly outlines of uniformed men with rifles sticking from their shoulders faced our way. I shuddered. Two of them stepped closer for a better look. I sensed their pompous arrogance. Within seconds, as if having seen enough, they walked away.

Moments later the military men returned, with them an odd man in civilian clothes. He stood next to me, his black leather gloves and matching boots seemed to spit at me.

"*Guten Tag*," he said in perfect German. No one responded.

"How many of you are there?" he continued. "How many?" he said a bit louder. Again none of us answered.

"You," he said as he shifted his spit-polished boots toward me, "I know you can understand me. You have come to the end of your journey. Tell me then, how many men are in this car."

I didn't move my head and hesitated as I tried to wet my lips, then hoarsely whispered, "Dead or alive?"

"What do you mean?"

"For . . . ty . . . six," I struggled to say.

"I see," he said, then faced the other officers.

I did hear him say, "You have come to the end of your journey." *Why am I not glad? This isn't Siberia.* With a childlike effort, I positioned my bare foot near the loose boot hoping it would look normal.

A burly older man, with thick fumbling fingers, unlocked the sliding bars. The door crashed open. No one stirred. A Russian soldier bounded onto the platform holding a bucket and mop. He threw the mop aside, and from a spigot in the foundation wall drew enough water to give the bucket a quick slosh. He then placed the full bucket of water, along with a dipper, in the center of the platform.

"Water!" I gasped. No one moved. I attempted to sit up, only to roll back and whack my head on the steel bars. When no one else made an effort, the soldiers dragged several, face down, toward the bucket on the platform.

The men in brown yelled and stomped and tried to wake the sleeping. I heard groans and mumblings. A few bodies stirred; none made it to the bucket. One soldier poked the listless with the mop handle, another used his boot on the ones who crawled in the wrong direction. Two soldiers repeatedly kicked the bodies that failed to move, snorted and cursed. Finally they realized the futility. In disgust, they dragged the additional dead to the pile of the other three corpses.

When the captors became aware that none of the living could sit and drink, they placed an enameled wash bowl, filled with water, on the platform. One of the brutes yanked two listless men by their collars toward the water bowl. He simultaneously let their heads drop into the bowl, that caused it to flip over and spill the water. Snarling with hate, the ruffian took the empty bowl and smashed it over the men's heads. He then stomped off to retrieve the full mop bucket and sloshed the two as they lay helpless. He dowsed us all, one bucket full after the other. No one stopped him. Chuckles all around.

Being dowsed with cool water did revive the dying. Slowly, for several hours, with a new resolve to live, we helped one another drink. The men in brown had a job to do and made sure all of us were attended to. In controlled intervals, we passed mugs of water to each man. Eventually, all drank a full mug of water.

—

The pompous German-speaking ass reappeared. He called out a name from a list. No answer. He called the name louder. Again, no answer. One man gently elbowed the fellow next to him. The speaker stepped toward him, bent to shake his shoulders, and asked again, "Auerbach?" The young soldier barely nodded. Guards pulled him by his shirt sleeves to one end of the platform. Subsequently, the ass called all names. They dragged the men and deposited each on the platform in the order called. The dead, also called, didn't answer. It tightened my belly to realize they'd never again answer their children's call, nor their wives'. When all were accounted for, they again passed the mug down the row.

"Is anyone sick or wounded?" boomed the next question.

My heart stopped. . . . *A bullet.* . . . *this is it.* No one said a word or raised a hand. A few of my brothers glanced at me.

"No one?" A bit more emphatic.

Timidly, I raised my hand. The spit-shined fellow did not call me from the ranks, but squatted to look over my foot. He made no further comment. My angst remained.

The Germans, guarded by six soldiers, sat back to back in two rows; a group of obedient mutts. My exposed foot obviously now a point of stares. A truck hauled the eight dead men away. Their boots appeared again a half hour later.

The quiet crept on. The drizzle saturated our clothes. Ominous clouds clung to the mountain slopes. An old woman, pushing a wooden wheelbarrow, approached the loading dock. She scooped several armfuls of folded clothes out of the wheelbarrow and dumped them on the dock. She jabbered and waved her arms, then turned to one of the officers and handed him the tally.

A one-size-fits-all baggy trouser, along with a rope to hold it up, landed in our laps. A shirt and underpants added a personal touch. At least the outfit had no horizontal stripes. Next, they commanded us to remove our boots and socks. The boots, carefully kept in pairs, joined the ones from the dead. The socks left the platform in the wheelbarrow pushed by the washerwoman.

With great patience, the captors encouraged us to drink every half hour or so. Gradually, like a once-wilted vine, we revived. Apparently the men in brown knew this routine well.

—

Toward the afternoon, an enticing smell of fresh-baked bread wafted toward us. All heads turned to search for the source. I didn't know I was hungry. A man, dressed in white linen, dropped a sack of dark loaves onto the platform. We intently focused on the fellow cutting the hard-crusted loaves of rye bread into chunks. Going down the line, a soldier doled out a chunk to each. Without saliva, the bread had no taste, and proved difficult to chew or swallow. Our captors realized this and allowed each to dip our portion in the pail of water. Every bite slowly revived the taste buds. Although soggy, at the moment it was the best thing I ever ate. Again the men in brown showed patience and gave us plenty of time to eat, sip more water, sit quietly—a pleasant thing. *I'm still alive.*

After a full day of sitting, we were ordered to stand. Most of us had not stood in five days. I dreaded to exert pressure on my foot, but didn't want to be singled out. The men teetered and staggered. Most hunched over and reached for the cattle car's bars to hold on to. More than one man dropped to his knee. In due time we shuffled forward; our newly issued clothes under our left arm, the right hand on the man's right shoulder in front of us. A single column of men groped their way down the platform steps, crossed the cobblestone road, slowly tottered through a rutted alley, and on toward a river's edge. The earlier mist increased to a heavy drizzle. The runoff water, mixed with waste, also made its way to the river. Reconstituted smells from dark alleys, mossy rock walls, and outhouses introduced the town. People in the street stopped and stared. Others peeped at the strange barefooted march from behind thin window curtains.

At the riverbank the washerwoman awaited us, still blathering and waving the new tally. Several long, halved logs, parked on flat rocks, served as benches on which we placed our new garments. We were ordered to strip down. Our uniforms formed a useless heap in the weeds. Undergarments became a new cache for the washerwoman. Naked, standing in line like begging pups, we held out our hand to receive a small block of lye soap and a tattered rag. Now, the last bit of dignity peeled from us, rag and soap in hand, exposed to our last pimple, we stumbled into the frigid river. The washerwoman craned her neck, not missing the show—her jaw still flailed.

The river's flow proved too brisk for two of our men. Wading into the river, they stumbled and slipped on hidden rocks, lost their balance, and rolled down river. A sure signal to all not to take the river lightly. Two of our men near the mishap, forsook soap and rag, and scrambled to help the two back on their feet. The uniformed guards stood, arms folded, and chuckled at the early evening's entertainment.

The bone-chilling water rinsed my bleeding foot, and emphasized the pounding in my head. When I looked down at the rushing stream I lost my balance and fell. I crawled to a depth where I could stretch out and let myself be dragged by the current. My body gently wrapped around a boulder, as my arms and legs flowed free. A thousand fingers massaged the weariness and former death grip from my neck and back. Every pore inhaled the rejuvenating newness.

After the washing, we dressed in our new garb and returned, by lantern, to the depot. A pair of boots and two worn rags, replacing our socks, awaited us. The replacement boots, all worn, looked all the same size. Some of the brogan's soles had separated from the leather. Some missed a heel. In others, the air flowed through the soles. I could not tell the left from the right; they were shoes.

I had worn my brother's boots since my call to active duty. He died of a bullet to his head within months of the Poland campaign. My brother had painted a white patch on the upper inside of each boot. On it he methodically printed his full name and serial number. My mother, who had received his few belongings, urged me to try them on. They fit much better than the stiff new issue. Now, they too were history.

Again we sat on the depot, this time mere bodies. The uniform we fought under part of a heap. Things we treasured confiscated. Like helpless and frightened infants, we keenly sensed our vulnerability and nakedness. All we needed to drive us further down was a given number. *Hell, even a dog had a name.*

When I pulled the new boot on my good foot, an officer, pistol on his belt, decided to have a look at my mangled toes. The recent walk to and from the river forced new blood to mix with the filth of the street. My foot's infection had spread to beyond the ankle. New hope for a future came when the interpreter stated, "We will have a doctor look at this." *No bullet for now!*

First, a pair of medics at a military post took a look. It didn't take them long to conclude a quick fix wasn't within their skills. Soon, my hands tied to the cargo bed of a vehicle, they transported me to the town's doctor.

The doctor greeted the interruption with a frown and a huff. Up in age, and slightly hunched forward, he didn't make eye contact. With a gentle voice and few words he pointed to where he wanted me to lie. The driver watched with stoic indifference. I lay sprawled and stared at the cracked plaster of a low ceiling. The doctor studied my vital signs, then gingerly washed my foot and bent to have a close look. He probed the wounded area with the backside of a scalpel, noting where my pain sensitivity ended. From a drawer he pulled two straps. The gentle doctor positioned my arms on the examining table and strapped me down. When the ratchet clicked its last click, I could no longer rise to see the goings on.

The doctor started to poke and snip, causing increasingly more pain to charge through my body. I attempted to claw at something while cold sweat poured from my head. With calculated coolness, he tightly wrapped my ankle then clamped the wounded foot to a hard surface. He rummaged through his toolbox. Within seconds he began to saw my bones. Great slobbering gasps of spit, air, and screams burst from me. Blankets of black clouds flooded my brain. Repeated jolts of pain kept me from fainting. The guard stood over me, pushed my head to the bench with both hands, and held it there. When hell received its satisfaction, a noisome smoke invaded my nostrils—burning flesh. I wished I'd died on the train.

—

My recovery bed became a straw sack at the town's temporary post, where the captors doled out food twice a day. An impersonal young soldier brought my portion to the barracks. In the morning bread and hot tea. In the evening more bread and hot vegetable stew with assorted bits of meat or pork fat. On other days a bowl of gooey oatmeal satisfied the pangs. The interpreter checked on me the second day. In a matter-of-fact tone he snapped off instructions.

"Drink as much water as you can. Walk to the latrine when you can stand the pain." He pointed to a padded crutch, made from a tree limb.

"Sir," I said to the interpreter, "what did they do to my foot?"

"The doctor amputated your big toe and the first joint of the one next to it."

"How soon will I walk again?"

"That depends on how hard you work at it," he said, as he walked away. *At least I would walk again.*

My foot, wrapped with gauze and protective rags, looked like a giant club. To protect it, a block of wood stuck out the bottom, and one thinner out the front; primitive, but sufficient. The barrack guard, the only person to check on me, sneered each time he made his round.

I'll be hopping from now on, maybe for the rest of my life. A sobering thought. I lay down and contemplated the tent ceiling. Black-encircled holes, peppered the area where the stove pipe exited the canvas roof. During a sunny day, the holes sparkled. At night, as new sparks spewed from the pipe, more holes burned into the canvas and stared down like red-encircled demon's eyes.

Sporadic sleep left much time to think. Plenty of fluids did their job to fill the bucket next to the bunk. Much pondering, thinking and staring, morphed me into a keen and calculating cat. I noticed the smallest details. Everything interested me, but much also irritated. An idle mind is definitely a cauldron in which the devil can stir. A mental crash loomed. I considered my options.

With the straw sack folded under my head, I laid out two scenarios. One of a miserable cripple having lost his self-esteem, his family, and his sense of belonging. He could not see five meters in front of him because of self-pity. He lived a slow death, moped about and despised all of life, and all who spoke to him. He withered away into a blue funk and deep depression.

The other man I pictured, not yet middle-aged, was in good health except for his foot. He realized the futility of trying to return and be with his family, but had hope. He would not give up and let his hardships consume him. He would make an effort to see beauty in human beings, even though some were as brainwashed in Russia as they were in Germany. This other man also knew, with certainty, that in the vast country of Russia there must be trout streams, singing, classical music, and friends. I jumped from the bunk.

Frantically, with crutch under one arm, foot throbbing, I grabbed the pee bucket and headed for the latrine.

"I'll use the damned outhouse from now on, if it's gonna kill me," I said loud enough for the tent flap to open and two faces stare at me.

The third day, a military medic checked my foot. He swabbed the wound and made it burn like hot pepper. After he applied salve, he rewrapped it. The same evening the barracks filled with Russian soldiers, some I remembered seeing on the platform. Now off duty, they boasted, shoved, and romped about like a group of schoolboys. The air inside the tent soon thickened with the same stench that permeated the mattress, and the same reek the Russian soldiers exuded when first captured. Everyone in the tent seemed to light a smoke. Some rolled their own, some lit stubby pipes. *Makhorka*, they called it. Part tobacco and horse manure I guessed. Next to my bunk, shrouded in sickening smoke, four men played cards. They passed around a bottle protruding from a rag. The cork rolled to the floor, no need for it. When the stuffed rag quit supplying support, one of the fellows stumbled out of the tent to seek the secret stash to keep the party going. The big-eared comrade noticed my gawking. He smiled through glazed eyes and offered me a swig. Why not? I took a swallow. They all grinned and motioned for me to take another, and I did. Soon after, I enjoyed the best night of sleep in months.

4

I threw my crutch on the woodpile. Like a determined youngster I hobbled along, ready to kick the world into shape. Feeling quite frisky, I volunteered to tend to the barrack stove, clean and shine shoes, and keep the place spiffy. It didn't take long for my volunteer spirit to turn into twelve-hour shifts in the kitchen and maintenance shop. Most of the soldiers showed little hostility once that crazy German became a benefit to them. When I finally forced myself to wear my boots, they shipped me out.

Again, my wrist had to be latched to the side of the truck's cargo bed, as it wormed its way for hours through narrow and pathetic dirt roads. At last, it halted at an intimidating wrought-iron gate. Another steel gate! The surrounding mountains, dressed like hooded monks with chiseled noses and cheekbones, hovered over the valley. I remembered the map of our grade-school wall. The Ural Mountains hugged the frame on the right side. Even then, a young lad, I knew they were far away.

At last I became an *It* . . . a number—Z88. A numbered slave at a coal mine. The place looked dead, a yawning grave, black and barren. Aging trestles, defunct rail cars, and other decrepit mechanisms formed the bones. Weathered shale and rocks the skin. Stark and clear, I saw my destination and future lay before me.

Surprised, two of my army buddies greeted me. The three of us joined several other squads of German prisoners at the mine. None of us newcomers received orientation orders as had the earlier groups of prisoners. Maybe they added us to replace the dead?

A fellow, with a white stripe sewn on his sleeve dropped a bundle of work clothes at my feet. He examined my eyes to see if I was of a right mind, wrote something on his clipboard, and then showed me my windowless abode. I went to work the same day.

"You'll soon figure out how to get around," my buddies told me. "Stick close to us."

"When does the day start here?" I asked.

"At the second blast of the steam whistle, we fall in, squads of twenty, four rows of five men. They'll shove you around until you get it straight."

The guards addressed us by our number. "Hey, Z88!" The number painted on the issued shirts garnered more respect than the person wearing it.

If, in the morning, one of the prisoners fell in late, we all were late. Not a good start of a day. They counted us at the feeding station. They counted us when we reported to work. They counted us to reenter the prison compound. Counting stole most of an hour of precious free time each day. When the prisoner count came up short, they ordered a recount to verify the first count. If still off, they searched all the shacks until they found the sick or dead. As a penalty, they doubled the wasted time and added it to the workday.

Paper, apparently scarce, had the guards pencil notes and numbers on a wooden board. When the information became useless, they scraped the board clean with a pocketknife.

Blood did flow through my veins, but I did not live. I existed. I had no melody in my heart, no spring in my step. The dull surroundings drove home the hopelessness and added to my gloom. Not a wild flower bloomed—not enough soil on the ground to support one. We worked twelve hours a day, six days a week, plus assemblies, that generally kept the lid on joviality, camaraderie and spunk.

The distressing scream of the steam whistle, a red-eyed vulture surveying every move, mounted high on the trestle, regulated our lives. After a few short weeks we became zombies, head hung, shoulders hunched, always alert for the next whistle blast. The long hours, the menial work, the monotony of the everyday activities made us walk, think, and talk at the same pace. No need for planning.

From my workstation I followed the sun's path, relating my timekeeping to its position and to a particular landmark. This kept the day in order and my mind alert. When the sun dipped behind the wooden-legged tipple, I knew we had to fill six more rail cars before the next whistle. I used each landmark to anticipate the whistle's scream, the dead tree, the smokestack, the crack in the mountain. I wished I had my watch.

At midday, when the sun climbed above the dead tree, the whistle blew. I left my post and walked to the water spigot to fill my tankard. Next, I joined the men in single file and headed to the supply station to receive a slice of dark bread. Studying the mysterious chunks of filler that poked from the slices confirmed my hunch. The baker added potatoes, chestnuts, slivered beets, and other chopped stalks of edible produce. If one's slice showed obviously smaller than the others', no one dared to argue with the fellow doing the slicing. One grunt, dirty look, or huff by a prisoner, resulted in the forfeit of your slice.

A step or two farther along the serving line a hole in the board cradled a lard bucket with a broad knife. Each of us smeared a gob of granular fat on our bread. Often the fat ran short. We scraped the sides and bottom of the bucket, if so inclined, chasing away the roaches that always competed for the last dabs. To make the acrid lard more palatable, we added a pinch of salt from a cracked crock wrapped with a rusty wire to hold it together. A hunger never satisfied makes all food offered always look good, smell wonderful, and taste great.

—

When the sun shortened its arch, deceptively ushering in the dark and cold, I knew my willingness to live would be tested. All German soldiers dreaded the endless Russian winters.

We, the captives and our dwellings, were fenced separately within the overall compound of the mine. Our shanties had low ceilings, barely enough to stand erect. Most of the little shacks were tucked into the hillside and faced west. In years past, they housed poor mine workers. Since the war brought new laborers to replace local men fallen in the conflict, the mine also became a prison camp. My orders to live alone near the assembly area became a good thing; fewer steps on my gimpy foot. To do the daily chores by myself, like hauling coal for heat, evened out by being close to the pile. One other benefit, I could tinker whenever the time allowed it. The extra straw-covered bunk and tattered wool blanket, became a place for a friend to sit.

An old man, not a prisoner, lived in my shack before me. He lived contently, being close to his work. The story told, he never traveled farther from his shack than to the small town down the valley. If he had any possessions, they sure disappeared before I moved in.

The old man worked at the mine since he was fourteen years old. The old soul died having a coughing spell. The hapless fellow, congested with coal dust, coughed nightly while sitting on a round stump outside his shanty, now my shanty—and my stump. His coughing suddenly stopped as he fell off the stump and rolled over dead. He ruptured a blood vessel in his brain, they said. Poor soul, gone, and all of forty-four years old. *How sad,* I pondered, *I'm thirty-six! A shack to myself and my personal stump to sit on.*

One evening, by the flickers of the oil lamp, I tried to plug a hole in the rear wall to keep the wind from whistling. In frightened disbelief, I found hidden, in a crevice of the rocks, an old and worn cigar box. I blew off the dust, flashed my eyes toward the door, listened for steps. Trembling, I opened the box. In it I found an illegible note, a very small silver spoon, a sea shell that mysteriously reflected the light of the flickering oil lamp. And—my heart stood still—a pocket watch!

Like a child, bubbling with excitement and shaking with an unfamiliar fear, I returned the box and its contents to its hiding place. I wanted to shout, but forced myself to lie on my bunk.

When I could no longer stand the suspense, I checked to see if the door to the shack was clicked shut. Eyeing the door, I stepped sideways along the wall to retrieve the watch. The watch's glass face showed cracks in multiple places. The winding knob felt fully turned, but the watch didn't tick. Afraid to snap open its face and the glass fall out, I sat and stared at it. I heard my heart thump. *I need tools to see what's wrong.*

The next day's evening called for a hot fire. The stovepipe glowed red. Through a crack in the vent I stuck a piece of barbed wire, which I found in a junk pile, into the throbbing coals. It soon glowed bright orange. A good whack with the poker on the sharp edge of the stove flattened and cut off short pieces at the point of impact. When dropped into cold water the pieces returned to their former hardness. I created a hook, a sharp needle prod, and a tiny screwdriver. Excited and ready to probe the broken watch, I crawled into bed.

Boris, a simple and honorable man, and I became friends. He worked as the only maintenance mechanic for the entire operation. When he looked at me I saw clear to his heart. His talk was straight forward, his actions kind and thoughtful; a man with no guile. He never thought of himself superior or in position of authority over me. He had a bear's shoulders, bushy eyebrows, and sported a huge mustache. His calloused hands assured a viselike handshake. Boris's eyes formed the sky above his bright smile. He chuckled when he tried to teach me a bit of Russian. He would rear back and laugh at my waving my arms, bringing rare smiles to my existence. Eager to learn, I spent as much time as I could with him during the brief breaks. Soon, having like interests, we found a way to understand each other. We built a bond.

I watched Boris heave and prop, bang and bend, crawl under equipment and weld with sparks attacking his clothes and body. I saw him run to equipment breakdowns. He continually gave all he could to the company. And, he always had time for me. He showed interest in a plan I devised to modify my work station. My job, if not totally asinine, proved to be an unnecessary use of manpower. I scooped up coal that spilled from the conveyor as it ascended out of the bowels of the mountain. The right-angle turn in the flow of the conveyors presented the point of spillage. I asked Boris to come on site so I could explain my modification idea. He watched me work, considered my proposal as he twirled his walrus mustache. Finally he grinned. That, a good sign. He uttered but a few words, then soon, as if shifting into high gear, he launched into a lengthy discourse that exceeded my comprehension. I stood and watched him. He finished his one-sided conversation by slapping me on the shoulder.

"I do work—weld—put up—Sunday . . .Yes?" is all the Russian I could piece together. He understood, winked, and walked back to the shop.

For weeks I didn't hear from anyone about my suggestion. Finally, a couple of starched shirts came to observe me on the job. Huddled together, pointing, they took a few notes and left.

On a Monday morning, again weeks later, Boris brought a new fellow to my work station who took over my job. In thirty-seconds I showed and explained to him his new position. I walked back to the shop with Boris, a little puffed and grinning.

The modification finally received approval. The only hitch, we couldn't get all the steel needed. Improvise was the order. Things looked up! Boris and I completed the project before the nasty and everlasting hold of winter. They sent the new fellow into the bowels of the mountain. The authorities smiled. Winter howled. I worked indoors with Boris.

Production improvements always warranted consideration, and most often were implemented. However, suggestions on improving safety were scoffed at. I asked Boris about that.

"Why not take care of the men?"

After a huff, Boris answered. "If you're dumb enough to smash your thumb with a hammer, would you do it again to remind yourself how good it felt?"

"Well put," I said.

—

Late one evening, while I systematically dismantled the ailing watch and had carefully spread its components out on the extra bunk, I heard footsteps approaching. I panicked. No way to hide dozens of parts. Without a knock, greeting, or introduction, the night guard plunged into my shack. He squinted his eyes to adjust to the lantern's light.

"Report to headquarters an hour before roll call in the morning." He said. Then, curious why I sat on a stump facing an empty bunk, he leaned forward to get a closer look. Not saying a word, his eyes widened and his eyebrows raised. In growing panic, I rambled a few words in Russian and gestured at the process of me repairing a watch. My jabbering and pointing stopped him from raising questions. Satisfied, he shrugged his shoulders and continued his round. *Does he think I stole the watch?* Dejected, I sat, unable to continue.

About an hour later the same guard tromped in again, this time he grinned. Out of his pants pocket he pulled a pocket watch, similar to the one I worked on. He indicated, with his own version of universal gestures, that he wanted me to fix his watch as well. Again, things looked up. The thought of where my watch came from or to whom it belonged did not bother him. All he wanted out of me is fix his watch.

A day later, "Is it ready?" he asked as he stuck his nose in the shack. When it wasn't, his face fell with disappointment as that of a schoolboy.

"It's next on the list," I assured him.

The blow to my watch had caused the glass to crack and to dislodge the winding spring. Given the tools I made, the fix became easy. I secretly carried the watch every day, hidden in the double seam behind the knot that held my pants up. No one, except a few of my fellow prisoners, knew the watch existed. My life lit up.

To know the time brought a small part of self-worth to our frayed dignity. We duped our captors, a gratifying victory. We had no control over any portion of our day. With a watch, however, we were able to allocate certain segments of time to activities such as bathing, doing the wash, or playing chess. To snub that damned old steam whistle was our greatest achievement. The guard's watch also resumed ticking, ushering in a new flow of projects for the mad German to tackle.

—

I didn't fail to heed the guard's instruction to report to the management office. Long before the next morning's whistle, I leaned against the office building and waited to meet whoever wanted to see me. The morning started cold and raw, and dark as a raven's tail. The dampness in the air crept through my layers of clothes and brought on shivers. I had to clamp my jaw tight to keep my teeth from rattling. *What wrong did I commit?* I asked myself, feeling robbed of an extra hour of sleep.

Next to the office door, two coal buckets, full and ready, awaited the first person to arrive. I studied the buckets and noticed that one radiated a faint glow onto the stuccoed wall. All being deathly quiet, I ambled over to the glowing bucket to have closer look. *Hot coals! What a way to be pampered.* I leaned against the wall and straddled the radiating bucket. The bun warming only lasted until the main gate creaked. I slunk back into a less-noticeable pose on the other side of the door. Out of the dank and dim a neatly dressed man approached.

"*Guten Morgen!*" he announced.

"*Ja*," was all I countered.

"Grab that hot bucket." He pointed with one hand, while he fumbled for the key to the door with the other. Erect, and shoulders back, he walked toward his desk. I followed meekly, bucket in hand. Without asking, I poured the hot coals into the black enameled stove and closed the lid. Dutifully I returned to the outside and retrieved the heavier bucket. My bad foot, though much stronger, made me totter. The man sat and watched. I placed the full coal bucket near the stove and fed the glowing embers with a heaping shovel full.

"I get room warm?" I said, shrugging my shoulders.

"Good. I see you don't mind getting your hands dirty," he said. "Sit and relax." If an average Russian, he sure didn't resemble Boris. His hair glistened black and stayed plastered to his head. Thin eyebrows and a sharp nose gave him the look of a crow ready to peck. He didn't introduce himself. I guess it wasn't necessary when confronting a nobody.

He tried to speak in German, but was limited. I answered in simple terms. Several times he became irritated and walked around his desk. He wanted me to ramble and reminisce.

"Franz," he started afresh, leaning back in his chair, "you're nearly forty years old. You're healthy, and yet your military rank is only that of a mere foot soldier." He looked at me, and when I didn't have an immediate answer, he continued, "Why were you drafted so late in the conflict?"

"I don't know," I said. "As a master precision tool and die maker, I had to supervise men on difficult projects."

He shifted in his seat. "According to our data, the plant you worked at designed and manufactured parts of German weaponry."

"That is correct. And, as you probably know, so were many other manufacturing plants."

"True. Going back to why you were called to duty so late, can you give me a more precise answer?"

"Just a guess," I said, "but I worked on a vital part of a specific piece of weaponry."

"And?" He said, not flinching and focusing hard on my facial reactions."

My stomach churned. At the German plant, I had been sworn to hold all phases of the development a secret. He had me squirming. I felt like a juicy bug, ready to be devoured by this crow.

"We finalized development of the MG42 machine gun."

"Aware of that," he said, sliding to the front of his seat. "Need specifics," he spouted.

Why does this bore-hog offend me so? If I tell him more, they still can't fit it all together. So I answered.

"The trigger mechanism."

"What was wrong with the previous one in the earlier machine gun model?" He asked.

"It was too slow."

He glared at me. "Why? Didn't it kill enough men?"

"Not my decision, Sir."

"Did you and your team achieve your goal?"

"Yes, in early 1943 the weapon went into a revised production."

"I know, a devastating piece of machinery. We have many of them confiscated and are using your technology as a springboard to an even better weapon."

Yea, sure, I said to myself.

In control now, he got up and strutted about like a cock bird. He faced me with an artificial smile and said, "Since you were in charge of the development team of such an efficient piece of weapon, I admit to say that your skill is highly underutilized here at the mine."

He looked at the wall clock and summarized the meeting by complimenting me on the modifications to the production line. Then he concluded by saying, "I'm sure your motivation and engineering savvy will continue to be a benefit to the Soviet people."

I hustled back up the hill to make the morning roll call.

What a dumb meeting. I pondered. *They show me a little more interest. Hell, . . . the pay is still zero. I get lice like the rest.*

5

At the camp, personal grooming revealed one's self-respect. A man letting himself become shaggy and unwashed signaled a sure sign of depression. They allowed us to trim our beards and hair with the community scissors, a tool big enough to cut a rope. With those sheers, even the most fastidious fellow couldn't be finicky. In warm weather, we pruned our heads and faces close enough to see what might be crawling. When lice made a comeback, as they often did, a straight razor, supervised by a guard, did a better job than the sheers. With nothing to read and no congregating permitted, the long winter nights had dastardly effects on each man. The cold, little food, lack of daylight, and the stress of long hours in the shafts turned the faces of my fellow prisoners into carved folds of drawn pallor. A surly face, a hanging head and curt statements, can make a loner out of a good man. One-word conversations became the norm. Depression was an evil we all battled, an evil that stalked the depth of one's mind, a real adversary that couldn't be grasped with hands or destroyed with weapons. We had to get hold of ourselves, look up, pull our shoulders back, and keep eating the miserable slop offered. Men died because they gave up. Hope was not a word we used. As the months and years crawled on, I coped because I liked the fellow I worked with.

"Only one person at a time at anyone's place," was the rule. My close friends and I unwound playing chess on the day off. We straddled my spare bunk with the game board between us.

The chess board, a sheet of tin, had been granted us by the guards. I painted the squares by mixing coal dust and lamp oil then baked the tin on the stove. Light colored stones and black nuggets of coal made pawns. The black figurines I carved from coal and then rubbed them down with lard. The white figurines, also carved from coal, I painted with paint I used to keep the men's identification numbers visible on the issued clothing and headgear. It pleased the guards to see their squads looking sharp.

This extra duty of freshening the numbers enabled me to befriend many of the men, some of them Russian priests and dissidents who bucked the System. Rarely did I received a thin slice of bread.

The buzzword around the camp was, "if it needs rigging, talk to Franz." The guards stopped by to see what contraption I brought to market, or to talk and get warm during the blustery nights. My gizmos and doodads ranged from clothes hangers to rat traps. One of the few pleasures came from my personal rat trap. After leisurely nibbling on the bones of a rat for a little extra protein, incinerating the skin gave me great satisfaction. It avenged my frequent nightmares of the ordeal on the train. I also made traps designated for our outhouses which could accommodate a family of rats. The traps staked near the kitchen's disposal bins were very small; a clandestine operation. Once trapped, the rats could crawl away and hide, but could not get loose. The prisoners volunteered to check these traps on a rotating basis. A hungry belly looked forward to rat guard. With a fire going year-round, all one needed was a stolen dab of lard and pinch of salt—close your eyes and smile.

—

The community coal pile reminded me of an anthill—our center of commerce. The coal pile never dwindled. Plenty more in the bowels of the mountain. We schlepped one small bucketful at a time. Stockpiling coal in the shack was against the rules. The efficiency of the stoves left a lot to be desired. We had to get out of the sack during below-zero nights and stumble to the coal pile to keep from freezing to death. It appeared all I did was heat the tin roof overhead.

It's a good thing man is never satisfied, I said to myself. The wish to stay in bed all night prompted a new strategy. The wheels churned. The next couple of weeks I collected rocks and stovepipes from unoccupied shacks.

My new project began to evolve by elevating the bunk using flat rocks under each leg. Next I raked the lingering coals and clinkers onto my short-handled shovel and slid them outside my shanty. The strange red glow reflected off the tin wall and lingering drifts. I knew it would attract curiosity, and it did.

"What in the world are you doing now?" came the cry from one of my friends toting his bucket. "Are you setting up an altar to the Siberian gods out here?"

"Hey, you trotting zombie," I hollered, "come in and help me. And don't run your mouth out there where everyone can hear you."

"Okay, okay," Georg said as he stepped inside.

"Help me take these fire bricks out of the stove, would you?"

"You must be the craziest fellow I ever met," he replied. With borrowed welding gloves we removed the still-hot bricks.

"Now, help me lay the stove on its back," I said. His interest pricked. We struggled, but managed to lay the heavy stove down with the fire door up.

Georg scratched his head as he looked at the pile of rocks and stovepipes inside my shack. "Now, pray tell, what are you going to do?"

"Thanks for the help. You can go on to your place," I said.

"Me, leave now?" he said raising his voice, "I wouldn't want to miss this next maneuver for anything."

In silence he watched as I shoved and snapped a series of stovepipes together. I placed them along the east wall to an elbow in the corner, then under the bunk, and finally out through the wall.

"You see," I said, "I elevated each section of pipe a little higher than the previous one, all the way around."

"So . . . why all this contraption?" he asked.

"Heat and smoke rises. As long as there is a draft, it'll follow the pipe."

"And?" he said.

"You see, Georg, the heat from all that pipe will keep my butt warm. It will heat the rocks I'm going to pile on the pipe and especially under my bed. When you get up for the fourth time at night to stoke the fire in your stove to keep your ass from freezing, I will have gotten up only once.

"No rule against storing rocks," I went on. "Help me cover the pipe under my bed with the big ones over there. Rocks warm slowly, and they cool slowly. I'll be as warm as a loaded diaper all night."

"Well put, Franz, but you're a wild man. If you couldn't change things, you wouldn't be happy."

"Changing things keeps me sane. Let's see here, before we stack the rest of these rocks, let's bring the coals back in and find out if this contraption actually works."

We added the embers and more coal and opened the air vent —the stove inhaled. Georg shook my hand and smiled. He added more coal and said, "Now she's talking."

"Thanks for the help," I said.

"Yep, no problem. I've got to go and add this bucket of coal," he said. "I wish you all the comforts of that loaded diaper."

—

As in previous winters, when the cold and growling bear dug in with determination, the spigot supplying water during lunchtime stopped flowing. We had to hoof it down the long hill to the cafeteria where the locals ate their meals. Except for the hike down and up, we thought it a better place to eat than sitting outside under a shed roof. There, inside the mess hall, we saw women for the first time in many a month. I didn't want to stare and ogle and be seen as a lecherous boor who dragged in from the lonely mountain. To me women were still interesting. That, a good sign! The ladies all wore kerchiefs tied behind their ears to cover their hair. None wore jewelry. Most were older and fairly portly. With the mine at the edge of Siberia, some ladies had round faces and Mongolian features. Certainly, none of them ever flirted or mingled with us the Germans. Our food was doled out by the older women. They were polite, but they never engaged in long eye contact or lengthy conversations. We, the outsiders, had no part in the fabric of their lives.

We ate in fifteen-minute shifts and had assigned tables along the wall farthest from the kitchen. I liked sitting against the outside wall and able to observe all the goings-on.

To keep up our strength and fight the cold, every man jumped at a chance to do an extra chore to cadge a few additional ounces of bread or kasha, the coarse Russian oatmeal. On rare occasions, especially during an extended blast from Siberia, the guards instructed the women to ladle out an extra scoop of soup and a somewhat thicker slice of black bread. To have a chunk of bread stashed in my pocket was a good feeling.

We survived on soup—everlasting, daily watered-down soup—and that pasty mush of oats, which always lacked salt. Soup with less water became a pulpy stew, prepared with vegetables grown and preserved during the summer. A hot, steamy bowl of sugar beets and greens, with an occasional small chunk of sow's belly, was my favorite.

Fish soup posed a different situation. The fillets of the fish satisfied the locals. The carcass belonged to the Germans. The "chefs" threw the gutted fish's remains into the stew mix. All sizes of fish bones, fins, and small bits of fish hid among the lumps of potatoes and mysterious strings of dark greens. We chewed and chomped and ate it all. It was difficult to finish eating within the allotted fifteen minutes. Being forced to chew and eat slowly made you think the belly filled. To receive a whole fish head in your serving was the top prize.

At the edge of Siberia, the everlasting icy wind cut clear to the marrow and stayed there. For months, I never really got warm. Only at night, the warmed rocks under me, curled in a fetal position, brought the needed rest. The additional clothing issued amounted to quilted pants and jacket, plus a fur cap with earflaps. Many men slept wearing every piece of clothing issued, even the *Valeki*, the foot warmers. These felt boots, slipped over the foot, came up to under the knee. If they got soaked during the day, the thick material didn't dry overnight, which guaranteed cold feet the next day. To battle the frozen blasts, we wrapped our faces with a face cloth long enough to go around the neck and face twice. Two long strips sewn to one end tied the wrap in place.

The shanty, so poorly constructed, swayed and trembled from the fierce winds. Snow swirled through cracks of the thin walls. I wasn't surprised, after lighting the lantern in the morning, to see a dusting of fine snow covering part of my room.

In warmer weather the wise prisoner probed, braced, and tested his shack. He stuffed crudely braided ropes, twisted from common weeds, into cracks. Smaller cracks he daubed with a mixture of grass, mud, and lamp oil. Rocks on the roof kept the tin from flapping. Although one side of my shack hugged the mountain slope, the wind found cracks even an ant could not find. Snow on the roof should have provided insulation, but either the wind blew it off, or the heated tin melted it. When Siberia tested our efforts, we often found the shack spewing forth the crude fillers in the cracks.

Every winter presented a new test of will and stamina. The forlorn howls of wolves reverberated from the canyons and slopes and emphasized the piercing cold. Cold, such as I never before experienced. The wide broom of Siberia relentlessly scoured the side of the mountains that hovered over us. It swept the snow from open areas and piled it on the lee side of shacks and other buildings. We rerouted paths to keep from having to tunnel through drifts. Icicles hung from mustaches and beards. To linger and contemplate in the outhouse proved to be impossible. The coal pile often fell victim to those creeping snow monsters. Drudging through blinding gusts to fill the bucket was bad enough; having to uncover the coal pile in addition made no sense. We got smart. By beating on our coal buckets we sent a signal down the row of shacks, a signal to team up. Together we tromped to the pile and cleared the drifts only once.

During blizzards, we strung ropes to help guide us out of the compound. After such a storm, guards reclaimed the rope, measured every meter, and returned it to the guarded supply house.

The wind, the cold, and the dark continually tested our resolve. More than once, even rocks placed on the tin roof were no match for the fiercest blasts. For hours, the tin on the roof and sides would flap violently. If not skillfully secured, it tore loose —not to be found for days.

One workday morning, as I shoveled through a huge drift in front of my door, I discovered a large section of someone's roof wrapped around the corner of my shack. While the bear still howled, I knew someone faced a dire predicament. Several men and I set out to find the crippled dwelling. Icy crystals stung the face as we groped our way through whipping swirls until we spotted the pitiful shanty. The door swung and flapped. Inside, men already there, tried to rouse a young prisoner. His shack mate sought shelter earlier at their neighbor's place. A hole in the roof gave the blizzard a chance to spread its blanket of death. The younger man opted to stick it out. He sat on the floor, barely alive, his head hanging, fully clothed, and wrapped in everything he could put on. His back pressed against the cold stove and covered with snow. We carried the man next door. His feet and arms already stiff, we tried to rub life into him. Soon his pulse ceased. Six of us reported late; the entire prison camp had to make up the time. The gratifying reward, however, none of the men minded; we were brothers who mourned one of ours. When the workday ended, two carried the young man to the far edge of the compound. There, along with the other corpses, he awaited burial when the spring thaw arrived. Periodically, we covered the taunting stack with snow and then poured buckets of water to encase it in ice. When the swallows returned, we buried them.

6

Women. Sure they are precious and part of every man's life. Sure, the men missed them. All had special women in their lives, a spouse, a girlfriend. The men often swooned while sharing memories of a darling back home. When we left our women, the war raged. The separation brought with it deep worries about their welfare. I missed my wife and children with a gnawing in my soul.

The air raids in München whined and threatened so often that most women and children fled to safer areas of the country. My family's evacuation took place while I trained in France in basic hand-to-hand combat and small weaponry. During a brief furlough, before I reported to combat duty, I hugged my family the last time. We loved, we warmed each other with tears and hugs, and we struggled to stay warm in an old building to which Friedl and the children had been relocated. Deep down, however, a wretched grip on our hearts told us that we soon must part.

The call came to join the eastern front, a two-thousand-kilometer battle line, in a vast country. I dreaded to face the Russian bear. It made me shudder.

—

At the gulag, during free time, one could spot a handful of the men pacing the barbed-wire perimeter like caged animals. No one had heard a word from home in years. "Do not write letters," the guards ordered. "This is a labor camp! No written communication shall leave this compound until further notice!" We existed as nonpersons, numbered, a sprocket in the operation.

We, the German prisoners, called the place a camp. Calling it a prison had a demoralizing ring to it. We did not pay for any crime or misdeeds; we fought for our country when called to do so. This fact our captors could not swallow, and understood less. Even some of our men, diehard Hitler followers, realized that the protector of the Master Race could not save them. Being slave laborers for seventy-two hours a week without pay was our lot.

In the evenings, I often found myself talking to my family while sitting on the bunk. At night I dreamt of lying in fields of daisies with Friedl's head nestled in the crook of my arm. I dreamt of the Bavarian Alps radiating their splendor. My dreams became the soul's down pillow.

During the first months of action, Friedl and I wrote each other regularly. Soon Hitler's front line started to crumble. We retreated more than we pushed forward. The letters from home skipped a day, then none for a week. The last letter arrived about a month before I was captured; it tore at my heart more than any previous letter. Friedl told of meeting a farmer's wife with four young children and her husband off to war. The woman tried to keep the farm productive and needed help with sewing and mending clothes. Friedl, in exchange for her labor, received a few fresh eggs and a liter of milk a week. In closing, she stated she is expecting our third child.

That day, when I read the letter, I sat on the hay cart and faced west. The last bundle of hay made a good cushion to lean against. Kruger, our last horse, had died. An eerie quiet hung in the air that day; plenty of day left for killing. Gnats crawled up my nose and in my ears. I stared repeatedly at the sentence that mentioned a third child. I shed my last tear on that cart as I grappled with the wretchedness that had engulfed our lives. *A new baby, no job, mending clothes for milk. What am I doing here?*

I had my reply letter sealed and ready, ready to hand to the runner who also brought food and drink to the front. . . . The runner never came.

7

Each prisoner at the mine kept his own jerry-rigged calendar. To be sure we stayed on the same track, we often called out to one another the full date: "Hello Max, powerful day, eh, this fifth day of March nineteen-hundred-and-forty-eight." I kept a record of days by burning a dot with the hot poker on an old beat-up board. My board had a bad case of the chickenpox—four years' worth of dots.

During the crunch years in Germany, my position at work entailed the oversight of secret military projects. Hitler's henchmen thoroughly had scrutinized my background for prior deviant behavior or any opposing political associations. To keep me "behaving," government snoopers, as I called them, visited the plant and stuck their noses in everything. Many times, an inspector lingered around my work station, subliminally pressuring, but never engaging in conversation. Their presence left me fraught. I and the team were patted down daily before we left the plant and repeatedly warned not to speak to anyone about our project, not even to our wives. Even away from the plant, faces, clearly not from the neighborhood, became casual additions at the tavern I frequented, as well as at the clubhouse where all us fishermen bragged and socialized.

At the mine I made a tactful effort to dispel the guards' mindsets that all Germans were Nazis. I often reminded myself, "Keep a grin on your face." Being mad brought no positive results. To keep the mumbling to yourself proved better for the mind, and the belly. A bowl of cabbage soup became more precious than an opinion or freedom itself. Many of our men did not have a fight with, or animosity toward, the Russian people. Everyone worked hard, natives and prisoners alike. We, however, worked longer hours, pulled our own teeth, tended to our own sick, ate a few fat rats, and buried our own dead.

—

Nearly five years elapsed since I last felt the unnerving pressure of snoopers. Now in Russia, the same so-called inspectors came to observe the operation of the mine and its interrelationship with the prisoners.

While seated on narrow plank benches at the supper table, dipping bread into a runny gruel, we noticed an attractive young woman walking toward the maintenance shop. "Check it out!" Not a spoon hit the side of the bowl. Jaws dropped. The woman wore a white, long-sleeved blouse and a pressed pair of tan trousers. Her hips conjured up memories. She held her head high, proud to show off her lustrous black hair cascading to her shoulders. Not wanting to be seen as a group of lecherous men, we only stared until she glanced our way. Without a doubt, she did not walk from the mountain village nearby. She carried a black briefcase in one hand and gestured with the other to the armed guard who followed her. *He thought he was showing her around.*

The next day the attractive woman came to observe the operation of the kitchen, including the serving of the prisoners. We watched her crane her neck, intently focusing, noting all dirt and cobwebs on her writing pad. The women in the kitchen did not grant her a look. To them she was a nonissue, a pain. The snooper checked the supply room, and, standing in the corner of the chow hall, studied the employees performing their tasks. The expression on her face said, "Don't give me any sass. I got the pad and the pencil!"

Several days later she still stirred resentment. She inspected the fence around the prison compound and was later seen emerging from the shafts below, wearing a gray, long-sleeved cloak to protect her spotless outfit. The second time she visited the maintenance shop, she talked with Boris at length. When he pointed his thumb in my direction, the subject of the discussion had to be me. I didn't have any vested interest in that godforsaken coal business, nonetheless I felt rubbed raw by this high-nosed stranger. She looked at me, but didn't see me. I was Z88. She made my stomach churn.

The snooping became personal. She and her guard entered our compound. They marched up and down our one-meter-wide boulevard and surveyed the shacks, the bath stalls, and our highly ventilated outhouses. Unashamed, she visited each of the prisoners inside their shanties on our time off. *How insensitive,* I thought.

The first evening she interviewed—interrogated—over a dozen men, about ten minutes each. At least she had the decency to leave the men alone long enough to get a night's rest.

"Where is she today?" I questioned my friends. "What does she want with us?" I griped. "Those commies know everything already, right down to the number of the warts on my ass."

"Ah, but she is a looker," Hans and Georg agreed, as if that made it all right.

"She also wants to know how we're treated—food, work, and so on," said Georg.

"I wasn't going to complain," said Hans, his eyes darted from left to right. "My good sense told me, swallow hard and keep your trap shut."

"Watch out, Franz, when your turn comes. She is a charmer. She's got that sultry voice and deep-purple eyes that worm their way into the soft spot of the brain, and she is gorgeous."

"How'd you manage to keep from slobbering if she's that good looking?" I said to Georg. "All you've talked about the last four years is how you missed Elsie and the cookies she let you taste."

Following the weekend, the classy woman picked up where she left off. Agitated, I awaited my turn. Several more days passed. I knew by then she had spoken to all the other German men. *I don't like this. Why not me? I want her out of my hair!*

Before I crawled under the covers, I reached for the willow twig and stuck it in my mouth to soften it. Slumped and disgusted, I sat, brushed my teeth, chewed, and spat. The night soon crawled through the cracks and carried its penetrating dampness with it.

Next February I'll be forty-one. My son will soon be nine. We used to celebrate birthdays . . .

The following day, after the evening grub, I sat on my stump, hooked my boot heels on the edge, and leaned against the tin wall of my rickety hovel. Cool breezes whisked my hair. I flipped up the collar of my shirt. The scraggly and stunted trees around the camp, lucky to have escaped the ax, had turned brown. The dry leaves rustled as they cried out for life. A chilling dread enveloped me as I ruminated on another winter in this hell on earth. To the north, two ominous mountain peaks reflected the last rays of sunlight. God put them there to reign over this valley, holding back, or, if they decided, funnel down the wintery blasts straight out of Siberia. . . . *They considered the man who had lived in my shack, old at forty-four.* A shiver shot down my spine.

Inside, I stretched my weary bones on the straw sack and pulled the rat-frayed blanket over me. I let go a chest-full of bottled-up nerves trying to shake the anxiety the inspector caused. Soon my fists clenched and pressed against my sides. My chest heaved with a wracking melancholy. Breathing became shallow and quick. An incredible wave of agitation had hold of me. My eyes rolled into my head. My sanity started to slip. Black and red spots danced over me. Despairing and cramped into a knot, I shrieked, "Let me go!" as wiry arms, many of them, overpowered me. I fell, deeper and deeper, into a cavernous pit.

Hours later, sprawled on the dirt floor of my shanty, I pulled my hair to check if still in this world. My shirt hung on me limp with sweat. My blanket was flung to the far corner of the room. Exhausted, I rolled to one side and struggled to get up. My uneasy legs managed to get me to the edge of the bunk.

I stared at a beam of early morning sunlight streaming from a hole in the eastern corner of the shack. The round beam lit up the door hinge and moved gradually lower toward the dirt floor. Mesmerized, I watched. Minute after long minute, the bright spot crept down, met the floor, then moved in my direction. *A light moves in my direction!* I vividly recalled the night's nightmarish battle, the falling into the abyss, then being cushioned by an enveloping pillow taking over my struggle. The little light beam brought a calm, a slow and gentle healing. The rising Sunday sun outside added to this strange joy. Through damp eyes I saw my violin hanging on the peg. I heard its soft melodious sounds. Then, almost in disbelief, I stepped into the new day.

8

"Ah, Boris," I said, breaking the quiet.

"Yes?"

"Have you seen her today?"

"Who?" he asked.

"The inspector. You know, the one who has floated around here for the last week or so."

"Oh, her."

"I didn't see her all day Sunday or today. You think she's left?"

"I don't think so; her guard is still here. Saw him in the cafeteria joshing with the ladies."

"Where is she staying at night?" I probed.

"I know the guard sleeps in the temporary accommodations next to the office building. I doubt she stays there."

"Then she must have a place down in the village."

"I would say so," he concurred.

"What do you think her overall purpose is for coming around here?"

He didn't answer right away. Then he said, "It's an everlasting game. A constant push to improve production and compete with the other mines."

"You mean the government tries to supervise each mine from Moscow?"

Boris cleared his throat, "Well, generally, they have a good handle on everything. The management here does whatever the higher-ups dictate." Boris tried being diplomatic. He had a life ahead of him and would spend it right there at the maintenance shop.

"Where is she from?" I pumped.

"I think from Moscow; at least the last guy came from there," he said, not looking in my direction.

"How often do these analyses take place? I've been here nearly four years and this is the first I've noticed."

"Yeah, you're right," he half mumbled. "Usually about that often—four, five years."

After a few moments he said, "Thinking back, the last time someone stuck their nose into our operation many changes followed afterward."

From a drawer he pulled an old plan. "See," he said, "this is a drawing of the prisoner's compound. We built the fence around it about five years ago. We also added the outside lean-to to feed the prisoners in warmer weather."

"A request from the crew here?" I asked.

"What do you mean?"

"I mean, did you men here refuse to eat with the enemy?"

"No, no," he said. "The notion to separate them came from the big shots. They thought we'd have confrontations. You see," he continued, "many of the people working here lost brothers, husbands, and sons since the attack by you Germans."

An amazing fact hit me. Boris did not show any ill feelings toward me. He looked me straight in the eye while talking.

"Boris, did your family suffer any loss?"

"Yeah, my wife lost a brother; killed early in the war. My brother lost a leg and part of the feeling in the other one. Stepped on a mine. His buddy with him got blown to bits."

"Horrible," I said.

"And you?" he questioned.

"Boris," I said, "I wore my brother's army boots until I was captured. They fit better. Every morning, when I put them on, his name and serial number stared at me."

"Was he discharged?"

"No, he got killed . . . my only brother. Shot in the head in Poland soon after he got drafted."

Boris put the plans back in the drawer. "Franz," he said, "one other change they made after the last inspection." He waited for me to ask.

"What was that?"

"At the time I had a real good helper here in the shop, a fellow from East Prussia. The NKVD picked him up when he couldn't prove Russian citizenship. A good pipe welder, also good at welding aluminum. He escaped when the Nazis were after new blood for the war."

"What became of him?"

"I really don't know," Boris said taking a deep breath. "All I do know, he left with the last inspector." Boris quickly glanced at me.

"Did they replace him?" I asked.

Boris seemed reluctant to expound, but answered, "I worked alone for a while." Then finishing his thought he said, "No use to complain around here. A man like me, with no big-city education, better not complain. This job isn't that bad. For many years I did put in my time down in the shafts."

We continued to work in silence. I did not like the silence. It wasn't like Boris not to communicate. I asked, "So, did you get new help before I came along?"

"Yeah, a few fellows in and out. Most of the time I ran the place by myself. I remember coming to work sick one day—collapsed right here on this floor."

"Did they find you?"

"Yeah, when I didn't show for midday break. Two of the comrades stormed in here ready to rat on me. They expected to catch me doing work for myself." Boris walked over to a spot and pointed to the floor. "They found me lying right here." He thought for a minute then continued. "They cleared a spot on the workbench, picked me up, and laid me on it, while I heaved and spat up stuff. To be kind to me, they rolled me on my side and stuffed a handful of rags under my chin and cheek. Very thoughtful, don't you think? For added comfort, they plunked lumps of coal along my ribs and hips to keep me from rolling off the bench. I heard the whistle blow to go home, but I couldn't get up. Long after dark, I finally mustered enough strength to drag myself out of this place. At the gate, Yelena waited." Again he stopped and looked into space. "Help for the shop came soon after that episode. They brought the old man in, the one who lived in your place."

"The one who died on the stump before I got here?"

"Yeah, poor guy, totally worn out, coughed his guts out all day long; too weak to get a good breath. He didn't have anyone to take care of him."

"Why didn't the authorities put him in a sanitarium?"

Boris looked at me. "Because he still had a few days of work left in him."

It took a while for that unsettling statement to let go of its grip on my gut. "Boris," I said.

"Yes, Franz?"

"I know we are from different countries, and we're supposed to be at odds because of the war and such. . . . Boris?"

"Yes?"

"I'd be honored to call you my friend." Before he could say something, I continued. "If I have to stay in these mountains until I die, I hope it is here with you—in this shop."

He squeezed his lips together and smiled. Wow, that big, round-faced man had dimples.

I felt a comfortable calm. Occasionally I glanced over at Boris and caught him looking at me, smiling. *I have got me a friend!*

That evening, I rolled my tree stump to the west side of my shack and watched the sunset. I didn't bother to feed the fire in the stove. As I leaned against the tin, my eyes drooped and my body ached from standing all day. The town below exhaled coal smoke from home-fires being stoked. The valley gradually surrendered to darkness, as the fading day crept up the mountains. The peaks watching over us still glowed, reflecting the setting sun. Streaks of splendor highlighted the horizon. I sat, at peace; not a troubling thought.

Suddenly, a stark silhouette of a capped man walked into the streaked sky. The black outline of his image grew larger. From his shoulder stuck a rifle resembling a skinny crow. Determined, he tromped up the hill. A smaller silhouette, that of a woman, trailed close behind. My heart stopped.... *She is coming for me.*

"Brunner," the guard called, seeing my outline in front of the shack's reflecting tin.

"Yes, sir," I said as I jumped erect.

"At ease. The lady wants to talk to you."

"Certainly, where do you want me to go?" I answered, already feeling violated.

"Inside," the guard motioned to the door.

I stepped aside and gestured for them to enter ahead of me. The guard balked—a prisoner does not follow the captor.

"Don't you have a lantern in there?" he inquired in a stern, accusing tone.

"Yes, sir. I will light it. Yes, sir."

I reached for a strand of soaked twine.

"What are you doing in there? Come out here and let me see you!"

I hopped back outside, twine in hand. "Sir, I was about to light the lamp."

"How?"

I cleared my throat, then said, "I soaked this twine in lamp oil. I stick the end into the embers to get a flame."

"Go on," he snapped.

He watched intently as I moved about in the dim shack. When I reached for the poker to stir the coals, he hollered, "Halt!"

Immediately I straightened and dropped the poker.

"What do you need that for?" He growled.

"Sir, to stir the coals so I can light the end of this string."

"I see," he said a little humbled. "Get on with it."

I did not respond. I felt his eyes bore into my back. I inserted the string into the red glow of the coals. A short puff, the string flamed up. I lit the lantern, then turned it low.

"Turn it up," he hollered. "What is the matter with you, anyway?"

"Nothing, sir! Nothing."

I don't know why he kept getting more ruffled. Maybe all that, "Yes sir," stuff got to him; or from being made to look a bit dense. The woman stood by the door. She seemed to enjoy the competition between authority and servant.

I raised the wick, but was compelled to say, "Sir, there is very little kerosene left. With the days getting shorter, I'm worried I'll run out before my next allotted tin full."

"Turn it up! . . . more . . . all the way," he barked.

"Yes, sir." I knew it would get mighty dark in the next few minutes.

The important lady chose to sit on the spare bunk, dressed in a starched, white blouse neatly tucked into a light tan skirt. She could not hide being a woman.

The guard stood by the door, the lantern blazed away. The lady surveyed my lowly abode. No one uttered a word. The guard noticed the stove lying on the ground. His eyes followed the stovepipes, propped and covered with rocks, stretching along the wall, around the corner, and under the length of my bunk.

"This is not safe," he hollered. "You'll burn this place down!"

"But, sir," I calmly replied, "this will be the fourth winter this way. The pipes heat the rocks under my bunk. It saves much coal for the company. The heat does not go straight through the roof."

He looked at her as if seeking a partner to jump this mad scientist, but she vaguely looked in his direction and said nothing. He shrugged his shoulders and finally shut up.

The black-haired woman, her eyes ever searching, studied my simple existence. She studied my crude clothes hangers. The drying underwear. She tilted her head and contemplated a small painting propped on a crude shelf on the wall. Her eyes moved to the chessboard and studied the carved figurines, all along issuing the aura of a snob. She even noticed my willow twig toothbrush prominently hanging on its nail. Still, she did not speak a word.

To avoid an uncomfortable lump in the straw mattress, she shifted in her seat. As she leaned forward, her blouse offered a glimpse of her fullness. She stopped scanning and focused only on the little painting.

"Who is that?" she said with the allure of Marlene Dietrich.

She looked directly at me when I answered, "My wife and children." Our eyes locked. That short moment invaded my soul.

The lantern sputtered. Immediately the guard's eyes flashed to it. I briefly turned my head, but as being pulled by the moon, I faced her again. While the guard fiddled with the lantern, she spun her web.

The flame crackled a few more seconds, then with one last sputtering gasp, it quit. It was dark.

"Leave the lantern here and find more lamp oil."

"Yes, ma'am," he said, as he groped his way along the ribbed tin wall toward the door. "Are you sure you're going to be all right with him in the dark?"

"Yes," she assured him, "you know, I come prepared for all situations."

He clicked the door shut then eagerly hoofed it down the hill.

The darkness matched the deathly silence. I felt the rhythm of my heart against my shirt collar. My brain grappled with her statement "being prepared for all situations." She brought her satchel. Surely she didn't need such a big one for a pencil and writing pad.

"What is your name?" She asked, penetrating the silence.

"Brunner," I replied.

"Full name," she said a little sharper.

"Franz Brunner."

"Franz Brunner," she repeated, surprised at her pronouncement of my name.

"What part of Germany did you come from?"

"München," I said, then listened to see if she could repeat as I said it.

Sure enough, she repeated, "München," with the perfect inflection of a German.

She waded through a script, wanting to know my age, my trade, and the names of my parents. The few seconds of silence that followed the routine blared with tension. In the darkness, I discerned the rustle of her starched blouse as she moved on her seat. The smell of the day's sun hung fresh in her laundered clothes. The previous peep of her cleavage, coupled with the silence and darkness, alerted me to a delicate wisp of perfume. I realized my weakness.

"Tell me, where did you work?" she continued.

A stab in my gut. *Here we go again. Stay focused!* She noticed my hesitation.

"In München, at a manufacturing plant."

"What did you do there?"

"I am a machinist." I knew she goaded me to where I did not want to go again.

"Franz," now suddenly on a first name basis, "the war has been over for more than three years. Don't be holding anything back."

I tried to stay levelheaded and said, "I don't quite understand what you are asking."

"Franz," she said, the timbre in her voice even more alluring.

I felt her lean forward . . . in perfect German, she said, "We know your background, and know exactly where you worked. I also know, so far, you answered correctly. So please, don't start deviating from here on."

I kept silent. My belly didn't like threats. The darkness oozed a suffocating blanket.

She continued in German. "Did you paint the picture on that little shelf?"

"Ah, yes," I stuttered, shocked in the change of subject. *Watch out! She is as ruthless as she is good looking.*

"What are your children's names?" She continued, trying to relax the mood.

"Peter and Dolores, we call her Dolli," I said. Then added, "Friedl is my wife's name."

"I can't speak your Bavarian dialect, but I do hope speaking in German will relax you. You're a bundle of nerves, Franz."

There in the dark, I imagined being a plump roach, slowly and deliberately coaxed into a spider's web.

"How did you manage to paint that painting?"

Again, she circled the prey. Yet, again—whether the war was over or not, I had determined not to be wheedled out of military information. Not by some secondhand inspector.

"Did you paint it from a photograph?"

"No," I said, "from memory."

"Relax, Franz. Tell me about the painting. I'm not here to harass." Her voice dripped with kindness. "Where did you find art supplies in this forsaken place? In the dark I still see the picture. Quite different, I may say."

I coughed, knowing I committed no crime, I revealed my method. "As you may imagine, the black and other deep colors are mostly coal dust. The white paint, used to brighten the colors, is leftover from painting the squares on the chessboard. I swear I got permission for the paint."

"I'm sure. Don't worry," she said, "I know you cannot make yellow from white and coal dust."

"Ah, yes," I cleared my throat. "Some of the yellow comes from three bird eggs I robbed from a nest. I ate the whites. Mixed lamp oil and a bit of white with the yolks."

"I perceive you are a man who can work around obstacles. Tell me, how did you achieve the other colors?"

"The green came from chewed vegetables. The purple from beets, much the same process."

I sensed her lean forward. Her voice somewhat nearer. I imagined her eyes.

"I'm Tatiana Popova," she said almost in a whisper. "Call me Lana when we're alone and having conversations like this."

The warmth of her breath wafted clear to my brain. Stunned, fully alert, I swallowed hard and waited. Then she asked, "How did you get the rich red in the painting?"

"It's blood, mixed with a little yolk-powder," I uttered. "Not blood from the rats I kill."

"Who's blood is it then?"

"Well, . . . it is my blood. I know that sounds crude, but it is the only way I still feel connected to my family." She didn't comment.

At that moment, I heard the guard huff back up the hill. Without a knock, he ducked his head and burst into the room, the door slammed shut behind him.

"Where have you been?" She scolded.

"I first tried the storage shed, but the fellow in charge had gone home. Here, I got a cupful out of the maintenance shop."

"Did you steal it?" she probed.

"No, no," he stuttered, "the night guard let me in."

"Since when does the night guard have a key to that building?"

"Oh, he doesn't. We found one of the doors unlocked."

Please no! I groaned.

While I held the lit end of the twine, he filled the lantern and aptly trimmed the wick with his pocketknife.

When the lantern flared to full brightness, the lady strained over her pad, furiously writing. It sure impressed the soldier. She stood up, flipped her hair back, brushed some wrinkles out of her skirt, and in a commanding voice spouted in Russian, "That will be all. If we have further questions, my comrade will be seeing you."

She stepped ahead of the guard, glance at me and said, "Good night, Brunner."

"Good night, ma'am." She vanished into the night.

I sat puzzled, not quite able to grab the gist of the entire interview. Her presence lingered. *"Lana," she wanted me to call her.* I turned the lantern low. The new chill in the room called for a scoop of coal. Like a trained zombie, lacking meaningful things to do, I cleaned my teeth again, snuffed the light, and bored holes into the darkness. The tension ebbed. The heat of the stovepipe under the bunk exuded its magic.

9

The late season rains kept the mountain grasses green, pleasantly separating the fall colors of birches, maples, and oaks. At the mine, however, soil had long ago disappeared from the well-traveled paths and picked-over ground, leaving a lifeless landscape of loose shale and rocks. I felt like an old-timer among soot, rust, and naked rocks. Years earlier, I learned to channel the rivulets of runoff away from my shack. To put your boots on in sooty mud does not make a good start of a day. The issued wool cloak kept the wind and cold from stiffening one's bones, but it didn't keep a drenching rain from soaking through. Our caps kept heads warm, but didn't keep the water from running down the back of our necks.

After the snooper's visit to my shack, a relentless rain lashed down from the mountain gaps and promised to stay awhile.

"Nasty out there, eh, Boris?"

"Mm," he answered, noticeably not his friendly self. I walked toward him, but he didn't turn to meet my eyes. His round face was unshaven; dark circles under his eyes underscored his weariness.

"What is wrong, my friend?" I asked.

"Ah, Franz, my heart is heavy."

"Why, Boris?"

"I had to spend the night here in the shop. You know I can't rest here. There is no place to have a good sit, let alone lay down and sleep."

"What is going on? Why did you spend the night here?"

"The commander ordered me confined to this shop for three days. They'll throw me one beggarly meal a day. My wife doesn't even know what's happening."

"Why? I don't understand. Has this happened before?"

"No. Not to me. To others. When they're being reprimanded, they spend their punishment in lockdown. Since I'm such a big shot, I get to do my time in here," Boris said as he kicked the coal bucket.

"Why? What have you done?"

"I want to be with my wife. She is the only comfort in my life," he almost shouted. "My baby girl will be four years old tomorrow, and I won't be there. Franz, I'm so tired I could die."

"Tell me, what this is all about?"

"I forgot to lock the back door over there. I don't even know how it got unlocked. The boss man does not look kindly on fellows with responsibility failing to live up to it."

Dumbstruck by the news, I decided my poor friend would be better off not knowing the circumstances.

We spoke few words that day. Before Boris closed the shop for the night, I asked, "What do you suppose your wife did when you didn't come home?"

"I'm sure she came to the gate last night. Probably waited there well into the night."

"Would she come with your little girl?"

"Oh yes. She wouldn't leave her home alone."

"Boris, let me do something for you after it gets dark."

"What?" he asked.

"Let me borrow your slicker and hat and I'll sneak down to the gate after everyone has gone home. If Yelena comes again tonight, I'll tell her the situation."

"You can't go to the gate; you're a prisoner here. They will do worse things to you than they did to me."

"Don't worry about me. I want to do this. We need to ease Yelena's mind. No one will be watching for someone traipsing around; it's raining too hard."

At closing time, Boris handed me his hat and slicker and said, "Tell her I love her." He nodded his head and looked comforted by the prospect.

I tucked the hat and slicker under my cloak and sloshed to my shack. The whistle soon signaled the evening grub. Resembling a tight bunch of bats, the men and I stood packed under the mess hall's low overhang waiting for the door to open. Intermittent sheets of rain continued to pour as darkness squeezed in. I checked out shadows and lighted walls, and devised a route to the main gate before I returned to my shack.

On drenching rain days, the guards didn't bother to count the prisoners before they reentered the compound. Over the years, less attention had been given to prison security. The gate to our compound merely leaned shut. The rusted lock no longer functioned and hung for appearance only. I'm sure the snooper made note of it.

Excited, I stuffed the stove to last the night, hung my cloak and cap to dry, slipped on Boris's raincoat, donned his cap, and ventured into the soggy night. The rain pelted my face, *a perfect night to do this little deed for Boris.* If spotted, his hat and coat, not having a prominent number on it, would provide enough disguise until I vanished into the dark. I hoped, on such a cold and dank night, the guard had crawled into a warm furnace room for a snooze. *Don't bet on it!*

The hard rain peppered down. The wind flapped the rubber slicker. I had trouble discerning nearby sounds. To locate the roving guard was paramount. To head straight to the gate would be pure folly. The few sorry lights shining hung on rickety poles and created spooky shadows among the dripping buildings, alleys, and paths. The wind in the cracks and corners of overhangs added an eerie wail. As I squatted among crates and other discarded implements, my covered head and eyes barely showed above a trash container—I heard a cough! The guard. He carried his weapon butt end up to keep the rain out of the barrel. Adhering to a strict routine, he made his way around the buildings and then down to the main gate. When he sloshed back toward the company offices and into darkness, I eased my way toward the massive main gate.

I waited and strained to see. Out of the dark and gloomy night slipped a woman, under a large black umbrella, with a child glued to her skirt. Guarded, in small steps, she eased toward the gate. When the two came within a long stride from me, the woman whispered, "Boris?"

"Yelena?" I said in a tone that would not alarm her. "I'm a friend of Boris. He is fine—nothing's wrong." I let the few words settle.

"But, but . . . something is wrong. He is not home!"

"Listen. Listen please, nothing is wrong with him. All he did, he forgot to lock one of the doors to his shop. He's being punished for it. He has to spend two more nights at the shop with orders not to leave."

"Who are you? You're wearing his coat."

"Yes, this is Boris's coat and cap. Boris desperately wanted to get word to you. He isn't hurt or sick, only under shop arrest."

"Who are you?"

"I'm Franz, the German prisoner who works with him."

"You are putting yourself in danger," she said.

"Boris is my friend."

"Boris talks about you. He is so happy he finally has good help in his shop."

"Your husband wanted me to tell you that he loves you."

"Oh my! I love him so!" she said, a quiver in her voice.

To the little girl I said, "Your father wishes you a happy birthday and he will be home to kiss you soon."

"Thank you so much, Mr. Franz," said Yelena. "Although my Boris isn't with me, I can sleep tonight."

—

Before I reported the good news to Boris, I stopped by my shack. With a resolute purpose, I grabbed my bedding and wrapped in it the chess set. I also removed the straw sack and blanket from the spare bunk. Wadded together, it made a huge bundle.

At the maintenance shop, I leaned the bundle against the door and slipped to the rear window. A lantern flickered inside. Boris sat on a box, his elbows on his knees, his large hands cradled his face. I tapped on the glass. He jerked out of deep thought, saw me, and hurried to the door. One hand on my shoulder, he read my face, awaiting my words.

"I met with her," I said right off. He dropped his big hand and let out a long breath.

"She came with your girl—I told your little one that her father wishes her a happy birthday." The big man smiled. "Yelena told me she loves and misses you. I told her why you're away from her. She shook her head."

As tears welled, he uttered, "Thank you, my friend. I wish, someday . . ."

"Boris, please don't. . . .To see you smile is payment enough."

I dragged the bundle to the far corner, out of sight, and unrolled it.

"What's all this?" He asked.

"I brought my spare bedding. You need to sleep—recharge. You're a wreck."

"Why two straw sacks?"

"I'm staying the night to keep you company."

"Oh no, you can't do that. We'll both get into real trouble."

"Boris, it's all right! I'll sleep against the back wall. You see this blanket?"

"Yes."

"My chess set is in it. We're going to play a few games, then lie back and have a good night's rest. Don't worry! No one will miss me at the shack. They haven't checked on me in years. I'll be out of here before the first whistle. No one will be the wiser. Deal?"

"Uh . . . deal. Sometimes you make me nervous."

We arranged the straw sacks, on opposite ends of the shop, out of sight. In a far corner we laid the chess board on the dirt floor between us, sat on wooden boxes, relaxed and enjoyed the game. It didn't matter who won or lost. Being together as friends mattered—two men at peace—One a free man, the other a prisoner. Both lives scarred by war. The future laid out—

tomorrow the same as yesterday. Another day older and weaker in spirit. Ever groaning and aching toward a time when a man's purpose is dead and the body broken. Always creeping toward his final rest, and finding it only when covered with shale.

Boris broke the stillness. "Franz," he said.

"Yes?"

"I have known and worked with many men, but I have never sensed genuine kindness toward me from any of them. Why you?"

"Boris, you're my friend."

"Good night, my friend." His forlorn look said it all. A lost man without his family.

"Good night, my friend."

10

Boris rested well when I rose, long before the first whistle. I rolled my sack and blanket and skipped out of the maintenance shop back to my place. I didn't say a word when I left, expecting to see him shortly when the workday began.

In the hollow and dark of night, while everything still dripped from the night's downpour, I heard the gate in the fence squeak. I knew none of the men traipsed around at such an hour. I had been back only minutes, and barely had time to unroll my bedding, when the sound of approaching footsteps tensed my body. Without a knock a guard burst into my place.

Surprised to see me dressed, he said, "What are you doing up this early?"

"It wasn't the best of nights," I mumbled. "Why this visit?"

"You, come with me. Someone is waiting."

"Waiting for me?"

"Hey, shut up. I have already said too much. Let's go!"

The guard pulled me out the door by my sleeve and herded me down to the front office. From there, two men grabbed one arm each and dragged me to a waiting small troop transport.

When I heard the metal tailgate slam shut, a padlock on the end of a chain click, I realized all too clearly that I was nothing more than a number, a prisoner.

"Wait!" I shouted. "Are you moving me? What about my things?"

The two uniformed men, totally unconcerned, jumped into the cab of the truck and drove off.

This is mindless! I had a gut feeling that this hurried event is going to change my life in a new and odd way. A great wound opened. It wasn't because of leaving my willow toothbrush or the rat trap, or the little painting. . . . I left my friend.

A train whistle saturated the early air with sadness. The truck shifted into a lower gear as it entered a town. I slipped my watch from its secret pouch. It showed ten minutes to seven.

When the tailgate dropped, I, the cargo, jumped from the canvas-covered vehicle. One of the men gripped my arm and led me to the same platform where long ago a carload of half-dead men were dragged from a steel cage. No soldiers this time. Instead, a scarf-covered woman sold hot tea and black bread. The truck driver handed me over to a uniformed railroad man who expected my arrival. With a smile and a friendly hello, he motioned for me to get on the train. I could have run, but where to? So, like a little lamb, I stepped onto the train.

I saw her— Lana, the interrogator. She turned, obviously having watched for me.

"Good morning, Franz." She smiled.

"Yup," I answered.

"Won't you sit?" she asked, pointing to the slatted bench opposite her. Bewildered as a threatened puppy, I sat, our knees almost touched. Her unopened briefcase lay beside her. The whir in my brain made it impossible to focus. Befuddled, I looked at the ceiling.

"What am I doing on this train?" I asked, not making eye contact.

"We've arranged to rescue you," she proclaimed with a cheerful lilt in her voice.

"Rescue!" I almost shouted.

"It's all right. I know you're puzzled. Please calm down. I'll be with you through this little upheaval." Her voice attempted to calm me. "We recognized your training and skill was underutilized at the mine, so a good position is awaiting you."

Miffed, I stared out the window seeing but a blur. Like a grandmother, she showed enough savvy to keep quiet, letting a little boy pout as long as he wanted. Even that irritated me.

When the pouting became childish, I ventured a glance in her direction. Staring at the floor, I noticed her high heels matched her black skirt. I found her legs nonchalantly crossed, and, after a heart-skipping peek, noticed her hose disappear above her knees. Again I looked out the window before I continued the visual journey. She didn't say a word; perhaps amused by my juvenile shyness.

On her lap laid her jacket, her folded arms resting on it. On her left hand she wore a black onyx ring set in gold. Her long-sleeved blouse glistened silky white. Cloth-covered buttons traveled up the center to her neck. The tightly spaced buttons struggled to hold a clean line as they explored her full bosom. To complete the feminine display, a little decorative lace on the collar formed a pedestal on which her captivating face rested. In less than a minute I perceived all her ample features and converted them into a Rubenesque motif.

The mysterious woman's raven black hair hung to her shoulders, spilling forward on one side. The early sun flirted with her full lips. Aware that once I looked in her eyes, she had the power to dismantle me. Her voice had been reassuring enough, but my pulse still raced. Not only was she very attractive, but I also didn't trust her.

She waited for my uneasiness to subside as I stared out the window some more. I *had* to focus on the situation at hand, not on tiny buttons climbing over bosoms. To counteract my masculine wonderings, I forced myself to imagine sitting opposite the older and portly matron named Ursala at the cafeteria—full double chin, two missing front teeth, one eye looking toward the wall. The haze cleared. Reality sharpened.

In contrast to her stylish dress, my pants were held up by a rope. The area of the pants over my bony knees showed off the maintenance shop's grime that hadn't responded to many washings. My hair stood in all directions. The morning yuck still stuck to my eyes, and my shirt read Z88. I looked worse than a scruffy old dog, not at all convinced my smell didn't match the look.

The train started to move. As it passed buildings and trees, flickers of sun highlighted her pale rose cheeks. Her lashes' shadows enlarged and deepened the eyes.

Mama Ursala, I thought, *how sweet of you to flash your toothless gums at me. . . . Get hold of yourself, you old fool.*

I finally exchanged her gaze.

"I'm sorry for being so fidgety," I stammered. "I feel out of place and so unkempt."

"Franz," she said as she tapped my knee, "I understand. Don't worry about that."

"Where are you taking me?"

"I have permission to take you to Moscow," she answered, being proud of herself.

"If you got permission, who asked for it?"

"I did," she stated. Instead of leaning back and flashing a look of self-confidence, she leaned a little forward and looked at me with a reassuring and tender smile.

Mama Ursala! My mind blared out again. *Stay focused!*

My skepticism eased a little when she spoke in German. She almost whispered as she used all her persuasive and personal charm, "Franz, life is going to be much better for you. You have given much to the mine and its operation. Your willingness to cooperate, improve production and the lives others, was noteworthy."

I leaned back and perused the paneled ceiling again.

"I have talked with them," she continued. "We've compiled your profile. At your new position you can start to earn pay and have a chance to better yourself."

"I need to go home," I said. "I have nothing here in this country that says I belong, no heritage. Not even a pair of shoes."

"Franz, Germany lost the great conflict. There is little left."

"My family is there. They need me," I said.

"You must give yourself some time here. Things will get better for you, I have connections."

Slumped in the corner, I rubbed my forehead; totally aware of a major and maybe sad point in my life.

This government is not going to let me go! I felt it in my gut. I also knew I had no say about any of it.

"Miss . . ." I stammered.

"Franz, I told you to call me Lana."

"I can't; I don't know you. You call me Franz because I am your prisoner. You have authority over me."

"Yes," she said. "Although I have a good civilian position, I have no power over you. Your power is in your heart and mind. When the war carried on, yes, you were a prisoner. Now you are a civilian. You are allowed to pursue what Russia has to offer."

As long as I dance to the Communists' tune, I said to myself.

"Yes, I know more about you than you do about me," she confided.

"Why didn't the others get a chance to a better life?"

"Your background, as we discovered, was more noteworthy."

Here it comes, I thought.

She shifted in her seat and relaxed her shoulders saying, "Recently, and for the last several years we periodically received updates on you, and others, as they researched your history."

"Who are the 'they'?" I asked. "Did they mess with my family?"

"Mr. Brunner," she said, showing some frustration.

I had hit a nerve. She didn't want to discuss her job while this little cat-and-mouse game continued, but answered anyway.

"The 'they' are the intelligence apparatus of our country doing its job. The Nazis had their spies throughout this country; we have ours in yours. Since we are back to a more businesslike conversation, you can call me Miss Popova."

A long silence followed with no eye contact. We both pretended to enjoy the scenery. The slatted seat seemed harder.

"Why did you turn Boris in for leaving the back door to his shop open?"

"I didn't pursue that infraction," she said. "The night guard is who reported it."

"Is that what is expected of the citizenry of your country?" I asked. "To report to the higher-up people? Do the night guard and Boris have an ongoing personal conflict?"

"Not that I heard or read about," she admitted.

"Then why would he not mention to Boris what he had found and let it go at that?"

"Well," she said, "in our society, the ones who are organized and perform their duties properly do tend to get promotions more readily."

"In other words," I said, "the hell with being a friend; being a snitch and two-faced is a desired quality?"

With a sigh, she countered, "Mr. Brunner, the Soviet people are human beings in pursuit of peace and happiness."

"Well said, Miss Popova, but how often are these goals fulfilled?"

More silence, as we looked over the countryside. She seemed to be contemplating her own statement.

"How is your foot?" She suddenly inquired.

"My foot?" I said somewhat startled, "I learned to walk without a cane. Although at times I wish for one. A cane does make me more sure of myself. I also realize, the more I do without one, the stronger and more steady I become. I manage. To walk on a balance beam is out. A two-meter-wide sidewalk is more suited."

Miss Popova allowed a spontaneous chuckle and said, "With needing a wide sidewalk, everyone would think you are the town drunk." We both smiled. The chill disappeared.

Our conversation meandered from the weather, to classical composers, to food, and was often interposed with periods of silence. I shifted and slumped, stretched and yawned.

"Sorry. I'm having a hard time relaxing on these hard seats. Never been blessed with enough cushion, you know." She smiled.

"I believe the next stop will last a good thirty minutes. We can get off and move around, see about a drink, maybe get a bite to eat."

"I'll stay on the train. You don't want me to tag along."

"Nonsense, Franz, I want you to start feeling your new freedom."

"Freedom? With the number Z88 on my shirt!"

"I won't snicker. Wear the shirt inside out."

"The next thing you'll have me do is sport a cravat with it." We both chuckled.

The train's whistle screamed as it signaled the stop ahead. Miss Popova peered out the window and seemed eager to do something different.

"You are aware, I'm sure, that I don't have any money," I said. "Isn't it proper in Russia for a gentleman to pay for the lady? I don't want to embarrass you. It's bad enough I look like someone who lives under a bridge."

"Mr. Brunner, your company is more important than what someone may think in this upcoming knot-on-a-log town."

Yeah, I thought, *nice talk. The train'll stop, and you've got to keep an eye on me.*

Another short whistle, one last puff, the train came to a halt. She let me get off first. I helped her step to the ground; quite a step for a lady in high heels. She firmly gripped my hand and several strides later still held on.

With no depot platform, the busy streets merged right into the train station and immediately drew us into the town's activity. The city's clamor conveyed life and encouraged us to strolled from the depot. Local women sold everything from trinkets to treats. Some peddlers, realizing a train had stopped, came hustling from the side streets to be part of the action. The hiss of the locomotive stitched together all the hustle, clamor, and smells.

No more than twenty meters into town, we heard a singsong voice proclaiming, "Fresh bread! Good and warm!" A stooped woman, her head covered by an oversized scarf, waved a small loaf of black bread at us. A leather strap, slung round her neck and shoulder, held the large basket from which a dozen or more loaves smiled at us. Black loaves, brown loaves, some as long as my arm, others meal-size, still others showing bits of brown onions poking from the crust. We decided on a light-brown loaf sprinkled with coarse salt.

A few more paces into a side road, another industrious woman, her hair tucked under a dark red scarf, roasted chestnuts in a kettle. The hammered copper kettle sported a coating of encrusted soot and other baked-on sauces. The cauldron rested on a wrought-iron spider with a wood fire under it.

"Smells good," Miss Popova said to the typical babushka.

A wrinkled old face, flashing one tooth, looked up. Her eyes grinned and squinted from the smoke. Next to her, on a rickety three-legged milking stool rested a beat-up tin cup. Not breaking her look at us, she took a sip from the cup, and then warmed its contents by adding from a bigger can that hung on a makeshift hook on the side of the large kettle.

"Tea?" Miss Popova asked.

Yes, said the nod.

"Would you sell us some?"

Again she nodded, got off her stool, handed me the stir stick to the kettle, and shuffled to her house. She returned, a bit hunched over and grinned with two tin cups. Much obliged to do a little business, she poured each a generous cup from the hanging can while I stirred the chestnuts. The hot tea tasted bitter and strong—a treat nonetheless. She motioned for us to sit on a bench along the wall of her house. I pressed my back against the sun-baked wall and savored its soothing heat. The smells and sounds, the friendliness, the warmth of the day, the entire experience was reassuring.

Suddenly, as if on a rescue mission, the woman jumped from her stool and ran to the house. Within seconds she returned, stirred the nuts, and then handed us a half empty jar of honey. I smiled as I flipped the metal clasp open and plopped a generous glob into my mug of tea. After I sloshed the tea around, the bitterness became divine.

When Miss Popova noticed how much I savored the sweetness, she offered to buy the jar.

"You don't want that sticky jar," the woman said. "I'll get you a fresh one. Here, stir." Again she jumped. I stirred. Miss Popova paid the woman while I looked the other direction.

Before I sipped the last swallow, Miss Popova took hold of my left arm and stuck something in my hand. Instinctively I pulled back. "Ssssh, take this. Put it in your pocket. You pay the next time," she whispered. "When we're back on the train, I'll bring you up to date on money and things."

Although she tried not to make a big issue of it, I still felt like a five-year-old learning to use money and count change. Miss Popova never showed any smugness over these small humiliations. I appreciated that.

"You need to carry money from now on."

"Why are you doing this?" I asked.

"To add to a good day." She smiled. "Tomorrow we'll have plenty more time to talk. In a few minutes I'll be retiring to my compartment for the night."

"For the night?"

"Yes, we still have a full day, and part of the next, ahead of us on this train. I'm sorry, no money is budgeted for your own sleeping compartment."

"I understand," I said. " Will I see you in the morning?"

With a smile she said, "Certainly. Do try to relax. I have a hunch tomorrow will be an even better day."

There, I sat alone. *I could jump this train!* A few folks had settled in on the other end of the car. No eyes strained to watch me.

No more than five minutes later, Miss Popova peeked around the corner. "Excuse me for disturbing. I brought you a pillow and a blanket out of the cupboard in my compartment. Again, have a good night."

"You too, and thanks for the bedding . . . and the honey."

11

A slight jostle, as the train pulled from another stop, announced the new day. All night long my body couldn't decide whether to collapse or squirm. My morning's disposition resembled that of a foul dishrag. To my surprise, new folks seated nearby witnessed my morning grunts. It took a few mind games to turn myself into a human being.

"Good morning!" said Miss Popova peeking around the corner. "Look, a little wake-up treat."

"Good morning. What have you got there?" I asked. "You're mighty chipper."

"Yes, life is good. I am heading home. And, I might add, I'm having breakfast with an interesting man." After a quick smile, she added, "I'll put this plate of buttered bread on your lap, but it doesn't mean you get to eat it all."

"Fair enough. Where in the world did you drum up this treat?"

"The dining car. I had to do some sweet talking to win enough to share."

"Sweet talking must come easy to you. I can visualize the fellows caving in—oh so ready to please and accommodate." She smiled, accepting my words as a compliment.

"Wait, I'll be back in a minute with a pot of tea."

I sensed a little giddiness when she poured the tea. She pushed her flowing hair behind her ear and leaned forward to retrieve a slice from the plate. Her nearness communicated a fresh splash of perfume as well as the woman the blouse failed to cover.

"Many country folks drink hot milk for breakfast," she said. "Some add honey or molasses. At home, we often drink a hot brew of roasted barley and malt."

"Are you married?" I asked. "You mentioned at home *we* drink. I hope you don't mind me asking."

"You have sharp ears, Franz. No, I am not married. I do have an eleven-year-old daughter, though."

"A daughter? How precious. Is she with relatives while you're away?"

"No, she doesn't live at home. She is quite an ice skater. She is at a high-skills government facility near Leningrad. A school where most of our Olympic-caliber skaters are trained."

"Olympic caliber! Well, how about that! Impressive. Does she come home on the weekends?"

"No, I'm sorry to say. They keep the young people for ten months of the year, with full room and board and a high-quality education."

"Do you miss her?"

"Oh yes," she sighed. "She is my joy. So smart and pretty."

"I'm sure, like her mother."

"Thank you. You're kind." She looked into her teacup, holding it with both hands. I sensed her yearning.

I leaned back and rested my head against the paneled wall. "Yes, a daughter is her mother's joy. A joy held close by a love that is unwavering; a mother's love, none more true."

"You're right. In this world of strife and war, a person must cling to the good that originates from within," she said. Her voice faded as if thinking out loud. "Not everyone has the privilege of loving someone, or is even capable of doing so."

Liking the direction of the conversation, I said, "Do you believe a man can love the same way?"

"I never fully thought of that. I know her father loved her, but then, a man also shares his love with his mate. What do you think? You asked—you are a father."

"Well," I said, hoping to set the proper tone. "Instinctively a mother will always be closer to her child than its father. After all, it is her own flesh and blood. A mother will always protect, forgive.

"A father loves the child, for it is his offspring. He is also drawn to a role of being the provider and protector. I agree when you say, 'a man shares his love with the wife and the child.' However, in a purest sense, the way it ought to be, a man should love his wife more. He is with her till death does part the two. Children will leave the home and begin the cycle again. The man's goal is accomplished when the child leaves home, but his love will not fade. The mother always has a harder time letting go."

"I agree." She continued, "It was so in the beginning and still is in most cultures, except where people are enslaved."

Enslaved? An interesting point. I wondered if she wanted me to comment on that. I had been enslaved for four years, but that had nothing to do with her point. So I changed the subject. "What is your little girl's name?"

"Irina," she said smiling. She shifted in her seat.

Since she knew all about me, I felt comfortable asking, "Is your family from Moscow?"

"No. I was born near Königsberg," she said.

"That's in East Prussia. You grew up in a German home?"

"Yes, my father is a stern German. In school we all spoke only German from the first through fourth grade. After that, the emphasis changed to learn Russian. However, many children also spoke Polish at home. As children we communicated in all three languages."

"Interesting," I said. "Did you ever hate that you had to learn them all?"

"No, not really. Anything learned is gained. It afforded me this position," she said with confidence.

"Tell me a little more about Irina. What happened to her father? You said he loved her."

She glanced out the window. "Oh yes, he did." Realizing the conversation may turn too personal, she said, "I'm sure doing most of the talking. You are, you know, the mystery person."

"Me?" I chuckled. "What's the mystery about me? You told me that you know all about me and my family."

"Yes, true. But a few things we're not sure of. I for one, I know there is a whole lot more man behind that hard facade. You know how mysteries are, everyone always envisions an ending." She tilted her head and looked at me.

"It seems the ending is in place. Hitler lost the war, and I'm stuck in Russia," I said.

"Don't say stuck. We want you to learn to love our country," she said, injecting all the charm she could.

The train's passengers nearby stifled any deep conversations we may have had. Miss Popova never made another mention of Irina's father. Her continuing charm and openness tempted me to called her Lana, but I didn't.

The train took advantage of better-maintained tracks and traveled much faster. Two times during the second day the locomotive took on water and coal. We got off to stretch our legs. With a handful of money in my pocket, I bought more bread, some apples, and a handful of prunes. Miss Popova did the negotiating. I did the paying. A blip of self-worth returned when I stuck my hand in my pants pocket and felt several coins and paper money.

Weary and sapped from yet another night of sitting, I faced the third day with measured zeal. The nearness of Moscow, the many new ears and eyes seated nearby, and the business at hand, dampened our conversation.

BOOK TWO

12

"Mr. Brunner, welcome to Moscow. Please give this opportunity a chance. I know the last four years were rough. Here is a chance for a new start. We want you to become part of our society, begin to enjoy life."

"Yes, I'll keep an open mind." I said with little conviction. "You have made similar statements before. Do you understand how difficult this is? How can I seek personal satisfaction when deep within me is the need to be home?"

"Mr. Brunner," Lana Popova continued, "you can have that dream. No one is going to be able to take it from you. The reality is you are here. Again, please give it a chance."

"One main point I have to learn," I added, "is that I do not have any choice in the matter."

She didn't comment.

The train rolled to a gradual stop. Again she tried to calm my anxieties. "Remember the war wreaked havoc on the Russian people as well. I'm sure you have contemplated your situation and found that to return to a fragmented and devastated Germany, at this point, is hardly possible. We have many German men employed in various industries, some of whom are quite happy and even have started new families."

At the word *family* my stomach tightened.

—

Moscow, like a giant whirlpool, engulfed with thousands of people on foot and on bicycles, didn't impress me. All scurried about, resembling a horde of rats gleaning a newly harvested wheat field. I didn't spot a single bright shawl or sporty coat. Everyone looked dressed the same, a gloomy gray.

Miss Popova led the way. I hobbled along as best I could. Beeps and honks fill my ears. We scampered toward a tram island in the middle of a busy thoroughfare as we weaved around cycles, horse-drawn carts, cars, and small three-wheeled motorcycles.

"Hurry," she shouted, "let's jump on."

We clung to a fully packed tram plastered to the outside as a leech would to a pimple. One hand gripped a worn handle, and only one foot found room on the crowded running board only centimeters above the road. "Ding-ding" rang the familiar sound as the tram scurried along. We hung on. After folks got off, we gradually squeezed inside the tram—standing room only.

"This is insane," I muttered. "Like München during mad hour."

"Ah yes, big cities are all the same."

"I guess there is no use of me asking where we're going and how far it is to get there."

She looked at me with a pleasant smile and announced, "We are going to Leonev Square, a small suburban city, a short trek outside of Moscow. It is a quiet place, with a few quaint shops and taverns along a bold river. Mostly professionals and their families live there."

"Professional? Why me among the privileged? An ex-prisoner, surely a bad fit."

"Mr. Brunner," her voice a bit exasperated, "Things are different now. All your immediate needs will be met."

"Miss Popova," I pleaded, "this sounds all well and pleasant, but you know where I need to be."

Responding like a mother comforting a child she said, "I understand. With time all things will work out." After a pause, she continued. "The next stop will be the end of this tram line and the end of our long journey. Take note, Tram Number Eight will take you to your apartment and will also take you back to the city. Here is the key to your new place. I'll walk with you to the door," she said, closing the matter.

My heart hammered. A disquieting future laid before me, a package wrapped in darkness. The number on the door read "8."

"I'll be back at eight in the morning to take you to breakfast."

"I'll be ready."

"Good night, get some rest," she instructed.

I glanced back and watched her disappear into the shadows. I stood alone, left to face the imaginary wolves of night, the ghosts of a strange city.

A lone street light managed to cast whimsical streaks of light onto barren trees and buildings. I inserted the key. Once inside, I turned to look out the window. It vaguely revealed the trolley stop. Miss Popova did not sit on the bench waiting for a ride back to the city. The sidewalk glistened, as a fresh skiff of snow sealed the evening.

In the dim room I fumbled and found a thin chain hanging from a ceiling light fixture. The walls exuded a lingering smell of fresh paint. I stood and surveyed my new surroundings. The floor throughout consisted of wide boards, beautifully laid and highly waxed. The simple, but ample, furniture looked new. The wardrobe intrigued me. It contained everything from freshly ironed white shirts to jackets, sweaters, underwear, and socks. Socks! Not foot rags as I'd worn for years.

The hat rack displayed a felt hat that fit me perfectly. From pegs under the rack hung two overcoats and a soft-fiber scarf. Neatly parked on the floor, two pairs of dress shoes and a pair of tall, laceless rubber overshoes, awaited approval.

I perused the contents of the washstand. The thoughtfulness to details showed a vague eeriness. Every grooming article a man would need laid fastidiously displayed and properly organized. From razor to strop, to baking soda and toothbrush. From soap to hairbrush, from scissors to cufflinks. All placed on white linen cloths.

A kitchenette, including a small table and two chairs, brought to life the far wall of the apartment. On a wooden cutting board, covered with cheesecloth, lay an inviting loaf of bread and chunk of cheese. A good sized bread knife beckoned me to partake.

A single-spigot brass sink hung on the wall. Under it, a variety of small tubs and buckets looked at me. The small gas cookstove showed off a brand-new copper teakettle. When I opened the oven door, a pair of felt house slippers greeted me.

I was tempted to start a fire and burn all my old clothes, but decided to drape the ratty rags on the short rail outside the door, begging dogs to drag them off during the night. I hoped so far no lice or other critters had crawled into my new environment.

All the freshness around me had my body scream for a good scrubbing. Two burners on the stove, one for the teakettle, the other for a pot, soon filled the wash tub with warm water. When my head finally hit the feather pillow, a weary mind recalled and pondered the momentous last several days.

I am a Z88 . . . I came on tram Number Eight. . . I'm in apartment Number Eight. . . She is coming at eight in the morning. . . . A ghostly quiet hovered. The room remained cold as a morgue. The dim street lamp pitched a few warm splotches onto the stark wall. I stared at the ceiling. A giant number eight floated in my mind, a racetrack, never ending. Round and around I whirled. Spinning, whizzing by, in an endless race.

At six, the alarm spooked me to a ninety-degree position. The clock's bell chimed loud enough to wake all of Moscow. Hard to say which annoyed less, the steam whistle of the past or this brass monster with its two bells on top?

I heated a kettle of water to shave and wondered if I still knew how. My beard had grown toward the wild side since the last delousing. I eased real close to the tiny mirror above the sink. A worn and hollow-cheeked face stared back. The loss of weight caused my eyes to sink into their sockets. Deep wrinkles crossed my forehead and streamed down my cheeks. The receding hair and graying temples mingled with the scraggly beard and mustache. *Still living!* I reassured myself.

It took forever to shave. I decided to leave a thin mustache. I aimed to look dapper and be dressed with the best provided— white shirt, tie, cufflinks, the works. My hair, a bit unmanageable, resembled one who should be conducting an orchestra.

At five till eight I slipped on the new topcoat, donned the debonair hat, and stepped outside. Not much snow had fallen, but enough for all to look clean and pristine. I ambled about the gardens nearby to peruse the new surroundings and take note from which direction Miss Popova arrived. My pocket timepiece showed two minutes till when she rounded the corner of a nearby building.

"Well, look at you," she announced. "I knew a smart-looking gentleman was behind all that fuzz and baggy clothes."

"They didn't trust us with real mirrors and straight razors, you recall. I didn't know I could trust myself either this morning."

She scanned me from top to bottom. "Your outfit fits you very well."

"Did you have anything to do with gathering all the necessities and the sharp new wardrobe?" I looked at her smirking.

"In a way I did, I described you to my friend in a letter. She did all the shopping."

"I knew a woman had something to do with it," I admitted. "Right down to the felt slippers hidden in the oven—definitely a woman's touch."

"Slippers in the oven?" she asked, with eyebrows raised.

"Yes, grinning and ready, those slippers spoke to me. I tried them on right away, even before the bathrobe."

"The bathrobe?" she grinned. "I better watch out, I may have described you too well. The next thing I know, you and my friend will check out what goes with the bathrobe and the slippers." We both laughed.

"I feel good," I confessed. "I even wield a little money in my pocket, thanks to you."

We started to walk toward the tram stop and then beyond. The sun struggled to capture the morning. Tiny tuffs of snow clung to the crooks of twigs and branches. All glared new—unexplored—a mystical start of the new day as well as new life. Soon we strolled along a river, its water reflected the morning's streaks of gold and pink. Soft puffs of wind shattered the water's docile gleam urging on ripples to titillate the new day. The exhilarating freshness of the air added to our giddiness. I steadied my gait with the umbrella, while she placed her arm in mine on the other side. If someone had looked at us, they would have thought we'd been together for years.

A beautiful old stone bridge led across the river to a brick-paved plaza, graced with benches, small tables, and chairs, scattered about under stately linden trees. Their branches, like comforting arms, gestured to sit. The plaza's inviting shops sold everyday necessities and goodies to indulge the affluent.

A pleasant waft drew us to a nearby bakery with its muffins, rolls, and breads.

"I don't want to be a nagging brat, but could we buy some?"

Miss Popova smiled, a genuine smile, full of assurance as if to say, "I will take care of you."

"Viktor is famous for his finger breads," she announced. "It's a small, skinny loaf of white dough, dipped into a buttery solution, then baked."

"I'm as hungry as a bear," I almost blurted. "Last night I was a little nervous to cut the bread and cheese your friend left on the table. Wasn't sure how long it has to last."

"Cut and eat! Don't let it mold." She said. "For now, let's buy a half dozen finger breads and then stop at Anna's and top them with a dab of cheese or fresh butter."

I paid for the goodies. Yes, money in one's pocket makes the man.

As I broke the small loaf, Miss Popova produced a pocketknife from her purse.

"Here, use this. If you like it, you may keep it. You told me how much you missed yours."

I looked at her in disbelief. "I don't understand," I stammered.

"I hope you'll take it as a token from me, especially since I didn't present you with the fuzzy slippers!"

"This is a beautiful knife," I said. "Stainless steel blades, bone handle. You don't want to do this."

"Yes, I do," she said, "it's a little big for me to carry. It belonged to Josef."

"Your little girl's father?"

"Yes," she continued. "She is too young and surely wouldn't have any use for it later."

"This is a treasure for her to have," I said.

"That may be," she continued, "but, I want you to have it."

For long moments I looked, handled, and studied the knife. I started to see this mysterious woman in a different light. *Why me,* I thought. *Is there no other man in her life?*

"Thank you," I said at last.

We ate in silence, sipped black tea, the pot kept hot under a quilted cozy.

"Lana, I hope I'm not too nosy, but what became of Josef?"

I had not planned to call her Lana. It came from someone other than a dejected prisoner. I was relieved to at last having lowered the shield of suspicion.

"Franz," Lana said, as our eyes connected, "I will tell you about Josef, but let's walk some more. It's too chilly to sit outside."

We again crossed the old bridge then chose a path paralleling the trolley tracks and the river. The grass covered water's edge and seasonal plantings were ready to meet the coming winter.

The graveled path kept time with the river as it meandered along. Occasionally a bench invited one to sit and face the languid flow. An alluring place for sure. I envisioned myself lost in its charm during the days ahead.

We had walked in silence for some distance when Lana spoke. "It happened along a river, about this size, when I held his hand for the last time. Mother had little Irina for the day. Josef completed basic training and had notice to report for active duty. I took him to town that designated morning in the family horse-drawn buggy. We were glad to have the whole day to ourselves. Neither of us knew then we would never see each other again." She looked straight ahead, her eyes in distant thought.

"The pleasant day came to a disquieting end when we started our way to the train station. It was Josef's hour. Before he boarded the train, he peered into my eyes and whispered, 'I can never fight my own people. If they make me, I'll have to run.' Josef's family has a long German line on his father's side. His mother's is Polish. Both sides of his people lived in East Prussia for several generations. My mother's family originally came from Macedonia. Both Josef and I were born outside of the city then called Königsberg about a half day away by horse and wagon." She slowed her pace and apologizing said, "I'm sorry. I don't know why I'm telling you all this. It must be boring to you."

"Lana, your story is most refreshing!"

"Well, good. I'll go on then. I grew up with Josef, but I never much liked him. Always a pestering young tyke, worrying the girls. The older we got, though, the cuter he became—at least I thought so. Of course I never told him so. They selected Josef and me to receive higher education, while most of the other children left school to learn a trade. Early every Monday morning, our fathers switched off to take us to the big city school for the week. On Fridays one of them always be waiting to take us back home. We never saw each other all week long. The boys and girls lived in separate dormitories as well as separated classrooms. When I first noticed that Josef liked me 'in a special way,' I was only fourteen. It happened in my father's buggy coming home one cold and frosty Friday. We each had our own blanket to wrap in. As nature would have it, our knees touched, our hands found each other's under those cozy blankets. A fire was kindled in me. I venture to say in him as well. After that spark, we searched for every opportunity to touch.

"Although our parents cooperated by taking us to school and back, they did not often visit each other's homes. I know my mother noticed a change in me. I brushed my hair a lot more often. She never said a word, but I knew that she knew I was in love."

"You're not going to stop now," I said. She looked ahead, her chin raised and smiled.

"For three years the fire never abated. Every time we touched, even as Josef helped me into the buggy, I practically melted. It seemed to me the fathers paid more attention to us, for they sure turned their heads a lot to check to see if we were 'all right' as we rode in the back of the buggy. It wasn't until my father finally could afford to rebuild the lean-to room, which had suffered damage during the Great Conflict, that Josef and I had the opportunity to add to our fantasy romance."

"Yes?" I said, in anticipation to hear more.

"At last, I got to embrace my dream. Are you sure you want to hear this?" Lana said with a sheepish grin.

"Of course!" I declared. "Sounds as if the dam is about to burst."

"Well," she continued, "as you put it, the dam did burst. My father called on a few trustworthy men from nearby families to help. Josef's dad worked for the railroad and could not help, but Josef could. As the men erected the structure, they became familiar with the routine around our house. Josef also noticed that my job, other than kitchen and laundry duties, was to pen up the chickens before dark. This wasn't a big thing, we only had a few. One day as he got ready to go home, he startled me as I rounded up the hens and said, 'Tomorrow take care of the chickens *after* your folks thinks all the men went home.'

"All day long I tried to figure out why he said that. The next day, I lingered a bit longer in the kitchen until all the workers had gone home. Dusk had crept in when I headed to the chicken coop. As I rounded the coop, there, Josef waited with arms wide open. He scooped me into his arms, kissed me wildly, as we stumbled toward and into a soft pile of hay in a nearby shed. Soon I felt a lifetime of bottled up rockets explode in my body. I could not believe, all I had imagined for so long became reality. I floated in such a whirl that I forgot to call the chickens."

"I gather it was worth the wait," I said.

"At that point, yes, the highlight of my life!" she concurred. "Realizing our romancing took a little more time than the chickens would require, Josef quickly whispered, 'the same tomorrow,' as he hurried off."

"What a wonderful love story."

Lana reached for one dead leaf still clinging to a tree. She placed it in her hand and tenderly touched it, looking off into the distance.

I let her memory seep gradually back to the present before I asked, "Did Josef get to know his little girl?" I quickly added, "Forgive me. You must think you've shared enough. I am sorry."

"I did share more of my life with you than I've ever with anyone else. I know what I tell you will not come back to hurt me."

We resumed the walk, aimless, stepping on our shadows in front of us. Then she spoke again.

"Soon after the men completed the house repair, I received a notice to come to Moscow for my internship. Josef took a position as a draftsman in Königsberg. Sworn to secrecy, he could not tell me more. Upon arriving in Moscow, I had morning sickness so bad I couldn't hide the fact I was pregnant. My supervisor called me aside, and with a few cutting words told me to 'get an abortion or leave this employment.' I went to my apartment frightened. Rest did not comfort me. I pondered three choices, the abortion, to leave town and tell no one, or to be with Josef. To be with Josef was my wish—to leave my employ was my choice. I knew Josef wouldn't be able to support me or the baby. Family traditions and beliefs would not have allowed us to live together. So, I worked as a maid in a convalescent home, a bit outside the city, until the baby came. The baby in one arm and dragging my suitcase with the other, I took the train back to Moscow and asked for my previous job. It worked. The old woman who advised me to abort had died. The new person in charge checked the old records and made room for me.

"I made the correct choice, don't you think?" she said.

"Yes, no need to second guess." I said.

"The early years turned out to be especially tough. Josef lived too far away to visit regularly, but we corresponded often. The baby and I took the train to see him once. We even made plans to get married. Then, as I told you, he got his conscription orders and all the plans fell to nothing—as did the leaves from these trees."

"You said the story ended. Do you still love him?" I asked.

"I came so close to fill my life with a precious and lasting love those long years ago. I could feel it. I had it in my grasp. The howls of war tore the heart-written poem from my fingers. Never again did I find a new love. Do I still love him, you asked? Sometime I shiver. Not from the cold outside, but the void within. My work consumes me. Staying busy is a way to cover the emptiness. I'm not complaining. I like my work.

"Yes, the story ended when they found him. He had been absent without leave. They shot him without hesitation and sent his belongings to his mother. She is the one who let me have a few of his things. One was his pocketknife."

"You shouldn't have . . ."

"Please," she said, "I have my daughter."

"You said a while back that you know what you told me would not come back to hurt you. I am honored you feel that way, but who would hurt you?"

"In my position, I do the watching of others. All too often, others are watching me. Everyone is always ready to chew and spit out to get ahead."

"Do you want to get ahead?" I said.

"Me get ahead? To have more phony friends clawing at me? Frankly—no! The System starts to stink the higher you climb."

I let her last statement rest. We had had a great day to that moment. No need to undo friendship with a political debate.

"Franz," she said, "I enjoyed this day. It is so refreshing to talk without reservation. Take the day off tomorrow. Look around, discover! The following day, however, I'll be at your door at eight in the morning. You need to start your new position. See you then."

"I'll be ready. And thanks again for the pocketknife."

13

On the day of work, Lana and I took the Number Eight tram halfway to Moscow. From there we boarded a shuttle trolley to a huge industrial complex. Old brick walls and buildings with corroded window frames and broken glass stared from every side. Rusted iron steps and catwalks connected and hugged all the structures. Metal roofs, peeling and rusted, showed patches of smeared tar where halfhearted attempts were made to keep the rain out. Chimneys and smokestacks evoked a menacing dread of one being overpowered. Soot and smog wrapped it all.

Lana must have known my thoughts when she said, "I hope now that the war is behind us, the government will concentrate on revitalizing these old factories. Over a hundred thousand people work in this area. Employment here has been a vital part of family lives for generations."

"I understand. Why can't anyone grow a tree around here?"

"There is a place and time for all things, and this is a place for working," Lana said as if part of a lecture. Then she added, "We're not getting off here—not yet."

"At least in the Ural Mountains the wind blew the smoke out. I feel sorry for the folks here, spending a lifetime among in this smog."

She left that remark on the trolley. We rode in silence for another kilometer or two, when to my surprise the environment shown trees and shrubs. The greenery, not too old and thoughtfully planted, flourished among the more modern facilities. I slowly chewed on my previous remarks. Besides bicycles, a few cars lined the designated areas.

"We'll be getting off at the next stop. Note, the same line will take you back," she said, making sure she had my attention. "This evening, on the return ride, I'll point out some of the essential places you may want to patronize; the Chinese couple who does laundry, a barbershop, a place to buy sliced meat, a small hall where you can read the current news."

"The fact is sinking in fast, I will be sticking around a while," I commented. "Guess I'll have to learn to fend for myself. I can brew tea and slice bread!"

"Vera, the woman who helped supply your new flat, will check on you occasionally." Lana added, "As long as you promise not to ask her to warm your fuzzy slippers." We both hopped off the trolley grinning.

—

Lana flipped her badge for reception. Within seconds a thin man appeared. He guided us down a long, dimly lit hallway to a double door, held open for us to enter.

"Comrade Grozny will be with you shortly," he said, then walked off.

I stood, overwhelmed by the glass-enclosed atrium. The glazed room tended to merge with the outdoors. Terraced gardens and ornamental trees overhung a small fishpond bordered by ferns and flowers. I was taken by its beauty. Lana noticed.

"This setting is pleasant all year long. In the spring, when most flowers show off, it is breathtaking," she proclaimed with pride.

Above a marble fireplace loomed a portrait of Stalin, to me a stark reminder not to get too chummy or comfortable in this land of many faces and eyes.

Grozny appeared to be well prepared. Only one folder marred the otherwise immaculate desktop. Lana and I sat facing him.

Lana conversed in a formal manner and referred to me as Mr. Brunner. He addressed her as Comrade Popova. The two spoke fast, using technical vocabulary, and left me clueless for most of the conversation. Whenever Grozny directed a question toward me, it was simply stated. Most questions required either a yes or a no. Obviously they had discussed and decided my appointed tasks previously.

When Grozny picked up the phone, we knew we had been dismissed. A gentleman in a white shop coat appeared and asked us to follow him. He led us into another building and up a flight of stairs that opened to a balcony, a type of catwalk that overlooked a manufacturing plant. Methodically, we promenaded around the entire facility, looking down on the workers and machinery.

"From here, the plant manager and his supervisors study the workers and workflow for optimum efficiency," the guide announced. "As you can see, not one workstation is hidden from view."

Yes, complete trust, I said to myself.

Upon circling the entire facility, we descended to the main floor to meet the head supervisor, a Comrade Ulanov.

After a polite handshake and a courtesy smile, he began, "Mr. Brunner, we're pleased to have you as our employee. We've researched your background and found it exceptional, especially in machining and product development. Before and during the war, this plant manufactured a variety of weapons and related parts and mechanisms. We're still in this process, although not as vigorously as before, always implementing new designs and upgrades derived from our capable intelligence system."

I guess you are, I thought. *Stealing all the engineering you can from superior weapons you confiscated.*

"We are also in the process of changing over to products for civilian use, primarily engines, generators, trucks, and mass transportation vehicles. Any questions so far?"

"No," I said, without hesitation. This job certainly looked better than the one at the mine. *If I'm forced to do so, I can work on weapon systems, but I'm not volunteering, and I'm sure not suggesting improvements,* I said to myself.

We entered a neat and noise-dampened room.

"Mr. Brunner, this is the Experimentation Room. Prototypes are refined and perfected here. The X room, as we call it, will be your main station of work and focus. We expect you to add your expertise with product development and testing as we generate new parts and prototypes, bring them on line, either in this facility or one of several others in the Soviet Union. Part of your work may also be with our engineers in designing production lines." Ulanov looked at me expecting a response.

"Thanks for your confidence," I said. "Sounds challenging."

"Yes, it may well be." He continued, "We expect you'll need some time to familiarize yourself with the machinery and testing equipment."

The X room had its own entrance, a short walk from the trolley stop. Its equipment showed some modern technology and was kept spotless. Mr. Ulanov assigned me a small desk and went on to show me my locker in the adjoining room. "If you have further questions, your immediate supervisor is Comrade Gagarina."

Miss Gagarina looked to be near retirement age. I suspected her drawn expression caused the perpetual frown and wrinkles. The woman's dull, gray hair, pinned into a tight knot on back of her head, promoted her Romanesque nose to be the main attraction and the perfect saddle for her pinch-on glasses. Her face revealed eyes that failed to find satisfaction in life. Her desk, in the far corner of the X room, offered her an easy view of everyone. Piles of machine parts, trays of small tools, and items with notes and drawings tucked in between, covered her desk. She hunched over her work as a hen over her chicks and mumbled rarely more than a greeting.

From day one, the majority of fellow employees, acted aloof and vague, said little, and often ignored me. I represented the enemy. To some an ever present threat to their position, to others a reminder of great pain and loss the war inflicted. At first, no one in the X room let me see what they worked on, much less asked for advice. Whenever I approached, they turned their backs to me and pretended to be busy. I stayed determined not to let it bother me. The lack of cooperation forced me to approach Ulanov directly, instead of Miss Gagarina, with my observations and ideas for the plant. That, of course, did not sit well either. It led to Ulanov calling Miss Gagarina to his office. He must have persuaded her to show me at least the civility of listening. Her attitude changed to forced congeniality.

As time passed, I gained respect with some of the workers in the plant. I had helped many make their tasks easier. At long last, shift leaders and department heads came directly to me when malfunctions occurred. On several occasions I redesigned the workflow and eliminated enough hourly labor to have some promoted. Miss Gagarina, however, shrank back into her jealous shell and moped around, totally ignoring me.

I never did learn what the average pay was; obviously a subject everyone kept to themselves. As for me, my pay amounted to a mere pittance. Then, why should they have paid me at all? Why, I had free housing, a pile of coal, a pair of work boots, a laundered shop coat and two shirts per week, a morning snack and a reduced cost lunch. Exactly what any zombie needs. With what little pay I took home I squeezed out a bottle of beer a day and even an extra bar of soap to wash out my underwear in the sink. If I continued to keep my mouth shut and danced to the tune to suit the Big Eye watching, I could be assured a free casket when I died.

—

My energy level stayed fairly high, even compared to younger people. However, about eight months into my new career, I started to see confusing images. A new pair of glasses improved my eyesight, but they didn't do away with my feeling disoriented and frequent headaches. I came to work tired and arrived home physically drained, with my feet numb and tingling. Often I fell into bed nauseated and without eating.

When I didn't show to meet Lana for our Saturday evening walk, she came to check on me. Receiving no answer after knocking, she hollered and then entered. I struggled to sit erect having severe stomach cramps. Lana knelt on the floor to check my eyes and pulse.

"Can you walk?" she asked.

"I think so."

"We are going to see a doctor!"

I knew by now that tone of voice meant business. She didn't wait for me to get dressed, but threw my robe over my shoulders. I could not have made it to the trolley station without Lana's assistance. Exhausted, I collapsed onto the bench.

At the doctor's office Lana rang the emergency bell. A woman, not much taller than a child and dressed in black, answered. Apparently not fazed by the sight of a desperate man holding to a woman, she announced, "The doctor is at the hospital on an emergency call. I know he would want any patients in need to report there as well."

We crossed the street to catch the a trolley. The one already at the stop started to pull away. Lana waved frantically at the conductor to wait for us, but he didn't. She stepped into the trolley's path and forced it to an abrupt halt.

"Hospital!" she snapped.

I collapsed upon entering the hospital's door. I last remembered the bright lights overhead as they spun in circles. When awareness returned, I rested on my side, my head in a tray. Two tubes entered my mouth. I knew Lana to be present somewhere in the room.

"Franz, can you hear me?" Her blurred voice came from a cave.

A grunt was all I could muster.

"You are in good hands," she assured me. "The doctors pumped your stomach and forced fluids in to flush any remaining poison. When your head clears, you and I are going to find out what got you into this situation."

I heard the word poison, but only got the gist of Lana's statements. During the night the tubes were removed. I still sensed Lana in the room.

"Lana?"

"I'm here. You rest."

"Lana, are you really here?"

Lana came to the bedside, placed one hand on my forehead, and whispered, "I am here. How are you feeling?"

Comforted by her presence, I said, "I don't think I'm going to fade away, not yet. Thanks to you, we kicked the Grim Reaper in the arsch."

"My, my, you are getting well. Almost sounds like the old Franz. Did you understand what I said when you first woke up?"

"I think I got most of it. Let's see," I thought. "The doctor thinks I got poisoned. Is that it? . . . My head . . . it's about to bust."

"That's right. Rest. You're doing fine," she said. "Whenever you're able, maybe by tomorrow, we can try to find out how it all happened."

While Lana spoke, a nurse came in, forced me to drink a beaker full of a bitter concoction, pulled me to my side, and rammed a previously prepared injection in my rump. I didn't wake until hot tea and sliced bread arrived at the ward the next morning. When I looked, Lana sat near, still smiling.

"Good morning, Franz," she said, with a singsong lilt in her voice. "Can you hear me?"

"Yes, I'm glad to see you."

She changed her tone to more businesslike. "Franz," she said softly, "it's early Monday morning, very early. I hope you are in a frame of mind to do a bit of thinking. Please try to direct me through some scenarios."

"I'll try."

"If this is not an accident, but attempted murder, I have to have a handle on it before the start of work this morning. If the culprit finds out you're in the hospital, he or she would remove all evidence. Franz, if someone is doing this to you, they want you gone for good—to die. Think hard. Who might that be?" She slid her chair close to my bed.

"I don't know. A while back, not many liked me. Now, the folks have gotten used to me."

"Franz, I believe a single person did this to you. If it were accidental, more people would be sick." With a slight tone of panic she asked, "Think Franz, think! Franz, are you still with me?"

"Yes, I am thinking who has lately extra pleasant."

"Extra pleasant!" she snapped.

"Yes, to decoy their deed."

"Well, is anyone coming to mind?"

"Not really."

"Then think about who was nasty to you lately. Someone who hates to see you around. A person who talks behind your back or makes snide comments in your hearing," Lana prodded, grasping at anything.

I had a hard time staying focused. Situations of old kept popping to mind.

Her face now very close. "Franz?" Warm breath brushed my cheek, her hypnotic voice, low and clear, whispered, "Focus, Franz. Someone who feels pressured. Have you made anyone angry? Have you stepped on someone's toes? You know what I mean. Does anyone feel threatened by your popularity? Is anyone agitated thinking you may get ahead of them at work? Can you think about someone worried you may replace them?"

The last question lit a flare. "Miss Gagarina!" I blurted. "She don't even look at me, or talk to me any longer."

"Are you positive?"

"Yes, she may be worried I'll take her job."

Before Lana rose from the chair, she gave me a quick kiss on the forehead and said, "Bye."

Did I deserve that kiss? I thought. *Do all intelligence agents kiss their clients?*

I focused like a stalking cat on how the old witch mastered her deed. . . *Poisoned.* . . . *Slowly.* . . . Gradually the spilled sack of marbles quit rolling, as fresh adrenaline rushed my brain and cleared the fog. My bones and head ached every time I took a deep breath or moved.

The nurse, syringe in hand, was prepared to sock it to me again. I refused the pain killer. "I have to think," I told her. The last time I lay on a sick bed, two of my toes were the problem. The offer of a hard drink had been a welcome one. There in the Moscow hospital, I welcomed the pain.

Slowly poisoned . . . a little at a time . . . every day. I studied my daily routine and habits. Methodically I groped through every possible plot. A simple scenario fell into place.

On the wall of the locker room hung a long sink. We, the X room gang, used it to wash our hands and drink of its good, cold water. Above the two spigots hung various-shaped mugs and drinking cups. I claimed one as my own. Two, sometimes three times a day, I'd take the cup off the nail, let the water run a few seconds, then get a drink. However, I never first rinsed the cup. All mugs hung by the handle, none hung so they drained.

That's it! She is putting something in my mug! That is why the old witch is always first at work.

I raised up on my elbows. My eyeballs about popped from the pain. I wanted to shout, tell someone! The world spun. The pain slapped me down. My lights dimmed.

My bed stood in the middle of a ward of a dozen patients. Monday evening, still feeling wrung out, Lana pulled a chair close to the bed.

"Let me share the highlights," she started. "I got to the plant the same time Comrade Grozny stepped out of his car. We entered the building together. Once through security, I confronted him with my request. He agreed. Comrade Ulanov delayed Miss Gagarina from coming to the X room while I searched her desk. I found no suspicious liquid or powder."

"You looked for liquid?" I said in amazement. "That is exactly what I think it must be. Lana, let me tell what hit me after you left this morning."

Face to face, eyes wide open, we inhaled each other's breath as I developed my theory.

"Very plausible," Lana agreed. "Franz, tell me, does she drink beer?"

"Not that I know of. I never noticed."

"Well, I found three bottles of the stuff in her desk. One was half empty. She must sip it on the sly. Did you ever smell it on her?"

"No, as I said, I don't get that close to the woman. She could be nipping."

"You know, Franz," she continued, "those bottles do not have to contain beer. They're easy to open and shut with those rubber-tipped ceramic plugs on them. If we go with your assumption, one of the bottles may contain the poison."

"The two full ones may be beer," I suggested. "They're there as a decoy to draw attention away from the half-empty one."

"Very good point," Lana agreed. "Good thing I didn't remove any of the bottles. I need to catch her in the act."

"How are you going to do that?"

"Well, when you didn't show this morning, Comrade Ulanov told Comrade Gagarina you'd be out for the day. He made it sound more feasible by telling her, "Miss Popova is taking him to tour Plant Number Four."

Now, if your theory is correct, she didn't put poison in your cup today—we messed with her routine. Tomorrow, however, thinking you'll be back, she'll be up to her old trick."

"Still, how are you going to catch her?"

"I have a notion that might play well. I'll be at the plant long before she arrives. If I remember correctly, the lockers face the sink."

"That is right."

"You think I can fit into one of the wall lockers? Don't answer that! I'm talking it through. From inside the locker, I'll get a good view through the vent slots."

"I wish I could be there. To see the old spinster squirm would do me good."

That evening Lana worked out the strategy at Comrade Ulanov's apartment. He agreed to ride the tram to work so his blue bike would not signal him being there. The shop was left dark. Ulanov hid behind a machine to have a clear view of Miss Gagarina's desk. Lana, meanwhile, hid in my locker to monitor the wash sink.

Miss Gagarina as usual arrived early, hung her coat in her locker, then went to her desk. She promptly opened the bottom desk drawer and pulled out the half-full bottle. She then reached for a pencil in her pencil cup, held the bottle to the light, and stuck the pencil into the bottle as if to fish for something. She promptly shuffled to the locker room and put the pencil into my cup. At that moment Lana jumped from the locker. Miss Gagarina dropped the pencil and pretended to wash her hands. Ulanov entered about the same time.

The pencil turned out to be a piece of copper hydraulic tubing, which she dipped into the poison to the desired depth. To keep the liquid from draining she held her index finger on top of the tube.

Slick, I thought. Why she worked in a machine shop and not for the MVD I did not understand. The old sadist played me like a fish on a line. She could have upped the dose and had me keel over anytime she chose to. Ah, but the joy of doing it slowly.

14

The one and only time in my life I was forced to use a bedpan it prompted me to get well pronto. Once my head quit spinning, I became aware of a particularly large nurse who assisted the other patients in the ward. I had become fed up with having to urinate into a bulky bottle every hour. When the need to perform the other function arose, I reckon my turn to meet Miss Kong, as I called her, had arrived. She jerked the blanket off of me, locked her massive arm around both of my legs, and lifted my bottom off the bed. After she rammed a bedpan under me, she wrapped her capable arm under my armpits and yanked me into a sitting position—all in less than ten-seconds.

Being in the middle of the room, and the only one in sitting position, I had a good chance to look around. Now I, the dominant object, felt like an admired bouquet. All eyes watched. To relax in such a precarious situation is well nigh impossible. I dare not grunt, or even distort my face, in fear some of the women in the ward might think I winked at them. If that humiliation didn't sit bad enough, when the mission was accomplished, Miss Kong rolled me to my side, jerked one leg straight into the air and with a cold towel, resembling a mop on a mission, gave me one good wipe. I didn't want to ask whether she hated Germans, or if the routine complimented the charm and hospitality of the establishment. It became clear to me to get out of bed, do or die, the next time the need arose.

When Lana heard of me getting out of bed, she asked for my release and brought me to my apartment.

"Continue to drink plenty of liquids. A spritz of cider vinegar and sugar in a glass of water would also help," said the doctor. "In addition, I recommend one glass of red wine a day."

"Can I afford the wine?" I asked Lana.

"Franz, don't worry about the cost of all this. Doctor's instructions, you know. The State is paying for your hospital stay.

I've made sure your position is not in jeopardy and your pay is continuing as we sit here."

"Thanks," I said, feeling fairly recovered, compared to a week earlier.

"Any development on the Miss G. matter?"

Lana eased over to the stove. She tried to dampen her next words. "The lab report confirmed arsenic." Again she hesitated, sliding the copper kettle onto another burner. "All I want to say at this juncture is that Comrade Gagarina has been relieved of her duties and is being detained by the authorities."

"Good. The witch will be out of my life." Then the truth hit. "Arsenic! It'll be with me a while, will it not?"

"I posed the very question to the doctor who delivered the lab report to the office."

"And, what did he say?"

"There will be some residual symptoms, however, the chance for a complete recovery is good."

After I pondered the facts, she added, "Franz, I can see it in your eyes your mind is cranking overtime again. That means you are on the mend. If the mind is willing, the body will follow. I would be happy to be part of the healing, the healing of your body, and your heart, if you let me."

"Heal my heart? That'll take some doing."

"Think positive. I've got something that will start the process," she said with confidence.

From one of the small chairs in my apartment I watched Lana saunter toward the bed, revealing the slight sway of a full-bodied woman. With one hand on the bedpost, she flung a coy smile coupled with a come-hither look. Seated on the bed, she produced from her purse two narrow cards.

I realized fast it wasn't the day for healing the body. "Come here. Take a look at these."

The two cards looked alike; only the handwritten number differed. Then the name Tchaikovsky registered.

"You and I will attend an all-Tchaikovsky concert," she said. "We'll hear the *Fifth Symphony* and *Violin Concerto*."

"Lana, that is the most exciting news I've heard in years."

"I thought it would cheer you up."

"I love it. I love Tchaikovsky, and I love the violin!"

"The concert is on Saturday, I'll be by to see you earlier in the day. We'll have a pleasant afternoon before we head downtown."

"Great. I'll look forward to it." With deep curiosity I asked, "Why are you so concerned about my well-being? You have spent countless hours on a simple, leftover POW. Plus, now this?"

"Well, to complete what I have started is important to me. I want you to be satisfied and a benefit to our people," she said smiling. "You deserve a little special treatment. You're a great guy. I enjoy your company. I hope before too long you'll feel the same about me."

"Lana, I have had much time to think, especially while not working. I know where I would be right now were it not for you. First, I'd probably be dead, poisoned. At best, still stuck at the mine. Lucky me, a lovely lady had been assigned to my case. It could have been some fat old guy, all slouchy, with rank cigarette breath. Lana, I am honored you enjoy my company, and I do enjoy your company. I admit, being with you positively rounds out my week and boosts my fractured manhood."

"That's indeed good to hear. Healing has begun. Is there anything you need before Saturday? Is Vera keeping you supplied with the essentials?

"Essentials? Yes," I said. "Vera is quite a woman."

"Franz, what's that mischievous smirk?"

"Oh, nothing," I said grinning, "bread, cheese, linens, you know."

"Aren't you wily," she quipped, knowing the comment was in jest.

The Moscow Symphony Orchestra sprawled before me; as large an orchestra as I had ever seen. The quality of the performance overwhelmed me. It filled my soul. I had difficulty holding back tears. It also opened a void in me, an immense longing. Lana's words came to mind, "It is time for your heart to heal."

As we strolled from the massive concert hall, Lana placed her arm in mine. "Why has the music affected you so?" She asked.

"I do not quite understand it either. The performance truly was exceptional, and wonderful. The music itself always brings a tear of joy. Tonight, something different penetrated. It felt like a religious experience. Heavenly voices streamed through to my soul. Much like a gentle river caressing every eddy and cleansing every pebble. I experienced a tremendous yearning to hold on, but unable to grasp. When the last note subsided, the feeling slipped away. I felt so alone, so incomplete. Lana, tonight is the first time I've heard music in over six years. I didn't know how much I missed my violin."

"Your violin?"

"Yes, I used to play. Never professionally, only for the joy of it. Before the children came along, my wife and I patronized various evening spots that featured live music. At times I'd fill in for the violinist. My wife loved to play her concertina. Whenever we traveled, that little squeezebox came with us. She'd play the hit songs of the day as well as the old favorite beer-drinking songs. She'd sing along and yodel. I, I'm more of a classical musician, playing the Italian masters' love songs, as well as gypsy music of Liszt and Dvorak."

"I see music played a big part in your life." Lana gripped my arm all the more. "Franz, would you think wrong of me if I asked you to come to my place? I know, it sounds like a schoolgirl's trick, but I have a little more healing for your heart."

"Lana, I would never think of you as brash or brazen. If you're still as charming as right now, I'll even consider staying a while."

She stopped and faced me, lowered her voice, and said, "You may get into the henhouse, you old fox, but this chick knows her way around her coop." We both chuckled and ambled on toward the tram.

—

As I surmised, Lana's apartment was a few hundred meters from mine. An open stairway led to her flat. Before we entered, she placed her index finger on my chest and said, "For the healing of your heart, remember?"

"I know . . . the healing of the heart." I smiled.

Lana switched on a simple light near the door, took my cool-weather jacket, and hung it over the desk chair.

She motioned toward the sofa. "Make yourself comfortable." When she entered the kitchen, I ogled all I could take in. The decor exuded an inviting warmth. Not excessively feminine, more of a motherly touch than sophisticated or professional. A piano graced the middle of one wall, forming the focal point of the entire room. The desk chair, the piano stool, the couch offered the only seating. I suspected not many people came to visit.

Lana entered with a pot of tea, two cups and a sugar bowl on a tray. She gracefully placed all on the small table in front of the couch. Then she brought the desk chair for herself. The wall clock's ticking, the spoon stirring the cup, added the only sounds. All seemed pleasantly charged when I broke the quiet. "I should be the one sitting on the chair. Please, you sit on the sofa."

"I'm fine, please, stay put."

We chatted about the tea, the cups, and the tray it was served on. No doubt the evening had the ability to turn in several directions. We needed time to divert our physical notions to matters of the heart.

"Does Irina play the piano?"

"Yes, she is taking lessons when she's home."

"I venture to say her mother plays also, for the keyboard is uncovered."

"I do." Lana crossed her legs making sure her skirt covered the knees. "But, I'm not nearly as talented as your wife."

"My wife, I would say, lost all her joviality long ago." Making eye contact, I said, "From what I see, you spend your time either at your desk or playing the piano."

"I read too," she added.

I left the couch and walked to where she sat and held out my hands, I said, "Lana, would you play for me?"

Relieved, she took my hands and rose. "I hope I'll not disappoint you."

"Lana, the only way you would disappoint me if you didn't play. Play for us. Play from your heart."

I sat again on the couch. After she found the center of the piano bench, she drew her shoulders back and relaxed. The expectation drew me closer. From the corner on the couch I beheld her classic profile, enticing, *the* forbidden fruit. She switched on a small crystal light on the piano. Spellbound, I watched. One loose lock of black hair kissed her cheek; the rest fell to her shoulders. The twinkle of the crystal light coaxed tiny shadows from her long eyelashes to transform her dark eyes to shimmering red wine.

Beginning with the first note, a chill rushed through me. Soft and tender grace not only revealed her talent, but her soul as well, as she flowed with elegant ease through Beethoven's "Moonlight Sonata." Again, I could not contain a tear.

Lana concluded by resting her hands on the keyboard, tilting her head, and smiled.

I reached for her hand. "So beautiful, absolutely beautiful. Is that what you meant when you said, 'I have what would help heal your heart?'"

"Yes, I trust it made a start."

"Oh Lana, I hope I'm going to be sick for a while. I could never get enough of such music, played so well and by such a charming person." She seemed pleased.

We nibbled on sweet crackers. I refreshed our tea. The serenity of the evening compelled me to ask her to play again.

When I opened my eyes, a calm stillness surrounded me. The only light glistened from the small crystal lamp on the piano. My feet laid stretched on the sofa, my shoes neatly placed on the floor. A thin blanket covered me. My watch showed a bit after three in the morning. I slumped back unto the couch.

Now what? Should I leave and go home? Wake Lana? I decided to let the night play out, hoping to fall asleep again and be awakened by the special lady. I stirred when a faint rustling came from the kitchen.

"Lana," I whispered, not wanting to startle her. "I must have dozed off. I'm so sorry."

"That's quite all right," she assured me. "You were tired. You did have quite a couple of weeks, you know. I hope you rested."

"Your playing wooed me into heaven, where I stayed all night. At peace and satisfied like a baby in its mother's arms."

"I am glad. I'm making fresh tea. Are you awake enough to have some with me?"

"Wide awake. Thanks," I said. "May I freshen up a bit?"

"Go ahead. The place is yours."

"Thanks."

The washroom reflected Lana. The black tile on the floor spoke of the color of her hair. The handmade rag rug, fashioned mostly of rose-colored strips, told of her cheeks. The large, white cast-iron tub along a rich red wall, elevated by brass paw feet, emulated her skin and luscious lips. Above the small radiator hung one bath towel. A brass spigot protruded from the wall above a white washbowl sitting on a black wrought-iron stand. The entire bathing nook exuded her mysterious charm.

Lana waited at the table. The completeness of the setting, cups, saucers, plates, and teapot matched her womanhood. From a linen-lined basket peeped several warm slices of bread. A slightly chipped glass lid covered the butter dish, while a dainty silver spoon stood erect in a bowl of jam.

"Isn't it amazing how a drifting vagabond like me wound up eating breakfast at your place with his shoes off."

"Don't put yourself down. Relax! It's my pleasure you're here."

"Lana, do you have to report our meeting here to the authorities?"

"What do you mean?" She said, somewhat disturbed.

"You know, I had such a wonderful time—falling to sleep and all. Do you have to let someone know?"

"Franz, relax. As far as my life goes, I report very little. What others inform me about, that I have to write-up." She looked at me hoping I understood. "I can tell you this," she reduced her tone to a whisper, "sometimes the System stinks."

15

Lana, smart and beautiful, lived alone. Any social life she pursued likely ended by being exposed and scrutinized. Her befriending me certainly prompted an even deeper look into my past. I had to remind myself not to get too philosophical, but make the best of every day. I liked the thought that Lana felt at ease around me. I enjoyed being with her. For better or worse, I got along.

Before I returned to work, Lana emphasized not to reveal the reasons of my absence. "The superiors all know the facts. Anyone in the manufacturing area will not be barefaced enough to ask for details," she said.

Without much ado I fell back into the routine. The X room hummed along well without the witch. Generally, the folks in the plant were about as enthusiastic as the machines themselves. Joviality stayed outside the shop. Often, instead of keeping up with the machine's production, the operator slowed it down. Lethargic motions of some employees, a sure sign of alcohol influence, not only followed weekends, but showed daily. The bottle to some had become the confidant, a partner. Life for the vast majority churned on and on, and evolved into absolute boredom. To be seen as ambitious or ingenious translated to a threat to the other workers.

When a problem arose, or a suggestion needed approval, I had become the one who approached Ulanov. Along with my responsibility of keeping the plant's equipment productive, several other sister plants also had needs. Because of the increase of work, many projects stayed incomplete, buried on my desk. Frustrated, I left the job with a knot in my gut and became increasingly more irritable and curt with Lana.

"Franz, you're sort of aloof lately. You're not responding or are as free as usual. Is something troubling you? I look forward to these Saturday evenings together."

"You noticed? I'm sorry, I didn't mean to drag it home."

"Drag what home? You want to tell me?"

I exhaled a chest full of tension. "Sure. I'm frustrated. Can't seem to get caught up."

"Oh?" She responded.

"Yes, the more I do, the more they find to pile on. Maybe since the poison didn't kill me, they figure they're going to work me to death."

"Funny, not really," she said.

"As production increases, new demands arise. We failed to bring on an assistant, promote a sharp mind, one who can think, show some decisiveness. As you can imagine, everyone is fat and happy. Why should they worry as long as this fool German is doing it all."

"Franz, I hate to see you so stressed. Have you talked to Comrade Ulanov?"

"No, the increased productivity makes him quite comfortable in his catbird seat."

"Do you want me to get involved? Do you have a suggestion?"

"You know young Nikolai? He has an excellent head on his shoulders. He is always nosing around and interested in what I am doing. Too bad, he is only seventeen, certainly not old enough to warrant respect from the others."

"Franz, if he is leadership material, let's start him now."

"That change order would have to come from someone other than me."

"I agree," Lana echoed.

"If I only had someone as conscientious as Boris."

"Boris? The maintenance man at the mine?"

"Yeah." I said with a sigh.

"Hmm," Lana thought. "We brought one of your fellow compatriots into the maintenance shop after you left. I forgot his last name. I'm fairly sure they called him Werner. He worked as a welder in Germany."

"Sure, I know him. One of our machine gunners. As much damage as he did to your side, it's a wonder the Red Army let him live."

"All I know, he is working out fine. Going back to Boris, I find that an interesting idea."

"Zlatoust is almost 2,000 kilometers away. Do you think he would want to leave the area? All his family is there. He's lived there all his life," I said.

Lana studied my suggestion. I found it a bit of a stretch to think that Boris might be called to Moscow.

"Boris and I worked well together." I said. "Every idea I had, he'd jump right in and run with it. He is a mighty good mechanic, curious and forthright enough to fall in line with the operation here."

"I trust your judgment," she said.

"Lana, if you could pull this off, please make it worthwhile for him and his family. He is a good man. He has given his life to his work."

"I'll start the wheels turning. Meanwhile, Franz, don't let the workplace get to you. I'm comfortable with the way I've always known you."

—

The seasons changed—my mundane existence dragged on. I stared at the third winter in Moscow. When the days shortened and the barren ghosts emerged and hushed the joys of bloom and warmth, my soul clambered to grab hold of a reason for going on. I found the strolls along the river the best therapy. In the dreary evenings of winter, the purling waters of the river seemed to be the only thing alive. The drab hours of the early dusk turned to long nights, adding time to think. Lana, however, had an inherent knack of rounding out my week, months, and the raw edges of winter. She always steered me through the days when the pit of depression loomed and gently eased me back to life.

As always, the days again lengthened and folks stirred like starving squirrels. I again tipped my hat at friendly smiles along the graveled paths. I loved the sun's warming rays. It blessed my soul to see the leftover mounds of snow succumb to their last melt. *One more winter behind me,* I pondered. *Round and round I go—a mule treading grain. Dependent as a caged rat. My clothes hang on me like curtains on a hat rack. My shoes leak. . . . But . . . I'm alive!*

Nikolai, the young man at work oozed energy. A strapping young fellow with shoulders that promised strength as a man. Totally unassuming and curious, capped with a shock of reddish-blond hair that always sported an unruly cowlick in back of his head. He was not afraid to smile and show a few crooked teeth. I didn't learn his deep-set eyes were sea green until much later. He communicated well with his fellow workers, and was one of several apprentices in the plant. For his age, given the opportunity, he demonstrated to be quite an accomplished lathe and milling machine operator.

Nikolai knew I admired his enthusiasm for learning. He, in turn, tried to please me. Not that he wanted to be promoted, I think, but because he had pride in his work. Nikolai noticed I had a different approach than "The System" did in accomplishing the everyday challenges. He latched on to the idea that not all problems can be solved solely by following a standard procedure or format. In Nikolai, I saw a young man who would go against the grain if he thought the cause justified it. I didn't know if more like him hovered out there. To me he was refreshing.

Sitting opposite him at the end of the long lunch table, I watched him unbuckle the strap of his cloth satchel. Unabashedly, he'd unwrap part of a loaf of bread, a piece of cheese, and a chunk of hard, smoked sausage. The crinkled wrapping paper showed it had gone through the same routine many times before.

"Don't you like the lunch here at the shop? It doesn't cost all that much, and it isn't bad," I said.

He tilted his head a bit and half mumbled, "I know, it's not bad."

"So, you think it's too expensive?"

"No, that's not it. I chose to get a few extra roubles in my pay envelope."

"Why does a young man need extra roubles?"

"I don't have my own place, you know. I pay my sister for a small room."

"Don't you get a housing allowance?"

"Yes, but living with my sister saves me money."

"What are you saving for?" I pressed. When he hesitated, I said, "Nikolai, say it's none of my business. You don't have to answer me."

"I know, Mr. Brunner. I don't mind the questions." Nikolai continued, "I hope you also are going to answer some of my questions."

"I will. I tell you what, let's meet at the bicycle rack for a short chat every other day or so. How does that sound?"

"Perfect. Why every other day, and why outside?"

"Let me say, I'm the foreigner and probably never alone. If you know what I mean."

"I know exactly what you mean. Great. I'm excited. Meet you at the rack."

"At the rack—today!" Smiling, he went back to work.

Nikolai starved for a paternal figure. I was old enough to be his father. We had our casual chats at the lunch table in the presence of his friends. The meatier talks we tackled at the bike rack.

During the ensuing months. Nikolai opened his heart at the rack. Although he lived with his sister, he didn't much participate in her family's life. He revealed his disappointment for not being selected to become a mechanical engineer. His grades at the time were fine, but because of his family's social status, he was denied additional education.

Nikolai was twelve years old when he last saw his father. His father and most of his friends disappeared one night. Not long after, his mother, his older sister, and he found themselves on a collective farm in the Ukraine. At fourteen, upon completing the basic eight grades, he ran away. He continued his story during the short periods at the rack.

Nikolai spilled his heart. His trembling voice revealed a deep hurt as the words rushed out. "The authorities picked me up when I tried to get work papers. They said if I could find someone to take me in, they would give me my papers. If not, a juvenile work camp stared me in the face. I gave them my sister's address."

Enough information for one day at the rack. We quickly parted. If someone watched, I didn't want to be seen engrossed in deep conversation. At the next rack meeting he'd start precisely where he left off.

"While the authorities checked on me, I stayed at a correctional center and performed menial tasks until word came that my sister would take me in."

"Nikolai, let me be your friend. What we talk about no one else will ever know." He smiled, hopped on his bike, and peddled off.

I couldn't help but grow close to this young man. He was still a child, yet determined and focused at the vulnerable age of seventeen. Nikolai did not cower to the authorities. He knew not to spout denigrating remarks in the hearing of his friends or even his sister. I found him to be a young man with strong principles. *A dangerous trait in this land,* I thought.

"Nikolai, you never told me why you want to save money?"

His eyebrows furrowing. "Mr. Brunner, to do what a man wants to do, he needs money."

"Any plans on what you want to do?" I asked.

"The options are coming clear to me as I listen to . . ." Nikolai hesitated, dropped his head, and stared at the ground. I didn't say a word. I knew he stood at a crossroad—wanting to reveal something different, something shocking, something deeply secret.

"You were saying . . .?" I said after a moment.

"I started to say that I listen to radio," he said in a measured way, not sure if he wanted to continue on the subject. Taking a deep breath, and a forced smile, he said, "I'll tell you about it another day." He peddled off.

—

Vera's note on the small table read, "Lana wants to share a bowl of stew with you tonight."

In my world of routine I welcomed the chance to spend extra time with Lana. It always outweighed sitting on a bench counting ducks in the river's eddies.

"I heard a bit of news about Comrade Gagarina's case today," Lana volunteered.

"Is she coming back to try again?"

"That won't be the case, I assure you. The arsenic she used on you is also used to process certain metals at several of our sister plants. The strange truth is, she diluted the potions and literally played with your life. Apparently getting great pleasure seeing you gradually waste away and become too sick to perform your work."

"So, it wasn't meant to kill?"

"Oh yes! It was going to kill you. Being diluted, it would have taken a while."

"Thanks for telling me all that. I think I'll skip supper."

"The big question remains," Lana said, "where did she get the stuff? If from one of the other plants, who gave it to her?"

"Do you have to find that out?"

"Sure. We cannot have even the smallest amount in the hands of civilians. We have many dissidents in the country. You can understand."

I wanted to jump on that last statement and start a good argument, but I treasured a pleasant evening instead.

While I helped clean the dishes, Lana asked, "How is the job going these days?"

"As much work as ever," I said. "The stress is easing a bit. I don't know if it's a better attitude or the hope of Boris's coming."

"The Boris deal may work, but it may drag on a while," she said. After hanging the dish towel she smiled confidently and said, "Let's go over to Mikhail's Café. Sound good?"

"It's a fancy place, isn't it?" Surprised at her suggestion. "I faintly hear the music drifting across the river when I walk and the wind is right."

"It's not that fancy. If we hurry, we'll get seats inside. It's still a little nippy to sit under the trees outside."

16

The old bridge to Mikhail's Café displayed beautifully chiseled stone, echoing the centuries past and promising to endure centuries to come. The bridge had been built wide enough for a horse-drawn wagon. A knee-high ledge hugged its sides. One could sit on the ledge and let a buggy squeeze by. Viewed from any bench along the river's edge, the bridge was a charming structure. Now mostly used by pedestrians, it provided access to the quaint shops, taverns, and specialty stores that supplied and satisfied the whims of the affluent party members living in the area. Lana and I made our way to the café guided by one feeble streetlight at each end of the bridge. The waters below whispered with a thousand garbled voices. The spring thaw forced the river to lap near the top of its banks. Even in the dark, I heard the gurgling swirls as they rushed among boulders and newfound eddies. The thought of falling into the icy water gave me a chill.

"Lana, I don't have the money to patronize these places," I commented. "By the way, does anyone ever get a raise in this country?" She smiled.

The music floating from Mikhail's drew us to its arched entrance. A friendly fellow seated us at a table for two with a fair view of the musicians. We both ordered a glass of red wine and then settled to enjoy the music and watch the people.

"You know, the State ought to pay for this glass of wine. It is part of my rehabilitation as ordered by the good doctor."

"Maybe you ought to run up a tab here. Submit it, and see how far you can get with it." Lana grinned.

"Yeah," I continued, "all we need is for you to find an ailment. Then both of us could do this every night."

The room filled with tobacco smoke. Some sucked on hand-rolled cigarettes. A few ladies flashed their smokes held in long Bakelite holders. I spotted pipes dating back to the nineteenth century, while others sported the short, modern type that stuck straight out from the mouth. The smell of it all was certainly a lot more pleasant than the reek in the barracks, years ago.

Straight vodka reigned in most men's glasses. Some of the good folks obviously settled in to stay the evening, as reflected by the cork sticking from the bottle on the table. One rosy-cheeked fellow, his chin resting on his chest, sat slumped against the wall. The trio played on—one violin, a cello, and a balalaika.

Many men and women turned their heads as they recognized Lana. All made a simple gesture of greeting, but none spoke to her.

"Do you come here often? The folks here act as if they know you."

"No, not often. Most all of them I know as neighbors."

"Lana, tell me, the work you do, does it sort of keep you on the sidelines? Keep you from being who you want to be?"

"What do you mean?"

"I mean, is the real you different from how the people see you? You must know your position creates much curiosity. It seems to me people are reluctant to get close. Either they are in awe of you, or they are afraid of you."

"Franz, you have a keen sense of your surroundings. The position I hold, as seen by ordinary people, is not one of high esteem. I'm not always welcome. As an investigator for the State, people are leery of me. By living in this neighborhood for a good many years, folks made me into something that I am not. I once had a great time socializing, had many friends. As the years moved on, even my friends became wary of me. I'm sorry you noticed. Sure, I'm troubled by their reactions. Even if I changed careers, their conjured-up opinions would hardly change."

"How long have you lived in this neighborhood?" I asked.

"It's been close to eight years." Pausing a minute, Lana continued. "We, my little girl and I, used to visit other families. Together we patronized the park regularly. Everyone seemed pleased and cheered for us when Irina won her first figure skating competition. When she kept on winning, and received regional recognition, some of the warmth and close friendships seemed to dissipate. About that time, my neighbors also learned about my investigative work. They started to respond to me in an aloof manner. Then, when Irina was chosen to enroll at the national skaters' academy, which offered advanced schooling along with ballet instructions, all contacts by former friends gradually dropped away. Slowly, I increasingly felt more alone. Not even Irina's friends paid any attention to me any longer. Not that I need their attention, but to be spoken to at times would be pleasant."

"Lana, I don't want to say I'm sorry, but I understand. I know you don't want to chase men or women for the sake of making new contacts. Most men, I venture to say, probably feel you are above what they would ever expect to have as a lady friend."

"How is that?"

"You are a striking woman. A man would assume any advances on his part would only result in rejection."

"So, what are you saying, Franz? You surely don't want me to become someone who I'm not?"

"Of course not. I didn't mean for you to lower your standards. You do need a companion to divert some of the ill attention. I'm sorry if this sounds cold, but with a dynamic and debonair male companion, you could fall into a new circle of acquaintances."

"You're right. Maybe I've been announcing 'no chance' for too long."

"When Irina comes home, does she mix with her friends?"

"Not really. It seems the attitudes of the parents poisoned the minds of their children. It has become more noticeable each summer when she's home."

"Have you considered moving?"

"Yes, I have, many times. I even asked for a transfer to another city, but to no avail. In this country, when you have a comfortable place, it is expected for you to be satisfied. There are too many folks who want to move up, as far as housing goes. I know it is not wise to be nagging for a new place for reasons no one else even cares about."

"Let's say you had another child or your mother comes to live with you. Would that qualify you for another apartment?"

"I would certainly have a reason to make the application. However, no guarantees. My apartment is rated to have two adult occupants. I'm fortunate to have as much room as I do, since Irina is gone for most of the year."

"Let's have another glass of wine; the government is paying for it anyway," I proclaimed. We chuckled.

The musicians kept the atmosphere charged. Their melodies rang of a regional flavor, with the balalaika leading. The violinist sported a hoary head, which complimented the great feel he had for Tchaikovsky and Rachmaninov. The cellist played his instrument with the bow or, depending on the tune, plucked it like a base.

"Do these fellows play every evening?" I asked Lana.

"I don't know. Let's ask the waiter."

The waiter, appearing more courteous than necessary, answered, "This particular trio only plays on Friday and Saturday nights. During the week, various locals get together and play for a little pocket money." Having our attention, he volunteered a few more pointers. "An old mandolin player, quite good, lives at the edge of town. He comes around but doesn't play unless a violin player accompanies him."

"Why is that?" Lana asked. I wanted to know as well.

"He says he feels more at ease when accompanied by a violin. Why? None of us ever found out."

We left Mikhail's long before midnight. She clung tight against my side as we crossed the bridge. The moon played peekaboo from behind the fleeting clouds.

Before parting for the night, Lana drew near and playfully ran her fingers under the collar of my topcoat.

"This debonair fellow you want me to find. Where do you suppose I should start looking?" She caught me off guard—exactly her aim.

"Ah . . . well," I mumbled, clearing my throat, "most often we seldom see the obvious. The person you're looking for may be at your office, or in your daily life, not yet playing the role he is destined to play."

"What if I only think about him? Does that count?"

"Listen to your heart—does he live in there?"

Lana grabbed my collar and pulled herself even closer. She pressed her face to my chest and murmured, "You always have a special word of comfort. Thanks for understanding."

"Good night, Lana. Thanks for a special evening. Hope you let me share again soon."

"Soon. Good night," she echoed.

The dim streetlight could not hold her. She disappeared among the shadows of the budding trees.

Whom does she think about? Am I too vain to hope it's me?

When Lana reported for an assignment away from Moscow, I missed her. Although we didn't see each other every day, I always knew her to be close by. When she stayed gone for more than a week, I felt increasingly alone. One haunting evening, after my daily stroll, Mikhail's Café drew me across the bridge. I don't know if the music beckoned me or the need to be around people.

The mandolin player of whom the waiter spoke sat at a table for two, his mandolin case stood in the chair opposite him. He seemed to enjoy the lone musician's balalaika tunes. At a break, I mustered enough courage to speak to the man sitting alone with his mandolin.

"May I sit?" I asked. "I see you've brought your instrument. Will you be playing for us?"

"I planned to," he said with a friendly smile. "I'm waiting for my friend to show."

"Do you and your friend meet here regularly?"

"Regular?" he grinned with raised his eyebrows. "At my age, I hope, a bowel movement is a regular thing. Anything else, I take it as it comes. Tonight, I'm glad I got here."

"Good points," I said. "I love your candidness. To take life as it is handed to you is something most of us haven't yet mastered."

"Are you new in the neighborhood?" he asked. "Haven't seen you here before."

"Been living here for several years. This is only my second time in this place."

With a tone of satisfaction he said, "Cozy place, eh?"

"Yea, I appreciate the music. Play myself." I volunteered.

"You play?"

"Yea, haven't in a long while."

"What do you play?"

"I try to play the violin."

"Why don't you bring your fiddle tomorrow and we'll strike up a tune or two?"

"I can't. Don't have a fiddle."

"What happened to it?"

"Nothing, it's back in Germany."

"Germany? You said Germany?"

"Yea, haven't looked at a fiddle since '43."

"You weren't raised around here, was you?"

"No, I'm a leftover war veteran."

"Are you lost?"

"Lost, yes, because I'm not back home."

"Why don't you go home?"

"I don't know how."

"Huh. I'd like to hear you play. I got an old fiddle at home. Probably badly out of tune. May even have a little mildew on it. Are you interested in trying her? Can you make it tomorrow around seven? Right here?"

"Sure thing. I'll be here, unless the bridge washes away."

"That bridge?" He laughed. "It's been there hundreds of years."

I never got to hear the old mandolin player that evening. I left the café with a spring in my step. I wished I could have stopped by Lana's to tell her all about it.

The next evening didn't come too soon. I waited for the old man on a bench outside the café. *I hope you had a regular day to make the trek to Mikhail's.* I chuckled to myself. My eye stayed focused on the bridge for a glimpse of him. The fading day soon dashed all hope of meeting him as nine o'clock slipped by. Dejected, I again looked inside Mikhail's. He wasn't there. I trudged home. I never felt more beaten. All hopes shattered of ever again playing a violin. I had words of encouragement for Lana. Why could I not find any for myself? I needed her.

Before I reached the door to my place, a strong conviction said, *try again tomorrow.*

After a long, dull day at work, I again waited on the bench. My heart full of tension as I focused on the bridge. I recalled his sincerity, his excitement in his eyes when he spoke to me. . . . I waited.

Then, as out of a mirage, I saw the old man struggle to negotiate the slight incline to the center of the bridge. He sat. Carefully he leaned two black cases against the short wall. I walked toward him. He beamed when he recognized me.

"I knew you'd be here." He said wheezing and short of breath.

"I knew you'd be back," I said.

"Let's find a better place to sit and see what's in there." He pointed at the violin case.

Backing up to a bench, he bent forward and then plopped down to sit. In a few moments he calmed his trembling. Finally, he reached for the case. I watched him. His face revealed a lifetime of struggle. Fifty years ago he must have been a strapping and handsome fellow. That evening, as the day waned, I saw a broken and weak man. His deep-set eyes glimmered with kindness. The fading light emphasized chiseled wrinkles in his face which certified the years of starvation and hard labor. Gnarled fingers and knuckles, deformed by arthritis, told of pain and exertion.

The cuffs of his well-worn coat hung in frayed shreds, and the sleeves showed evidence of a dripping nose. His trousers dragged the ground but exposed enough of the badly worn shoes to see the small toes scraping the ground.

"Good to see you," I stammered, as he wiped the dust of the case with his sleeve.

"I'm sorry I stood you up yesterday. . . . I couldn't make it. Not one of my regular days." He grinned.

"I understand. I knew you didn't forget and must have had a reason."

"Here," he said, "you take her out. She won't fall apart."

I unclipped the case and liberated the instrument. Then as if having delivered a baby, I wanted to kiss it, but kept my excitement within. In the waning light, the glow of the instrument's fine wood warmed my soul.

"May I check if it needs tuning?"

"Sure . . . what's your name?"

"I'm Franz, Franz Brunner. And yours?"

"Peter."

"Good to know you, Mr. Peter."

"No, Peter, call me Peter."

We sat at either end of the short bench. He watched and flashed approval as I gingerly lifted and held the instrument. I tuned the violin. My heart flipped. Not a word was said. The violin exuded a pleasant scent, one of wood smoke blended with a touch of dampness.

When the violin heeded my adjustments, I looked at him. He twitched his chin, as if to say, "Play. Try her out."

The world faded into oblivion. A warm sense of completeness flowed over me. I could not tell how long or what I played. When I stopped, Peter nodded in grateful agreement, his eyes damp. The look of contentment on the old man's face told of an awakening of a time in his life long ago. With one hand on my knee, he said, "Oh my! Let me tell my friends." He struggled to get up. We entered the café.

Peter didn't sit down to wait to introduce me. When the local musicians ended their tune, he walked to the front and announced smiling. "Let me tell you about a violinist, his name is Franz." He motioned for me to come to the front and play. A little reluctant, having an audience, I managed to cradle the violin and bowed. Slowly, I let the voice of the instrument fill the room.

I rejoined Peter at the table, "Thanks for the privilege of letting me play tonight. I hope someone gets to play this beautiful instrument more often," I said, then laid the violin and bow on the table. "It truly has a wonderful sound."

He looked at me and then at the violin. With a glint in his eye, he said, "She is yours, take her home. She was dead. Today she is alive again."

"You can't mean that—it ah, it's your violin. A precious possession I'm sure."

"I mean it. She is yours. As sure as my name is Peter. Take her with you. Please."

"Why, I . . . I don't know what to say. I'm honored. Thank you!"

I left him sitting in the smoke-filled café. I don't remember walking home. Once safely in my room, I stared at the gift in disbelief. With quiet tears I reflected on the man. *Peter, the man of few words, unselfish. Where did he come from? Why did he call the violin a she?*

17

The months went on. I hoped to spot my friend Peter to thank him for his precious gift, but never did.

Playing the violin generated a rebirth in my life. It led me to spend most all of the free time at home. The programmed walks with Lana no longer highlighted my days.

"You're a little late for our stroll," she remarked one evening. "I know, you're playing the violin a lot."

"Yes, I am. I have much catching up to do. I don't mean to neglect our time together, but minutes turn to hours in a hurry."

"I can understand. Have you met with Peter since?" she asked. "I know you'd want to play a few tunes together."

"No. I've looked for him for months. I need to tell him of the joy his instrument brings," I said. "As far as a playing partner, he would have to suggest that."

"Franz," she said, "you're not a timid man. Make the suggestion and then see where it leads."

"I might, if I ever run into him again. I really don't feel I belong in his group. I may play if invited. But, honestly, I'd be happy playing sitting on a bench next to the river."

"That wouldn't be such an odd thing. I have seen many a musician who squirreled together a few extra roubles that way."

"I don't know, Lana. I'm not exactly a bum."

"No, on the contrary, many artists and musicians experienced discovery by taking their work outdoors. One never knows how proficient one is until the public judges."

"I'll have to think about that. I don't know why I would want to be discovered. With work piled at the plant, all I want do at night is relax, play a tune, and drop into bed."

"That reminds me," Lana interjected, "I spoke with Comrade Ulanov about Nikolai being prepped to be your assistant. 'At this time it would be premature,' he said. 'He is about to be called to serve his tour in the military.'"

"No, Lana! Why? Things are going backwards. He is the help I need now. He finishes tasks I would otherwise spend hours to complete."

"I know your next question is about Boris's status. Am I right?"

"Yes, I didn't want to be a squeaky wheel. Years ago, while a young apprentice, a wise old fellow told me, 'The squeaky wheel may get the grease, but usually it is also the first one to be replaced.'"

"You're not a complainer, Franz. I don't know about Boris's status. All I know is, the background work has been done. I don't think he or his family have been contacted."

"What are they going to do, spring it on the guy the day before he is supposed to move?" I wanted to add, *"Like you did me the day we left the mine."*

"I don't have anything to do with that part." She closed the conversation.

—

Nikolai and I continued our short talks at the bicycle rack. I sensed a renewed urgency had hold of him. He knew of the upcoming call into the Armed Forces, making him even more eager to meet and share.

Again I reminded Nikolai that our chats can never send a signal. "Even a look around to see if someone is watching could send a signal," I warned.

"I know," he said, "but it seems we never get enough time to finish what I want to know or what I want to say."

"In time, the little snippets will fall into place. Do not keep a written record."

"Yes, you told me before."

The short conversations took place while he fiddled with the lock on his bike. On other days while he pumped the tire, or he'd slowly ride alongside me while I ambled toward the trolley station. Sometimes, I would slap him on the back and we'd both laugh to portray a jovial relationship. All to decoy the serious matter of our talks. To Nikolai, this was great discipline. He seemed to enjoy it immensely.

"Listen to radio?" I would ask, continuing on a statement he had made in an earlier bike rack conversation.

"At night in bed," he responded.

"Sister know?"

"Speaker under pillow."

From that bit of conversation I deduced he discretely listened to a radio broadcast that either offended the rest of the family or it was of a nature Nikolai didn't want the others in the house to know about. When he told of the speaker under the pillow, I figured it must be a permanent setup. So, I continued the conversation.

"You change sheets?"

"Yes."

"Music?" I asked.

"Voice of America."

Voice of America! I wondered. I didn't know about it. However, the word "America" made it sound much against the State's dictates.

Nikolai, not sure of his sister's or his brother-in-law's positions on political matters, chose to stay in his room and not be drawn into revealing his detestation of communism.

At work, under the guise of explaining a problem, slick Nik, as I wanted to call him, drew me a quick diagram of his makeshift rigging. It showed how he pulled the wires out of the room radio, far enough to unhook its internal speaker. Then, within a split second, he hooked to, and activated a secondary speaker under the pillow. All my war buddies would have been proud of this young man.

During work hours, I frequently made short comments to Nikolai about my background. Small snippets of information, like my take-home pay back in Germany, and other comments about free commerce. Nikolai, in turn, would have questions ready that evening at the bike rack.

"In Germany, how much pay?" He'd ask.

"Food, room, play."

"Play?"

"Shoes, music records, beer, save."

His eyes wide and half-opened mouth showed his astonishment of me being able to save money on top of the small pleasures mentioned.

The exchanges at the rack went on for months until Nikolai received his call to the military. I pieced together stories of times he pedaled his bike to the potato fields outside the city looking to steal a meal or two. Many people did the same at great risk. While in the potato patch, one never knew the person walking toward them. It could be the authorities, or another poor soul wanting to steal a meal's worth of potatoes.

Nikolai's duty to the family at home included to get in line early to buy bread and whatever meat, bones, or sausage he could gather. His sister got in the same lines. No one ever figured out he and she lived in the same household. On lucky days the two would come home with a double ration of bread.

I grew fond of the young man. I thought about his life and eagerly waited to piece together his secret ambitions. He became part of my day. He was like reading a book with only one minute worth of candle light at a time.

One day, as I walked by the lunch table, I had to make a comment. "Nikolai, don't you get tired of eating smoked sausage every day?"

The other fellows laughed and said, "That is the same sausage he nibbles on every day."

"It beats eating rats," another said. They all had a good laugh.

One of his friends added, "The peddlers keep raising the cost of pigeons. Why?" He went on to say, "If they kept the price low, folks would eat more pigeons."

"Yea," another said. "It sure would help reduce the white stuff on Stalin's statue." More laughs.

In a way, living by myself, with cheese and bread provided, a steady job, and the humdrum of days months and years, I failed to see the ongoing shortage of food. I saw the lines. I heard the grumbling. I relished having a meal at work and a snack for supper. Vera added fresh fruit and, when nothing else was in season, a bowl of rock-hard prunes. My little table always had something to eat on it. By Lana's instructions, I'm sure.

Vera confided to me that she lived in the basement of a large apartment complex with five other cleaning women. Her husband had died of tuberculosis years earlier. The women's living space amounted to a curtained off cubbyhole each, artificially creating a veiled privacy. All six women came home at night to one stove, one sink, one light bulb, and a hole in the floor in the corner that served as a toilet. Vera was not a homely person—thin and tested, yes. She had big hands, hands that had known a lifetime of hard work. Icy blue eyes gave her hollow face a glow. Loose-fitting clothes hid her feminine curves.

"I hope you don't mind me taking this chunk of leftover bread," she asked, embarrassed. "I left you a fresh loaf."

"What are you planning to do with that dried-out piece?" I asked. "Are you going to feed the pigeons?"

"No, Mr. Brunner, I'm taking it home. I hoped you wouldn't mind."

"Are you going to eat it?" I pressed.

Sheepishly she looked at the floor and said, "Yes."

"Now, Vera, sit down a minute," I said.

"I'm not allowed."

"Why? Who told you that?"

"It's part of my orders—not to mingle or have lengthy conversations with the people I work for. I have already shared many things with you. You're a kind man."

"Never mind me. But, Vera, you started to go home, right? You're through for the day, right?"

"Yes, Mr. Brunner."

"So, come and sit down. I won't harm you."

"I know that," she said. "I can stay but a minute. If someone saw you come home, and me still in this apartment, I'd be in big trouble."

"I understand. Are you hungry?"

Feigning all is well, she said, "I'll be all right."

I lifted the cloth to uncover what she had placed on the table. I cut the loaf in half, as well as the cheese and the summer sausage, and handed each part to Vera.

"I cannot take this," she protested. "If I'm seen taking from an apartment, they'll think I'm a thief."

"Vera," I said, "let me do this. Listen—listen, sit for a second. I know what your worry is. Hear me out. I'll sit at the bus stop bench at eight o'clock tonight. I'll wrap what I want you to have in brown paper and leave it leaning against the wastebasket alongside the bench. You mingle somewhere and watch for me. After I return to my place, you come to the bench, sit, and rest a while. Pretend to do something. As you leave, reach and take the brown bag with you."

"I understand. I must go now. Good night. May God bless you, Mr. Brunner."

I didn't quite understand the blessing stuff. I thought only priests can do the blessings.

—

Gradually, as if peeling back the pages of a decaying book, I more clearly witnessed the daily struggles of people as they sustained their meager existence. The masses still stood in long lines as they had been since my arrival in Moscow. However, I never before saw the whole picture. I decided to observe and absorb life outside of my own. The war drained the sap out of all. Through the tram windows I frequently saw souls who didn't make it through the night. Their draped bodies on stretchers were being shuttled into covered trucks. Starvation ravaged the young and even more so the old and frail. Over and over, I realized I lived a sheltered life. I decided to venture out, out of my realm, my self-imposed borders—to meet the desperate.

One evening I stepped off the tram at a busy intersection with shops and markets on both sides of the street. All had closed for the day, sold out. The same stop where long lines of shoppers waited every morning. I brought my laundry bag and pretended to look to buy food. Many elderly and crippled persons did the same. A bent-over man came shuffling out of an alley. Noticing my empty sack, he pointed to where I could buy. Halfway into the alley a group of people scattered. I stopped an old woman and asked her where I may buy what she had in her sack.

"Too late," she said. "I got the last half of the rabbit."

"Is he coming back?" I said.

"Probably not in a while, not to this spot."

"Why not?"

"You know, he has to keep moving. Don't want them to catch up with him."

"What else did he have to sell?"

"Who are you? I'm not a telling you nothing, since I don't know nothing." With a huff, she shambled off.

Apparently there existed an underground network of barterers and peddlers. The elder people knew their rounds. Peter, my old friend, emaciated and weak, came to mind. *Is he hungry?*

—

The misery and want, the continuing uncertainty all around, dispirited me. I found it difficult to play cheerful music. *There is nothing sadder than a sad violin player playing sad melodies.* I realized what I did to myself. So I quit playing. I forced myself to walk more, watch more of life. I made an effort to glean from the beauty around me, to stay out of the pit myself. My instrument stayed at home. I hit the streets and paths with a purpose. I flicked my cane, mimicking Charlie Chaplin. The simple motion with each step brought back the joy of walking.

Further and further I ventured from my apartment. I passed by the newer and more modern housing for the privileged. I came to an old church. Two grand spruce trees graced a crumbling portico. I wanted to stop and commune with the old structure, but I moved on. Gradually, the manicured shrubs and trees disappeared.

A pulsing inner drive took me beyond all previously self-imposed limits. The decorative plantings coddling the elite, abruptly disappeared and vacant plats turned into garden plots. Gardens as small as a grave were spaded over and scattered among the small stone houses. Most homes, built alongside the dirt road, had low walls and few windows. Crumbling stucco revealed the craftsmanship of stone masons long ago. For extra insulation, the window sills showed packed dry sod or dirt mixed with fibrous cow dung to keep it from blowing away. Children made paper flowers and pinwheels to stick into the dirt to brighten the day. Fluttering rags of smoke danced from chimneys. Fences of all sizes, patched together of boards and odd wire, dissected the vacant land between the pitiful structures. Inside these fenced yards, smaller, less-secure fences had kept pigs and chickens in times of plenty. Now all empty. I did not see a single animal, not even a pigeon. In the small pens, no grass grew, bare since before winter set in. The pig wallows were glazed over where snow melt had formed puddles—the pigs long gone. Often, against one side of the stuccoed houses leaned a row of primitive animal cages, stacked two or three tiers high under the overhang. All empty. *Where are the rabbits? The guinea pigs?* Many families probably brought their few remaining animals into the house, afraid they'd be stolen by the hungry. The shrinking coal piles in sheds had to be barred and locked.

Disheartened by the bleak and squalid images of mere survival, I trekked along.

A whiff of coal smoke, mixed with garlic from someone's cabbage soup, perked me up. Every time I saw a blip of human activity, I rejoiced. A few folks scurried about. A woman carried a small pot of food to share with the aging or bedridden. Another took down the last armload of clothes from the line. One beat and fluffed the feather bedding, hanging over a board fence, with a woven cane paddle. Spring, however not yet visible, signals life. Spring always brings hope. It brings a sense of triumph in the hearts of man, having survived the claws of ice and hunger. New sprouts promise newness, a throbbing and expecting. Even the dejected regenerate in the spring.

For the first time I experienced life among the average Russians. I had spent my entire Sunday observing a new and different world. I felt the slow and faint pulse of a people that the elite at Mikhail's Café had long discarded. When the shadows lengthened, and a tattered sky promised to usher in an early night, older folks made their way to crude benches along the western wall of their dwellings. They sat, their backs against the baked stone wall, and absorbed the remaining warmth in the wall. I tipped my hat and shared greetings to all as they observed me, the stranger.

Totally unexpected among all I'd observed, a black instrument case leaned against a bench. Next to it sat a man, both hands on his knees, eyes closed, his back against the warming wall. I slowed my pace.

"Peter?" I asked.

Slowly the man raised his head. His eyes had a look of gray and a distant expression as they tried to focus.

He mumbled with gasps of unbelief, "Is that you?"

"It's Franz." I assured him. "I had no idea I would find you here. I've been watching for you at the bridge."

"Yes, come sit." He waved at the other half of the bench. "I think of you often. . . . Hoped we could talk some more. . . . Too weak these days to make the long trek."

"Are you ill, Peter?"

"Well, not really. . . . Nothing a good bowl of stew wouldn't cure."

"You're hungry?"

"Not exactly," Peter answered. "I've been wanting more to eat for so long . . . don't know what hungry feels like." He paused a while. I kept quiet. He wanted to say more. Between deep and quavering breaths he labored to speak on. "This winter . . . everyone ran out . . . a lot earlier . . . of what we put up. . . . We're cooking the seeds . . . meant for our gardens. . . . The breeding stock wound up in the pot. . . . Even if we could buy a pair of rabbits . . . it'd be a month or more before they'd have . . . enough meat on them to put in a stew."

He stopped talking to draw several labored breath. "We old folks . . . can't get to town early enough."

"Don't you have family or friends around here?"

"I've got friends," he said, "but they're all getting along in age. . . . My daughter-in-law lives not far from here. . . . I asked her son to go . . . buy some meat. That . . . was three days ago. Haven't seen him, . . . or the meat."

He looked at me, struggled to raise his head, took another trembling breath, and continued to lay bare his heart.

"I need something that'll give me a little getup in my getup . . . a good bowl of soup . . . made with them good bones . . . all that marrow in them . . . that . . . that'd do me right."

"That does sound good," I echoed. "Say, listen. Any place close by we could have us a hot bowl full?"

"This is Sunday, isn't it?" He said.

"Yes, it is."

"Well, . . . there's a place at the tram stop. . . . They play cards there on Sundays. . . . The fellow who runs the place . . . always has a pot of something heated."

"How far? Can you make it there?"

"Not that far. About a kilometer. . . . Over there. Around the bend. . . . I reckon I could make it. . . . May have to stop a few times."

"Come, you'll make it. I'll help you. Let me treat you to whatever good he might have cooking."

I helped Peter up and held on to him until he had steadied himself.

He pointed at the black mandolin case and said, "Let me put it in a safe place." A few minutes later he returned from his house.

Slowly, with the sun at our backs, both of us depending on a cane, ambled toward the establishment.

"I'm surprised the city tram comes all the way out here."

"Not often," Peter said. "Twice in the morning . . . and twice in the evening."

"What's the number of the tram?"

"Twelve," he said.

We ducked into the cozy *gasthaus* and chose a small corner table. Only one card game, and two fellows watching, filled the room with its liveliness. A couple of heads turned. None seemed to know Peter.

"It's been a long time since I been in here," said Peter. He motioned for the cook to come over as we plopped onto a chair.

Hot vegetable soup simmered in the pot that day. With a hardy grin, the cook served us each a bowl full. Steam and an enticing aroma hit our nostrils. With a slice of dark bread in one hand, and a spoon big enough to be called a ladle in the other, we slumped down to savor every swallow. Fresh parsley and black pepper added taste to the carrots and potatoes, while many yellow puddles of grease floated in the bowl looking up at us. Noticing we enjoyed the soup, the cook came back and waited for a comment on his masterwork.

"That's what I call soup," said Peter to the cook, who nodded and left smiling.

We hovered over the hot bowl. Slowly, as the world ticked on, savoring every spoon full. A glow of satisfaction showed on Peter's face. We both relaxed and enjoyed every minute. Before the bowl showed its bottom, Peter leaned back and said, "Thanks for helping out." He took a tired breath. "I can see you're not exactly overfed yourself."

"I'm doing fine," I said. "Peter, I enjoy your company and the soup."

"While we're talking about food . . . my friend Olaf . . . went to check the traps." Peter crumbled the last chunk of the bread into the bowl. After swallowing a spoonful he continued, "I live with him and his wife . . . you know."

"You started to say, 'check the traps.'"

"Yup, hate to admit it," he said almost in a whisper. "He went down to the river . . . see if he caught us a big fat one."

"Are there plenty of them?" I asked.

"Plenty?—I say not . . . about as scarce as hen's teeth." Peter looked at me. "Have you had a rat?"

"Yes, I have. Not ashamed to say so. . . . Roasted, with enough salt, he is right good."

Both of us sopped and slurped the remaining dabs of soup. The bond between us got tighter. We lingered, feeling the warmth of the soup coddle our belly.

"Will it get better when things start to grow?" I asked.

"Yea, it'll get better." He thought about it a moment. "It'll get better for the ones . . . that were able to keep breeding stock through the winter. . . . A healthy pair of rabbits will soon fill the cages . . . but, stuff needs to be growing to feed 'em. . . . There'll be gardens, I suppose . . . if folks got seeds left."

"What about the State?" I said.

"The State, huh? . . . I suppose I can tell you this: . . . Sometimes I think we'd be better off if they left us alone. . . . At least we'd grow what's needed . . . take care of each other. . . . The young folks got . . . got to depending on the State too much."

I thought Peter to be a man with few words, but between shallow breaths, he kept on talking. Obviously he hadn't shared with anyone for some time.

"Yesterday . . . both of us, Olaf and me, . . . tottered to the river," he said. "Old, you know . . . kind of feeble. . . . I went down to the eddies . . . no green cress yet . . . guess it's early. My buddy . . . he tried to catch us a pigeon. . . . Took the last of the day's bread . . . to lure one to the snare."

"How do you snare a pigeon?" I asked.

"You can catch one if . . . if you move fast enough. . . . Old Olaf, I've got to laugh . . . laid his snare loop . . . on the ground . . . the old bread inside the loop." He paused to chuckle and ponder. "I shouldn't laugh. . . . I'm older than he is. . . . Well, . . . more than once a pigeon got in . . . the loop, he said. . . . I guess he was too . . . too slow to jerk it tight . . . around its feet, you know. . . . A good chunk of bread gone. . . . Well, he tried.

"Interesting," I said. "You live year-round with this older couple?"

"Yea, I tried living alone . . . did it for years after Olga died. . . . I guess Olaf felt sorry for me. . . . He asked me to move in with them. . . . Got me a comfortable bunk. . . . A little coal stove. . . . I share all I have with'm."

"Peter, tell me, when we first met and I played your violin, you said, 'Take her home, for she was dead and is alive again.' What did you mean by that?"

"Franz," he said as he took a painful breath, "the violin use to be Olga's, my wife. . . . She made my heart sing when . . . when she played. . . . I miss her!"

18

Every Russian winter lasted longer than the previous one. Every year my brain had to re-digest the same realities. The Russian winters robbed warmth of living. They stole the daylight. They took away the green. They invaded the walls, the bones, the soul. They never let go. They grabbed and pulled you down and laughed at you with a cold that shattered stone.

Every morning, like a slinking cat, I trudged to the plant in the dark and returned home long after sundown. So, when the snow finally thawed, my innards and my attitude did also. The life-giving fingers of the lengthening day always managed to turn my dark funk to a childish giddiness. Every year I found renewed strength to click my heels and play the violin outdoors. Daffodils along the river's banks showed their bashful smiles and proved revival was at hand. During the blustery days, my walks with Lana were brisk and short. However, as the days lengthen, we lingered a bit longer, walked a little further, and often sat on a bench overlooking the river.

"You know, Franz," Lana said as she moved closer, "when the daffodils look at me with their heads tilted, I'm reminded Irina will soon be home for the summer."

"I know you can't wait to see your little girl."

"She is growing up . . . and she's not home for me to experience it."

"Lana, would we get in trouble if we picked a few of the daffodils?"

"No, as long as we don't wipe out the lot."

"I'll pick two for you, all right?"

"Why two for me?" she asked.

"One for you and one for Irina."

"Irina is not home yet, why not one for me and one for you?"

"I don't know. Are you going to put mine in the same vase with yours?" I raised my eyebrows.

"Yes, I have the perfect vase." Lana's voice lowered to almost a whisper. "We'll be in it together. . . ."

"Comforting thought," I said smugly. "Please, don't fill the vase with cold water. I have been chilled enough since I've come to this city, or the country, for that matter."

"Don't worry, spring has sprung. I'll help you thaw out." She flashed a coy smile.

"Do you think I've got more thawing to do?" I played along with her coquettish remarks.

"Yes," she slipped a little closer. "There are parts of you that have been cold too long."

Not quite positive as to where this little talk would lead, I put my arm around her shoulders as we absorbed the fading red of the western sky. She didn't object to my arm, slid a little closer, and pressed a bit firmer against me.

"It is getting chilly out here," she whispered. Pretending to search for warmth, she slipped her hand between my topcoat and vest. "I'll pick my flower, and you pick yours," she said, "and I'll use my vase—with warm water! Will that suit?"

"Good. Anything but cold."

We walked to her place. Each carrying our daffodil, her arm tugged in mine.

The door to her apartment closed with a faint click. The lingering sun's red streaks, defused by the window glass, dappled the otherwise dark room with dancing shimmers. Lust took over the moment. Drugged by the wine of her hot breath, I inhaled her luscious lips. Our tastes mingled. Desire burned, blinding my brain. An intoxicating want rippled through every muscle of my body as I floated in a sea of passion.

"Come, my daffodil," she murmured. We stepped over our coats on the floor. Her probing fingers found their way inside my shirt while she coaxed me toward the bathing nook. Playfully, she pulled back its silky curtain and lit two candles. The white tub seductively waited. The scintillating flickers revealed two matching towels hanging over the tub's edge. *Two towels.* . . . A flood of raw expectations saturated my mind.

From an alabaster flask she poured a dribbling of bath oil into the tub. The room filled with its aphrodisiac. I inhaled the fragrance, the moment, her very essence. A seductive finger under my chin pulled me close. Her head tilted back as her eyelashes rested on her cheeks. She pressed her firm body against mine. Our lips caressed. Fire shot through my veins as she reciprocated every touch, drenching the moment with unbearable desire.

The magical dance continued as her blouse, now only partially buttoned, invited a response. Soon it fell to the floor. My lips found the liberated offering. Skin met skin. A ravenous pulse of lust now in control. In the glint of the candlelight, she responded, firm and throbbing, heaving, wanting. Our souls mingled into one, one desire, one goal.

"Fill the tub, the vase," she moaned. "Warm water . . . nice warm water . . . and be my strapping daffodil, . . . *my* daffodil!"

The all-consuming deluge passed. Throbs of dull thunder pulsed in my veins as the waves of hot lava slowly subsided. The bedroom shimmered. We lay spent on down pillows. The lace curtains fluttered in quiet approval. The glimmer of a single candle on the nightstand exposed her satisfied form, voluptuous, depleted, at peace, having escaped the world. A smile twinkled through her lashes. Her flared nostrils and slightly parted lips showed fulfillment. There, in the crook of my arm, lay the goddess of the deep.

The stage had been set since that one strange and eerie evening in the shack. She had been mesmerizing then as the oil lamp flickered and revealed her beauty. For years, we shared thoughts and feelings in an ever-more-relaxed and personal way. We laughed, we cried with joy as she brought me back to my music. During those years, desire built, but it always had to be suppressed. Through her sharing, she became a different person, a person alive with a sensitivity and a meaningful past. I learned about her struggles and realized the role she could not shed. However, she was always a woman. And, without realizing it, I was evermore drawn to her; to a point where I pondered and visualized being with her for the rest of my life.

—

Early the next morning I entered my apartment, attempting to clear my mind to go to work. I couldn't focus. I mulled over the sudden and dramatic change that had crashed into my life.

For the first time I showed late for work. Alexander, one of the apprentices, said, "Comrade Ulanov looked for you."

"What did he want?"

"He wondered where you were. He showed a big fellow around the plant."

"A big fellow? Did you ever see him here before?"

"No," Alexander assured me. "They stood in the X room when I got here this morning," he said.

The door swung open.

"Boris!" I jumped out of my seat. "My friend, my friend! It is great to see you!" I slammed him in a bear hug.

"I see you know this fellow," said Ulanov, with a grin. "I've already shown Boris the plant. You two make up for lost time. I'll see you both in the morning."

Boris and I found a spot at a lunch table, far from the crowd. Old times flowed.

"Franz, you opened my eyes to many things after you left. I did much thinking."

"Boris, whatever you gleaned from our friendship, and particularly my suspicious nature, don't let it lead to disappointment. There are plenty of good things to life."

"You're right, I don't have to look far to see folks worse off. I hope this trial period here will lead to something better for my family."

"I bragged about you to Lana and Ulanov enough times," I assured Boris. "They agreed that, if all goes well, the State will reward you and your family."

"That's good. Meanwhile, I'm gonna miss my two women." He paused a second. "And who is this Lana?"

"That's right. Let me connect a few things for you." I took a long drink of water from my mug. "Tatilana Popova is the interrogator from back at the mine. Remember? She is the one who dragged me here to Moscow. She still keeps a check on me. I understand I'm one of her assignments, but we have also become good friends."

"Interesting," Boris said, stroking his mustache. "I imagine you weren't exactly happy when they yanked you from your friends?"

"Yes, totally peeved. I miss my buddies. And, missed you my friend."

Boris's arrival turned out to be a pleasant distraction. It helped calm the whirr I in my head. Late that afternoon, Ulanov called me to his office.

"Sit down, Mr. Brunner. I see from the smile on your face that you're happy to see your friend."

"You can be sure of that."

"Starting tomorrow, I'll put him in the shop to familiarize himself with the flow of work and the plant as a whole. After a week or two, he'll be under your tutelage."

"That will be great," I agreed. "You will see for yourself the energy and knowledge he'll bring to the operation."

"I'm pleased to see the camaraderie between the two of you. Having a ready friend will help him get used to his new environment faster."

"Mr. Ulanov, are his wife and daughter coming?"

"Not yet," he said cautiously. "I would expect they'll be here shortly after the trial period." Mr. Ulanov walked to the door with me, laid a hand on my shoulder as I left the room.

—

Lana hung up her blouse when I entered her apartment. She turned to me, her warm lips met my embrace.

"Franz," she said smiling, "let me get covered."

"Why? That is quite a greeting."

"You are too eager. I didn't plan it. You're a little devilish boy, pouncing in here while a lady is undressing."

"Ah, but how pleasant to snitch a piece of rich chocolate."

I let the moment pass and plopped onto the sofa. "What a day I've had. I didn't have much time to glow over last night. How about you? Did the vase play on your mind?"

"The vase, my heavens! Thank goodness I stayed busy. Franz, I'm exposed to you, open and wanting, turned inside out." She unpinned her hair, ran her fingers through it, and sat down. "Tell me of your day."

"I was late; for the first time, mind you. Then Boris walked into the X room."

"Boris?"

"Yes, isn't it great?"

"Boris. Interesting. You did have quite a day," she agreed. "My day . . . nothing big like that. Except, we learned that comrade Gagarina got the arsenic from a chemical engineer at the other plant. We also traced other potions that fellow let slip through the checkpoints. Some of those doses made their way to a group of dissidents. I'm sorry you had to be the sacrificial pig, so to speak, but we nipped a possible major headline in the butt."

Lana chose the couch, patted the cushion for me to join her, and said, "You trumped it all though, you had me spinning all the day."

"Good," I said, all smiles. "Where do we go from here?"

She answered in a calm and satisfied tone. "I don't quite know. We need to keep the symbol of the daffodils alive!"

"What do we do when their season ends?" I said.

"My sweet Franz, what we have will never be out of season."

"Lana, you are precious. I've grown accustomed to you. I need you on this journey. I didn't know how lost I was until last night."

"I feel the same," she confessed. "I had been lost in a sea of demands and expectations. You have stirred in me a need I didn't know still lived." She rose and said, "Wait here, I want to show you something I did early this morning."

She came back with a thick lexicon and let the book fall open. Two pressed daffodils rested between its pages, placed facing each other, their stems crossed.

"You see, Franz, the seasons may end in the field. Here in this home these two daffodils will be preserved between these pages. When we're old, we'll open this book and recall the days of our beginning."

"Lana, you never cease to amaze me. Behind that tough professional is a soft and sentimental heart. Continue to share it with me, please."

"I want to and more." Her full lips sealed the promise.

—

In the evenings I played the violin while Lana flowed through the love songs of old on her piano. We kept the symbol of the vase alive. The weeks drifted on. Nature's perfume, this time from lilac, discreetly plucked from the tended gardens around Lana's apartment, now filled the room.

"I received a letter from Irina today," Lana announced. "She'll be home in less than two months."

"That is wonderful! Are you excited?"

"Why, yes, I have been expecting this letter."

"Lately, you haven't mentioned her coming much," I said. "I hope I'll become her friend."

"I wrote to her about you. Told her you were kind and debonair and made me feel special."

"What did she say?"

"Not much. I guess she wants to see for herself."

Imagining Irina becoming part of my life worried me a bit. She was old enough to have her opinions.

"How current is the picture of her on the piano?" I asked.

"It's three years old. I don't have a more recent one except for a newspaper clipping."

The heading read: "IRINA POPOVA WINS TITLE." My jaw dropped. In the clipping I saw a lovely young lady. She represented one of Russia's hopes of an Olympic medal.

"Why have you not told me of all this fame?"

"Fame is not the point in this country. National pride, to elevate the State to the world, is all that is at stake. The thing I fear, my little girl has spent her life building a house of cards. She built it tall, but it is still a house of cards. Any mishap or a mistake in concentration can bring it to the ground. The pressure these young girls are subjected to is horrific. Franz, she is all I have. I'm so proud of her, but also afraid. As her mother, I have got to be strong, strong for her. I cannot let her feel the anxiety I carry in my heart. She is only fifteen, still a little girl."

"Lana, don't let what could happen spoil your happiness. Let's rejoice in her accomplishments. I've learned in these last seven years that without hope there is no future."

"I know you're right. I can't help but worry."

"Let's get this house ready for Irina; she deserves it," I said. "All of my stuff I'll take back to my place."

"Franz, I love your presence here."

"Thanks, but the focus now should be on your girl."

"Well, I guess you're right. A little at a time, I'll start bringing out her favorite things, fluff them up, and lay them around."

"I could cut a mat for that newspaper article. You may even have an old frame to put it in."

"I'd like that. I do have a frame."

We added rearranging and redecorating to our routine. The extra smiles brought comfort.

19

From the very first day of Irina's homecoming, I sensed her reticence to even look at me. The lack of courtesy and cold demeanor was apparent in the short conversations with her. Either Lana didn't pick up on this, or she welcomed her daughter's demeanor. I couldn't tell. Lana did not encourage Irina to accept me as a friend of the family, at least not in my presence.

I gradually removed myself from their time together and convinced my dulled brain that after Irina returned to Leningrad, life would flow back as before. The situation forced me to weigh the long-term outlook of our romance. *Is it now possible to ever return to Friedl? Gone seven years, a long time. . . .*

When Irina returned to school in Leningrad, I tried to rekindle the intimacy. However, Lana had changed. Her grave looks concerned me.

"Are you worried over Irina?" I asked. "You look a little peaked."

"I have not been feeling well. I am pregnant."

The bomb, a direct hit, blew out my lights. After the shock waves subsided, I managed to put a few words together. "Other than not feeling good, aren't you excited?"

"Are you?" she countered.

"Well, yes! It will be a beautiful baby," I said.

Lana got up and entered the kitchen. Her back toward me, she pretended to be busy. The ticking of the clock pulsed in my ear.

I searched for words. "This sure changes everything again. My stay in this country now has purpose. We'll have some planning to do. I'll ask Ulanov for that raise. We're going to . . ."

"I'm getting an abortion!"

A dagger pierced my heart. I saw a baby wrapped in newspaper and thrown unto a rubbish heap. I felt as if *I* was being aborted.

"How? . . . How could you?" I gasped. "It's my baby too!"

She kept her back toward me. Her decision final—case closed.

Her casual statement and position crushed me. I slithered out of her apartment and into a void . . . an absolute nothingness.

—

Several weeks stumbled by before Lana left word with Vera that she wanted to resume our walks. In a way, selfish or not, I welcomed the chance. We had shared every Saturday afternoon for years. Now, however, after eliminating a part of me, our wills differed. Her company and discussions became a filler to round out the week. On selected occasions I enjoyed her playing the piano. We were in a holding mode, groping to justify our meetings.

"Franz, you have been aloof, and, I might say, avoiding me. I had no idea that terminating my pregnancy would have such an effect on you."

"Lana, a baby is life. Look around; is there life in this world? I mean LIFE. A bubbling of joy flowing out of love. Our baby could have been the glue to our relationship. I guess I'm naive; my opinion is not worth considering."

"Don't say that. I've watched over you. Your welfare means a lot to me."

"Yes, and I thank you. But, have we lived? Have we exposed our soul to each other? Have we become one in mind and spirit?" Not often did I leave Lana speechless. She held to my arm as we walked on in silence.

Lana slowed her pace and made me face her. "Franz," she almost whispered, "my nights have been a disaster these last few weeks. I hate the turmoil I've caused. I miss you!" When I didn't answer she continued. "The sad thing is, I can see you don't believe what I'm saying. Oh Franz . . ."

I was too bullheaded to admit that I felt her pain. However, my heart had changed direction.

The previous regularity of eating together and other fun times shriveled to a mundane, platonic relationship. She no longer had the mesmerizing pull on me. Whenever our eyes met, the passion was barely there. I tried to make excuses and not be with her, but she always insisted. The thought of her having to keep a log on me and my whereabouts had an enormous dampening effect. Every fiber in me wanted to get rid of the life I lived.

—

Finally, after three months, the authorities let Yelena and Zina join Boris in Moscow. A thoughtful Yelena brought the crude little painting of my Friedl and the children with her. Boris, right after I left, discreetly entered my shack and confiscated it before his comrades wiped out all evidence of the mad German.

Boris and I devised a way to get the little painting to my apartment. I hung it so I could gaze at it from bed. Vera agreed not to mention it to Lana. The years had dulled and faded its colors. Still, I found myself talking with what was left. . . *What is the baby doing? Tell me—is it a boy or a girl?*

—

When Nikolai finally got his notice to active duty his supervisors approached it as a matter of fact. The other apprentices expected the same in their near future. The older men smirked and were glad the ordeal now behind them. The government guaranteed their civilian job when they got out, as it also would be for Nikolai.

I for one felt slammed. Slammed to the mat. Not only was Nikolai a tremendous help, but he also became like a son to me. I found that our bike rack meetings rounded out my day as well as his. I missed him. Although Boris was now part of everyday life, still, a friend was gone. I considered the time away Nikolai had to face. *Two years,* I thought. *Will I still be stuck here?*

Day after monotonous day, months dragged on. Work became a drag. Other young apprentices tried, but didn't replace Nikolai.

Lana never came to my place again. I'm sure Vera, her personal representative, kept her informed of all the amazing adventures I participated in. What a joke!

The summer of 1952, after I hung the faded painting, I concluded that I must escape. Escape, discreetly and without permission. I despised the constant tiptoeing on glass bubbles. I wanted to be free and shed the oppressive Soviet culture. "Free!" It felt good to say the word out loud. The last four years shifted from total incarceration at the gulag to a giant house arrest. The wire fences and steel gates switched to eyes, spies, curiosity, and reports. With clear purpose, I channeled every thought, all energy, and cunning toward the escape. I did not know how many months or years it would take, or exactly how to accomplish it, but I was determined to succeed.

My first thought was, *I need money*. The exact words Nikolai said three years earlier. America was his focus, mine was OUT! "Freedom!"

During the years in Moscow, I only put a paltry sum of money aside. Necessities, like resoling shoes, or a gust of wind ruining my umbrella, often gobbled up most of the small stash I may have had.

Lana encouraged me to play the violin in the open in front of the world. "Go where the people are," she'd say. "Play your heart out! You'll have admirers who'll enjoy your music. Not everyone who loves music can afford to patronize Mikhail's Café. You'll be happy, and someone else as well."

My brain agreed. *I could collect a little money playing for the folks!*

Whether Lana calculated my visibility to make her job easier, or she sincerely wanted me happy, I did not care. However, on every occasion we did get together, I saw her eyes, searching, searching mine for a hint of forgiveness. *Yes, I can forgive,* I thought. *But, I'm on a mission.* Forgiveness, I found, was a soothing balm on my daily struggles. I never came out and said the words, but tried to be personable and understanding. It did sooth the wounds, but I had a purpose, a shift in direction.

I moved most of my violin playing outdoors. A bit reticent, but managed to calm my nerves by thinking of the goal. *A little money to help get me out of here.* Within weeks, increasingly more people stopped to listen. The violin case laid open for donations. At first I played from a bench at the river's edge for less than an hour. Then, I stood under various trees and played. Eventually, I settled to sit on the low rock wall of the stone bridge, a high traffic area. Always, the violin case laid open. People joined by bringing pillows or small blankets to spread on the nearby grass. Peter's violin sighed its songs of love and intrigue to the folks and river below. Spring, summer, and autumn, the one-man concerts became part of the neighborhood's daily energy. The world and time merged to create a gentle and tender peace. Summer sunsets reflected off the waters as swallows darted above. I played on. Lovers strolled by, listened, then ducked into the shadows to steal a kiss and embrace. Always, the music—the air—the birds—the sun—the water—the wind drew near to God.

For nearly three years the violin case lay open on the ground, begging. thankful for all tokens pitched in. Special requests always added extra coins. Sunday evenings during pleasant weather, a larger than usual crowd gathered to attend the free concert. Victor, the baker, gladly exchanged a pouch of coins for paper money. I hid my stash in my shoes and in the lining of my coat. The downtown merchants eagerly traded a large bill for a stack of smaller denominations. In my heart I knew Lana instructed Vera to keep a watchful eye for new things I bought. I also realized if I didn't spend any money, Lana would surmise I hoarded it. Of course, her next question would be, "For what?"

"I hear you're getting to be quite a phenomenon out there on the bridge," Lana probed while she shared a bowl of stew with me at her apartment.

"Phenomenon? That is rubbing on a little extra sauce," I answered.

"I hear folks sit and listen to you, not even crossing the bridge to patronize Mikhail's."

"Come on now," I said in disbelief. "There are no seats on the grass, and I don't serve wine or cheese."

"Are you having fun out there?" she continued. I had my antennas tuned.

"Yes, I think I better learn a few new melodies or the crowd will soon get tired of me." I smiled naively. "I even saw Peter a couple of times. He sauntered by, tipped his hat, and grinned from ear to ear. What a wonderful old fellow."

"How are the tips adding up?"

"Great," I said cheerfully. "It reminds me of times long ago when I played along the river's edge in München. A young man then. Everyone lived in a tight squeeze. The early thirties, you know, no one could find a job."

"Victor tells me you bounce into his store, all happy, to change coins into paper money." Lana kept poking, smiling spuriously.

"That's right." I acted oblivious to her prying. "I can't carry a sack of coins to the store when I get enough together. I've been eying that phonograph downtown for months. I want the better of the two, the one with the built-in radio."

"Well, I didn't know that's your wish."

"Sure is. I need to upgrade my repertoire. Got to have a player to learn the new sounds. Sometimes I think I'm boring folks, playing the same stuff, you know."

"Come on, Franz." she said, "I heard you play. You must have hundreds of melodies in your head."

"Thanks. Having them in your head does not always translate into good music. For my own gratification, I need to learn something new."

While Lana had her back to me, fixing tea, I ambled about her living room and expounded on the various phonograph records I wanted to buy. Her attaché case lay open on her desk. An official-looking document with my name on it protruded from under a small stack of notes and other papers. Keeping up the conversation, I took a closer look. A transcript from the German government declared me dead. The same abortion knife stabbed my gut. Lana never said a word about it. *You play your game,* I thought, *so can I. Watch me!*

"When did you start using your cane again?" Lana asked, as I eased to the door getting ready to leave.

"Well, for a while now," I said. "As you may have heard, I fell a couple of weeks ago, for no reason, it seemed. I still don't know if I got my feet twisted, or if I had a sudden blackout. All I know is, I hit the ground."

"That's a little troubling, isn't it?" She looked concerned.

"No use making much of it. I don't mind using a cane." I grinned, donned my hat and turned to leave. "Good night. The phenom needs rest!"

Now that I was officially dead, I determined to carry out my plan that much more—and I didn't take all my change to Victor, the baker, any longer.

I am dead! Dead! I sat and stared at the little painting until the last winks of light faded and my family disappeared into the dark room. I had been gone for nearly ten years. It hadn't occurred to me to be declared dead. I considered it a form of closure for the government and a way for Friedl to go on with her life—to marry again. . . . *To marry again!*

—

To be rid of the grasp of Communism became my passion. I could no longer stand the business of Lana watching me. Lana the woman, aside from her KGB position, still had a hold of me. I could not deny her constant presence in my mind. When we did meet, I sensed her inner turmoil as she realized my interest in her waned. But, I started this move to escape and was bent to shed the hellish theater of falsehoods.

I purposely tripped and stumbled when Vera could witness. At work, I again started to use my cane to get around.

"Why the cane?" Boris and the others wanted to know.

"I have been falling some. Probably the injury to my foot," I said. "I sure don't want to fall into one of the machines out there."

I kept on faking the stumbling. I fell when I came to play on the bridge. The bump on my head, the scrapes on my cheek and hands told of the ongoing problem. To Lana, the spells signaled something seriously wrong.

"I'm beginning to get very concerned about your falling. Are you sure you're not blacking out?"

"It hits me so fast and leaves so fast, I do not know what to think."

With a worried look, Lana said, "We should see a doctor. You could have an inner ear problem. Or, I hate to say this, you may be having mini strokes."

"Thanks for painting these reassuring pictures. What about my foot? You know I have but three toes on my left foot."

"If it were your foot," Lana explained, "your cane would be all you need."

"I don't want to see a doctor yet." I played the man thing.

"Franz, you don't have to spend any of your money," Lana said with a slight dig.

"I know, I know. All is free. If it does not quit in a month, I'll go."

"Good," she said. "I'm going to hold you to it."

I had everyone in Russia convinced something physically wrong brought on the spells. Even the doctor. He rinsed out my ears, which did have several chunks of wax in them. He gave me some concoction to take daily to thin my blood. Back at the apartment, each day, I flushed a teaspoon of the stuff down the sink in case Vera kept a check on the medicine bottle.

Ulanov came to see me in the X room. "How are you feeling?"

"I'm getting along quite well. Often a week goes by without a spell. Then, as I think I'm improving, I find myself on the floor."

"Are you still seeing a doctor?"

"Yes,"

"Good. Keep me informed."

"By the way, Mr. Ulanov, could I modify my umbrella to a comfortable cane and umbrella combination. It's a bit awkward on threatening days to walk down the sidewalk with two sticks, a cane and an umbrella."

Ulanov grinned. "Go ahead. Use anything you need."

"Thanks."

I modified my large umbrella by cutting off the wooden grip and replacing it with a hollow brass collar and handle. In it I planned to hide money, matches, fishhooks, and line while on the run. To complete the project, I reworked the tip as well. When unscrewed, it gave access to a super-sharp stiletto and a screwdriver. Chunks of rubber kept it all from rattling. When the day of my departure came, I wanted to travel unnoticed, light, and fast.

20

Nikolai returned a man from his tour of duty. I was shocked the two years had swooshed by like wiping a runny nose on a sleeve. His short haircut, and defined shadows of a strong beard, along with muscular arms and neck, placed him solidly into manhood. Again we worked together and had our short meetings at the bike rack. As before, Nikolai kept his personal convictions close to his heart. The renewed chats at the rack included military adventures, but most often the old, secretive, and carefully worded questions and phrases remained as before. I could sense his present life did not suit for the long run. I still could not tip his careful balancing act of emotions and plans into a heart-to-heart confession. I felt compelled to find a spot to have a long private talk with him. Peter's neighborhood, with its many paths and cart roads, seemed perfect.

The day I ventured to find the appropriate meeting place, I faked a stumble or two, held to a light post here and there, a tree for balance, as I eased further from the familiar surroundings. I didn't walk in one direction, but circled back, rested, always looked to make sure no "eyes" followed. The small bundle under my arm held victuals for Peter, my friend, a little help before another winter set in.

Near Peter's neighborhood, the tracks of tram Number Twelve ended in a large, overgrown circle. A rickety waiting bench and a faded signpost indicated the line's termination. From there, I followed a narrow wagon road that lead to a river's edge. At the end of a footpath I found a halved log propped on river rocks. Tall weeds and bushes offered a secluded backdrop. From the primitive bench I could see a fair distance before the path weaved out of sight. A great spot for a meeting with Nikolai, my deep and troubled friend. Having met my goal of finding a meeting place, I set out to revisit my friend, Peter.

I found him chopping sticks and branches. He wielded a hatchet in partnership with a worn and battered tree stump. A gratifying sight; an exclamation point to my day. I had seen my father do the same.

I called his name several times before he ambled to the gate.

"My friend," he said, "it's good to see you. . . . What brings you to this decrepit neighborhood?"

"I started on an afternoon stroll. You living way out here gave me a reason to come this way. Wanted to see you before cold weather sets in. Brought you some dried peas and sausage to cook with'm."

"Aren't you something, Franz?" Peter wheezed, not hiding his joy. "Why are you doing this? . . . You hardly have enough meat on your bones yourself. . . . I thank you, though. . . . I'll share these goodies with Olaf and his wife."

"It's not much, Peter, compared to what you gave me."

"Ah, that was many moons ago." Peter looked off into the distance. "Many moons ago. . . ." The deeper feelings of his words were in the perceptible gaps. "Franz . . . it is a good thing, she lives on."

"Yes, all this time her spirit nudged me on. She has become part of me. Not only is she a joy to me, but also to many who've heard her music over the years."

Apparently not wanting to stir more memories, he looked down and said, "I see you got a new walking stick."

"Yea. I combined the umbrella and the cane."

"You like to tinker, don't you?"

"I've got to keep my mind cranking." Taking a deep breath, I continued. "They demand a lot at work. Still, not a day goes by, however, that I don't miss my family back home."

"The war is long over. Can't you go home now?"

"Maybe I can, one of these days soon. Thanks to her, the beauty in the black case, I've saved a few roubles."

"Wouldn't that be something . . . if your going back home . . . came about by Olga's violin?" With a trembling breath, Peter took hold of my sleeve and said, "It sure was worth it all the more."

I reached and took hold of his bony arm. He struggled to straighten his hunched shoulders, then looked squarely at me. Our eyes met. I saw clear to his soul, then gently said, "You know, Peter, you're a true friend, a friend who sticks." After a chocking dry swallow, I squeezed his hand and managed to utter, "Good-bye."

"Good-bye," Peter said. His voice quavered. He realized this good-bye was for good. "I'll be thinking of you, come pea soup time."

—

At the bike rack, as Nikolai handed me my dropped cane, I said, "I need to have a long meeting with you." I slipped a piece of paper into his hand. He didn't look down or make any odd moves as he hid the note from view in his palm. It read, "Next Sunday 9:00 a.m. Tram 12 east to Pavel. Walk east to river. I'll be waiting. Burn this note."

On the appointed morning I walked at a brisker pace to fight the chill in the air and arrived at the meeting place ten minutes early.

I heard the faint "ding-ding" and knew the tram had come and now pulled from the station. Before too long, a lone figure, Nikolai, dressed in a long, black coat and wool cap, walked in my direction. When assured he saw me, I turned so he'd follow me toward the bench.

"Good to see you." Relieved, I shook his hand. "Sit down. What do you think of this meeting place?"

"It's perfect." Looking around, Nikolai continued, "I'm sure no one followed. I'm sorry I'm late. A man trundling a two-wheeled cart had a mishap. A wheel came off. Turnips rolled onto the tracks and every which way. A couple of us got off the tram and helped the old fellow get the wheel back on and the turnips reloaded."

"It's not often we get to see something to chuckle about," I commented.

After a few moments of silence, Nikolai sensed the tension, but kept quiet, his eyes wide open.

"Nikolai, I'm making plans to escape."

Nikolai's jaw dropped. He tried to speak.

"The reason I'm telling you is that I've had a hunch for quite some time you're planning a similar move."

"Ah . . . ya," he stammered.

"You know, Nikolai, I'm placing my future, my life, into your hands by sharing this. Please hear me out."

"Why are you telling me?"

"Listen, I'm planning to leave during the spring thaw. If you planned to leave shortly after my disappearance, you might want to rethink it."

"Why?"

"You would have additional hounds on your tail. Everyone knows we're friends."

"What about you?" Nikolai asked. "What if I left before you? Wouldn't you be hounded more?"

"If the time span between the disappearances is long enough, I believe they wouldn't make a connection."

As if turning on a faucet, Nikolai unloaded his bottled-up secret.

"I think I've saved enough money to go all the way to America," he said with pride. "I haven't made up my mind whether to take a ship out of Leningrad or a train south."

"Why not straight to Berlin and on west?"

"Oh, no," Nikolai said. "Been there in the army. The border guards are real fidgety. The military has put tremendous pressure on the local governments for not being able to suppress the flow of defections of East Germans, Poles, and others into West Germany."

"West Germany?" I asked.

"Yes, after the war they split Germany in two. The bulk, or western part is under British, French, and American occupation. The rest is controlled by the Soviets and their puppet regimes. A ten-meter-wide control strip runs along the entire border between the two German sections. To the east of that strip is an additional five-hundred-meter-wide protective area, which is expanded by a five-kilometer-wide zone that forbids anyone to live in it. Only by permission can it be farmed and only during daylight hours. Isn't that crazy? What is worse, Berlin is two-hundred kilometers inside the East section. Half of Berlin is free, with much American presence there. However, no one can get into West Berlin without proper documentation, the VOPOs'll shoot to kill. The best way in or out of the free zone is by air. You can imagine the security madness."

"I didn't realize the mess in Berlin."

"You know, isn't it ironic, I served part of the time in the military as a border guard. I learned firsthand the checkpoint situations and methods of operation. I served a stint near Berlin itself. One time, forced to shoot at folks trying to escaped, I shot over their heads."

I had never heard Nikolai talk so freely. He stared at me and made sure I heard and understood what he related. His enthusiasm was punctuated with unrestrained gestures and body movement. To see him as free and full of expressions sent my spirit soaring, reviving my withered demeanor. With joy I soaked in everything he said.

"It's interesting you mentioned heading south. From where do you plan to sail to America?"

"Hamburg or Bremerhafen would be ideal."

"What about skipping into Austria first?"

"Well, Austria is not under Communist control. The borders are still guarded. Hungary, though not too sympathetic to the Soviets, has looser borders."

"If you decide to leave by ship, you probably couldn't sail directly to Germany either."

"Yes, that's true. I'd have to sail to Helsinki or Stockholm first. On the other hand, to travel by way of Hungary or Austria will put me way south and stretch my money."

"I don't want to stifle your dream, Nikolai, but, did you consider Russian roubles may not be worth much in Germany. You may have a hard time making the exchange."

"When I think about these details I get frightened. Deep inside I only want to get out. I wish I could follow a script."

"I know you've got what it takes." I placed a firm grip on his shoulder. " I can't wait for spring to come myself."

"I'm ready." Nikolai said. "The fuse is lit."

Curious about the occupied sector, I asked, "Is München in the western sector?"

"Yes, I'm positive of that."

"I'll give you my mother's address there. If you should wind up in a dire situation, look her up and tell our story. If nothing else, use her address to write to me. Wouldn't it be great if we met again as free men?"

"Somehow I think it is our destiny," he said. Staring far off, Nikolai continued. "Isn't it incredible? While along the border, I became the head maintenance man. Thanks to you, I could figure out how trip wires and alarms worked. I fixed malfunctioning gates and reconnected sabotaged signals. I also heard of plans to install spiral barbed wire fencing along all the western border, and that was several years ago. A couple of buddies told of unloading truckloads of mines. I don't know if I want to take a chance at crossing a mine field. To cut a wire and swim a river wouldn't be much. The mines do scare me."

"The mines should scare you. You don't want to get all the way to the border and then take such a chance."

"Mr. Brunner, if I can fix a sabotaged border gate, I can also sabotage one."

"Hey, good point," I said. "Why don't you clue me in on some of the details?"

Nikolai told me all he knew about the construction and electrical setup of various devices.

"Interesting," I said. "Who knows what I may run into when I skip town." I went on to say, "This may sound dumb, but what does it take to buy a train ticket? I must travel out of here by rail."

"Well, for relatively short distances, nothing but money. For long distances within the Soviet Union, it may take some form of identification. To head directly west into occupied territory, you can count on needing proper papers."

"Proper papers?"

"It's a document that states your place of birth, now live, and that you are a member of the Party."

"You know I don't have that. I'm a nonperson. Illegal. A war leftover. In Germany I'm declared dead. I feel about as insignificant as a budding mushroom on pile of barn mulch."

"I don't have civilian Party papers either," said Nikolai. "I have my military status card. It should get me to most cities within the country."

"Nikolai, is there some form of papers that would make me legitimate? You know, all I have is the ID card that lets me in and out of the plant."

"That won't do you any good." Nikolai abruptly paused. . . . "Mr. Brunner, my sister has all of my father's papers stored in a cigar box. She rarely looks in it. Both of us would be long gone before she'd miss the stuff."

"My son, could you borrow some documentation? We would both have the same last name!"

"You called me son."

"Yes, it feels good."

"It does, father," Nikolai smiled. We hugged, patted each other on the shoulder, and cried.

—

For years I had trudged on, collected coins, and kept nerves of steel. I had to live a lie. My mind wanted to withdraw but instead had to focus on not becoming a noticeably different person. Each evening I recalled my day to weigh if I had been too jovial or too moody. I could not show the excitement in me when the days of the spring thaw drew nearer. I developed difficulty sleeping.

All the effort of planning the escape made facing Boris an exasperating challenge. To appear normal with my friend took a soul-wrenching effort. For most of six years, he and I sat opposite one another at the lunch table. As my departure drew nearer, I gradually seated myself more often alongside of him to avoid eye contact. *What a shame.* Did Boris sense something different? I could not tell.

To keep the lie going with Lana, I continued our weekly jaunts. Sometimes on Sunday we'd eat together at her place, play a little music, and depart as friends.

—

In the summer of 1955, Irina, training for an international competition, suffered a horrific fall on the ice. She shattered her knee as well as her career along with the dreams of bringing home a medal to her country. Now home permanently, her previous surly demeanor toward me grew to bitter. Her boyfriend, Sven, fed on her animosity and seemed to egg Irina on to make my life miserable. Again, Lana did nothing to stifle or reverse the cold looks or snappy responses to every effort I made to warm up the relationship.

Sven, a lanky young man with deep-set, dark eyes, straight black hair, and a wispy mustache, seemed to enjoy his role as antagonist. One late summer night, relaxed on Lana's ottoman, I heard him talking to Irina on the stone patio. The open window, hidden behind a shrub, made it possible to overhear part of their conversation.

"Why does this guy keep hanging around?" He asked Irina.

"He's known Mother since I was a little girl."

"He is nothing but a bastard without a country. The likes of him killed my father. I tell you what," he lowered his voice, "you give me the nod, I'd have no problem of getting rid of him for you."

I sat up straight and checked my surroundings. A cold shiver crawled up my spine. I felt exposed, vulnerable.

"Anything the matter?" Lana asked.

"Yes, I . . . we need to talk!"

"Franz, what's wrong? Are you in pain? You look frightened."

Feeling choked, I coughed. "Can we go for a walk?"

Under a group of trees, out of hearing, I abruptly stopped and faced Lana.

"I overheard Sven make a monstrous and vile suggestion. That fellow, that . . . that unpleasant . . . friend of Irina . . . wants to kill me!"

"No . . . not . . ."

"I heard it! The window is open. He is waiting for Irina to give him the go-ahead."

"Franz—"

"I killed his father, he claims—or the likes of me. I've been through this before. Now, after all these years do I still have to watch my back?"

"I'm not dismissing what you're saying. The fellow may only want to impress Irina."

"Impress? Phooey! Lana, it's bad enough you haven't shown any concern about how your darling daughter has flaunted her dislike for me. That little snit has been delighting in snubbing me for years. What is it? Haven't you noticed? Don't you care? Do you gloat with enjoyment when she gets under my skin? Now her punk-kid friend makes death threats?"

"I'm going to check into it."

"Yeah! Check into it. Shit!" With a huff I walked away.

—

I not only lived a lie, but from that day forward I felt hunted. At my place I propped a chair under the door handle every night.

I valued two things in Russia, my real friends and the plan I had in motion. My resolve to escape renewed a yearning for my own people. My imagination became saturated with images of a time and a love I once enjoyed. I spent every waking moment conniving and plotting. I felt strangely exuberant, young. Fooling Lana and her ilk stirred within me an exhilaration and a drive to succeed. Yet, I had to keep up the pretense, the lie, the blackouts, and now the watching of my back.

—

Nikolai couldn't hide his excitement. When the time for his escape drew near, his hands trembled and fidgeted trying to do his work. I knew his dilemma. The others in the X room noticed as well.

"Nikolai, you have been acting like a man in love," I said in front of the others.

"Why, what makes you say that?"

"You're a bit antsy these days. Looks as if you can't wait for the day to end so you can be with her again. You've got to relax; women want a confident man."

"What's her name?" The others asked. "Have you set a wedding day yet?" They all roared with laughter.

That evening, leaving the plant, Nikolai said, "Bench. Eight Sunday. My day has come!" He walked on. No time at the bicycle rack.

Almost two month had gone by since we had our first meeting at the bench. The appointed morning burst with beauty as the gleam of dawn sprang to life. Playful darts of early light painted dabs of brilliance unto treetops, roofs, and chimneys. The stillness let me hear my heart's pumping. I was happy to be alive, happy for Nikolai, his day. Not a good-bye, but a life coming to full bloom. Even the birds seemed eager to witness the thrill. I never felt more convinced that he is making the correct decision.

Nikolai stepped from behind a tree as I approached the bench.

"How are you, my son?" I said.

"Good to see you, father." Nikolai took a deep breath and almost choked with excitement. "Tonight, I'm leaving on a late train for Kiev. From there, several shorter trips heading west. I'm not carrying much—warm clothes and rain gear, one loaf of bread, and three smoked sausages."

"You have been living on that for some time now. Did you practice to see if you could survive?"

"Maybe subconsciously, but not really."

"I'm so happy for you, son. You've been patient for a long time. I'm proud of you. I am a lucky man to have shared so much with you."

Nikolai pulled an envelope from his coat pocket. "Here are my father's papers. I had a chance to snatch them several days ago while taking care of my little nephew."

"Great! What a help. I see, my new name is Lev Sakharov."

Nikolai clued me in on the various documents. "Some, you'll likely never need. You'll notice my family lived in Penza when the political zealots hauled my father away. I don't want to tell you what to do, but you may want to visit there."

"Why is that?"

"If someone questioned you, you could at least tell a few things about the city. It'd give your identity more credibility."

"Good point."

"By train, Penza is only one full day from Moscow."

The conversation ended. All that mattered had been conveyed. A stillness clutched our souls. I looked toward the heavens as if expecting orders from above. We rose from the bench and embraced.

"Father," Nikolai said. His chin trembled.

"Son," I could only whisper, my breast full of pride, sorrow, and gladness.

Abruptly, he walked away. At the end of the path he looked back. Without a wave or any other gesture, he ran toward the trolley stop. I sank to the bench, now strangely cold. A wave of exhaustion clouded all surroundings. Smiling, I raised my chin. Tears trickled to my collar.

—

The walk back to my apartment led me near the old church I had admired since my first trek to Peter's neighborhood. I felt the need to be alone, to be shrouded in the sanctuary's cocoon of solitude. Lana had talked about the religious cleansing by Stalin. How he persecuted and disposed of many Christian leaders to atrocious gulags. To me, surely that time had passed.

Entering, I did not hear the door; however, the click of it shutting behind me reverberated throughout the old sanctuary. A shiver of awe rippled from heart to toe. Darts of colors, from a few remaining shards of stained glass, carelessly sprinkled down the pealing walls. The sparse light spoke in strange whispers as it also revealed the desecration. All sorts of debris laid scattered on the magnificent marble floor. Puddles of water from recent rains created ugly blotches encased with snakelike edges. The missing window panes and holes in the roof invited pigeons and bats to find refuge. Everywhere drizzled mounds of droppings verified their presence. Long pieces of guttering, stacked along the edge of the sanctuary floor, told of icy winters of years past. An assortment of empty crates and dusty sections of makeshift platforms desecrated the altar area, dishonoring the glory of God. My back slid down the wall until I sat on the floor. No human eyes watched; yet One watched. Time took a break. As if bathing in lukewarm water, a complete calm washed over me. . . . Restful images, imaginary melodies, reassuring voices, entered my being. Assured, I clicked the door shut behind me and stepped back into the bright day.

My room felt strangely cold and empty. I missed a friend. I tried to play the violin that special Sunday, but couldn't. I tried practicing being Lev Sakharov, but couldn't. I felt lost, helpless and spent—and yet satisfied. Nikolai will soon be on a train toward freedom.

—

On Monday morning, acting rejuvenated from a day of rest, I said to anyone listening, "I need Nikolai to finish this grind. Have you seen him?" Two men stated they hadn't seen Nikolai.

"He's usually one of the first to work. He may be out in the shop. Gocha," I said, "would you go and find him for me, please?"

Ulanov found out Nikolai didn't show for work. "Mr. Brunner, do you know of any problem that might have caused Nikolai to be absent?" he asked so the others in the X room also heard.

"No, not really," I said. "He wasn't sick on Saturday. Maybe a bit antsy, though."

"Why do you say that?"

"He's got a new girlfriend," one of his coworkers blurted.

"Yes," I said, "the fellows teased him about it."

"If he does come in later, send him to see me."

When he didn't show Tuesday or Wednesday either, Ulanov sent one of Nikolai's friends to visit his home.

I never heard another word out of anybody. Several weeks after, I asked Boris if he heard something about Nikolai.

"No, nothing worth repeating." After a pause, he added, "He was contagious. I've been thinking. I miss him."

"I miss him a lot. Didn't know how valuable he was to me. . . . Boris, what do you think happened?"

Not looking at me, he mumbled, "Franz, if it's a job change, he would have asked for a letter of recommendation. Between you and me, I think he fled." Boris lowered his chin and added, "I hear thousands of folks are leaving for Western Europe."

"Hmm, that is interesting. I tend to agree with you, but I'm not going to offer such a scenario to Ulanov. I'm sure he has his own conclusion."

When I didn't play the violin on the bridge, I practiced being Lev. I needed to learn to act and look the typical Russian—somewhat older, unkempt. I planned to take my old coat. I wanted to look poor, slightly hunched forward, with the coat pulled up at the back of the neck and unbuttoned in the front. Something heavy in the pockets to help pull it down. Lev needed to be a man of few words. When confronted, people needed to think he was tongue-tied. A speech impediment would hide his accent and present a somewhat backward man. I practiced speaking Russian with my tongue pressed against my lower teeth. I mumbled a lot.

December of 1955. The colors of autumn faded and Moscow took on the look of wilted bleakness. Like a mouse to a chunk of cheese, I again drew near to the solace of the ravaged church. A faint beam from a wintery moon mysteriously pierced the dark vastness of the sanctuary. As before, I sat on the floor, my head rested against the wall. Tensions soon melted. Memories of days long gone plucked at my mind. *Where is Christmas? Is there still a Christmas?* Faintly at first, I heard Friedl singing "*Stille Nacht, Heilige Nacht.*" I saw my last Christmas—the Christmas of twelve years earlier. Friedl taught the words and melody to my three-year-old boy. The Christmas tree stood in the corner. Tinsel quivered from the heat of the lighted candles on the tree. My baby girl cooed in the wicker cradle, her blue eyes reflected the sparkling magic. Sadly, in this heathen land of suppression, I had forgotten about such special times. . . . Christmas.

21

For a long time I had been one of Lana's "clients." I figured if I stayed in her face, there would be less reason for her stoolies to monitor my every move. Apparently the reports on my movements didn't suit, because she hit me with this question: "Why do you keep going to that old church?"

Bam! She startled me. I thought for sure no one in the dark of night had seen me.

"It's a devastated old building," I brusquely answered.

"I told you several years ago the State does not condone religious activities among the new progressive populace."

"What religious activity? There is nothing going on inside the old church. I feel a certain comfort in there," I said.

"What I mean is this. You are an intelligent man. Why would you want to seek comfort in such medieval superstition? This is a new world. This is a Socialist world. All of us embrace our progressive government. We know it will soon dominate the world! . . . Franz," she lowered her voice, "I recommend you not continue such worthless practice."

"Lana, why are you so hard on me? I'm a lonely man. I find solitude inside that church."

"Franz, all is going quite well right now," she emphasized in a subdued tone. "I tell you this in a hush, I did not report your recent stroll toward Peter's neighborhood. To me, it seemed innocent enough. So please don't start something new I may have to write a report on."

—

The small family painting gave me continued hope. I perfected my blackouts. I fell as I stepped off the trolley, causing a small commotion. I also performed an excellent fall at work. I collapsed and smacked my head against a milling machine. When blood ran to my shirt collar, the woman in charge of the first aid box stopped the bleeding. I fell in front of my door when

Vera stepped from the apartment. On and on, I continued to live the lie by day and practiced being the tongue-tied Lev at night.

At the appointed time, my demise would come from falling into the swollen river while having a blackout. "He drowned," they would say. "Washed downstream by the torrents of melted snow and spring rains."

—

The day before my departure the violin ceased its communion. I needed to think. The wind gusted playfully outside my window. The moon peeked through cracks of late-evening clouds. An occasional splash of rain did not keep me from one last walk. With every stride, new energy throbbed through my veins. I trod these paths for years and knew every bend and pebble. At the river's edge, I slowed, stopped to listen to the gurgling and menacing laps of the raging water. My grave.

As I neared my door, the streetlight behind me, my mind engaged in tomorrow's escape, a strange sound pricked my ears. I slowed my stride.

"Keep walking!" the words hissed. A vicious arm lock yanked my head back as an icy blade pressed against my throat. Without hesitation, my elbow uncoiled a violent thrust at the assailant's head. The cold blade sliced over my jaw. My blow knocked the man off balance and gave me an opening to stomp the arch of his foot. I felt the crush, followed by a choking wail. The assailant collapsed and rolled face down. I used both knees and forced his right arm back until it cracked. With his own knife point I pricked the skin under his ear and yanked the lanky punk erect.

"Boy!" I breathed, "If you ever grow up, learn not to mess with a soldier!"

I left the whimpering Sven slumped on Lana's doormat.

Over the wall sink, I dabbed my open wound with wine. A cold cloth stopped the bleeding. I did not bar the door that night.

That last day in Moscow I sat facing Boris and looked straight at him.

"Boris, my friend, is all going well?"

"Oh, yes! The family has adapted well. Yelena is happy in our new apartment. Zina is going to a good school."

"Do you ever write to your brother Ivan?"

Somewhat baffled, he said, "I don't write. Yelena writes. She does all the writing to relatives. I'm not good with words on paper."

"Do they all live in Zlatoust?" I asked.

"No, we all live in the small village Ivankov. We do get our mail out of Zlatoust."

I reluctantly pressed on to get his full attention. "Boris, I'm going to share with you a little of my background in Germany. Some of the stuff Lana was curious about since the day she visited my shack."

Boris shifted in his seat, glanced to either side, then looked down and fumbled with the spoon in his empty bowl.

"Back in my country, I was in charge of perfecting the trigger mechanism of the German MG42 machine gun. The big wigs here know about that. That is why they pulled me from the mine to work here so they could get a little more out of me. I hated working on that wicked weapon back home, and I sure didn't want to see the likes again in this shop."

Not knowing what to make of this odd conversation, Boris stammered. "Why? . . . I . . . I heard my brother speak of that nasty gun. He told me it gave him shivers when it rattled off hundreds of shells in seconds. Many of my brother's buddies didn't get away fast enough, paid a dear price."

"I'm so sorry, Boris." After a pause I said, "I'm glad I never had to actually work on the thing here. They try to copy the mechanism here, but I tell you, there are too many parts, and too many varied metals involved for them ever to come close to an equivalent gun."

Boris shook his head. "Why the continued push? All war machines are evil."

"Evil is hardly the right word," I said. "That thing, the way we had it tuned, fired over 1,200 rounds per minute. That is more than twenty rounds per second!"

"What was the use of all the killing?" Boris said. "They said we won, but life became a lot worse after the war than ever before."

I noticed his troubled eyes. I calmly continued. "Boris, if I became a Russian and stayed here the rest of my life, I would love to have the name Lev. Yes, it would be Lev."

His eyes half closed as he slightly turned his head, but kept focused on what I said. He became uncomfortable and tense, but kept quiet.

Boris needed to know a link of communication he later would understand.

"Boris, my friend," I said in a loving whisper, "kiss little Zina for me. Yelana. She is wonderful. . . . We have got to get back to work."

We did not speak again to each other that day, nor would we ever again.

—

When I arrived at the apartment, I found a note, written by Lana in much larger letters than her normal writing. The note said: "Franz, see me AT ONCE!—Lana" . . . *'At once' to you! Lana! You no longer have any dominion over me!*

BOOK THREE

22

There are momentous days in a man's life. The day a man chooses a mate for life. The day a man becomes a father for life. The day a man is forced to separate from his family. The day I chose to die was by far the most unnerving. I chose to fake my death. I had to be resolute and calculating. My nerves, as tight as a kettle drum, enabled me to hone awareness to its sharpest. The last meal, cheese and bread, was no different from thousands before. With ice in my veins, I tuned the violin, put on an extra sweater, coat, and the old woolen mantle, donned my felt hat, stuck my modified umbrella under my arm, grabbed the cane and violin, glanced one last time at the little painting, and then snapped the door shut behind me.

With total purpose, I strode to make my last stand. My eyes blurred with tension. I managed to smile at all who saw me. Over the years, about everyone within walking distance heard me play the violin. Many witnessed my blackouts and helped me get back up. I had become, one might say, a fixture in the community.

As always, the short wall was my stage. I pretended to tune the instrument to give my nerves time to control my trembling. Again the sweet sound flowed from the violin as it took over my spirit. I played until the crowd thinned and the last person receded into the night. To close out my life, and that of Olga's magical instrument, I offered Dvorak's *Ninth Symphony's* "Largo." Not a soul listened.

A few brisk steps brought me to the end of the bridge, where I jumped the short wall and disappeared toward the water's edge. Down, down I stumbled. The old cane I left at the foot of the wall along with the violin case on the cobblestones, open, the night's donations still in it. I nestled the bow between the rocks at the river's edge and made sure it was visible from the bridge. With inhuman purpose I smacked the violin against the rocks. A dagger gored my soul. I crawled under the bridge, the cracked violin under my arm. The angry waters lapped the rocks on the river's edge to within a meter of the bridge's underside. Dank and musty smells of decay carried a sense of doom. Chalky stalactites hung as fingers of death. Several times my foot slipped, filling my shoes with icy water. I pressed on. Once through, I groped my way to the grassy bank and into the shadows of the barren trees. Downstream, at a previously discovered eddy, I bent to partially submerge my beloved violin. "I'm so sorry, Olga." My heart ached as I watched her drift until she came to rest. One more little push, her neck still gasping for life, completed the burial.

Driven by a single-minded purpose I picked up my pace, a half moon whisked in and out of clouds. I wanted distance, away, away from hell. Saliva drooled from the corners of my mouth and mixed with cold sweat and hot breath. I caught an almost empty tram at a stop different from the one I normally boarded. The bulky old mantle disguised my hyperventilating. The switch from living to dead, from bound to free, almost proved to be more than my spirit could handle.

At the Moscow South train station a matronly woman smiled at my clotted speech and sold me a ticket to Penza.

Again my future found itself hitched to a train, a train in an endless country. I sat frozen on the end of the wooden bench of a full train. My arm touched the person next to me. Both hands rested on the umbrella knob. I focused on the floor.

My weary brain succumbed to the rhythmic sound of the wheels and the drone of conversation all around. A tap on my shoulder snapped me erect.

"Ticket," the conductor barked, not even looking at anyone. My ears felt red.

After that interruption, the people around me settled in for the night ahead. Everyone found their own odd way to relax and doze. I too wanted to rest, but freezing feet kept me from relaxing. My shoes and socks found a spot on the luggage rack overhead. I slid the mantle down to pool around my ankles and rubbed the cold feet with the wool cloak. Slowly my body warmed. At long last my nerves calmed.

I woke up when my elbow slipped off my knee. It was morning, far from Moscow. The new day yawned showing a slight shimmer of green on the hillside.

The few folks still on the train stirred, stood, stretched, then made their way to the privy. A young woman on the bench opposite hesitated to nurse her baby, with me watching. I gave her a reassuring smile. Then I nonchalantly retrieved my shoes and socks from the shelf above and put them on. I got in line to visit the iron restroom. A work of art. I stood and looked through the cast iron shaft mounted to the floor and watched the rail ties as they streamed by. *Good. I'm moving on!*

The young mother finished nursing and proceeded to burp her little one, having it lie on its belly across her lap. She pulled a piece of sweet bread and a jar of what appeared to be water, from her travel bag. When she noticed I had nothing to eat, she offered to share her bread.

"I'm fine. Thank you." My tongue against my teeth, I asked, "How much longer to Penza?"

She paused, noticing my impediment, but answered with a warm smile. "Mister, you'd do well to settle in for a long day."

She mentioned three stops in Penza. The first on the outskirts, the second at the industrial area, and the third in the center of the old city. She also informed me that, if I needed a connection, I should get off in center city.

The baby rested soundly in the cradle of the young mother's arm. Soon she asked, not threatened by my speech or demeanor, "Could you hold her, please? I don't want to take her to the restroom with me, she'd wake up. You know how noisy and filthy that metal cubbyhole is."

"I'll be happy to," I assured her.

"Thanks. I won't be long." I held the child in the crook of my arm, her tiny legs rested on my lap. As I looked at the angelic face, my heart melted. . . . *Is my little one an angel girl?*

The mother returned to her seat and asked, "Was she good?"

"She was an angel," I assured her, "because she is an angel."

"She is going to see her daddy for the first time," the mother confided. "I have not seen him either since the last furlough. We're to meet at his mother's house."

"Did you grow up in Penza?" I asked.

"Yes, I lived there until seven years old. Then, before the Great War started, they came and took my father away," she said softly as her eyes beheld the child.

"Did you know where to?"

"No, my mother tried to find him, but never did."

"Did others disappear?"

"I personally didn't know any, but mother told me of several more who left Penza."

I continued to show interest and said, stammering, my tongue pressed against my bottom teeth, "I'm so sorry. I'm sure your father would love to hold his little granddaughter. When they came to take your father, did they hurt your mother?"

"No, but when I came home from school, I found her sobbing. The next day in school my friend, Nikolai, told of his father being taken away."

My heart slipped to my belly.

"Mother said an entire family was hauled off. Although, some returned after several years."

The young woman, not shy and eager to share, told of her childhood. Twice, during the long ride, I got to play with the baby. I cooed and acted silly.

—

At mid-afternoon I stepped off the train, apprehensive of the reception. I bought the newspaper *Izvestia*. I knew any news about my drowning would not be in it. Even if it concerned them, the Soviets never did anything wrong, nor ever lost anything or anybody. The powers in charge are always correct, always praising their efforts and always deceiving. From a bench, looking over the top of the paper, I surveyed the surroundings.

Men pushed, women toted, young folks hurried, some loafed. I blended in. The warmth of the spring sun seeped through my coat. Judging from the paper's propaganda headlines, nothing major brewed. After a period of pretending, I reached through a slit of the coat lining for money. Emboldened by the distance behind me, I pulled the identification papers from the shaft of the umbrella. I didn't want to incriminate myself later, fumbling in front of an official.

To satisfy my gnawing belly I chose a tavern near the rail station, an establishment below street level. Behind the thick entrance door I found myself in a dim and stale-smelling eatery. The ceiling, barely over my head, exerted an unwelcome pressure. A large table in each corner filled the room. I slid onto a wall-mounted bench and propped my elbows on the table. The special of the day was scribbled on a chalkboard. A furry-looking fellow stuck his head from a window-like opening and hollered, "If you don't want what's on the board, we got cold meat, fresh goat cheese. Made it meself," he added with a toothless grin.

"The hash is fine," I answered as thick lipped as I could. "Add some bread to that."

The way the words slobbered out of my mouth produced the quick glances I expected. Two short sentences is all it took for the locals to formulate an opinion about me. I ate my swill of mushy potatoes, cabbage, and carrots in silence. I paid for the grub, stuffed the leftover bread in my pocket, and stepped back onto the street.

My new grip rapidly filled with necessities I needed for the journey. I added a razor, a small whetstone, soap, and some survival staples. I aimed to keep a clean face, except for a mustache.

At dusk I followed a meandering, narrow street and found a small sign that read, "Room for Rent." My options were an upstairs room with a coal stove, or a cubbyhole with bunk only. The cheaper one—a rough-cut lean-to attached to the stone building—was my choice. A lad took my payment for one night, so, I tried out my new name.

The night's chill brought back memories of the old shack. I needed my heavy mantle for extra cover. The next morning, while I sought the outhouse, I heard my name mentioned from somewhere inside the house.

"I'm not kidding." Someone said. "I heard it with my own ears. Wait around, he'll be in here to turn in the key before too long. You can ask him yourself." Whether they talked about me or another person, I couldn't be sure. I didn't want to take the chance. I grabbed my gear, left the heavy key sticking in the door, and squeezed through the gate in the backyard into an alley.

Penza, unlike Moscow, offered the charm of a hometown. Other than factories, a quaint place. The ancient cobblestone streets, stone buildings, and shops supported a simple life where average people could lived in harmony. Yet, the charm seeped from the buildings only. The faces of the folks revealed the drag and trials and a life-smothering spirit. People's chins stayed tucked, eyes made little contact with the world. One would expect, on a sunny day, as it was, some of the older men to sit around joking and jesting. Not until school let out, and children claimed the streets for their games, did the town come alive. Boys removed their boxy satchels and parked them at the edge of the town's square. Working folks steered clear as boys kicked around a worn ball. The girls, in giddy huddles, obviously discussing the boys, giggled and squealed. The younger children played hopscotch and jumped rope. Happiness briefly entered the town, and my heart. Then, I thought, *will they grow up and also succumb to the monotony of a system where no reward is offered for being energetic, inventive, and inquisitive. How sad. . .But, I'm going home!*

To blend in, I acted the part I had practiced, hunched over, coat pulled up at the back, a rolled newspaper sticking from the pocket. My new leather satchel hung from my hand as though it pulled me along. Few gave me a second glance.

I longed for a place to lie down without having to register my name. Every nook and alley between the warehouses became a possibility.

A heap of coal near a furnace or a boiler always translated to warmth. I snuck to investigate such a pile, then eased toward a short chimney which stuck from a shed attached to a warehouse. A metallic click opened the board door to a well-used, dark, and grimy boiler room. A large stove, recently stoked, radiated heat. *Not bad, . . . If I need it.*

As drawn by a magnet, I eased back to the rail yard. A glorious sunset helped celebrate my second day as a free man. With my legs stretched out, I leaned against a buttress made of great timbers that terminated one of several rail tracks. The display of reds, indigo, and golds showed off its splendor before fading below the horizon.

An old, unused water tank, with scraggly trees growing from its base, was also witness. The tank's arm, which once quenched the thirst of locomotives, precariously dangled, broken, over its edge. Barely visible was the fading face of Stalin painted on the side of the tank. The words under it read, "Together We Can." I had seen many similar signs. This one stood out. The old water tank had lost one of its boards, leaving a black gap coursing through the right eye of Stalin. I stared at the gap.

"I've seen that black gap through Stalin's eye before," I muttered out loud.

The quiet suddenly shattered as a steam whistle screamed. More than a dozen men poured out of a building behind me. Unaware of me sitting there, some men passed so close I could have tripped them. Within minutes, all returned to quiet. New sounds from nearby houses reached my ears. A door slammed, squeaky windows and shutters chimed in. Bolts and bars slid to lock entrances. Shoveled coal filled buckets. My eyes returned to the missing board of the water tank. Pondering, my free spinning mind slowly sharpened. *"I saw that evil eye before. . . . It was not on the train to Moscow!"* Methodically, I decrypted my only other train ride in Russia, the one from the battlefield.

Is it possible, I thought, my heart in my throat, *that we stopped here? I rested, propped against the bars, looking west. Right over there—yes . . . yes! I faced the sunset. That one-eyed Stalin stared at me then. . . .*

I developed the latent image and vividly also remembered a mysterious woman giving me water—giving me life. . . . *Does she live in this town? I must find her!*

As full darkness crept to cover all, befuddled by the new revelations, I stretched out on the soot-covered ground and stared at the starry heavens. After much pondering, I concluded it wouldn't be wise to spend the night in an open rail yard. So, I slunk to the previously discovered boiler room, warm, hidden, next to the coal pile. As quiet as I could, I stepped into the spooky abode and left the door ajar in case of a quick exit. The dark, darker than death itself, grabbed my gut. The furnace's three round, red eyes stared as it drew its raspy breath. Assured, I clicked the door shut and slid down the wall into a squatting position.

"Who are you?" Came a voice from an unseen corner inside the tiny room. I jumped to my feet, groped the crude wall toward the door. "Sit down," the voice continued. "It's warm in here. I could tell by your sneaking you needed a place for the night."

"I . . . I . . . I, you scared the stuffing out of me!"

"Relax."

"Ah, thanks," I said, forgetting my speech impediment.

"What made you pick this place?" The voice questioned.

"I saw the coal pile. Figured there must be fire nearby."

"You from here?"

"No," I admitted. "Only passing through."

"Me too." It must be the code of the hobos to say little and ask less.

"Rest," he said, "morning comes early. We've got to beat the fellow stoking this boiler."

"What time?" I asked.

"Long before the six o'clock whistle." He let me absorb that fact. "Hey listen," he went on, "I travel alone."

"Me too."

"I'm leaving first. You get that?"

"Sure thing," I answered. I didn't want to know why. At that point I've had enough conversation.

How far have I come? I asked myself, as I wrestled with reality. *How low have I fallen to lie with the rogues and the homeless?*

"Hey you!" said the voice out of the corner. "Quit your fidgeting. There ain't nobody in here after you."

I heard what the man said but couldn't calm down. The worry of being followed, the overwhelming journey ahead, the unsettled and eluding matter of the mystery woman, all saturated my mind. I questioned the worth of it all. The option hung open, get on the first train and head west. However, a grasp held me back—the one-eyed Stalin . . . the cup of water . . . the woman.

A wisp of cold air from the purposely left-open door woke me. I did not hear the "voice" leave. I rose, keenly listening, then ventured from the shelter. Too dark to read my watch, I walked alongside a stopped train's passenger car,—half past four. As I neared the caboose, my satchel hanging from my hand, a watchman jumped from the train yelling with menacing venom, "Get! Get out of here! I don't want to see you near this train again!"

The hounds of Hades behind me, I scooted across the tracks and into the shadows.

One last shout: "If I catch you trying to stow away on this here train, I'll have you shot!"

I scrambled for more distance. In my hurry, I bumped into a burly fellow with a shovel on his shoulder. "Hey, watch where you going!" he barked as he swung the shovel and almost knocked my head off. I kept moving on. Where to? I had no idea. Not fond of being accosted twice this early in the day.

The confrontations before the break of dawn, coupled with fatigue and not sleeping well, renewed my determination to find a resting place. A thicket, along the tracks away from the earlier altercation, next to an enormous water vat for filling locomotives, looked perfect. I dropped to the ground, crawled far enough from the graveled path and stretched out in tall weeds. My body told me to sleep, but tension keenly amplified all sounds. A rooster proclaimed his day. A steady drip nearby kept up its beat. Doors and gates clicked and slammed. Whiffs of coal smoke had me imagine women heating water, firemen stoking the boilers. I heard footsteps on the gravel paths, some shuffled, others thumped the ground. I ducked even lower.

Then, very close, I heard a squeak, a turning of a rusty faucet. My eyes darted toward the sound. Through the weeds I saw, no more than three meters away, the backside of a woman. Bent over, her pail on the ground, she drew water from a spigot mounted on the giant water vat. With the bucket full, she disappeared. Within moments, two more women came to draw from the great tank. Only a brief greeting between them injected a human side to an otherwise stoic morning ritual.

The spigot squeaked on . . . off . . . on. Women kept coming. The six-o'clock whistle blew. As if by an unspoken command, the pail ladies disappeared. Now, only workers scurried to various shops, warehouses, docks, reviving the day's bustle of a rail yard.

Again robbed of rest, I crawled from the thicket and drifted back toward the center of the town.

Here I kept moving, a man on the run, yet trapped. Trapped, because my mind could not shed the angel of long ago. I decided to walk far from the train depot. At the end of a rutted wagon road, a spring flowed from a rusty pipe out of a hillside. The lively flow spilled into a hollowed tree trunk. An assortment of broken pails and crocks, covered with dirt and dung, laid piled against the base of a short rock wall. I rinsed a shard big enough for a healthy drink, then quenched my thirst.

A surrey, stowed in a nearby shed, invited me to sit and lean back. I heard the spring gurgle. There in the shade, hidden from the world, the pastoral setting brought comfort to my troubled mind. Not a soul nearby, except a scarf-covered woman, more than a hundred meters away, making fir-bough brooms.

Glimpses of eleven years earlier gradually rebuilt the old scene. The mystery woman's face emerged. I saw her on the other side of the steel bars, somberly looking at me. The gold of the setting sun gave her face a glow and caused her green eyes to shimmer. Her uncovered hair, pulled back, revealed its pale hue. Her mournful look conveyed a distant hurt. A hurt that may have been responsible for the scar on her left cheek.

For hours I pondered and contemplated in the quiet of the musty shed, but always short of a next step on how to find her. Baffled and miffed, I dragged myself back to town.

Again behind the old newspaper, propped on a short wall, an uneasiness invaded my space. As I peeked over the top of the paper, I noticed a person glaring directly at me. When I fully met his stare, he abruptly scampered into an alley. I had been spotted!

—

The southern train platform of Penza offered several benches for people waiting. At the end of one, using the shade of the overhang, I faced west. Years earlier, when I lay in the cattle car, I had faced west. I sat on the stump in the Ural Mountains and gazed west. My family lived somewhere in the West. For many years I dreamed of an end to the Red Soviet's cycle, the red solstice. . . .

Jarred from my thoughts, I became aware of movement all about—a shuffling of feet, an occasional banging of a pail. Again, now at the end of the day, in the likeness of wind-up toys, women repeated the early morning scene of fetching water. One more drink for the goat, the pig, or the chickens. Maybe water to soak a load of wash, scrub down the children, or give the flowers around the house a drink. One poor woman carrying two large staved pails, tottered to keep the yoke from slipping off her bony shoulders. Evidently, as revealed by the women's varied ages, most of them had performed the task since they were big enough to carry a pail.

I pondered. *If this ritual has been going on for years, then . . . did my mystery lady also tote water so many years ago? Would she have gone to the spigot with only a tin mug? Surely, she had filled her pail before she turned toward the men on the train and handed me that life-giving drink. She had to be living close by to see the train pull in. She must have known we were Germans. She had to have brought the mug for only one purpose—to aid us. Obviously, she did not despise the men in the cattle car. Was she German also?—she despised the ones who locked them there. She must have feared being spotted aiding the enemy. What a woman! Does she still carry water today?*

I jumped off the bench and off the depot platform. With a clear vision and renewed purpose, I set out toward the decrepit water tank. I needed to look Stalin in the eye. There, in the fleeting light, in the exact spot where I lay eleven years earlier, I now stood as a free man. I turned to watch the women toting the heavy pails. A few trudged my way. All wore long skirts and aprons; their heads covered with shawls or scarves. One lady wore her shawl around her shoulders, her hair a pale gold, tied into a bun in the back. She disappeared among the warehouses.

No scarf! I almost shouted.

23

"I'm back," I said in a strong whisper. No answer. The boiler breathed; three red eyes confirmed the fireman had come and gone. My feet checked out the corner where the stranger had lain the night before, nothing but packed dirt and gravel, a little wallowed out as a hen would her nest. I purposed to lie down a spell, to figure an approach to meet the woman without a scarf. I fell asleep as soon as my head settled on the gravel mound.

Toward the morning hours a downpour awakened me. Rain beat the tin overhead like a hundred drummers. When I rolled to lie on my back, my hand fell into running water. The swelling rivulet meandered next to my head and out under the door. Alert, I wondered if the "voice" had returned after I came in, I called, "are you in here?" Not a word.

The coals in the furnace had died to an encrusted gray slag. Too dark to tell the time, the tip of my umbrella poked the remaining embers enough to read my watch. Three-forty. Too early to crawl out of this hole. Too late to go back to sleep. I planned the day.

When the roosters decided to wake the world, I had found my spot on the depot platform bench. A bone-aching drizzle took over the early morning. Soon, women again trotted to draw water. Everyone's head covered. I sat, my mind struggled at how to confront the woman with the uncovered flaxen hair.

"Are you lost? Hey, yes! You over there!" Startled, I turned around. A man dressed in a railroad uniform walked toward me.

"Are you speaking to me?"

"Yes," he said, "I saw you sitting on this bench yesterday, and here again today."

"I'm waiting for my sister."

"What train is she on?"

"Should have come in last night," I stammered and struggled to make myself understood with all the speech impediment I could muster.

"Where is she coming from?"

"Stalingrad."

"Stalingrad," he repeated. "Depends if she switched trains. Officially, fifteen-twenty is the next scheduled arrival from Stalingrad."

"Thank you," I said.

Fifteen-twenty would have been a nine hour wait on the bench. I stepped into the damp day. My new wide-brimmed hat kept the drizzle from running down my neck, and the rubber slicker did its job while I traipsed back to center town. The day's sogginess kept folks indoors. Runoff in gullies and ruts ran black with soot and grime. All else glistened, the dullness washed away.

Whiffs of garlic directed me to a tavern. Needing time to dry out, I stepped in and ordered a hot bowl of the daily stew to satisfied my hollow belly. My looks and clothes blended comfortably with the other haggard patrons. No one said a word, the dreary day didn't deserve it.

Back in the streets, a wrinkled babushka sold me an apple and a handful of shriveled carrots, limp and covered with a trace of sand. I spat out the grit, savored the sweetness as I gnawed on the carrots. The apple, also from the previous season, shriveled and rubbery, I saved for later.

The long day, while waiting for the evening's water pail ritual, drew me to the neighborhood that surrounded the defunct water tank. Paths and cart roads snaked through it much like in the area of my friend Peter. I saw gardens spots spaded over and small seed beds propped open and boxed in with boards. Tender sprouts of cabbage and tomato plants peeped at me. If folks saw my farcical-looking hat and cape, they must have figured me lost and from a different world.

Daffodils bloomed along the south side of picket fences and stone walls. I recalled the lustful nights to which I succumbed. I tried to come to grips with the mind of a man like me, who would, at such a time, forgo his integrity and submit to raw desire. Now, six years after those escapades, I envisioned my wife and children. I could almost touch them, as my heart yearned. Yet, I realized all too keenly, the thousands of kilometers of separation.

No one worked the soil that soggy afternoon. No one said hello. Only a few shoats, small and wiggly, had a smashing time as they wallowed in fresh mud. Later that day the clouds broke—another promised sunset.

I stationed myself on the platform bench to have full view of all activities. A different attendant worked the depot that evening. At last, the women started to appear to fetch their evening water. Only one woman interested me, the one without a head cover.

Then, what looked to be the angel of old appeared. At first a vague image, hair in a bun, shawl on her shoulders, she came walking toward the depot. She casually held the empty pail under her right arm. The setting sun behind her, her silhouette tall and slim. My eyes followed her every step. I watched her fill the pail and cross the tracks again. As she turned, and walked facing the sun, I stepped off the platform and hurried toward the old water tank. From there I watched her approach. I had imagined this moment—her face illuminated by the last glimmer of the sun. *Will it be her?*

While still at a reasonable distance, I emerged from the shadow. I did not want to frighten her. Without hesitation or breaking her stride, she continued to walk toward me.

When she neared to within speaking distance, I said, "*Guten Abend.*"

"*Sie auch,*" she answered.

"*Sprechen Sie Deutsch?*" I asked, my heart in my throat.

"*Ja* . . . yes," she stammered. She was so surprised she stopped her stride, hesitated, but continued taking smaller steps until she was at arm's length from me. The golden darts of the late sun lit her face. The scar on her cheek jumped into view.

"I'm sorry to startle you," I said. "I had to make sure it was you."

"Me? Why are you looking for me?"

"I want to thank you for a cup of water you gave me eleven years ago."

"You must be mistaken, sir. I don't know you." She started to walk away.

My heart met the pit of my stomach. I moved to follow her and said, "It was you, ma'am, I am sure. I'm the German soldier on the cattle car, on a train going east. You came and helped me drink from a tin mug."

She stopped, turned to look at me as she shifted the heavy pail to the other hand.

"I remember," she said. I watched her face recapture the distant scene. "Your arm hung through the bars."

"Yes," I almost shouted, "I want to thank you."

Having been convinced I didn't present a threat, she slightly twitched her head as if to say, "Follow me."

I let her gain about ten paces and then followed. She did not speed up. She did not turn her head. She knew I followed. At a modest stone house she entered the yard through a gate in the picket fence. She left it open for me to follow. I closed the gate behind me. When she faced me, she stood in front of a weather-beaten door with rusted hinges and a crudely wrought iron latch. The latch groove in the wood showed many decades of use.

"I'm sorry I acted a bit curt on the way," she said. "I didn't want to be seen loitering with a stranger."

"I understand," I assured her. "I appreciate you even listening to me. You speak German. I figured you did."

"You did?"

"Yes. You had pity on us."

"I did," she whispered. Pointing at a well-used plank bench, she said, "Come, sit down Mr. . . . ."

"Brunner, Franz Brunner." I remained standing. "Thanks, but I had best be going. The day is late and I expect you have chores to do. I wanted to thank you and not be a bother."

"Are you staying in Penza long?"

"I'm passing through here. Haven't chosen a train out as of yet."

"You must come back for a visit, if you could?"

"Ah, . . . yes. It would be my pleasure."

"Very well. How about ten in the morning?"

"That's good. I look forward to it."

I tipped my hat and wished her a good evening. A new lift entered my stride as I headed back toward the dark abode. On the way I stopped a young fellow to asked where I could pay for a bath. He didn't lose a step, but pointed and hollered, "Glinka's Laundry. He closes at six."

Being homeless and ready to change course when needed, I kept my satchel by my side. I hadn't had a chance to clean up or shave since I left Moscow. The bath stall offered no surprises. A boarded-up cubical the size of a two-seater outhouse. The evening star and her host of friends formed the roof. The items offered included one bucket, one spigot, and a dipper welded to a long dog chain. A few stout nails kept one's clothes from dragging the strange weeds growing in the corner. A box to sit on and meditate, or tie one's shoes, I considered a thoughtful touch. The rough board crate, off the ground enough to keep one from being spattered with mud, had grown a slick coating of green mold. The weathered board walls had shrunk enough to stick one's hand through. However, it was called a bathhouse—such it was.

The smell of lye soap promised to get the job done. Dipper after full dipper, the icy water coaxed the soap suds to tumble down my body and through the crate. Invigorating no doubt. I decided to scrub my undergarments, along with the shirt I had wallowed in the previous nights. After rinsing and wringing, I rolled them in my slicker. I shaved as best I could while I looked at the sickle moon. Refreshed, I hightailed it back to my hole. The fireman had already come. I hung the wet laundry over the door to dry.

I lay down and hoped to fool the ever present "Eyes" one more day. Little by little, I mastered the art of being a bum. So far I spent very little money and stayed well positioned to face whatever expense to get to Germany.

—

With a wedge of cheese and a small bag of dried apples I strutted to my rendezvous. To evade the curtained eyes of the neighborhood windows, I paralleled the tracks out of town, then angled toward her house along an overgrown fence.

She stood waiting at her gate and swung it open with a welcoming smile. Her hair again pinned up, but not as tight as the day before. A fallen loose strand over one ear softened her demeanor. Her long-sleeved blouse fluttered in the morning breeze. The long skirt revealed only a broad pair of slip-on shoes.

"*Guten Morgen*," I said.

"*Guten Morgen*! Come in," she answered.

The door, slightly ajar, swung open with a little push of her hand. I had to duck to enter. In the dim interior I felt the ceiling close to my head. A strange calm enveloped me as I observed the simplicity of her existence.

She pulled a chair. "Please sit. What brings you to Penza, Mr. Brunner?"

"I'm on my way west, Mrs. . . . ."

"Kunstler," she said. "Please call me Marlena."

"Marlena, a lovely name. I'm Franz."

To break the slight awkwardness, I placed the crumpled paper wrap containing the cheese and dried apples on the small table.

"How thoughtful. Thank you."

"I don't know where to begin, Marlena. I've been in Russia since you first saw me."

Obviously shocked, she said, "The war is long over!"

"Yes, but they forced me to stay on."

"Don't you have family in Germany?"

"Yes, a wife and three children."

"What did they think about you being held against your will?"

I paused to swallow hard. "My family thinks I perished in the war."

"Did you not write to them?"

"No use writing. At the gulag, where I was for four years, all mail was intercepted. I did write from Moscow, but never a response. Later I found out I had been registered as killed in action."

"I don't know how much more of . . ." She faded to a mumble as she pinched a slice of dried apple. "Please forgive me; just thinking out loud."

She may have been thinking out loud, but her reaction showed a deep and despairing disgust.

I had decided that if the authorities did not greet me at her doorstep I would reveal my soul. "Marlena, finding you happened purely by accident, a pleasant one for sure. I've worked in Moscow for more than seven years; under surveillance, I may add. Were it not for this turn of fate here in Penza, I would have been on a train toward Germany."

"Did you come all the way to Penza to search for me? Penza is not on the way to Germany."

"No, I did not. I didn't even know I passed through this town before. I chose to come to Penza to learn a little about the city. My false identity's address is that of Penza."

"False identity? Why? Are you on the run? Escaped?"

I saw her fear. Her face wide-eyed, and motionless.

"Yes, I escaped, Marlena. Please don't worry. I don't think anyone knows I'm here, nor do they think I'm alive."

"How can you be sure?" She said. "There are informers all over."

"They think I'm dead. Even if they thought otherwise, they'd be looking west of here and not in Penza."

"But, you are not dead. They don't have a body!" She sat erect pinching the same slice of apple.

To dispel her fear of harboring an escapee, I told her the details of my faked demise. She calmed down.

"Clever, in a strange sense. But . . . but you have been hanging around town for three days—three days! You mustn't be seen any longer. Someone will start digging."

"You're right. I feel as if an invisible clamp hangs over me. I know to move on, but when I realized I received the cup of cool water in this town, I had to stay to find you."

"Where are you staying?"

"Well, after the first night uptown, I crawl into a boiler room. Been there since."

"A boiler room? No wonder you had coal dust smeared on your face yesterday. How did you clean up, if I may ask?"

"At Glinka's, they have a bathhouse—uh, stall—in the back."

"Glinka's Laundry? Ah, yes, they do. I get my mending jobs from him." She said with a tone of gratitude. "I patch up workers' uniforms when they start to wear thin or tear."

"Is that what you do to earn your living?"

"In cold weather that is all I earn." She took a nibble of the dried apple slice. "During the growing season I work in the fields, as do many other women."

"I gather you have a hard go of it, especially during the winter months."

"Not all that bad. It takes all I earn, plus the vegetables I put in jars or store in the root cellar. Every year the winters seem to get longer. Maybe I'm getting older and fed up sooner with the endless cold."

I pondered the tireless discipline she must have to go on year after year.

"Let me fix a pot of tea," she said. "We could nibble on what you've brought. I have bread to go with it."

"Wonderful."

The warm tea, the home-baked bread, and a few nibbles of cheese and dried apples, dispelled all apprehension that may have lingered. As the day unfolded, an amazing level of comfort and trust settled over me. I sensed the feeling to be mutual.

The small house conveyed a simple and practical way to live. All implements needed for daily routine hung on pegs or were placed on shelves in an orderly manner. A bench, an old cupboard, and two straight chairs at the small table included all the furniture. A narrow, open stairway led to a covered attic opening. Securely fixed in the middle of the house stood a massive, tiled stove with a flat area on top. A rolled-up quilt and a pillow hung over its edge.

Daylight flowed through two tiny windows—one in each gable end of the house. An oil lantern stood ready in the center of the table. From the window above the water tubs one could observe the activities on the train tracks. The wide window sill showed off rooted pinches of last year's geraniums ready to plant outside to bring pleasure the coming year.

Marlena's graceful movements conveyed a rootedness and stability. She seemed to float. Her loose dress, gathered at the waist, revealed her slenderness.

"Marlena, did you watch the train, the one I was on, from this window?"

"Yes, I've been thinking about that. I stood there and rinsed carrots. A little later, as I left to get the evening water, I noticed your train still stopped. For some reason, I decided to bring my short tankard along." She took a tin mug off its peg and placed it on the table. I froze and stared at the life-giving mug. We sat motionless, silence our communication. The ticking clock kept time with my breathing. Then . . . slowly, hands trembling, I reached to caress the mug.

I struggled to suppress my emotions. "This is hard. I'm sorry, Marlena," I sighed. "Such horror took place to that point. Your act of kindness brought me hope; and life, I may add."

"I knew all of you were prisoners. I had seen cattle cars full of humans before. The sight of such treatment makes me shudder even now." Despondent, she shook her head. I sensed she wanted to speak of her burdens, but kept her composure allowing me to recount that day.

"I thank you again for the most wonderful drink of water in my life. None of us on that train had had water. Most men were delirious at that point, with death in their eyes."

The day was too pleasant to continue on about horror on that train. After a time, I asked, "Marlena, I don't want to get too personal, but where is your husband?"

"Franz," she murmured, "I once had a husband."

"I'm sorry," I whispered. "Maybe I should be going."

"Please, Franz, stay. I'm not ready for you to leave. I haven't had a conversation in German for many years." I watched as she struggled to continue. "It gives me a feeling of, of something new, a reawakening of my younger years. Sadly though, it also reminds me of a past I hoped to forget."

"Maybe we should talk about more pleasant things," I suggested.

"True. I think we both know a few happy tales."

"If we run out of tales, we can always make up some," I piped in. It brought a smile to her face.

"Franz," she put both hands on the table, "do you mind if I do a bit of ironing? I have to deliver this stack of shirts to Glinka's this evening. Of course, don't leave. You sit here and tell me all those happy tales you have buzzing in your head."

Marlena turned to the cook stove and snapped the wooden handle onto the iron. With a bit of spittle on her fingers, she tested its hotness. "Oh my. I need more coal."

"Let me get it," I said.

"Thanks. It's out that door, in the shed, in the far left corner."

I ducked through a narrow door and into a dim shed attached to the stone wall of the house. The only light came through the cracks in the board siding. As I felt my way toward the coal pile, a cat jumped and disappeared into ghostly shadows.

"Good thing I've got a strong heart," I gasped, coming back in the house. "That cat out there almost did me in."

"Oh, I forgot about him," Marlena smiled. "I keep him around to handle mice and other critters that eat the hay and veggies I store."

"You've very little coal left; did you know?"

"I know. Don't remind me. I'm trying to make it stretch. Don't know how I'm going to buy more right now."

"What do you do with the hay?" I asked.

"It's left over. I fed rabbits and a passel of guinea pigs last year. They hopped from the cage to the market or the pot. I also had chickens," she continued. "Winters are long and hard, especially on livestock. If you know what I mean."

Her ironing board consisted of a hand-hewn slab of wood, neatly padded and covered on one side. She propped the board on the table in front of me and started to press the shirts.

Speaking our native dialect comforted my soul. Her childlike glow revealed a renewed spirit. The ingrained suspicions and tension drained from us as the pleasant afternoon drifted on.

She spoke of the communal effort and work in the fields. How the harvest always ends up shipped to the cities. She spoke of her own ways and how she complemented her existence with crops from the small plot she cultivated. In the summer she ate aboveground vegetables. The carrots, beets, turnips, cabbage, and potatoes had to last the winter. She told of picking all the green tomatoes before the first frost, then laying them out in a closed cupboard.

"It does me good to the bone to find a red tomato that I had stowed still green weeks earlier. Especially when the snow flies outside."

24

Marlena survived because of her industriousness and ability to spread her reserves over the entire year. As I listened, I wanted to cheer her on. She did not speak to gain sympathy or pity. She did not move about with slouched shoulders, knitted eyebrows, or a sullen expression, but with strength, resolve, and a joy for having been given enough. She had fortitude and gumption to keep on plugging. In contrast, I questioned whether I matched her caliber or had I become a dejected and grumpy old man?

"Marlena, what will become of you when you no longer can take care of yourself?"

A wry smile crossed her face. "I guess I'd have to learn to eat less. If it ever came to that, the best for me would be for a friend to take me in. I don't want to think of the other option."

"What's that?"

"The State would scoop me up and haul me to one of these 'gated' homes, with steel gates and tall, gray walls—to which comes no mail nor friend. I'm not sure if I would even get such a benefit. My husband was a Jew."

"Oh, I see . . ." I mumbled.

"My Moshe," she said with a sigh, "the only man I ever loved and wanted. We'd planned for a short stay here in Penza to help his aging grandmother. We left our son Benjamin with Moshe's parents in Budapest. The little tyke barely started to walk. Such a sweet thing. . . ."

"I understand. I'm sorry," I said.

Marlena, compelled to reveal her soul, continued. "Not long after we arrived here, a commotion roused us from sleep. Three men smashed in the door, with drawn swords they stormed in and searched the house. One of the three ransacked the place. He took all he wanted, stuffing his pockets. He found the pouch that contained the cash for our return fare. The other two manhandled Moshe out the door. They dragged him to the depot where a truck waited. I ran after the men, screaming and scratching, trying to free my Moshe. They shoved him into the back of the truck where other men had already been tied. Frantically, I tried to rescue him but those ruffians overpowered me with ruthless force. One sneering brute slung me to the ground and kicked me in the ribs. Hysterically, I got up and ran after the truck. When I caught up with it and grabbed the back gate to climb on board, one of the guards on the truck smashed my face with his rifle butt and knocked me unconscious."

After a long moment she looked up and pointed her finger to the scar on her cheek.

"Marlena . . . don't . . . that is a beautiful mark." I rose from my chair and clutched her shoulders. "Marlena, it is a mark of great valor and proof of an unending love. You know, Marlena, if I had not remembered that scar, I would have never recognized or even found you."

"Thanks. I'm happy you came to see me."

We turned the two small chairs and looked out the open door, reflecting on the day—a precious silence. Birds dashed to their roost before darkness dropped its veil. A tender strand of friendship spun around us as late afternoon clouds thickened.

Marlena continued to spill her gripping story. "In less than a month after the abduction of Moshe, his grandmother died. She stopped eating, grieving herself to death. Several neighbors came and cried with me. Comrade Glinka helped dig her grave. She is buried right out there in the corner of the garden, wrapped in a linen sheet.

"I admit, I do become despondent at times. I've learned to be thankful, though. Mother Ruth grieving herself to death is all the sacrifice the Soviets will ever get out of this house," she said, looking at her hands and worn fingernails. I sat quietly, waiting for her to continue. "So, I keep on. I made the work itself my joy. I work the fields for twelve hours a day, tend to my garden and other chores. That does not give me much time to feel sorry for myself. I plod along."

"I gather your dream is to go back?"

"Oh yes, I dream. Every time I manage to save a few roubles, the cost of bread flour or coal raised more than I saved. I've no hope of ever seeing my Benjamin again."

"How much would the fare cost?" I asked.

"Oh my. A friend traveled to Kiev last year. She paid more than I earn in three months for that trip."

"Marlena, I don't know what to say. I'm sorry. Do you want to bring your son here?"

"Please, no! If I'd ever make it back, it'll be to stay. I write letters to ask about my son. No answer. I write to my parents in Germany, but never a response. I've received one letter in the last two years. This is unlike my mother; she loves to write. I'm not sure my mail gets out. I don't understand what the State has against me to be tracking my letters."

"I'm reluctant to say, 'never give up,'" I said. "The last time I said such words two of my buddies on that awful train hung themselves that very night. I'm going to say it again though, don't you ever give up. I'm convinced it is not meant for you to die in this place."

"Franz, I have tried to get a better job, I'm a trained bookkeeper. Somehow, always, the position disappears. My number never comes up. I'm numbered all right. Numbered to fade and shrivel away, one year at a time, then fall into a damp dark hole in the ground. By golly, they are not going to destroy me mentally before they dig that hole."

She stood at the stove, her back toward me to switch irons.

"Marlena, maybe, maybe I could help. Perhaps we could make the break together. There are plenty of ifs. It would take some planning, and, of course, money."

"How could I make more money? I've sold most of Mother Ruth's belongings. Always selling something in the spring to buy a couple of chickens and a rooster. Then I sell the eggs to buy a pair of rabbits. When the fields turn green, I gather the tender grasses to feed them. When chicks hatch and more rabbits come along, I sell them. Oh, I fatten one or two during the year to have a feast. I even salt-down two or three and hang them in the shed to have a little meat when the snow swirls. Am I complaining? Not really. The challenge makes life worth the living."

Marlena quit talking and stared at the wall. Suddenly, she perked up and said, "Make the break together? You mean leave this place and head for Hungary?"

"Yes, it's possible," I said. I walked around the room and looked out the window. "It is possible."

A fierce wind kicked up. Marlena announced, "I've got to run these shirts to comrade Glinka before it starts pouring."

"I best be going also," I said.

"Where to? Are you going to crawl back into that boiler room?"

"Well, I guess so. I'll be careful not to be seen."

"Why don't you stay here, at least until I get back?"

She removed the shawl from the peg in back of the door, wrapped the ironed shirts with it, then left the house. In the quiet room I pondered my offer. A dual escape was possible. There in the quiet, I set my will toward that end.

She returned from Glinka's. "Look, more shirts to work on. Isn't it great. How about this? Look!" She showed me a small handful of coins for her labor. "I'll add them to the jar. You know, Franz, those coins may be the beginning of my ticket home."

"Don't say maybe; say they are!" We both smiled. Her cheeks flushed from rushing back. The scarf kept her shoulders dry. Droplets of rain clung to her hair and face—she glowed. Her exuberance excited my spirit.

"Franz, I've been thinking while I delivered the shirts. I can't let you sleep in a sooty old hole. If you don't mind, you could cover the pile of hay in the shed with a blanket and sleep there."

"That wouldn't be right. What would your neighbors think?"

"I don't think they saw you come this morning. You came along the fence row. I saw you. All my neighbors within looking distance should have been at work."

"Are you sure it'll be all right?" When I looked at her face, I knew she meant it. "I'll stay until we figure out a way to pull off this dash to Hungary."

"Good, the cat can be your guard." She giggled.

Marlena laid the handful of coins on the table and pointed at the wall clock.

"Time to haul water. No respecting woman wants to be seen on the street when the men get off work." She covered her shoulders with the damp scarf.

"Your clock is a beauty." I said.

"Yes, it is." She grabbed the galvanized pail from the cupboard. "So far I didn't have to sell it. It would fetch a good sum. I dare not be without a clock. Nobody yet has trained the roosters to crow in the afternoon on a regular basis."

A gentle rain fell. I watched her from the window until she walked out of sight. I dropped onto the chair and cupped the tin tankard on the table. *She gave life to me. I must do the same to her.*

—

When Marlena returned from the water brigade, she announced, "We're having leftover vegetable stew. I'll get it heated. Would you shut the door and batten down the windows, please."

Using a long piece of straw, she fished a small flame from the stove and lit the oil lamp on the table and turned it low.

"I watched you, Marlena. Why don't you cover your hair when it's raining as hard as it is?"

"My hair is not a worry. I rather keep my coat from getting soaked. My hair—I normally rub it dry with a towel." With a coy smile she added, "I can't do that with company here. Don't want you to see me looking like a wild animal."

The ticking of the clock directed the rest of the evening. A serene quiet broadened our kindred bond and trust. My role playing finally came to an end. No longer had I to weigh every word. A deep weariness eased. I became Franz again.

The covered hay in the shed made a wonderful bed. I awakened as the area roosters contested for kingship, a pleasant cacophony, one of a basic life. Refreshed and eager to get on with the day, I waited for the first pulse of daylight to creep through the cracks. The cat lurked somewhere in the shadows, mindful of me, I'm sure.

Before a sound from inside the house, the smell of baking bread elevated the new day.

"Good morning," I grinned. "What do I smell? You sure have a pleasant way of waking the guests."

"We ate the last of the loaf last night. This is your lucky day. Did you sleep well?"

"With a personal guard cat, I could do nothing but."

Marlena's hair, loosely pinned into a bun, showed the damp of her morning's cleansing. The few untamed strands looked fresh and innocent. Her house dress covered her body with little effort.

"I've saved you a splash of warm water in the kettle if you want to shave."

"Good. Thanks."

A washcloth hung over the edge of a cutoff barrel perched on a three-legged stool.

"Sorry, there's not much privacy. I've been by myself so long I never think of privacy."

The simple warmth of the one-room house enveloped me. It radiated love and energy from every hanging skillet, every vase of flowers, every worn boot and sandal. I felt life. Life, graced by the woman who moved about with a purpose and ease. She smiled not only with her eyes, but also with her calloused hands, her proud shoulders, her home. Her every task reflected pride, which drew me to be a part.

"Are you ready to taste the bread? It is still warm."

—

The days following I made myself as useful as I could. When Marlena worked the fields, I prepared vegetables with minimum noise and made sure no smoke belched from the chimney. Outside work I did discreetly at night, away from the neighbor's view.

"I had a thought," I said to Marlena. "Are there any rivers or streams nearby?"

"Yes, the nearest is about one kilometer west of here. Why?"

"Well, I might try to catch a fish or two. The moon will be bright tonight." Smiling, I added, "I've become the resident bat. I only leave the house after dark."

"I'm sorry it has to be this way," said Marlena. "The ploy is working. I believe no one is the wiser."

"One other thing. While I prowl around I'll look for firewood. Can I use the bucksaw? The one in the shed."

"You can use anything you need to, but I don't have a fishing pole." Her eyes showed excitement at the prospect of fish.

"All I need is worms. I've some fishing line and hooks in the hollow handle of my umbrella. Figured if I had to survive in the open country, to catch a fish would be a good thing. I'm itching to give it try."

Soon after dusk I snuck from the house and clung to shadows of a winking moon. I scampered across the railroad tracks, then hugged the bank until I came to a culvert through which a good-sized stream flowed. The river's banks revealed a variety of sticks, dead trees, odd boards from fences and crates, all washed up by the recent snow-melt and heavy rains. Exhilarated by the sense of freedom, I baited the hook and flicked the line in the water. While I tied the other end to a sapling, I felt a tug.

Before the roosters had their say, I arrived home from my moonlight escapade with a sack of sawed wood and a half dozen pan fish.

Marlena raised up from her pallet on top of the warming stove and gave me an approving smile.

"No more buying coal," I said. "If I get busy, I can bring in a sack or two a night before someone else gets wise of the fresh cache lying along that riverbank. You go rest. I'll clean the fish outdoors."

I quietly buried the heads and entrails in the garden. When I returned she was propped on her elbows, still on her pallet, on top of the warming stove. "Franz, do you really think . . . me, possibly going home? I can't quit thinking about it."

"Marlena, I want to help." Her pale green eyes danced as those of an expecting child. "We must be realistic, if you have anything to sell, you need to start selling. I know this is painful to talk about. As not to raise suspicion, you need to sell a token or two every time you deal at the market. We can take very little with us. . . . Marlena, please don't sell the tin mug."

"No! I wouldn't do that," she assured me. "That mug brought you here." She put her head back on the pillow and hummed a childhood melody.

The days with Marlena rolled into weeks. The nip of a spring frost vanished. The hope of heading west became real in our hearts, and in the jar.

I said to Marlena, "Before some 'Nose' gets wise to your accumulating extra funds, can you find out the cost of a ticket?"

"And," she said, "we need a better hiding place for the jar. Don't you agree?"

"You're right. A scoundrel, thinking he can find extra money here, may decide to rob a single woman."

After drying the dishes in silence, she said in subdued excitement, "The hot water tank in the stove leaks. I haven't used it in years. Can we hide the jar there?"

"Great! Good place," I said.

"Franz, I hardly sleep at night. I feel like a little girl waiting for Christmas."

With the windows already shuttered, I got up and barred the door. Curious, she watched. "What are you doing?"

I smiled, took my coat off the back of the chair and spread it on the table. She followed my every move, eyes wide open.

"Franz? What in the . . .?"

"I'm going to show you money I saved for this journey. All of it by playing the violin the last several years."

"The violin?" She asked. "Didn't you say you worked in a machine shop?"

"Yes, but an old man gave me his deceased wife's violin. I played it for years out in the open. People came by and tossed a few coins in its case. I could never have saved enough to skip to the West on what they paid me at work. Remember, they wanted my skill while making sure I didn't go anywhere."

As I pulled the roubles from my coat, Marlena's eyes traveled from window to door to window.

"You need to hide this! You can't walk around, especially at night, with all that money on you." Sitting on her hands, she leaned forward. "I have never seen so much in all my years in Russia."

"You're right. Most are small bills. We'll hide it in the jar with yours. It'll stay good and toasty."

Our escape plans took shape and direction that night. Everything laid on the table—our earthly treasures and determination. The following days consisted of total focus. Words became fewer. The jovial chatter that sealed our friendship became secondary. We were on a mission.

"Does the ticket master at the depot know you?"

"I don't think so. I never noticed him ogling me or any of the other women."

"Ask him about the cost to Kiev. If you ask him for a price all the way to Budapest, it'll surely raise his suspicion," I said. "The old guy may not ogle the women, but he noticed me hanging around. He found it important enough to come from behind his desk and asked whether I was lost. I told him I waited for my sister to come in on a train."

"That is how it starts. The next time he would have reported you."

—

More weeks elapsed. Marlena sold most keepsakes, household items, and heirlooms. The jars slowly filled. Paper money in one, coins in the other.

"Marlena, we're getting close. You've got to start thinking about selling the clock. It is by far the most valuable item. I'm sorry. It will determine how soon we can leave."

"Grandma Ruth would understand."

"Don't sell it for the first offer. Tell them you have several interested buyers."

"Makes sense. I think I can play the game."

—

When the spring sun had warmed the soil enough for planting, hundreds of women again worked twelve-hour days in the fields. So did Marlena. From behind the window I watched streams of women, resembling a caravan of ants, as they tramped single file toward one of the many long buildings at the edge of distant fields. I stayed cooped up. Only the afternoon sun struck my face as it radiated through the open door. In the evening I helped Marlena sew and mend, always adding to the jar with great pleasure.

Marlena sold her clock. My cracked watch kept our routine going. The wall and cupboards looked stark. Her possessions shrank to a ghastly few—one skillet, one pot, two plates, enough utensils to stir, cut, and eat with. At night, I knew my job: gather wood and fish.

—

One rainy spring evening the gate squeaked, followed by a sharp knock on the door. Startled, I darted to the shed.

"Who is it?" Marlena called out.

A man answered. She opened the door. From the garbled conversation I deduced him to be her neighbor.

"I'd like to lease the idle strip of land this growing season. I want to sell more goods at the market," the man said.

"I had a similar idea." Marlena quipped. "What are you willing to pay?"

"Twenty roubles," he replied eagerly.

A deliberate long pause followed. With a hint of disgust, Marlena answered, "Twenty roubles, you can double that by raising potatoes only. If you grow snow peas, beans, and herbs, it could really be worth your while. Like I've said, been thinking about doing it myself."

Again, silence. It was the man's turn to counter with a suitable deal.

"Well, I'll double it to forty. I'll give you half now and the other half after the harvest."

"That won't do." She said very businesslike. "What if you decide to quit growing things, or wind up spending my part?"

"Comrade Kunstler," the man said somewhat exasperated, "you're hard on a man. I tell you what, I'll give you all but five roubles now, the balance I'll drop off at the end of the week."

"I'll accept that, I know you're good for the five."

I heard the chair slide, the door close. Soon Marlena stuck her head into the shed and beamed.

"I heard it all. You were marvelous. Who coached you to be so ruthless?"

"You're the one who got me started." She smiled.

We had enough to head west, and reason to celebrated with a mug of sweet tea.

25

Marlena spoke excellent Russian, German, and Hungarian. We decided to travel as brother and sister. I would use my Russian name, Lev Sakharov, and she her married name, Kunstler.

She bought basic-fare tickets. What food we brought I stuffed into my coat pockets. Two full days and nights later, sleeping sitting up, we arrived in Kiev.

For the next leg of our journey, Kiev and west to Hungary, Marlena did all the talking. I used my speech defect only when the need arose.

Many months ago, at one of the Moscow libraries, I tried to familiarize myself with the passenger train network of the Ukraine and Carpathian Mountain regions, but without success. The USSR does not provide such information for public study.

At the train depot in Kiev the ticket master sternly stated, "No trains are leaving Kiev directly to the border of Hungary."

Not wanting to push our luck, we settled to go on to L'viv, a distance considered local, which would place us within three hundred kilometers of the Hungarian border.

We bought the *Red Star* newspaper while waiting for our connection. I read, pretending to enjoy the afternoon as I leaned back to soak up some sun. Marlena knitted on a scarf—looking matronly.

The years of humdrum taught me patience, although adrenaline kept me on edge. As I scanned the paper, I was alerted by the word Hungary in a heading. The paper hinted that the Hungarian leadership failed to properly cooperate with the regime. It stated negotiations were under way. I had learned to read between the lines of Soviet news. We both knew the Soviets do not negotiate. Talk maybe, while stalling for a time to take decisive action.

"I'm a bit unsettled about that article," I mumbled. "Getting into Hungary may not be as easy as we figured."

"Hmm. We're here in Kiev. We've bought our tickets to L'viv. That's pretty close," she said.

"You're right, our direction is fixed. I sure hope I'm not pushing us into something we regret later."

"Franz, I'm with you." Marlena said with calm conviction. "Whatever you decide, for better or worse, I will never hold any unforeseen mishap against you. You know that."

Two hours late, our train rolled in. The passenger cars, as always composed the front of the train. I immediately noticed the rear portion of the train carried tanks and other military hardware. My skin crawled on my arms and neck.

"You see that," I mumbled to Marlena.

"I see. I guess we weren't far off about the article. You think . . ."

"I bet the tanks are heading the same direction we are," I said.

"Let's hope not."

—

On the train, we slumped and dozed, careful not to fall off the bench. The ride's only highlight was a sleepwalking man in uniform who punched our ticket. Upon arriving in L'viv, drained and weary, we checked the availability of a train to Chop, a small town in Russia, but right on the Hungarian border.

"To Chop?" The ticket master snapped. He straightened himself, his eyes alert, "No one goes to Chop. The border is closed. The closest civilians are allowed to travel is to Mukachevo." Perplexed, he raised one eyebrow and looked over his glasses at Marlena. His eyes darted at me sitting on a bench. Leaning forward he asked with a low and inquisitive tone, "Why do you want to go to Chop?"

"My brother and I want to help our ailing father set out the garden for the coming season."

Throwing his shoulders back, "No trains go to Chop! Set out the garden, eh?" He snapped with a slight sneer.

"I guess we'll go home and write him that we'll come another day."

"Lady, traveling to Chop is closed for good. No . . . more . . . trains . . . to . . . Chop!"

"Uh . . . yes, we understand, but he needs our help," she said as she walked away dejected, head hanging, all to the benefit of the grouch behind the counter. As we left the station, his eyes followed us.

"Are you sure you're a bookkeeper?" I asked. "All this drama. I think you convinced the grump."

She smiled. "Sometimes I don't mind telling a fib. The way those Commies sat on us all these years, I feel good about getting away with a lie."

"My feelings exactly. I say we wait until this smart-ass goes home, then you and I buy our ticket separately from the one taking over."

"Why buy separately?"

"Well, if the old goat recorded our request as suspicious, the next guy would be looking for a pair wanting to go to the border. Although Mukachevo is as close they'll allow us to get."

"I understand what you're saying. Traveling as a pair is out. Does that mean we've got to travel apart from each other?" She asked, a little alarmed. "Franz, I need you with me. It'll be a long trip to Mukachevo, maybe ten hours. The train has to go through mountainous terrain."

"After the ticket is punched we can meet and sit next to each other," I said. Marlena released a long breath and smiled.

While we waited for the grump to go home and a new ticket agent to take over, we calmed our buzzing nerves with mugs of hot tea. I used the stiletto stowed in the cane to divide the last hunk of the smoked sausage. We waited some more. I again read the newspaper while Marlena knitted.

At last, a slumped-shouldered fellow, squat and portly, so big he hung over the edge of his stool, took over the small ticket office. His bulbous and purple-veined nose proudly supported a pair of pinch-on spectacles.

"Mukachevo, eh. The next train will only have two passenger cars. they may be full. I can't sell you a ticket now," he said to Marlena.

"I still would like a slip that says I requested one. I'll come back, and if it's full, I'll wait for the next train," she said with a warm smile.

"I guess I can do that," he said. "You don't want to be in Mukachevo, lady." He said somewhat puzzled. "Lot of soldiers! Well, none of my business."

I waited a spell to take my turn with the new ticket master. Fumbling and acting unsure I approached the counter with a hand-full of money. "To Mukachevo, please," I stammered, laying on my speech defect.

"How's that?"

"Ticket. Muka . . . chevo," I said a bit louder.

"I'm not hard of hearing. Spit it out! Mu-ka-che-vo." Totally irritated, he yelled, "I can't sell you a ticket. The train may be full."

"Ticket to Muka . . . chevo, please," I said calmly.

"Didn't you hear what I said? No ticket! Now get!" With a nasty motion he waved me aside. Then mumbling he added, "Why do I get all the nitwits?"

Several moments later I still stood at the booth. "Are you from another planet?" Incredulous that I didn't seem to get it, he barked, "Let me see your identification."

Playing the nitwit act, I groped around my pockets and took a little extra time before I produced my papers.

He squinted his beady eyes. "Lev Sakharov, eh—Penza. These papers are outdated. Where is your Party identification? Why do you need a ticket to Mukachevo anyway?"

"Ticket to Muka . . . chevo, please"

"Shit!" He raised up to get nearer my face. "Do you have any Party identification?" I shook my head to say no. He pulled himself off the chair.

"Lady . . . hey lady!" He jerked his chin in the direction to where Marlena sat. "Come here, would you." Looking surprised and worried, she stood before the man.

"This simpleton here, he either can't hear or he's not all there. He wants to go to Mukachevo, only his mommy knows why, and I can't sell him a ticket until I know if the train is full. See if you can help. I can't seem to get through to him."

Marlena and I stepped aside to be out of full hearing. She said in a low tone, "Let me see if I can get him to come around." To impress the crank in the booth, she acted as if communicating the facts with her hands and arms. She motioned for me to sit on a bench and wait.

"Mister ticket master, the man seems docile enough," I heard her say to the grump. "Could you possibly give him a conditional ticket like mine? I'll watch out for him. I'll lead him back here to see if the coming train is full. If it is, we'll both try for the next one."

His frustration now allayed by Marlena's charm, he did as she suggested.

—

We boarded the train to Mukachevo long after dark. The train moaned and strained as it negotiated the endless climbs of mountains. Finally, the next morning we crested the last ridge. The brilliance of the early morning christened the surrounding peaks while villages and dales below stayed blanketed in mists of downy cotton. On the hillsides the greening of the earth squinted through a sparkling dew. Such beauty and hope of the expected regeneration gave my heart a lift. The bends in the track afforded a glance of the train's trailing end. What I saw instantly killed the beauty of the day. We hauled military hardware.

"It's beginning to add up," Marlena said. "The old grump warned me about lots of soldiers in Mukachevo."

"They must be coming along with the equipment," I said. "That's why he couldn't sell us a ticket. He didn't know how many were on this train."

At Mukachevo, Marlena and I stepped off a few minutes apart. She carried her travel bag and kept her distance from me. Military men streamed from the second passenger car, filling the platform. The soldiers stretched and yawned. Some broke from the pack to buy drinks and other habits from the ever-present peddlers. I drifted toward a jesting and jolly group to do a little eavesdropping.

"They say it's not far from here," one said.

"I don't know why we're having maneuvers in this forsaken place. Don't look like any girls around here."

"The ones that are here are all milking cows. . . . Ha, ha," they all chimed in.

After a reasonable stretch of time and a shrill whistle, the soldiers made their way back to the train.

We had managed to get as close to the border as the authorities allowed. As always, Marlena watched for persons who had nothing to do but look around. With no further specific plans, we each made our way into the narrow streets of town, always within sight of each other.

I ducked into a tavern and found a table. Marlena observed, but kept walking. She joined me minutes later.

"From what I can tell, no one is interested in us," she said.

The stale air, mixed with yesterday's urine from the outhouse, cooking grease and tobacco smoke, curbed my appetite. A rag, bunched on the table under our noses, showed hints of beets and other food particles. Crumbs and dribbles from previous patrons covered the rest of the tabletop from corner to corner. By the time the attendant came to give it all a wipe, my arm had stuck to the wood. The attendant's apron greeted us first, sporting results of a month's worth of hand wiping. His britches, held up by a pair of stretched suspenders and hitched way above his behind, revealed a well rounded anatomy. The rear view proudly balanced the front with its prodigious paunch.

The midmorning break proved to be a good time to relax, take in the ambience of a local establishment, eat, and have an early warm beer.

"The soldiers think they're going on maneuvers." I made sure my voice didn't reach anyone else in the room. "One fellow quoted his sergeant as saying that usually there is a backup of trains trying to unload. The backlog may take a day or so to clear."

"You think that will affect us?" Marlena asked.

"Well, if we hitch a ride on one of those trains under the cloak of darkness and jump off right near the border . . ."

"Hitch a ride! With all those soldiers around?"

"It may be a good option. I know from experience, when you get a group of fellows together, they distract each other and aren't as vigilant. A single posted guard is much more worrisome to the enemy than a jovial bunch."

"To hitch a ride scares me. A bit daring, don't you think?"

"Well, it would be bold. However, to hoof it from here to the border would also be mighty bold. We'd be like geese out of season." Thinking out loud, I continued. "Brazen may be good. If I were the top shirt in a military outfit, and knew the entire train carried men and equipment, the last thing I'd be looking for is a pair of shameless hobos hitching a ride."

"Brazen may be good then," Marlena concurred. "I wonder how we could climb onto one of those loaded flatcars?"

"Well, good point," I said. "I'm sure there is a way. We'll figure that out later."

Sitting opposite each other—nose to nose, we discussed what to do next. Adrenalin oozed out of our ears.

"First, each of us needs to stake out this town, the comings and goings. Then switch assignments and compare notes."

"Why can't we share what we saw?" she asked.

"Two minds, two sets of eyes, process things differently. A woman always has different perceptions," I said. Marlena pondered and seamed to agree.

Most patrons of the eatery left to go back to work. The fellow tending to the establishment was nowhere to be seen. Empty bowls cluttered the tables all around. I banged my dry mug on the table. This snapped the pear-shaped chef out of his loafing mode.

"Another beer?"

I nodded. Other than warm milk, it was the only liquid fit to drink.

"Great place, isn't it?" I commented to Marlena with a sarcastic smirk.

"Great place to get lost in." Thinking ahead, she said, "What are we going to do about spending the night? I really look forward to stretching out."

"Me too," I groaned. "It'd be beneficial if we each found our own place, not because I don't want to share a room and save money. You could talk to local women, find out what all this military stuff means to them. I could listen to other gossip. Might glean some valuable information."

Marlena looked at the tabletop and studied the cracks between the boards. A tinge of flush entered her cheeks.

"Marlena, look at me! I would never cast you aside. I realize we could save a little money sharing a room, but we need to gather as many facts as possible."

"I know," she whispered.

Before long more folks, dressed in work clothes, entered the tavern and settled in to fill the benches again. A couple asked to sit at our table. "Welcome," Marlena said. We switched to speaking Russian. The couple smiled and exchanged pleasantries then quietly continued their conversation in Hungarian. Marlena listened. I ordered another bowl of stew. Marlena nibbled on bread.

"Warm day outside." Marlena said to the couple in Russian. They nodded in agreement. "Busy town, especially the depot," she continued.

Again they nodded and smiled. Speaking slow and deliberate, Marlena asked if they spoke Russian.

"Very little," the woman stammered. "Sell potatoes here, go back to Hungary."

"Sell potatoes in April?" Marlena kept the conversation going.

"No, later. No, sell this year. Border closed."

"You can't come back?" Marlena asked.

"No, no more come, no sell."

Marlena expressed her disappointment over their predicament.

Back on the street we sorted through their conversation. The Hungarians had visited towns on a fact-finding mission and meet with various vendors. They had traded in potatoes for many years and had sold them as far into Russia as Mukachevo. The couple discussed ways to beat the system and not lose their livelihood.

Marlena and I searched out the town's side streets. She clung to my arm, as we lugged our worldly possessions. At the far end of a market we stumbled on a bathhouse. To wash with frigid water proved surprisingly rejuvenating.

We stayed on the move and continually absorbed and appraised the situation. At the end of a road we spotted an unused stable. A ladder led to the loft. From a hole in the loft, an attendant could fork feed into mangers below. I climbed the ladder, cleared cobwebs, and snooped around. Marlena kept watch.

"It'll make a good place to curl up for a couple of hours if we had to," I concluded.

The first night, however, I rented a cot in a room with two other men above a tavern. Marlena found a family who rented her a bunk in their washhouse. One of the two men in my room mumbled until he passed out. The other talked nonstop about his soldier son and his various deployments until I fell asleep. Marlena told me of listening to stories the entire evening and went to bed when the family did.

The buildup for "maneuvers" appeared to be the scuttlebutt everywhere. The State barred all rail commerce coming from and going to Hungary. The talk was that the main road through Chop at the border had been severed with crossing bars. A two-meter-tall electrified fence along the border kept folks at a distance. The fence divided yards and gardens and even divided fields and wagon roads. The locals on the border no longer could trade or visit friends on the other side, but were forced to use the border checkpoint.

Trains rolled into town and left for Chop about every three hours. The military supplied its own guards while trains were stopped. Rail employees performed their normal duties. Two men worked the caboose. One stuck his head out of the window; the other blew the whistle and waived his arm to signal a departure. Not all trains carried tanks. Always, though, the equipment flatcars were hitched behind the military personnel car. All trains returning from the border were empty.

"I don't think there is much guarding of any kind going on. After all, who would steal a tank?" Marlena commented.

"I know, but we still have to be very careful. We could be shot on the spot. The way it looks, the best option still is to ride one of those flatcars to the border."

"I know. I'm nervous," she confessed.

"Tonight, we need to study the lighting and shadows of the depot. Our stunt will have to be pulled off at dark."

Wide-eyed, Marlena said, "I hope it'll be as dark as pitch."

Thinking out loud, I continued, "After the soldiers had their break and get back on board, we crawl onto a flatcar."

"Sounds too simple," said Marlena. "I'm eager to get on with it though. I've had the trembles since this morning and haven't been able to shake'm all day."

"I know. I too feel as if an electric motor is running in my chest. It's not going to get better until we're over and beyond the border fence," I said. "Maybe a bit of rest in that hay loft would help."

"I agree. The worst that could happen, is we'd get run off."

Five hours later, we slipped from the musty hay barn unnoticed, our coats sprinkled with bits of hay. A heavy mist continued to fall. Our footsteps echoed off glistening stone walls. Droopy eyed windows stared at us. We stayed on the move, walking, tucked under the umbrella. Our minds sharpened with each step.

"I'm worried about those depot lights. Did you notice them last night? There are too many of them."

We walked behind the depot to study the platform's wiring. Black, pitch-soaked tape dangled loosely from the twisted connections. Ceramic insulators held the wire from the wall as it looped from the back of the depot, around the corner, to the platform lights.

"We need darkness to pull this off," I said. Again, I took a deep breath to shake the tension. "I could kill those worrisome lights. The commotion it'll cause would benefit. Play this out with me, would you? . . . Listen."

"I'm listening."

"Yes. . . . as our train starts to pull out, I'll kill the lights. Timing, . . . yes, this little act of sabotage takes exact timing, let me think. You stand in the shadows and watch the fellow in the caboose give the engineer the signal. When he does, you wave to me. No! Don't wave. Tie your scarf under your chin. I'll hold off yanking the wires from the wall until the locomotive gives a couple of heaves. The sudden dark will baffle everyone. You run and throw our gear onto the little platform on the rear of the passenger car. You hop on and I'll join you as the train starts to roll."

With the plan complete, we nervously shared the last handful of prunes and slice of black bread. Our hearts raced. Imagination weighed heavy against common sense. The rest of the dreary evening crept along. Every eye that looked at us felt like a sharp probe. Anxiety and fear distorted reality.

The first train after dark rolled in. We again mingled with the folks that got off and carried our bags with purpose to wherever the main flow of activity moved.

Finally the moment was right. Folks had disappeared into town. The soldiers were back on the train. . . . My stomach had wrapped itself around my spine. . . . Marlena tied her scarf. . . . Puff . . . huff . . . groan, the black monster eased into motion. I reached up with a borrowed hay rake, and hooked onto the electrical wire. One good yank plunged the station into darkness. I spotted Marlena climbing the little platform. I tried to run, but couldn't do what my brain demanded. I teetered and stumbled forward. Desperately I focused on not falling. The train groaned ever forward, gaining speed. An outstretched arm, one final reach, and Marlena's hand clasped mine. She pulled me toward the iron step and onto the little platform.

Hunkered down, we held to each other and waited for our nerves to settle. My head pounded. The loaded train strained on into the night. Black clothes, black train, black night all blended toward a dark unknown. Occasional boisterous outbursts by the soldiers inside the car kept our minds from being sucked into total fright.

I pointed at the tank on the flatcar hitched a few meters away. "Let's move on into the shadows."

Marlena, trembling, stepped onto the massive hitch that coupled the flatcar, and then hopped on to hold onto the tank. I followed. However, the rocking train, now moving faster than walking speed, slung me to one side. I tottered then slipped. Desperately I tried to grab hold of the tank, but only caught the cabling that secured the massive machine. I stumbled off the flatcar's side, but held to a cable with one hand. Like a stuffed puppet I scraped along the ground. My legs flopped, smacking the ground, in rhythm of the train. I heard Marlena's deep groans of panic as she tried to pull me back. Without warning my grasp let go. Horror gripped her face as she frantically groped the air after me. I slammed to the ground tumbling.

Out of sheer terror I scrambled to my feet. I couldn't tell whether I spat out gravel or teeth. In my daze I saw one flatcar roll by, then another, and another, then a boxcar. Driven to get back on, I staggered closer to the moving train. Chain ratchets zipped by my face. Then, my last chance, the caboose. With death-battling strength I managed to run along the train. The caboose, the last chance, started to roll by. One step from its end I grabbed hold of the narrow metal ladder welded to its side and dragged myself up. I latched my arms around the wrought-iron ladder tighter than onto anything ever before. In my mind, I held on to Marlena.

Did I see her wave?

26

Near the border the train slowed. The single track now was paralleled by a second one. Up ahead, on the second track, a huge locomotive's headlight steadily drew nearer. I knew Marlena hid under the massive tank. In full view, I stuck to the red caboose like a huge chunk of licorice. We rolled on. The big engine's light got brighter, as it waited for our train to pass. I turned my pale face away from the revealing beam. . . . The dark of night returned.

For several kilometers further our train coasted, ever slower. When it crawled along at walking speed, I lowered myself to the last rung of the ladder then dropped into a weedy ditch. Marlena must have watched. Within a minute she slid next to me.

"Are you hurt?" She grabbed my arm in panic. "You, . . . Franz, I'm frightened sick. You took a terrible fall."

"I'll be . . . I'm fine," I assured her, "the swaying, . . . I lost my balance. . . . I'm sorry."

Marlena held my hands. "It's all right. I'm grateful you're still with me. Back there, I thought I'd lost you. Franz, do you know how close you came to falling under the wheels?"

"I know. Scary, isn't it? . . . Other than a knot on my shin, . . . gravel inside my shirt, . . . I'm all right. Sure glad to be seeing you right now."

We lay stretched out on the side of the rail bank, panting, struggling to shake the stress. Marlena's head rested near my shoulder as we gradually absorbed the amazing quiet of the night. A brisk wind blew out the drizzle and scurried dark clouds by the moon. We rested, each to our own thoughts.

"We did it," I said at last. "I could rest here all night, but we've got to push on."

"I know you're right. If I remember correctly, coming through here before, the town of Chop was on this side of the track. So, I would say, the main road to the town will be there too. If we walk at a right angle from here we ought to come to it."

"I love your reasoning, Marlena. Let's find out."

Mottled moonlight led us across fields of recently plowed furrows ready for potatoes. A field of newly planted cabbage seedlings offered a handful of the tender leaves that satisfied like manna from heaven. In the distance behind us we heard the short steam bursts of a locomotive.

"Look! What about that? A road. Wide enough for two horses to pass," I proclaimed.

"Doesn't it feel good?" Marlena said.

"Yes. I think we're headed in the right direction."

We settled into a steady stride toward Chop. A town indeed small, and dark. Not a lit lantern anywhere. The crossing bar we heard about spanned the width of the town's main road. And at this time of night, its light overpowered the moon's.

Marlena and I scurried from shadow to shadow. "We have come to the end of Russia," I mumbled.

"Not quite, we've got a little more of it to conquer."

"True, true," I murmured. "A thousand meters would put us out of rifle range."

We slowed our movements. Chest tight, unable to fully exhale.

The next hour we studied the fence and as much of the main gate setup we dared to get close to. Two guards were on duty. One walking the rounds, one behind a window that faced the gate. More guards probably rested.

"Nikolai, the young friend I told you about, he described the electronic's connection box and said it is always on the hinge side of the gate."

"Then it is right under those spot lights."

"Yes, sure looks like it. The fellow inside the guard house can see the road and the crossbar. I hope there isn't a window that faces the fence. It'd be tough to mess with the wiring with a fellow looking down at you." That possibility tightened my chest even more.

We slipped through meandering paths of the slumbering town. Whenever a neighborhood hound yapped at us, we scampered like frightened rabbits. At last we encountered the border fence about a thousand meters south of the guardhouse. Its insulators warned of shock and death. The fence stretched on further.

We spotted the walking guard. The crunch of boots on gravel gave us the clue. He had made his turnabout and headed back toward the guardhouse. I followed him using the short grass on the edge of the path to soften my steps. Marlena, fifty meters behind, lugged the satchels and was ready to drop out of sight if the need arose.

After hair-raising minutes the guardhouse appeared. The guard walked on. I crouched and crawled on, easing toward the spotlight. The guardhouse had no side windows! Relieved, I scurried back to Marlena who hid in the eerie shadows of a sagging woodshed.

"All the pieces are in place. No windows on that side," I muttered. "Thirty minutes per round. Every fifteen minutes the guard comes back by the guardhouse. We have ten minutes or less to kill the electrical stuff, then jump the gate and scoot out of sight."

Marlena could sense my excitement and also the stress. "Are you sure we want to do this tonight?" she said.

"Let's get it done! A new guy started his rounds."

"One thing we don't know," she said, "how long is their watch?"

"Most likely two hours on, four off. He'll make four rounds. We should try to pull this off on the guard's third round."

"Why is that?"

"He'll be tired. His reactions and awareness will have dulled. Then, if for some reason I can't get it done, on his last round he'd be even more tired."

After the guard's second round, under a cloud-covered moon, we moved closer. I left Marlena and crawled on elbows and knees to where Nikolai said the control box should be. Ever closer I slithered toward the bright light and toward the gate itself. After long and frightening minutes I found a small mound of dirt. *Yes!* Under it the buried concrete box. I ate more dust as I wriggled back to Marlena. Only a minute later the guard plodded by to start his third round.

"I found the pit. Nikolai was right," I barely gasped, exhaling tension.

"Franz, I'm about to fall apart. It must be after midnight. Oh Franz, you took that awful tumble earlier and now you're out there crawling around dodging guards with loaded rifles."

"I know. Let's stay focused. It'll be over soon." I took a deep breath to gain composure and renewed confidence. "So, it all comes down to this: when the guy comes back, in about ten minutes, we both crawl forward. If by chance the guard is out of sync and sees me, you have to sneak up behind him and give him a good wallop with the brass knob of the umbrella before he gets a shot off. Knock him cold! A good whop." Marlena stared as the words sank in. "You have to do this."

"Yes, I will," she whispered.

"The guard has orders to shoot to kill. To shoot anyone endangering his assignment or mission." I noticed her pinched lips and frightened eyes. Her shoulders, normally confident and straight, slouched forward. She rubbed her trembling hands.

"Are you up to it, Marlena? You look doubtful."

"Franz, I can do this. I'm ready."

Once the guard passed, we crawled again along the fence to a dense bush, dragging the satchels. I pushed on further. My nose plowed through dead grass and last year's briars. I uncovered the box. The biggest wire served the motor that worked the gate; not a concern. A fused wire controlled the electrified gate and fence.

When I disconnected the electrified fence, a red light, in the middle of the gate, flashed like a fire truck. I quickly reconnected the wire. With the speed of a pelted rabbit I scurried back to Marlena. We both disappeared into deeper shadows, waiting, peeping through bushes and briars. No one emerged from the guardhouse to check on why the lights flashed.

"Woe, what an eye-opener!" I gasped. "I must have the wrong sequence."

We huddled low. The whirr in my brain, the thumping of my heart, the trembling, did not subside. One could have timed my pulse in my earlobe.

"We've got one more shot before our spunky comrade gets his rest. Are you still up to it?"

"I'm ready. This is almost more than I can handle, Franz."

"Remember, the minute you see the spotlights go out, you come running with the satchels. I'll help you over the gate. The wires on top wont shock us." I grabbed Marlena's shoulder. She nodded.

For the third time, we crawled into position. If the fellow on duty inside had leaned forward in his chair, he would have spotted me.

I tried to loosen the spotlight connection. It did not budge. When I rolled to my side to get more leverage, I saw him! The guard walked into the bright light and stood there. Totally out of sync with his routine. I froze. His gaze focused on me, positive at any second he'd raise his rifle and blow me to bits. Marlena thought the same. She emerged from the shadows, crouched low and edged forward. Like a cobra ready to strike, she rose. With unflinching determination, she raised her arms, the umbrella in her grip, ready to whop a quieting blow. . . . The guard reached for the butt of his rifle. . . . No, . . . a flask in his back pocket. With practiced ease, he tilted his face toward the stars and took a long swig. Taking his next step, he tottered. Marlena stepped back and let him stagger on.

Amazingly, he never saw me. He'd cut his last round short, needing to lie down.

I disabled the fence and kicked the feed to the spotlights out of its corroded connector. This also killed the warning light on the gate. Marlena came running with the satchels. Quickly, I replaced the cover over the box and piled a bit of dirt and sod on top. We climbed up and over the gate, ran down a slope before anyone checked on the power failure.

—

We strained on through fields and thickets to gain distance. On and on we drove ourselves, panting, stumbling, until all adrenaline burned from our weary muscles. The knees wobbled; yet we plodded on. At last, down on hands and knees, we collapsed in a low, growth-covered dell. My face met the ground. There, hidden from moon and night, we lay and heaved until exhaustion ushered us to sleep.

I awakened when a small twig landed on my chin. Instantly, I jerked erect, looked, and scanned the surroundings. The world was bright and glad. Birds chirped, flitted about, verifying life. Marlena lay nearby, asleep, the side of her face on the grass. I held the tiny twig and looked up. It had fallen from a nest that straddled the branches directly over my head. I settled back, listened and enjoyed the cacophony of spring. . . . *I too will build a nest. A new nest, and I will be glad in it.*

Weariness slowly eased from my muscles. Freedom entered my psyche like the soothing comfort of honey-sweetened milk. A reassuring, unseen hand on my breast said, "Lie there. This is your day. Rejoice in it!"

Clean, life-giving air caressed every crevice of my lungs. No coal smoke, no old potato soup, no hot machines, no unbathed crowds. Freedom invaded my very being—no dread, no anxiety, no shifting eyes. Though my ribs ached with every move, my wrist swollen, my legs stiff with fatigue, I inhaled freedom. Free of the weight of oppression, free of the grip that held me prisoner for so many years.

A cuckoo called his mate. To mind came Beethoven's *Sixth*, the calm after the storm. I had not heard a cuckoo since before my children were born. . . . *Thank you Peter, my old friend; you made this moment possible.*

A few steps from where we rested, a spring welled from the earth and beckoned us to drink. The small stream seeped from under the roots of an old elm. Its sparkling water quickly disappeared under newborn cress and other grasses. I swept aside portions of the growth and waited for the small pool to clear. We drank from our tin cup, again the symbol of life. The cool water gurgled down my throat, soothing, rejuvenating, touching the tense knots of aching muscles.

Marlena picked more grit from my hair. We washed our hands and faces and shook the dust from our garments. Slowly, we readied ourselves for the new day.

"Franz, you do not know how much I appreciate what you've brought to pass. I cannot tell you in words. I can hardly believe it. . . . I'm in Hungary. You are a wonderful man."

"And you, Marlena, you are a wonderful woman. Truly a tremendous partner. I cannot take credit alone for what took place thus far."

27

We walked for hours on a dusty road, not caring to which town it led. . . . Always west. . . . Distance, to gain distance from the border drove us on.

The pastoral peace broke when clomping of hoofs drew near. A wagon, pulled by two mules, came up behind us. Two persons sat on its bench. The wagoner called his animals to slow as they approached. When they came abreast of us, the woman realized we had met before in the Mukachevo restaurant. They halted the wagon and studied us as if seeing an apparition.

"Good to see you again," Marlena said in Hungarian.

The man took off his hat and scratched his head. The woman spoke.

"You are the folks we met in Mukachevo. How did you get here?"

"We got a ride," Marlena answered.

"I don't understand. Do you have relatives here? Did the border guards let you cross over?"

"We're from Budapest, and are trying to get back home," said Marlena.

"But, we heard you speak Russian."

"That is true, we came from Russia. We're going home."

Marlena's craftiness amazed me. She always directed conversations to suit her and the situation.

The woman said, "Why don't you hop on and save your legs?"

"Thank you." We climbed on board and plopped onto a rolled-up tarpaulin.

"Thanks for stopping," Marlena continued.

"Glad we can help," said the woman. "We heard nothing but bad news on the other side. Grigori and I feel let down after three days of maybes and right-out rejections." The man nodded in agreement, stroked his mustache and rearranged his hat. I nodded, but couldn't understand a word.

"We are sorry to hear that. What brought that on?" Marlena went on.

"The border situation is getting more ridiculous. We have traded into Russia for three generations. Now the fence. You should have seen the extra troops at the border gate. All over! Like ants on a disturbed anthill."

Speaking in Russian, Marlena turned to me and expounded on the conversation. I looked at her and knew she thought the same thing I did. . . . *Let's get away from here.*

"Is there a rail station in the next town?" Marlena inquired.

"The next town?" The woman chuckled. "It doesn't even have its own brewery."

"We're looking to exchange Russian roubles to buy a ticket to Budapest."

"You'll not make it to a train station today. Probably not even by tomorrow. A short train comes to our little town only twice a month since the Russians closed the border. You'll have to find a way to Kisvarda unless you can wait around for the little shuttle."

"How far is it to Kisvarda?"

"About fifty kilometers from our place. A little far on foot."

"I reckon we have to start walking. Sorry to be asking all these questions."

"Depending how many roubles you have," the woman said. "We could exchange some for you. Around here most folks use both currencies. Further west it'll be hard to find someone trading in roubles."

The conversation was light as the wagon rolled along.

"We could take you to Kisvarda, it's a two-day trip. The problem is, we have arranged for the neighbors to help set out the rest of the potatoes in the morning. Everyone will meet at the house early."

"You must grow great amounts of potatoes," Marlena said.

"Yes, we do. It is our livelihood. That is why it's hard for us to lose customers east of here."

"Can we help? You have been so kind."

The woman looked at her husband. He shrugged his shoulders and nodded. She continued. "We could use all the hands available. The soil is perfect for planting. If we don't plant before the next rain, we'd lose our edge when the new crop comes to market."

The mules clomped along. Their steady beat blended with the noonday sun. Mesmerized, I longed for a nap. The wagon weaved its way around hills and through small clusters of houses. Poor people tended gardens, hung out clothes, fixed, and mended. They waved as we rolled by. Some craned their necks to glimpse the two strangers. Finally, we turned off onto a field road. Grigori stopped the wagon.

"Do you want to find a place to stay nearby? If you're going to help us in the morning, you could come on to the farm with us." The man spoke. Amazing!

"Come on with us; my husband wouldn't have to get you in the morning," the woman said.

"We want to help, but don't want to be a burden."

"No burden. Come on, we've room at the house. I'd like to chat some more. You can help me in the kitchen while the men work the fields."

—

We slept soundly, worked hard, and ate hearty. The locals thought they picked us up along the way to have more hands in the fields. Grigori exchanged all of our money and even offered to pay us for our labor.

"No way," I protested in Russian, "I should be paying you. You have been a friend," I said. That made him happy.

After many steady and tiring hours, the fields having received their seed potatoes, a gentle rain fell to settle the earth.

"A good rain." Grigori said. "I think you brought it with you." He grinned, leaned back and picked his teeth with a whittled splinter. His crumpled socks and boots lay in a pile next to him.

The following day Grigori and his wife took us by buggy to the Kisvarda's train station. It still rained. On our way we laughed and relaxed. Our brimmed hats and rubber slickers kept us dry. Even the mules seemed to enjoy the day and didn't mind the cooling rain on their backs. We all spent the night at an inn, no frills. At the train station we shook hands and kissed each other's cheek before we boarded. Grigori glowed with gratification. He reminded me of Boris.

"I still don't know how you two beat us to the border," he said as he raised one eyebrow.

I smiled and put my hand on his shoulder. "I'll tell you Grigori, we took the train to the border." He pondered, head cocked, his bushy eyebrows drawn.

Before he asked me to explain I continued, "I'm almost ashamed to ask one more favor, would you please mail this letter for us? If possible, have it postmarked in Russia."

"Be glad to. We'll be over the border again next week. Is that soon enough?"

"That's perfect. And, thanks again for your kindness."

"Good-bye."

Dear Ivan,

I hope this letter finds you and your family well. I trust Boris is still working in Moscow. Be sure to tell him all is well on my side. I finally got my potatoes planted.

Best wishes and health,
Your friend,
Lev

I wanted Boris to know I hadn't perished in the icy waters of a raging river.

28

A two-day ride on bone-hard seats, propping each other up, brought us to the heart of Budapest. We scraped together enough money to pay for a plate of food and a lukewarm shower.

Benjamin, Marlena's son, answered the door buzzer. When Marlena recognized him, she fell to her knees hugging and kissing the boy's hands and arms. Bewildered, the boy stood rigid.

After the shock waned, Benjamin, who didn't remember his mother, clung to his grandfather and listened intently to tales of joy and deep sorrow.

The Kunstler's two-story apartment, although small, accommodated the two newcomers well. I slept on two long benches pulled together and covered with a pad. Marlena shared a room with her son. Within a few days I felt a pleasant harmony binding the family. The boy faithfully studied his school assignments and enjoyed playing his violin.

I approached Mister Kunstler and said, "I don't want to be a burden. I need to find a way to earn enough to rent my own room and then continue on my journey."

"I understand. But you must stay with us a while and rest." He gave me a pat on the arm.

"That's kind of you, but I can't stay. I must find work."

"Relax, Franz. Things will work out, they always do."

The warmth shown to me at the Kunstlers' made me feel part of the family. Within a week, Mister Kunstler secured a position for me at a local machine shop, a short train ride from the apartment. The Hungarian people were kind when spoken to, but many stared and looked frightened as they sensed deep undercurrents of change in their government. The months hurried by. Marlena and I found time to walk, sit by the River Danube, and quietly envisioned the days ahead. Benjamin, a pleasant young lad, played his violin with a childlike joy. I listened and smiled, and always encouraged him.

Summer waned. Russian soldiers moved behind the everyday life. The average citizen knew a change had taken place. An uneasy static hung in the air. The newspapers were all too quiet. The Danube flowed on.

"Isn't it a beautiful day?" I said to Marlena.

"Yes, it is," she said softly. "Do you realize, this is the first time we held hands for no other reason than to hold hands. Franz, I've grown accustomed to you being with me."

"Marlena, when we're walking together, our silent communion is wonderful, and yet so fragile." She squeezed my hand, conveying that she knew my next words.

"Marlena, you know, before long I must leave." I felt the jolt in her grasp.

"I know, I know," she whispered with head bowed.

We continued, a bit slower to cherish every step, every breath, and the very moment.

"I'm thankful to your father-in-law for finding that job. I have the means to move on. I've got to, Marlena. I need to see this through. I must find my family."

"I know," she murmured. "Franz, must it end?"

We stood and stared at the sidewalk, afraid to look up, afraid to fall to pieces.

"Must it end?" The words reverberated in my mind and sent a thin dart through my heart.

—

Another week passed. Mr. Kunstler placed a ticket in my hand.

"Take this, please," he said. "It's a ticket to Vienna. I think you ought to leave before too long. God knows I would love for you to stay. The Russians are rattling their sabers, and things are closing in. They must not learn you're here. I believe we all will be in for a hard time. We also must flee. Whether Marlena will go with us is not yet clear. As you know, she has a good position doing the books for my Lawyer friend. In any case, we will inform your mother in München of our whereabouts when it's safe to do so. By the way, I have plenty of Austrian groschen to swap for what you've earned."

Mr. Kunstler grasped my arm. I followed him to the far corner of the apartment. Away from the noise of the kitchen, he spoke to me like a father.

"Franz, I've become very fond of you. You delivered our precious daughter-in-law. Benjamin now has a parent. Only last year we fully explained to him the sad facts about the disappearance of his mother and father. We received only two letters from Marlena. The last one came eleven years ago. You are a Godsend. I also know what drives you. The police here are in the back pockets of the Soviets. For you to buy a ticket to leave the country and exchange money to a foreign currency is extremely risky. I have connections. It profits a Jewish family to always stay ready, to outsmart the claws of the bear."

"Thanks for everything," I said. We grasped hands. He looked at the floor, chin trembling.

—

When I stepped into Marlena's room, she sat and looked out the window. Rain fell. Occasional gusts splattered the glass, defusing the stark walls of the nearby tenement. She knew I had entered. She could not turn to face me. From the tremor in her shoulders, I knew silent tears bathed her face.

"I must go," I whispered.

Her voice quavered. "I know. You must find your family."

As if sedated, she rose from her chair and turned as we met. Trembling, she looked at me. I gently cupped her face and tenderly kissed her hair and cold cheeks. Like a soft down pillow I drew her to my chest. Her emerald eyes glistened with tears, searching and pleading with my soul. After an agonizing silence, I stepped back, our hands and arms gradually slipped apart. Then she stood alone, still reaching. I felt a great loss as I stepped from her presence—out, to face a new uncertainty—alone.

After Sopran, the last stop in Hungary, the train crossed into Austria. A uniformed man entered the coach. His outfit shouted, "Border Control." Everyone showed their identification. My nerves pricked. I wondered, *should I show my Russian papers or admit I have no papers? Should I use my slurred speech or speak normal Russian to go with my name? Should I show him my papers and speak clearly in German?* I chose the latter.

"Ticket and identification please," he repeated in German. He looked at my strange documents, pushed back his cap, eyebrows furled and wrinkled forehead as he studied my papers.

"Are you a Russian?" he asked.

"No," I answered.

"These are Russian papers, are they not?"

"Yes, sir."

"My Russian is not good enough to understand what these papers say. You speak German; why the Russian documents?"

"My father, who is long dead, lived in Russia with my mother when they first married. That was nearly fifty years ago. My mother was born in Vienna. She met my father in Budapest, to where she returned after my father passed away. I'm on my way back from Budapest, where I visited with Mother. Vienna is where I live now."

I do not know where such a series of lies came from. It sure impressed the gentleman in uniform.

I spent the night on a bench at the terminal in Vienna and waited to board one more train, that one, at last, to take me home.

BOOK FOUR

29

When I stepped onto German soil, a rebirth took place. As reality penetrated a debilitating and uncontrollable exhaustion flooded over me. I stumbled forward and fell to the ground, my arms landing on a bench.

"Help me. Can this be real? I'm home." I blubbered. The steam engine's gasps and hisses recalled the scene of twelve years earlier. Friedl and the children stood on this very platform to see me off. I recalled her words: *"Please come back to me. I need you here, next to my side."* We held each other until the train's short whistle forced us to separate. . . . A cold day in late 1944.

"Are you well?" said a man. Strong fingers gripped my shoulder. I turned to look, but could not focus.

"Is this your satchel?" he asked.

"Ah, yes," I stammered, recognizing its shape.

"Are you sick? Can I help you up?" Realizing the spectacle I caused, I raised my hand. With a strong grip the man helped pull me erect.

"Thank you, I better sit down. . . . In a way, I'm having a wonderful day."

He gave me a brief smile, nodded, then walked off. From the bench I watched the train pull out.

When I was able to control my emotions, I realized part of my weakness and trembling came from not having eaten in two days. Someone pointed me to a small Gasthaus.

"I can't take groschen," the waiter announced. "We don't have a bank in Karpfham."

"I see. I don't have any marks," I said. My first impulse was to reach into my pocket. "Could I get a plate of your special for this pocket knife?" He looked at me, not knowing what to say, he took the knife. "I'm sorry," I quickly added, "I'm only now coming home from the war." His jaw dropped, then disappeared into the kitchen. He came back with a mug of beer.

"I really would like to have something to eat," I said.

"I understand. This is to keep you company until I bring you a plate."

When he brought the food, I saw the biggest pile of *Kaiserschmarrn* I had ever been served. The piping hot pile consisted of fried potatoes mixed with sautéed onions, roasted bits of pork, scrambled eggs, all seasoned with salt, plenty of pepper, and caraway seeds.

I grinned. He smiled back. With great pleasure I devoured the pile. The server returned and laid a cloth napkin beside the plate from which my pocketknife slipped to the table.

"*Guten Appetit*," he said. "Compliments of the cook."

"Tell him many thanks."

—

The graveled road to Griesbach was the same my family and I walked twelve years earlier. Few words needed to be said then, as we anticipated the anguish of saying good-bye. A bitter east wind tore at our faces then. The baby in the carriage was wrapped to a point one couldn't even find her. Peter, the little trooper, wore mittens, a wool cap pulled over his ears and a thick scarf. All knitted by his mother. Friedl, her arm in mine, walked close to me. The cold air tested our souls, foretelling the death march.

This time, however, the hike back to Griesbach was one of joyous expectations. Although late in the afternoon, the sun radiated with a purpose. Fallen leaves had piled along the road's edge. My heart pounded. *I am going to hug my family.*

I knocked on the door, held my breath, and put on my best grin. It soon opened but a crack.

"Yes?" A woman's voice said.

"I'm Franz Brunner. Is Friedl home?"

"Friedl? Friedl?" The woman asked bewildered. "I'm Maria Holzknopf. No Friedl lives here."

"I know she lived here twelve years ago."

"What did you say your name was?"

"Franz Brunner."

Opening the door a little wider, the woman explained, "I moved into this forsaken, cold place about six years ago. A long time back. Let me think. What did they say the lady's name was who lived here?" She paused. "Is she a friend of yours?"

"Friedl Brunner is my wife."

"I believe her name was Mrs. Brunner. The folks in town here said she moved back to München, with her two children."

"Two children?" I questioned.

"That is what I heard. I'm almost positive."

"Two children? Not three?"

"I can't recall anyone ever mentioning three."

I took a deep breath. "I'm just now coming home from the war," I said.

Stunned, her eyes traveled from my head to my shoes.

"Why don't you come in? I'm sorry, I . . . I acted a bit rude," she said with renewed interest.

"I don't want to intrude, Frau Holzknopf, but I need to find out all I can about my family."

"I'm sorry," she said, "I know nothing about your wife and family."

—

Disappointed, but not crushed, I left Frau Holzknopf. In the twilight of the evening, I found a place to sit on the town square. Befuddled, I pondered the next step. Deep down I agreed with Friedl to take the kids back to the city. I should have expected it.

From the church tower, which rose prominently above all the other buildings, a bell announced the quarter hour. An unexplained unction, an invisible rope, drew me to the church. This time Lana did not hover.

My steps echoed throughout the cool sanctuary. The fading day added a peaceful aura. Only the eternal candle flickered. In the lofty tips of the stained glass windows played a remnant of daylight. I eased my way to the front pew and sat. I could hear my heart beating in the stillness. The quiet slowly melted my disappointment.

When I opened my eyes, it was early morning. I'd lain on the pew all night. The sun's first glimmers again danced in the tops of the colorful windows casting magical images of light over the gothic interior. I found my shoes neatly placed on the floor under the pew. I did not remember taking them off.

Griesbach with its centuries-old buildings crowned a modest Lower Bavarian hill. From its crooked roads and many balconies one could see rolling fields and meadows that stretched to the Alps. The town was stalled in time. Stuck, with nothing to do but farm or be fortunate enough to be born into a family who owned one of the small shops. A family, such as mine, had no future, but be stuck in bare existence, surviving.

The bank and post office shared the same building.

"Would you exchanged groschen for marks, please?"

"I'm sorry," the gentleman answered, "we cannot comply with your request, sir; we are not authorized to handle foreign currencies."

"What am I supposed to do?" I asked.

The man behind the counter hesitated a bit and then said, "We don't get many requests like yours. The only thing I can suggest is you see Ferdinand, the trucker. His garage is in that yellow building across the street." He pointed out of the window. "He often trades in Austria. If it's not a large sum, I'm sure he could help."

"Thank you. I'm sorry to have been a bother."

"No bother. Good day to you, sir."

Ferdinand had red hair and a ruddy face to go with it. A friendly fellow with a wide grin. I sensed a little dialogue could be fun. He happily exchanged my groschen and showed great interest in hearing my Russian imprisonment stories.

"Franz," he offered, "I've got to be in München next Monday. If you don't mind waiting, I'll give you a ride and it won't cost you a pfennig."

"That's great. I can't believe my good fortune."

"To be honest, the few marks you have in your pocket wouldn't have been enough to pay for a mule ride. You'll need that little cash when you get to the city." Taking hold of my arm he said, "Where are you staying, may I ask?"

"Ah, well," I stammered, "I fell asleep inside the church yesterday."

"You spent the night in the church? Come, you can stay in my shop if you want. I've got a cot there, a wash-up basin, and a toilet."

"Are you sure? . . . Great! Thanks."

"Come, I'll show you the setup."

—

Monday morning, when I heard a knock and a key jiggling the door lock, I jumped.

"Are you up to the trip?" Ferdinand hollered as he stepped into the shop.

"Give me a couple of minutes."

The cozy-warm diesel truck left Griesbach at four that morning. The cushioned seat offered a pleasant change from the hard slats on the train. Wartime stories, politics, and philosophy turned out to be the main subjects of conversation. The hours passed with ease while the new freedom invaded my speaking, my demeanor, my smile, and my soul. An incredible lift came to my spirit.

We said our good-byes at the Viktualien Markt, which is, and has been, in the heart of München for a thousand years. From there I caught a tram to my mother's part of the city.

30

More than eleven years after the war's end, the scars and ravages of the bombings in München were still evident. Most rubble heaps and bomb craters had been smoothed over to create vacant lots. The gaps between buildings still standing resembled a grimacing giant's many missing teeth. I also saw progress. Trolleys overflowed. Cars and vehicles of commerce created a bustle of life on the surface as they scrambled for position in traffic. With great interest I watched people's faces. The bleeding had stopped. I also knew many loved ones perished and many suffered crippling wounds. I could sense that sacrifices still gnawed and ached in the souls of survivors. Yet I also saw a yearning for a new day when life again would be special and tranquil. A longing for a time when neighbors would greet one another and Mozart's music would dance in their hearts.

With great anticipation I walked the last kilometer to mother's tenement. I could have changed trolleys and walked less, but I wanted to think, cherish the moment, and be ready. *My mother is in her seventies. The shock may be too much.*

Mother lived on the first floor. A mere twenty-two steps up. The cool and dimly lit building gave me a chill. I stood and took a deep breath. Slowly, I, the dead man, mustered the courage to climb the stairs.

I rang the old buzzer, head and ear tilted toward the door, and listened. Soon footsteps made their way down the long hall. I knew them to be Mother's, still heavy, a bit slower than once, but Mother's.

"Frau Brunner?" I said gently.

"*Ja.*"

"I'm Franz."

"*Ja.*"

"*Dein Sohn*, Franz."

She looked at my face. Her mouth fell open. When I noticed her eyes roll backward, I stepped through the doorway and caught her under the arm as she melted to the floor. I rushed to get a water-soaked cloth and on my knees gently wiped her forehead and cheeks. I sobbed. *God, my mother, don't let her die.* She felt clammy. Her pulse was weak. I freshened the cool cloth and placed it on the back of her neck. She stirred and opened her eyes.

"*Bis des Du, Franzi?*"

"Yes, *Mutti*, it is your boy." I softly assured her.

She raised her hand to touch my cheek. Slowly, trembling, her fingertips felt my face.

"You're not dead... You're...."

She fainted again. "Wake up, Mother! I have come home! I'm not dead! I've come home! Wake up!" I cried, my hands cupping her face.

Once seated on her chair, she felt better. Her deep, tear-filled eyes showed a glitter of joy.

"Are you hungry?"

"Mother, it's all right. Stay put. Let's talk before you jump up and start feeding me."

"Yes. Let's sit. Let me touch you; see if you're real. Slide your chair closer."

She held my hand and ran her fingers through my thinning hair. She felt my shirt and my arm. Silent tears flowed. We sat quiet for a long time, her head pressed against my shoulders. Her hands caressed my arm and hand. Periodically she patted my chest to make sure I was real.

"I'm going to put some meat back on your bones," she announced.

"You can do whatever you want, Mother," I said smiling. "I also need to see Friedl and my babies."

She let go of my arm and tensed up. "Franz, I have to tell you something."

"What," I interrupted.

Mother struggled, swallowed, then paused before she whispered, "They're all in America."

"What?"

A knife stabbed my belly. I got up and turned from her. At the windowsill I hung my head.

"America! The other side of the world." I gasped as I struggled to absorb the blow. "How long ago?"

"It will soon be two years."

"She and the children?"

"She, Peter, Dolli, and her husband."

"Her husband?" I barely held myself erect. Utter dejection flooded over me. I should have considered all this more thoroughly.

Mother came to the window, stroked my shoulders, and pressed her head to my side. "Be still, my son. You are home. You are alive. Friedl didn't know. You must forgive her. They declared you dead. She wanted to make a new life for the children. Times had been very hard for her."

Through the haze of sorrow I saw Mother's geraniums, proudly claiming both corners of the deep windowsill. Geraniums always graced my mother's windowsills. They *were* my mother. The flowers spoke to me with a warmth, a soothing comfort, in my darkest hour.

Long intervals between words kept our conversation at a crawl. Time hung there in the air, like a used, wet fishnet. The net had been cast into the once-rich waters. Now it hung there, at the end of life's day, empty. Everything had slipped away.

"Mother, do you know of a third baby?"

"Yes, I know." Again, after a lengthy pause and a deep breath she struggled to find the right words. "In the spring of 1945 she bore twins, beautiful girls, blond and blue-eyed. She placed them in the wicker cradle, the one you bought for baby Peter."

"And," I said, eager for her to continue. "Why didn't they go to America?"

"Because," she hesitated, then swallowed, "they died while babies. I never got to see them."

"No! Why?"

"Franz, they had little to eat, no coal for the stove, no money for milk for four children. The twins returned to Heaven. The first one died at four months old, the second at ten months. Friedl almost lost her mind. It wasn't anyone's fault."

"Except Hitler's," I blurted out.

In Russia I personally saw and felt the devastation of war. Never had I imagined it to be so heart wrenching for my own family.

Gradually, as I reasoned and rationalized and placed in order the segments of life as they had been dealt, I felt it necessary to thank God for what had been spared. I had acted selfishly, thinking I should be the one to have it all. Wisdom finally convinced me. The former things passed away; all things became new.

—

As darkness fell, a chill crept into the room. Mother pulled the string to the overhead light, and turned the radiator valve for heat.

"It'll get warm soon," she announced. "Let me heat a little soup for you. It's in the icebox in the hall. I fixed too much yesterday; I always do."

A soft poke of her heel kicked the door to the hall shut behind her. "I think you'll like what's in the pot, one of your favorites when you lived at home."

I smiled. "Mother, that was many moons ago,"

"Yes, but a mother never forgets. Her children are her cherished treasures."

She would not tell me what was in the pot. She showed an impish grin, while her dark eyes danced.

With a generous serving in my old soup bowl, she stood back and waited for my response.

"Griesnockerl Suppe!" I cried out with joy.

"Wait," she interrupted, then sauntered to the cupboard. "You've got to have a little *Schnittlauch* on top."

Again she stepped back, her hands together, smiled, and watched me indulge. The soup was indeed my favorite. No one can make soup as good as one's mother. In the beef broth floated small farina dumplings. The blend of her delectable broth and the dumplings, drizzled with chopped chives, created a wonderful harmony that soothed my starved taste buds.

"Mother," I said, "this soup would wake the dead."

"That is what you said twenty-five years ago."

"Yes, but it is still true. You are the best."

My mother found new life. She doted on me, all the while trying to fatten me up. Each morning she fluffed the bed in the extra room. Over the washstand hung two pictures, pictures of her only two sons—my brother, Alfons, and me, both matted in black. One evening, after Mother had gone to bed, I took my picture off the wall and reversed the mat. The color of death switched to the cream color on the other side. The very next day she spotted the change.

"I think I can make it from now on. All is not lost." She gave me a hug.

—

Mother's curiosity never abated. Having lived alone for years, any communication, more than "hello, how are you," presented a real treat for her—especially with a son who had been declared dead. We spent hours talking of long ago. We talked of what might have been. We talked of Russia. One evening she abruptly stopped and went to her nightstand.

"Look! This came in the mail a couple of months ago." She handed me a letter.

"See, it's addressed to your father. I wondered who would write and didn't know your father is gone." Still looking at the letter, she said, "I couldn't read it. Either it is bad handwriting or my eyes are failing me."

"Mother, this letter is addressed to me. It is from my friend Nikolai. He wrote in Russian, that's why you couldn't read it."

"The young man you told me about?"

"Yes, it's good news, because I now know he's made it to the West."

Nikolai's letter was short and to the point. He managed to get as far north as Hamburg. He figured to settle there for a while before he totally ran out of money. He was working for a construction company and was living with a Russian couple who also escaped. He hoped when I arrived at my mother's I would find her well. He closed the letter with many thanks and best wishes and hoped to hear from me soon.

I answered in German, except for the greeting, which I laboriously managed to scribble with the Russian alphabet.

Dear Nikolai!

I rejoiced reading your letter. Thank you. My mother is well. I'm out of funds also. My family moved to America. My children have a new father. I must find work as well. Going to America is out of reach, at least for now. I know you are planning to go there. I hope it will be soon. Please, Nikolai, keep writing. You are my friend, my son from a different time. In my heart I know we will see each other again, as free men. What a day that will be. Until then, keep in touch.
I'll be at my mother's.

With warmest regards, your father
Franz

Living at home with my mother provided the time to readjust. However, too much reliving of the past proved not conducive to a healthy mind. At first, the newfound freedom was difficult, sort of hard to grasp and negotiate in. I needed to learn that living can be done in the open. I had to learn not to look over my shoulders and allow myself to have an opinion.

"Mother, I know you don't want me to find work, but if there is a tomorrow in my life, I have to get out and create one."

"You'll be gone every day. I'm only now getting used to you being home."

"Don't worry, I'll be home every night."

I found work with my old company. A new plant replaced the bombed one. The company again manufactured camera shutters and other precision instruments for the medical field. They made a great to-do over my resurrection from the dead. I could have done without all the attention and wondered if the exposure would land me back in Russia.

—

My elderly mother shared a garden spot with many others her age, an effort by the city to stimulate and keep the seniors in the neighborhood content. The small plot was within a ten-minute walk of her apartment. An entire city block had been cleared of rubble, graded, and covered with tillable soil. Inside the fenced perimeter narrow paths separated the gardens from the adjoining one. Many built little garden houses on their plats, not only to keep their tools out of the weather, but also to have a place to sit and get out of the sun.

Mother's garden became a place to relax and a soothing spot to rest. In the fall I spaded over the rich soil for the coming frost to do its magic. A magic that digs deep with its long, icicle-clad fingers, loosening the soil to reward its worker come planting time.

I witnessed the wonders of creation. Swarms of red-breasted swallows flitted about and cheered one another on for the journey south. I pondered, *These swallows will fly south, will not carry a satchel or an overcoat, and never question their fate and purpose....*

I watched the leaves blow. They danced and swirled, driven by something they had no control over. Yet they too seemed happy as they settled under berry bushes, cuddled together to form a thick blanket to protect the roots from the pending grip of winter. Everything had a purpose, everything. *Who am I to think, without my family, my situation is hopeless?* Repeatedly, a gentle and explicit inner voice convinced, "Life is worth living."

31

"Mother, does Friedl ever write to you?"

"Yes, at Christmas and maybe a few times in between. The letters are always short. It seems their life is very busy, working to get ahead in the New World."

"Short letters. That's Friedl, always businesslike," I said. "She says much with few words."

"She hasn't sent me any new pictures," Mother volunteered. "The only one I have shows them on board a ship sailing to New York."

"New York sounds so big and so foreign. Mother, do you still have the picture?"

"I think I can find it."

Friedl looked well. I had difficulty transforming my mind's images of the children to the faces on the picture. Looking at the man sitting with them did not please me.

"Mother, the next time you answer Friedl's letter, are you going to tell her I'm back from the war?"

"Franz, I really don't know."

I pressed on. "What circumstances would have to be in place to make you tell her?"

"Now that you put it that way, the only circumstance at this point would be if her husband left her or died."

"I feel the same. If she is happy, it would be most unfair for me to appear." Considering further, I said, "The children, well, once they get older, I would have to let them know. Somehow, somewhere, I would want to see them."

"I agree, the children will step out on their own. You keep that hope alive." Shaking her head, she continued. "Franz, Friedl's new husband is an honorable man. He also fought on the Russian front as a machine gunner. After being wounded and having recuperated, they shipped him to the western front. The Americans captured him, then handed him over to the British. He stayed there as a prisoner of war until 1947."

"That is two years after the war ended."

"Yes, the British used many as laborers even after the war ended."

"Mother, isn't it strange? I'm beginning to feel somewhat connected to this fellow. What is his name?"

"His name is Alfons."

"Alfons!" I said out loud. "My brother's name! Isn't that something? Mother, I wore my brother's boots, you know. I looked at his name and serial number every day." *Alfons is his name, Alfons!*

"Remember, Mother, when both Alfons and I lived at home as young men? We rode the same trolley together. After we married, before either of us had children, we vacationed together. We climbed the tallest mountains in Germany together. Friedl brought along her concertina. Do you remember me telling you, Mother? We sang the night away—high up in a tiny shepherd's log hut. We soared as free as the eagle. Mother, do you remember?"

Let it pass. My still voice told me. *Let it pass.*

—

During the cold and dreary days of winter, I had time to revisit old thoughts of hunger, hopelessness, and monotony. It amazed me to see how a new and fresh outlook had me reconsider everything, even the weather. I discovered when one's spirit feels lifted and filled with purpose, there are no dreaded days. The cold does not go to the bone, instead, it exhilarates. I did not look at the snowy days as something I needed to battle, instead, the pristine purity, the glistening of absolute cleanliness, made me appreciate life.

On New Year's Eve, the close of 1956, I took a long walk. I crossed the Octoberfest Wiesen, on which, a long time ago, my father showed my brother and me how to fly our homemade kites. Sheep grazed there at the time.

I walked a tree-lined avenue to the intersection of Ruppert Strasse, where Friedl and I first lived after we married. We brought our babies home to that place. The apartment faced south. Its windows overlooked the train tracks that lead to the Südbahnhof. From there I shipped to France for infantry training. Twice I walked up and down the street and studied the refurbished tenements still standing. I couldn't identify our old place, or if indeed it still stood. I didn't have the stomach to talk to any of the shop owners who would have known. Instead of digging among the past and the dead, I felt nothing but gratitude for being alive and having all my limbs. I could have come home to absolutely nothing. I could have come home in a box. Not every woman and child left the city in time. I'm sure that men came home from the war to face that, nothing, no one.

When I returned to Mother's kitchen that evening, she asked, "Aren't you going to ring in the New Year down at the Augustiner Stube?"

"I hadn't even given it a thought." Changing the subject, I said, "Mother, what is Friedl's new married name?"

"It's Pfisterer."

"Did the kids take on the name?"

"No, they kept the Brunner name. I think Friedl receives a little monthly compensation from the government for raising the children as a war widow."

"That's great," I said. "The name Brunner will go on. Aren't you thankful for that?"

"Yes, I am. I told you all is not lost."

"That you did. Mother, the more I look at the good, the more rejoicing I do."

—

Spring came to my new world. it fluttered in like ballerinas showing off their yellow tutus. My heart soared. Wisps of warm breezes set in motion the smells of blooms. The swallows returned to their nests stuck to walls and ledges, for them a busy time of building and courtship. I planned to do the same. I found new friends and fished for pleasure, not for food. Work rewarded me monetarily and built a sense of self-worth. I bought a violin. I played for the joy of it, and on occasion for a little extra money down at the corner Gasthaus. The deepest satisfaction came when nature showed off its flowers and the garden grew. The world glowed more than ever before. Contentment nurtured me back to youthful exuberance.

One bright day, the postman brought a letter that showed an Austrian stamp.

Dear Franz,

I truly hope this letter finds you and your mother well. Do not think I'm writing from Austria. We are all still in Budapest. I am giving this letter to a friend, who is to travel to Vienna soon, to mail from there. I wanted to tell you, or at least mention the things that have come about.

The newspapers here don't say much, compared to their former reports of activities on the Soviet border. Among friends, many brutal stories are told. My father-in-law says the Soviets have taken over the flow of information and have essentially replaced our government with their ideologues.

My father-in-law has sent parcels of "good deeds" to several of his friends in Salzburg and Innsbruck. We have packed our bags and latched them tight.

The time is near. Mr. Kunstler does not want me to stay. He thinks all the signs are in place for things to get more oppressive.

Benjamin's violin has been "given" to friends as well. He misses it. He told me you gave him inspiration to play it often and play it well.

Again the time is near. Please do not write until you hear from me again.

Your much indebted friend who owes all to you,
Marlena.

After the takeover in 1956, the Communists tightened their grip on Hungary. Before the end of the year, Russia dominated the country as it did Poland, Czechoslovakia, East Germany, and countries to the Balkans. I worried about Marlena and the Kunstlers. For them to be safe, they should have left before the total takeover. I'm sure Mr. Kunstler could have managed to live under Communist rule, but, being Jewish, definitely not worth the chance. Even though their son had been murdered well over a decade earlier, the Jewish people had no guarantee of safety.

Coming home from work one evening I was surprised to see two daffodils in a vase on mother's kitchen table.

"Where did you pick those? I checked on yours yesterday, but they weren't even close to open."

"I didn't pick them," mother answered. "Someone carefully pushed them through the letter slot in the door."

A sharp ping surged from my heart to my toes. . . . *LANA!*

To keep mother from noticing my shock, I said, "Pushed through the letter slot? Isn't that a little strange? Do you have secret admirers?"

"Not that I know of," she said. "The stems had water on them, as if someone had pulled them out of a vase."

Lana! I felt gripped. Flashes of her mesmerizing eyes, her enveloping music, the music we shared on the featherbed, all came reeling back to a spring many years ago.

"Are you well?" asked Mother. "You look as if you've seen a ghost." She walked around the table to face me. "What is wrong?"

"Well, nothing to worry about, a flashback. I'm all right."

I pushed myself from the table and walked to my room. Sprawled on the bed, I tried to wrangle-in the visions erupting in my mind—the shack, her eyes, the hospital, her get-well kiss, Mikhail's Café, the red wine, the "Moonlight Sonata," the sleep on her couch. My chest heaved as I recalled the tub, the two towels, the swell and luscious lips, the candles and meshing of desire.

A stab in my belly recalled the abortion, the old church, and the all-revealing admonishment. "No!" I groaned out loud.

Mother tapped on the door. "Franzl, is something wrong?"

"I'll be fine. Had to lie down," I stammered.

The thought of Lana in München tore into me like the claw of a tiger. As much as I tried to shrug off the whirl of emotions, I could no longer see my new world as before. I looked behind my back and scanned for strangers. Not out of fear, but for the chance of a glimpse of her.

After weeks, the paranoia gradually faded and I regained normalcy in my routine. The corner tavern again became the hub, where my friends and I played cards, wrangled over politics, and planned the next fishing trip.

—

At long last, with renewed excitement, I opened another letter from Marlena.

Dear Franz:

At last I can write to you. It is not that I did not want to write, I could not. Our lives have been in an uproar since I wrote last.

After the new regime started to take a census, and the police confiscated guns and ammunition, my father-in-law sent his wife and Benjamin on to Vienna. Not long after, he told me to go to the train station after work and wait for him there. If he did not show by midnight, I was to come back home to sleep. He stayed at the apartment to meet the census takers. This went on for three days. He did not want them to think we had fled. We always left the apartment looking lived in—dishes laid out, laundry overflowed the basket, and shoes laid visible throughout the apartment.

When the snoopers finally came early one evening, my father-in-law informed them that his wife and grandson visited in the country, and I was still at work or with friends.

He then met me at the station. We left for Austria and met up with his wife and Benjamin.

When we arrived in Salzburg, we stayed the first night in three separate locations. I, with a family on the edge of town, the others split up. We pooled together and lived a while with a Jewish family who were distant relatives. I, with Benjamin, offered to move out to find our own way and place, but all thought it necessary to continue to decoy our whereabouts.

We did the same in Innsbruck and finally settled there in an apartment above a clothing store.

Benjamin and I are looking for our own place. May even settle in Garmisch, if I get a job offer there.

Please keep in touch and write to me at the address on top.

I'm so happy to be settled for now and closer to you.

I remain your grateful friend.
Thinking of you often,
Marlena

Corresponding with Marlena added a dimension of wholeness to my existence. I looked forward to receiving her letters. Although it was a long-distance relationship, she brought a little zest to my otherwise routine life. If a physical attraction played a roll, she never alluded to it. Her having moved to Garmisch, a bit more than an hour's ride by train, made it tempting to want to visit. However, the last chapter of my saga had to be written. She and I knew the stakes.

32

"I'm glad this is the end of the week," I announced to Mother. "If you can wait with supper until dark, I'd like to try my luck with the new flies I tied the other night."

"Going fishing? You go on. Supper can wait," she encouraged. "Before you run out, take this piece of mail with you. Addressed to: Herr Brunner . . . beautiful feminine handwriting."

With tackle over my shoulder I clicked the door shut behind me. The letter was not from Marlena. . . . *No return address?* I knew my mother often looked out the window to watch me leave, so I walked all the way to the trolley stop before I opened the letter.

Dear Franz:

Congratulations! You're home, and I trust you are doing well. I know this is a shock to you, but I have received permission to do some more fact finding in West Germany. I'll be visiting München the next three weekends and will eat lunch at Donisl's around noon on Sundays. Please come and join me.
I have much to share with you.

With warm regards,
Lana

Lana's letter didn't slam me as had the daffodils. *If* the daffodils were Lana's, they meant to dampen the shock. She would not announce herself that way if a couple of goons had come along to physically drag me back to Moscow. However, the old suspicions were rekindled, as well as the pleasant memories.

I put fishing out of my mind. Instead, I jumped onto a tram to get some reassurance from my friend, Alois, a cheerful fellow with a quick wit and a sharp mind.

I rang the buzzer to his flat. When he opened his door, I shook his firm grip. "Hey man, got a minute?" I said. "I need a favor."

"Sure. Come in."

I looked at him sideways. "What's the deal? Do you always answer the door in your skivvies?"

"I hoped to be surprised by a sensational dame."

"You! Give me a break. Who would fall for a fellow who reminds them of a bowl of prunes?"

"You should talk of prunes, old man, you've got a whole decade on me." We laughed. "I see by the gear you're dragging that you want me to go fishing with you."

"No. That's what I was going to do until I read this letter."

"Mail keeps you from fishing? Must be a bomb of a letter."

"Alois, I need a confidant, and maybe a little help. This letter is from Lana, you know, the KGB woman assigned to me to keep me lean, working, and, what she thought, happy."

"Yes."

"I told you how I got out of there. Knowing Lana, she found something that didn't let her rest until she got to the bottom of it—and she did."

"What are you getting at, Franz? From what you told me you covered all the angles when you supposedly fell into the icy water."

"Well, I thought so too. She is good at what she does. I must have left something uncovered. The puzzling thing is, she may be right here in München as we speak."

"Why should that worry you?" He said. "Listen! Franz, let me remind you again my friend—the KGB might be snooping around here, but I doubt if they are eyeballing you."

"I guess you're right."

"You think she's after your ass?" Alois asked.

"I don't know. She may want me back in Moscow."

"How do you know she's right here under your nose?"

"She is here, that's for sure. I know she spotted me and followed me home or she wouldn't have known where to send this letter. I got it today. Here, read it."

Alois digested the letter in seconds. His comment was fresh and honest. "'Fact finding' sounds interesting. What that tells me is *if* she's out to kidnap you, she wouldn't need but a day and not three weeks."

"Good point," I said.

"Looks to me like her business is not in this town. She only came to München to hook up with you."

"I tend to agree. But, I want to make sure I don't step into a trap."

"I know your past left you a bit jumpy, but what do you want me to do?"

"Well, tomorrow is Sunday. Donisl's isn't but a few blocks from here. Could you stop in at noon and see if she's with company. Even if she isn't, wait until she leaves the restaurant and watch if she teams up with someone around the corner."

"Got it. What's she look like?"

"She is sensational. But don't wear your skivvies." We chuckled.

"Sensational—in what way?"

"You name it. Looks, shape, legs, and style. I warn you, if you get close enough she'll lock you in with her eyes. Black hair frames her face and fabulously luscious lips. You'll wind up seeing them in your sleep."

Eager to play detective, Alois was ready. I was glad he didn't want me to pour over the words "share things." I had plenty of wandering of the brain by then.

To follow up on Alois's detective mission, he and I met that Sunday evening at Donisl's to better visualize what he saw at lunch time.

Settling in to eat our meal, I said, "You can't beat this combination: *Bier, Wurst, Kraut, Butterbrot,* and *Senft.*"

"Yes, that's what I had for lunch earlier." After a swig from his mug, he continued. "She sat right over there. I steered away from her glance. Her profile, however, from head to toe, nothing but sensational. You've got the eye, Franz. I watched when she walked in. She chose to sit in the corner, hoping you'd show up. I could tell. Then a man and woman asked to sit at the table. Other than greetings, I don't think she had any other conversation with the couple. I couldn't tell what she ate; not much, I noticed. She nibbled her lunch and nursed a second glass of wine until about one-thirty. I left before she did and blended in across the street. She did not leave with anyone, nor did anyone follow her or team up with her. She crossed the street and disappeared among the crowd."

"Thanks, Alois. I gather you don't think I have anything to worry about?"

"I think you'll be fine. Go meet with her."

The day following, soot and smoke hung thick in the air weighed down by a heavy mist. It was washday. The tenement seniors with the longest tenure often picked Monday as their turn to use the washhouse. Beginning in the wee hours of the morning, coal fires heated cauldrons of water to boil the wash. Soot-filled clouds of mist slunk among the buildings, invading lungs and saturating one's clothes with dampened filth. On the way to work, everyone on the tram hacked and coughed and wiped their noses on sleeves or tablecloth-sized handkerchiefs. It took folks at work until the ten o'clock break to warm up toward each other. The gloomy weather held on through most of the week and dampened most cheerfulness in me and in others.

"I'm glad the wind kicked up a bit," my mother volunteered. "Maybe it'll blow this dreariness out of here. You haven't been saying much all week—moping around, going to bed early. Is something wrong? Is the letter with the feminine handwriting to blame?"

"No, nothing's wrong. That particular letter is from someone I worked for in Russia. Couldn't figure out how they found me."

Mother opened the cupboard. "This may cheer you up—another letter from the Garmisch lady."

An interesting and pleasant letter arrived from Marlena. She had made new friends since moving to Germany and seemed to stay busy and fulfilled. A new and strange turmoil entered my mind. I wished I didn't have to answer Marlena's letter. Not at a time when I again stepped into the shadowy world of Lana.

—

The following Sunday, when I entered Donisl's, Lana sat facing the door. She instantly smiled when she saw me. My heart ramped up, but a knot also settled in the pit of my stomach.

"May I sit?"

"Please." She clasped my outstretched hand with both of hers. "It's wonderful to see you again, alive!"

"What a shock. This is so surreal." I stammered.

"No shock to me. You look well—well fed. You look ten years younger, I might add."

"Are you saying I've fattened up? It's all my mother's fault." Settling in my seat, I continued. "You haven't changed, Lana. Beautiful as ever."

"Don't tell fibs, Franz. The last three years have been testing me with a vengeance."

"Tell me something good," I said.

"One thing good, Franz, is you are alive and well."

"When did you first learn that?"

"I followed you leaving work and all the way to your mother's place."

"How often did you follow me around?"

"Only that one time. I saw you had settled in. I didn't need to know anything else." She sounded sincere.

"Ah . . . Lana, the daffodils. From you?"

She smiled. "The only nonthreatening way, I thought, to let you know I found you."

"Nonthreatening maybe, but you turned my world belly up. How did you even . . . ?"

"Franz, don't read too much into this. In Moscow you're officially dead, washed away by the icy torrents. However . . ."

"However what?" I squirmed in my seat. Lana didn't miss it.

"Nothing to worry about. Please, relax. At the time, I put a few things together for my personal satisfaction. I had to know the truth. My heart had to find you or the body downriver somewhere."

"Go on."

"For one, you couldn't have fallen into the river from the bridge and held on to the violin in one hand and the bow in the other,—and—to the homemade umbrella. I looked for the special umbrella in your apartment, but never found it. Then I considered one may have stolen it after you fell in. Then again, why would you have taken both your old cane, which laid on the bridge, and the new one?"

"Good work."

"I found other clues."

"Such as?"

"Well, I don't want to bore you. The good thing is you are here and I can look at you and be glad."

We nibbled our meal; she sipped her wine and I a mug of foamy dark beer.

Curious, I asked, "You hinted at other clues. Would you share them?"

"The phonograph player you wanted sounded logical. I knew you had been saving for it for a long time. However, on a normal day you wouldn't take along your cherished savings to the bridge. I searched the apartment for the savings; even flipped the mattress over to check for hidden pockets. I also ran into old Peter before he passed on, and he alluded to you saying that you may soon see your family again."

"Peter died?"

"Yes, about a year ago."

"I loved that old man. The last time I saw him he was mighty frail."

"I'm sorry. I thought you should know."

"I'm sad to hear. Peter filled an emptiness in my life; even though I wasn't allowed to see him as often as I wanted."

"Who told you not to see him?"

"Lana, the game is over. You are here. What do you need out of me?"

"Franz, please don't be surly. I don't need a thing out of you. I wanted to see you."

"Well, I apologize. I admit, it is good to see you also."

After several long moments I asked, "Why didn't you report your findings?"

"Franz, when I realized there was a chance of you being alive, I certainly didn't want the hounds after you. After I calmed down and put the circumstances in order, a hopeful feeling filled my every hour. I totally dismissed the few contentions we had and recalled the cherished times. The many good and wonderful times."

"You're right, we did have memorable times," I said. "You must have also known that deep down I needed to be rid of the System, and find my family."

"I know, and I understand. My position didn't give me much leeway. I had to do my job."

I understood and decided not to discuss her job any further. We each took a bite of our food and gave the moment a chance to redirect.

After a sip from her glass, Lana leaned forward and, with a slight tilt of her head, smiled. A warmth emanated, relaxing the tension. I had forgotten that smile. A smile, not defensive or coy, radiating from the velvet den of sensuality. It was Lana the woman, not Lana the agent.

"Is your mother well?" She snapped my brain to the present.

"Yes, she found new life doting on me." Still questioning her motive and direction, I said, "Lana, be honest with me. Why are you here in Germany?"

"Franz, I'm here, meeting with you, because I had the perfect opportunity to do so. You may not believe this, but I'm on assignment at the East German border, Berlin to be specific, to study and look into reasons and means of people defecting to the West."

"You come all the way on weekends from Berlin to München?"

"No, I have an assignment in Heidelberg for the rest of the month. I scooted down here hoping to see you."

"Well, I see." I didn't have words to add, so I showed interest in her assignment. "That Berlin thing, I didn't know it's getting more worrisome."

"The fences keep getting wider and taller," she said. "There is now a fence all around West Berlin. What is even more incredible, I know of a three-meter-high concrete wall is in the plans—straight through the center of Berlin."

"Why? I've heard of walls around castles to keep people out, but never to keep common folks in."

"You're right. Makes one think," she said. "So many of our educated and skilled people are risking all to reach the opportunity, as they perceive it, of having a better life."

"Do you think they are finding it, Lana?"

"Franz, I must admit, no one is coming back voluntarily. I always felt Nikolai headed for the border. Yuri, you may remember him, he left one afternoon and never returned."

"Lana, I want to ask this as a friend: Is a caged eagle free to fly?"

"I know what you're saying. The zeal of youth is wonderful. Yes, no one wants to be caged." She paused. "To be entangled is bad enough."

"How is that?" I asked.

"Well, I feel I'm entangled. Sometimes I wonder . . ."

I let the thought soak in. Lana ordered a second glass of wine. She shifted in her seat, ready to change the conversation.

"Youth—where has it gone, Franz?" Her fingers lifted a cascade of her hair to reveal the gray. "This silver is not a reward, it is payment."

"What do you mean?"

"Franz, I don't want to spoil this day. I had dreamed and waited too long for it. Other than being here, I have so little joy to share with you."

I relaxed my shoulders to ease the tension and said, "I remember moments in Moscow when you shared your soul. Lana, look around, no one here is even vaguely interested in us. Share, I want to know. I'm listening."

"Irina disowned me. She left home, to where I don't know. When I found Sven left in a pile at my door, I took him in and called for a doctor. He could not walk and hardly talk."

"He came up from behind and put a knife to my throat."

"Oh my . . .." Lana gasped. "I didn't realize . . .."

"I was wound a bit tight that evening," I said. "Stressed by tension and planning my move."

"I see now," she said gathering her thoughts. "I knew the encounter had to be with you. When I told the doctor of his fight with another man, Sven became angry. He wanted his injuries to be the result of an accident. Two days after they took him to the hospital a gentleman rang my door. Earlier the same day I heard of your demise. Already in a state of panic, I told the investigator more than I needed to. This brought a charge of attempted murder on Sven. He left prison when his cast was removed. He stayed with his family a week before being 'resettled' to Kiev to begin a new career. What career I do not know. Sven lost part of his jaw's movement from a blow which affected his speech. The result of crushed bones in his right foot left him with a noticeable limp."

Lana looked at me as if to say, "Did you have to be so forceful?" but said nothing.

She continued, "When the young man left Moscow, Irina was outraged. She became aloof and distant. The end between my daughter and me came when a farewell letter arrived from Sven. A week later an official statement said he hung himself."

"I'm sorry to hear that. I'm sorry."

"Enough of my sad story," she said. "I know yours must be a lot more exciting."

"Exciting? I don't know about that. It's an ongoing story of hope. You know I live with my mother. Well, since I'm legally dead, my wife remarried and they all immigrated to America."

"I thought something was amiss when you lived with your mother. What a shock it must've been. Are you going to follow them to America?"

"Well, she is my wife. At this point I can't see myself causing an uproar. My children, soon will leave the nest. . . . One day, someday, . . . I want to see them."

"You've weighed the options, I see."

"Ah, I suppose I have. I'm not bitter. It took me these last several years to fight my way through self-pity and rejection to finally realize I had not lost my family; I'm only out of touch."

Lana settled back in her seat, cupped her wineglass with both hands, tilted it slowly from side to side, and watched the last swallow.

"Franz," she reached across the table to touch my arm. "Can we meet again? Soon? I'll be returning in a week from tomorrow."

"Returning?"

"Yes, back to East Berlin. I hate being there. Before I go, I'd love to end my 'fact-finding mission' remembering the good days."

"Can we meet here next Sunday?" I said.

"Not sooner?" She asked softly and searched my eyes. "I had in mind an evening alone. Away from these crowds, hard seats, and worn wooden tables."

"Let us both digest what has happened so far, this coming week." I said. "Let's meet again next Sunday. How about nine in the morning; under the Glockenspiel? We'll make a day of it."

Lana reached for both of my hands, pulled them toward her, hung her head, and squeezed. "Thanks," she said.

Being the wretched man that I am, flashes of lustful pleasure bombarded my mind. I looked for justification not to fall again. But, she was right, . . . *Crowds, hard seats, wooden table.* . . . We had met where people and clatter blended, and tobacco smoke held it all together. Suddenly aware of the hard seat, my elbows hurting from resting on the wooden table, I wanted a change. . . . *Alone . . . soft . . . billowy pillows . . . undulating waves.* . . .

—

As well as the rendezvous with Lana went, I could not help but question my decision to meet with her again. She had not changed, still attractive, still persuasive, and bewitching. Lana once quenched my masculine impulses and so placed into my dull and meager life a sweet smelling rose, if only for a short while. Physical attraction always pervades. A fragrant marinade that seeps and invades and overpowers seemingly platonic relationships with its sly and steady penetration of desire. *Have I grown past that?* . . . She also represented the past, the imprisonment, the uncertainty and mistrust.

In fairness, I paused to reflect on Lana's human and gentler side. I believed in her sincerity to find me well. I sensed she had lived with a longing to see me again. I also was convinced her visit wasn't for one quick fling. My own heart was stirred to realize a deep connection, a deep need for a communion, a joining to become one. . . . *Am I destined to fulfill this need?*

—

The Glockenspiel, part of the clock built into the tower of München's old administration building, makes the heart of the city. It depicts carved dancers that spin round and round. Long ago, they enticed the city's inhabitants to emerge from their self-inflicted incarceration during the days of the Black Plague.

Lana and I met on the wide sidewalk at the foot of the tower. I trusted Lana had come, as I did, to seek a new day, uninhibited and free. A day in search for common convictions and mutual understanding.

"You smell these pretzels?" I said. "Let's start the day simple. Fresh butter on a pretzel, washed down with hot tea."

"Simple." Lana smiled.

"You know, Lana, at first I had doubts of meeting again."

"Why?"

"Why? Well, . . . I'm not sure if I'm ready to start a journey I may not be able to control or slow down." I paused a moment. "It took time to blot from my mind the tumultuous years as a prisoner. I don't want to go back there. I don't want to recount, or be reminded of it. . . . Lana, I can't help it, but you are part of that time."

"But, you did decide to meet me."

"Yes, you alone, Lana. You and me, and not the System," I said.

"You mean you wanted to be with me, the person, not one that has to write a report?"

"Why yes, no reports. That, that is what drew me here this morning. No report. The more I thought about the years past, I realized I can't lay my distain for what I've gone through on you, or any one person." I held her hand facing her. "After coming back to Germany, I had to learn to dwell on the newness of my country. I had to reclaim the freedom I once preached to you."

"Franz, don't think I didn't hear your words about freedom long ago. I stayed up nights and tried to envision a world without constant dictates from one authority or another. The best nights of sleep came after I spoke to you freely about my youth and first love." She smiled as she recalled. "And," she continued, "even though I was emotionally on edge, I still slept well when I let go and revealed my heart about my neighbors and how they shunned me."

"I'm glad you did. Yes, I remember those times," I said. "Would you say we were free then, even if only for a short while?"

"Yes, those moments we were free. That is why I rested. I trusted you. I didn't have to fill out any report. You were like an anchor. A rock I could hold to."

We sat, enjoying the sun and each other. The languid morning, among people and life of the city, added a comfort that made it easy to continue to share.

Lana looked down at our clasping hands. "Franz, I'm so sorry about terminating our baby. Your response destroyed me. I . . . I could not wrap my mind around your reaction. After that poor decision on my part, my days shriveled to nothing; my nights to a cold emptiness." Lana's words faded to a whisper.

"Lana, when you first mentioned you being pregnant, I saw you as the mother of my child. You . . . you and I had a future. We were going to . . ." I took a deep breath and softly continued. "I recalled a few months earlier you said to me, 'What we have will never be out of season'. When I heard of our baby, those words became alive. Then suddenly, with one statement, they were smashed."

"Yes, I know those words well." She hung her head. "One foolish decision doused it all. "I'm so sorry. Looking back, Franz, my action wasn't worth the saving of that retched, almighty job."

"Your cold statement killed me, Lana. That day is when I set in motion a mindset, a determination, an unrelenting drive to be rid of all that coldness, that . . . that insensitivity."

"I know. I know," she whispered.

I felt Lana's hands tremble. Tears trailed down her cheek. "Lana, look at me, . . . that was a long time ago. I understand now." I reached to wipe her tears. "I'm sorry, I should not have been so cold."

"But, during that time when you withdrew, I also knew I had lost you." She pinched her lips. "I lost you. Nothing I did after any longer gave me any satisfaction. I wallowed in misery." I pulled my chair along side of hers and put my arm around her trembling shoulders.

Slowly we rose and walked from the sidewalk café. A pair of pigeons hopped in and delighted in a few pretzel crumbs. A deep breath cleared the tension. Again, as in years past, Lana tucked her arm into mine. The radiating sun encouraged us to stroll on. Not a word said, we let time remove to old. Neither one of us needed to ever let it rise again. Silence did the cleansing.

From the trolley, we switched to a train which brought us to the Starnberger See, a large lake, about thirty kilometers south of the city. The change of scenery, the clear water, sailboats in the distance, inviting benches combined to set the stage for peace of mind and more silent communication. Lana's face glowed in the afternoon sun. The breeze played in her hair. Her lashes' shadows cast a dreamy appeal.

"Lana, you said you don't like your assignment in East Berlin."

"Well, it's not because I'm away from home, it's more of the constant awareness of what I'm doing that is affecting me. I've tried to understand why people are leaving for the West. As I mulled that over and over, I realized the futility of my job." She looked at me searching. "You've made it Franz. Why can't . . .?" She didn't, nor did I finish the sentence, but it lingered in my mind.

We leisurely strolled along the shore, holding hands. Holding hands was new. A touch that seemed more affectionate than arm in arm. Her hands and fingers conveyed a new sensation, a quiet invasion. The mere touch of her fingers radiated understanding and forgiveness. I felt drawn—woven to her. The moment didn't require words. Witness to the silent closeness were a pair of brilliant white swans dancing at the water's edge.

"Lana, what are you thinking?" I asked as we settled to sit under a whispering willow tree.

I held to her hand, softly she said, "Franz, dare I say? . . . You are my rock, my every thought. I need you. . . . I . . ." Her head dropped, afraid to say more.

"Lana, today you became new to me. I realize we were destined to meet again. Emotions and desire is not the only pull. I also realize time will wash and rinse away the old barriers."

"Yes, time will wash away the old. . . ." She looked up, her eyes damp with tears, and said, "Franz, I love you!"

I had no words as she melted in my arms.

—

Monday afternoon, my mother, all perky and curious, said, "I'm glad you told me you might stay gone all night. I would have worried myself sick." Her questioning eyes met mine. "I hope you and your friends had a good time."

"It was great! Hadn't had a day and evening like it in a long time," I quipped, hoping Lana's perfume had dissipated during the day at work.

—

I answered Lana's first letter after our rendezvous. When others arrived, postmarked from Moscow, I was tempted to answer. However, I faced a wall. I couldn't see myself jumping deeper into a relationship thousands of kilometers apart.

With Lana on my mind, my enthusiasm to write to Marlena waned. When she sensed my vagueness, she reduced her responses. This saddened me. Lana also stopped writing. All options seemed to slip away. Friends at work and at the lodge filled my days, but the nights were long. I felt alone. Imaginary visions of my family, on another continent, emerged and added to my frustration. The hope was there, but I had years more to save toward a visit to America.

—

The week after my fifty-second birthday, I again received a letter from Lana, this one however, showed a stamp and postmark from West Berlin.

Dear Franz,
I hope this note finds you and your mother well.

I'm back in Berlin, this time West Berlin. I've made a major change in my life and in my career. In Moscow I felt like I was withering away. I could not stand it any longer. I welcomed my reassignment to Berlin. To be nearer to you was the grand prize.
I plan to come to München soon. There is so much new I need to share with you. Hope you will be happy to see me.

With love,
Lana

Only a week later, I answered the buzzer on a Friday evening. Lana stood at the door. Flabbergasted, with no other options, I invited her in to join Mother and me at the supper table.

"A pleasure to meet you, Mrs. Brunner." Lana announced with delight. "Franz told me about you for many years."

"I'm glad to finally put a face on the lady with the nice handwriting."

The only word I said thus far was, "Lana!"

33

The conversation between Lana and Mother rolled on like that of old friends. Leaned back in my chair, I absorbed it all in astonishment. My mother, obviously enjoying herself, kept on asking questions. When I pulled the string to turn the light on and went to the radiator to add a little heat, Lana got up and hinted that she must be going. I walked with Lana to the trolley stop.

"I didn't want to say anything with Mother present, but—"

"I know. I know. My appearance," Lana interrupted.

"Yes. You cut your hair. What happened?"

"Franz, I shed my biggest burden I ever dragged around."

"What are you saying? Your hair? I . . . I don't . . . ."

"I quit the System—made a run for it. I defected to the West." Wide-eyed she continued. "I couldn't keep it to myself. I needed to tell you in person."

"In your letter you mentioned a career change. You, you actually left Russia?"

"Yes, isn't it great?" She let escape a quick giggle.

Stunned. I plopped onto the trolley stop's bench. Lana sat close, her voice low and positive. "I cut my hair to add to the disguise."

"Disguise? Who are you hiding from?"

"Dmitri, the man who had been assigned to be my aid during the years of chasing the human traffickers. He is extremely frustrated and revengeful. With me having defected to the West, he sees an opportunity to gain a few points by hunting me down. To have me snagged, the System could prosecute me for treason." She paused and held her breath in nervous tension. "I have to be vigilant."

"Lana, this is insane. Can't you contact the authorities and escape this hound?"

"Well, I got a job that pays the rent. I can't leave the city," she said. Lana, rung her hands, took a deep breath, and continued. "I know Dmitri. He is a stalker. One of the best. Seen him hang around at places I did before my escape. He is looking for me, I'm sure."

"So sad. Why dress like a refugee here in München? You always looked so chic."

"Sorry. Walking to the train station to get here, with Dmitri out there, I had to blend in."

"Do you see an end to this looking over your shoulders?"

"Oh, he'll eventually get reassigned. The Know-it-alls in Moscow realize there isn't much to counteract the defections. I have to wait it out." She breathed a long sigh. "I have a few of my pretty things tucked away. I can't wear any of them now. At this point there isn't even anybody to impress." She briefly looked at me and smiled. Excited like a schoolgirl, she continued. "I left my place on the East side in a hurry. Couldn't take a chance to walk back there but only once. I managed to lug some treasured possessions to the new apartment in the British sector."

"You hopped from East Berlin to West Berlin and stayed?"

"Well, I personally knew some of the crossing guards because of my former job. Since I came right back the first time I crossed, they didn't think much about the second time I crossed over.

Once I permanently stayed in the West Sector, the move became more of a challenge. My first priority was to hide from my former team. Other than my hair and simple dress, I acted like anyone else that jumped the border. With sheer luck, I got a job at the immigration center because I speak three languages. The place where I stay for now it isn't much, but I'm hoping." She smiled, giving me an inviting glance.

Lana didn't seem sad or worried about her situation. However, I saw a forlorn and lonely woman. A woman who may have hit bottom materially, but who was on an emotional high of hope.

I rode the tram to the train station with her. Her one-day visit ended. Holding hands, we kissed good-bye.

"Are you going to answer my letters?" She asked, her hands under my arms as she slightly pressed her body against mine. "I'm now only a day's trip away."

The stage was set.

—

Like a restless tiger I took to the streets of the city. I walked and walked, then walked some more. The reemergence of Lana proved to be the turning page in my life, and the beginning of a new one. This time she did not show up at my door to satisfy her curiosity. She did not come to meet my mother; it was obvious she came to see me, and for me. I believed the quick half day visit was to seal my trust, to gain my devotion, to win my love. I also knew my time of pondering, weighing the odds, had run out. I had begun to see only the Lana of compassion, of understanding. I recalled how she clung close to my side as we walked the dimly lit streets of Moscow. I remembered the trust she placed in me, telling of her younger days, her disappointments of the two-faced comrades at the office. She seemed glad to share her struggles. I'm convinced the State had not ordered her to be by my side, her every waking hour, as I recuperated in the hospital. She did not have to share her meals and music when the rot of my mere existence worked to overwhelm me. Even then, I had the distinct feeling that she searched for a friend, a partner in life and for life.

My mother, aware of my struggle, offered no suggestions. I appreciated her wisdom. I, and I alone had to choose. I wrestled with the decision on whether to wait until I visited my children. . . . Or, . . . I chose a fresh beginning. The time had come. I needed Lana.

—

I asked my boss at work, "Walter, do you remember when I first returned from Russia? I asked you to let me accumulate vacation time."

"I do remember. You had plans to follow your family to America."

"Right. I hoped for an extended leave when the time came."

"I gather the time has come?" Walter asked, somewhat surprised.

"Yes and no. I do want to take some months off, but not to go to America. I need to work through some personal issues. I trust it'll be fine with you and the company?"

"Ah, well . . . Yes." Walter stammered with a halfhearted smile.

—

I pulled my heavy travel bag from the train and onto the square pavers of the platform in Berlin. West Berlin, an island of freedom in the dead sea of Communist-controlled East Germany. The station's bustle fed my excitement. People were alive, exuberant, and bubbling as they met friends and relatives not seen in years.

"Franz! Franz," an excited voice cried out. Lana weaved her way through the crowd. "I didn't see you at first, Franz. My heart is about to explode!"

"I'm here. Calm down, calm down, be still. Hold me." We stood clinging to each other. The world and its clamor abated. The new openness overwhelmed me. Holding her in my arms was different from ever before. It felt like being enveloped by the comfort and security of one's own home; a oneness in mind and soul. The shield had dropped. I felt victory over the old separating barriers that had never before let us commune with such joy.

"Franz, I've waited years for this day, the day you would come to me!" With complete innocence she looked at me. "You came to me! You can't imagine what this day means to me."

"Lana, this day *is* our day. The beginning to many. We're going to shape them—together!"

"Yes!" she cried out, as tears of joy flowed. "I could not have waited another day. Only memories kept me alive." Lana gripped my arm as we walked from the station.

Her flat, two flights up, was small and cold. The naked walls glared. Two chairs and a small metal-legged table, along with a cupboard for dishes, a gas stove, and an oak icebox completed the kitchen. The closed casement windows dampened the noise rising from the street below. In the bedroom, a shear curtain covered the window.

"Not much, is it?" she said with an inflection of shame.

"Lana, you are the one who fills these two rooms."

"I could only pack what a normal business trip would require. Although, I snuck as many personal treasures I could without raising suspicion."

"So, how did you handle the call back to East Berlin?"

"At first it tightened my gut. I despised the work during the previous stint. But the more I thought about it, putting you into the equation, the more I rejoiced at the opportunity."

"Did you plan to defect earlier?"

"Yes, yes!" she said. "The thought had entered my mind after I found you safe at your mother's. The time we spent together only reinforced my love for you and the need to be with you."

"I'm so happy this is happening," I said. "I never would have suspected this. You always showed loyalty to your work and the System."

"True. You know what, it was you and your staunch defense of a free people that started the questioning years ago. Even way back on the train coming from the mine, I admired your convictions."

"You still gave me a hard time."

"I know. . . . Those types of putdowns also bothered me, but they reinforced to my superiors my loyalty."

"You mean you even had to report trivial actions and short conversations?"

"Not all of them. I had to report when others were present, and document them in writing," she said with a hint of exasperation and disgust.

Lana stirred, obviously uncomfortable with the tone of the conversation. She took a deep breath and smiled. "Let's leave the past."

"You're right."

We shared a small bottle of lemon soda, cold from the icebox, using the same glass.

"This place is stale and clammy. Everything is so stark," she said as she opened the valve on the radiator. "Nothing looks and smells familiar. The few clothes hanging on the hook behind the door and on the bedroom wall don't do anything to warm up this bleak place. To see your hat and your violin helps. It reassures me you're here for real. My man. My love, why don't you unpack and add a little warmth?"

"You are so sweet when you beg me like that," I said smiling.

It seemed like half a lifetime since I shared a coat hanger with a woman. I draped my jacket and button-up sweater over her blouses. To touch and cover those silky garments made me want to touch, protect, and love this woman. I knew, had I truly died in the icy waters she would not have left her apartment, her life's one comfort, to come and live in a bare, upstairs flat in Berlin.

"What's going to happen to the rest of your belongings in Moscow?"

"I suspect all has been cleared out by now. Dmitri, as vengeful as he is, made sure of that. Chances are, if Dmitri doesn't get a promotion, he will also fly from the nest. Still, every morning before I leave this building, I put on a shabby coat over my work outfit and put on a black-rimmed pair of glasses."

"Sad you have to play the game even as a free woman."

"Not for much longer, I hope. I've checked my back and watched my trail. Nothing's going on. From now on I'll have you, my personal escort." She said with a coy smile.

"While these walls get warm, let's stretch out on the bed."

We laid close and held each other. Her breath was sweet in my nostrils as we absorbed the stillness. I felt her pulse against my chest. Her eyelashes batted my neck. The silence gently wrapped a oneness around us.

"I need you," she whispered. "I am so alone without you . . . hold me."

—

Lana insisted I meet her supervisor at work in the British sector of the city. The building served as a processing center for escapees. She and nearly a dozen others directed desperate people to temporary shelters. Lana verified and processed legal papers and then created proper documentation for an orderly evacuation to West Germany and beyond. Her language skills helped speed up communication. She obviously became an asset to the process.

Back at the apartment, breaking a blissful silence, Lana said, totally open, "You know, before I defected, each time, as I returned to my room in the East sector, I tried to understand the 'why' of the great exodus.

"It's called freedom," I said. "A chance for personal and spiritual enrichment. Lana, your move took a whole bunch of fortitude. I'm fifty-three. I know you're not far behind. You could have played your role and retired with relative comfort."

"I know, but I had you. You were out there!" She said with excitement.

I came to the bed and knelt on the floor to face her. "Oh my sweet thing," was all I could say.

She reached and held my face with both of her hands. "I could not let my life dwindle toward meaningless oblivion, toward ravaging despair, and end up in a ward," she said, her voice broken. "I love you, Franz!"

"I love you, Lana. I need you." She pulled my head to her bosom as tears of joy bathed the moment. Softly I said, "We're together. We are sealed, Lana. Our love is the glue." The moment was precious as it lingered, giving the words their time to blend with the joy within.

We both went to the kitchen to prepare a pot of tea. "Franz, I'm through dodging, tiptoeing. I want to settle. To be with you is all I need."

"Yes, settled. Settled is a good word," I said.

"I know you look forward to meeting your children," Lana said excitedly. "That should be our first goal together. It is part of your purpose, your saga. I want to be part in seeing its fulfillment."

"That's a big goal. I love you for wanting to help me see it through."

—

We explored the city of Berlin with pleasure and curiosity. One evening, leaving the din of a busy thoroughfare, we ducked into a quiet side street. The last darts of the setting sun struck the gables and chimneys ahead of us.

"Before it gets dark, I want you to see what the fanatics have begun to do to this city."

As if dropped from the sky, there in front of us loomed a wall that sealed off the road. A wall ominous in size and threatening. We walked parallel to the taunting structure.

"How could any leader in this day in history think such a cold structure will stop the exodus of people? If anything, it will generate even more defiance and determination."

"Sickening, isn't it?" Lana concurred. "This hideous thing, when finished, will stretch through the heart of the city for over forty kilometers. That's besides the one-hundred-forty kilometers of razor wire around Berlin."

"It's insane!" I breathed in disgust. "It'll cut off families, friends, and all that is normal."

"You're right. People lost their livelihoods not being able to cross over." Annoyed, eyes wide, Lana continued to make her point. "Let me show you exactly what I mean."

From a terrace we saw the madness unfolding. Over in the East sector, bulldozers had cleared a hundred-meter swath, eradicating all structures and trees. Beyond that, one could still see devastated and crumbling buildings scarred by the bombings of more than fifteen years earlier, a stark comparison to the rapid renaissance of West Berlin. The wall in progress stretched down the center of roads, leaving only a segment of the road for use on the West side. Makeshift floodlights glared on the eastern side as men worked into the early night, ever adding to the ugly barrier.

We walked home in silence. Lana heated yesterday's potato soup. I cradled my violin and added to the sadness we'd witnessed.

"Is it ever going to end?" I asked, dipping buttered bread into warm soup. "Over eight million Germans dead and twice as many Russians. Six million Jews annihilated. Countless Poles and Allied Forces slaughtered and maimed. Yet the killing goes on. Innocent human beings wanting to better themselves are mowed down trying to cross a border. Lana, this is after the so-called war to end all wars!"

"Yes, I know," Lana concurred. "To this day tens of thousands with dissenting voices still vanish to the unknowns of Siberia. Thank God we're not one of these. We are alive. We have our limbs. We have each other." She concluded with a smile.

"You're right."

"Why don't you play something to cheer us up while I wash the dishes?"

34

The barren apartment soon became a home. Perky geraniums, floral curtains, a cross-stitched tablecloth, and pastoral paintings added a smile to our simple life.

Within a month, four stout men hefted Lana's secondhand prize up the thirty-two steps. We giggled tuning the old upright. I practically crawled into the thing while she struck the keys. In gratitude for being rescued from the junk heap, the old piano soon returned melodies that coddled the soul.

The reunion of Lana and her music lifted her spirit; confirmed by the mellow lilt in her voice and lightness in her step. Our love danced with harmony and passion. The old lexicon lay permanently open, displaying two dried daffodils, stems crossed.

—

Lana brought home a typewriter with its keys jammed and bungled up.

"See if you can do something with this thing," she said. "If you can give it new life, and we get the word out, I believe you can make a few marks."

"Hey, I like your entrepreneurial spirit. Part of freedom, you know." I grinned. "To earn a little money wouldn't be bad," I said. "For a fellow like me, only getting in the groceries and peeling potatoes gets old."

I fixed the typewriter. The extra few marks reminded me when Lana put some money in my hand on the way from the mine to Moscow.

—

In Berlin, the dividing wall temporarily dampened the flow of escapees. Within months, however, the exodus rerouted itself to more rural areas and to less-guarded sections in the border fence.

Lana introduced me to the staff of a makeshift infirmary. A place where the wounded who got shot or injured, while escaping, were treated. She had contact with the workers there because her position at the immigration center. All the folks at the infirmary required follow-ups and needed help to resettle. The volunteer's clinic was hidden from the busy thoroughfares and not regulated by any government oversight.

Her frequent visits to the clinic gave me an opportunity to accompany her. I recognized the value of such a service to the downtrodden and offered my free time. Soon I became part of the operation. My mind struggled to think of the many who were shot, dragged back behind the security zone, and left to die for lack of medical attention.

The clinic operated in the American zone and received funding and manpower by a joint effort of volunteers of the Allied Forces. The doctors gave of their time while off duty. An average of two GIs a day donated blood. As a volunteer, my job consisted mostly of a helping-hands position.

—

Lana and I became one in spirit. Our words flowed from the heart. I knew before she spoke what was on her mind. Being involved with rescue missions, we heard fascinating stories of daredevil escapes. In the evenings and on our walks, those stories became the bulk of our conversation.

"When I first came to East Berlin," Lana said, "I established my base in the Soviet sector. It didn't take long to piece together that several sophisticated networks and rings of operatives worked behind most of the high-ranking escapes. I imagine they are to this day."

"I gather you no longer try to crack their plots?"

"No, not at all. Back in those days I dreaded to fill out report after report, always having to admit I didn't make any headway. My entire effort became an embarrassment. I lost my zeal. However, strange as it may sound, I found myself cheering for the brave souls' success. Amazing then, and still is, those rings of operatives reach into every city east of here and even to Moscow. To move people, they modified supply trucks, created false bottoms in rail cars and delivered folks right into the center of Berlin. They recruited enough men inside the military to gain access to tear gas and even uniforms. They worked in teams with stealth and sophistication. Two or three would subdue the guards on duty while another drove the truck through the gate. They always knew how to disarm the electric fence or cross-wire the gate to have it open for an easy drive through. I know of an operation that uses fishing vessels to shuttle escapees. They'd switch them to Swedish or other Western boats in the middle of the Baltic Sea."

"So it wasn't only an individual's effort to attempt to cross the border? Interesting," I said.

"No, not always. Hired teams often directed the mission. On occasion, when an escape failed, the Soviet puppets took the wounded back to their respective towns and paraded them in the streets, bandaged and bloody, for all to see in hopes to discourage others."

I never saw Lana so emotionally charged, like a pot boiling over.

"I heard the saboteurs and operatives most often referred to as the S-gang," Lana continued. "The name of Mr. S often emerged as the mastermind behind most of the innovative stunts. No one I know has ever met this 'Mr. S.' I never found out his full name or out of what area or city he operated. I do admire his cunning, his sophistication, and that he never intentionally harmed an adversary."

We kept walking along the stark wall. Its imposing mass gave deep credence to Lana's stories. She continued.

"After I found the apartment I sneaked back to the East sector to retrieve more of my belongings, like I told you. I wasn't scheduled to return to Moscow for several more months. Since I spent the last of my money on the deposit for the flat, I had to have a job. I had known about the processing center and decided to use its services for myself. While there, acting all new and helpless, I asked where to find work. I was given a form to fill out. When the man glanced at my list of languages I spoke, he had me sit down and wait a moment. After a few more questions, and a ten-minute interview with an older man behind a big desk, I got my current job."

"Just like that?"

"Yup!" Lana stopped, slipped her gloved hands under my Loden coat collar. "You know the major deciding factor in my defection?" She asked, then softly answered herself. "You drove me crazy when you didn't answer my letters from Moscow. I could not let you slip away."

"Lana, I'm not going to slip away. I'm sticking. I want to be a part of your life, our life. All new and fresh. I'm ready to join in helping the gutsy folks who risk all. I want to be part—"

Pop—pop—pop . . . shots rang out—close by—on the other side of the wall. Searchlights scanned near us. A blip of the light's beam illuminated a person's hand on top of the wall grasping for its edge on our side. We rushed to see fingers desperately clinging to the wall, clinging to life itself.

"HILFE! HILFE!" I cried out to anyone near.

Two young men came running.

"We've got to help him! Pull him over." I screamed, pointing at the person's hand, high on the wall, cramped and holding on. "Can the two of you push me up?"

In no time I stood on a pair of shoulders and had hold of the desperate man's hand. Pulling on the hand achieved nothing.

"Can you shove me higher." I yelled.

Within seconds my shoe was cupped in a trembling, strong hand that pressed higher and higher until I pulled myself onto the top of the wall. . . . The determined searchlight prowled another path. . . . The man hanging had carefully chosen a spot of the wall under construction. The shadow of a large piece of machinery hid him from spotlights and more gunfire. I lay in the open on top of the wall. My black coat did not signal to the sniper on guard. The clinging body's other hand was wrapped in the loop of a rope, which he apparently had slung over the uncompleted wall. He hung there, too weak to pull himself up and conquer the wall. While the searchlight made its round, I kneeled, grabbed hold of the man's coat collar, and yanked his body until it sprawled on top of the wall.

"*Still! Das Licht kommt wieder!*" I warned in a coarse whisper.

Collars up, we covered our white skin and lay motionless. The light scanned passed us. One more heave and one leg flopped onto the wall. I reached for the other leg. It was limp, wet. Blood dribbled out the bottom of his pants. I pushed him over the top and gently let him drop to more than two men at the bottom of the wall who waited to catch him. . . . The searchlight prowled again. . . .

"I'm coming down," I yelled, as the blaze of the beam hit my face. The beam stopped and scanned back to where my face had been. Shots ended the encounter as my feet touched the ground.

"My Franz! My Franz," Lana cried out.

"He is losing blood! His left leg!" I breathed, cutting and ripping open the man's pants to find the injury.

One of two wounds below the knee showed more torn flesh than the other, a ricochet from the same bullet. With Lana's scarf we tied off the leg above the knee to slow the blood loss. All involved in the rescue knelt around the man, observing and ready to help.

To everyone gathered I said, "Thanks for helping this stranger. One more free!"

"Glad to do it." Was the general response.

"We'll take him home. I promise he will see a doctor."

One man helped carry the man to our apartment. The wounded fellow was a ghastly pale. When Lana held his head and had him drink a cup of hot tea with honey, his color returned, and the fright in his bulging eyes eased. If rescue had not come, he would have crumpled into a pile at the base of the wall—on the wrong side. "One more fool who did not learn," they would have taunted.

Both of us felt capable of stabilizing the man until morning. We cleaned and bandaged his wounds, slowly loosened the tourniquet, and watched over him throughout the night. Bedrich was his name, a Polish fellow. He spoke a smattering of German.

Early in the morning he ate all the bread and butter he wanted along with hot milk and honey. We took him to the clinic. Holding to the two of us, he managed to hop to the subway station and on to the hospital. The crew spotted us as we approached the building. The door swung open and a stretcher on wheels waited. As Lana and I wheeled the stretcher into the ward, all attention focused on the new arrival. A woman and a bushy-haired man in white coats hurried to met the gurney. As if running into an invisible fence, the man with the unruly hair abruptly turned to walk away. Lana didn't notice the strange action. I too didn't gave it thought at the time.

Bedrich recovered well. The bullet had nicked the bone, but not enough to require a cast. After a week's worth of rest, he rejoiced being able to hobble around on crutches. His cheerfulness was contagious, and always the center of the lively card games. One could hear him cackle from every corner of the ward. He initiated a game he called crutchball. A simple game of soccer kicked only with one's crutch and on one leg. The day before his release he joined us at home for supper. As tears glistened in his eyes, he clutched our hands and thanked us for saving his life. Lana explained the new documents and directed him to several charity organizations that would help set him on the right track toward freedom.

The volunteer work at the hospital was gratifying, especially during hectic times when those with multiple wounds arrived. Within minutes of a call for help the volunteer doctors and nurses came to a screeching halt in their Volkswagens or bicycles. They washed up and hustled to the operating room as if wolves were after them. Before their arrival, the one full-time nurse diagnosed the injury and then gave the doctors her initial findings. Most often the need called for bullet removal, a blood transfusion, setting of bones, or first aid for burns. During calmer times, patients lay and recuperated along a full-length window wall on the south side of the building.

A certain U.S. Army supply truck driver sparked my interest. Ferdinand Zimmermann, a strapping young American soldier, said his home was in Wisconsin. He originally was an immigrant from Ulm, Bavaria. I enjoyed conversations with him from the day we met. He plucked a string in my heart. He enlisted in the army to serve his new found country. Zim, they called him, drove his truck route from Hamburg to Berlin two days a week, the clinic being his last stop. A simple cot suited him well enough to spend the night before he returned to Hamburg. He enjoyed helping folks during the hours he stayed who'd risked their lives to be free. He always told of his blessings not having to take such drastic actions to enjoy his freedom.

"Zim," I said, speaking in German, "How did you wind up in America?"

"Well, it's sort of an unexpected thing. I was in eighth grade in Ulm when one day my mother received a letter from her long-lost brother in America offering to sponsor us. Pay for the trip and all."

"What do you mean a long-lost brother?"

"My mother had lost contact with him during the war. We always moved a lot, changed addresses. An American soldier from Wisconsin started the process. He played soccer with us kids in Ulm. When he said he was from Wisconsin, the word stuck in my ear. My mother had mentioned it before. She came to the playground and talked with the American soldier. He promised Mom to find my uncle when he got back to America. Two years later a letter came and everything changed."

"Your father go with you?"

"I had no father at the time. He never came home from the war." He hung his head for a moment then smiling said, "It was a good move, though. I got me a new dad in America. I didn't remember my real dad. Mom got a few letters from him, but then they stopped."

"Have you any sisters?"

"Nope, no sisters or brothers. My new dad really spoiled me, spent much time with me. He was firm though. Made me conscious of others and proud of my new country."

"Those are good things. You can't ask for a better dad." I kept him talking.

"Yep, you got that right. My mother loves to cook and dote on him. As I've said, it was a good move."

"You like army life?"

"Yep, it's good so far. Don't get to see my folks that often. I got to visit Ulm, the place where I grew up. Got to see my old school friends. Kicked a real soccer ball around. We had a great time."

This young man had it all together. Love for his stepfather and mother. Love for his new country. Love for his job as a soldier. . . . *He never knew his true father and all things turned out well.*

"Zim, who runs this hospital?" I asked, changing the subject. "Is it the head nurse?"

"In a way she does. I think behind most of the stuff going on, the flow of hurt folks coming, it's the guy with the bushy hair. He sure does plenty of flitting around on his machine away from this place."

"What do you mean?"

"He drives a NSU motorcycle—with a side car. Hauls wounded folks to this place."

"Who does he work for?" I tried not to show too much curiosity.

"I don't think anybody knows. He doesn't talk much, but he smiles a lot. He is mighty tight with some army folks, British and American. They meet often when he is in. His office is behind the two mirrors in the wall."

"What's his name? Do you think I could meet him?"

"He is hard to catch," said Zim. "He wants to blend in, I think. I don't see too many hanging close to him. He's friendly but keeps his distance." He continued. "I've heard the nurse call him Lev. Don't sound like an English name. He must speak English, though."

"Ferdinand doesn't sound English either and you speak English." We had a good laugh.

—

Christmas of 1961 culminated with gratitude. Lana and I got married. The justice of the peace rounded up two witnesses. A small sum of money for the marriage certificate sealed the ceremony. My purpose in life found its fulfillment. Contentment became the ultimate reward. Lana became my rock, together in spirit and goals.

That Christmas in Berlin also rekindled childlike hopes and dreams. Lana shopped the specialty stores to find her favorite goodies, which she hadn't had since she left her childhood home. She baked gingerbread cookies and a Christmas loaf. A dark molasses bread with raisins, nuts, and fennel seeds. We sipped hot, spiced red wine. Lana called it *Gloegg*.

On Christmas Eve we held hands during the midnight candlelight service. The pastor's words of comfort were on the coming of the Christ. Leaving the church, she turned to me and said, "Sweetheart, I must confess, the singing tonight was special. I closed my eyes and saw angels sing. I saw them through the same heart as you must have seen them when you found solace in the old church in Moscow." She whispered, "I'm sorry I shattered your Christmas dream then."

"Sweetheart, the old has passed. We promised not to dwell on it any longer."

"You're right; all things are new." She placed a small item, wrapped in brown paper, on the table. "Here, my love, a little something from me. Smiling, she looked at me with the flicker of the candle in her eyes. Open it. Go on." I took my time. She watched in silence.

"Awesome. Great. Thanks," I blurted out. "Sweetheart, this is a mighty fancy watch for an older dude like me."

"Older dude? Come on now. You can out-shimmy most youngsters. You are my debonair man, my rock, who is worth all I have. Merry Christmas—my man," she said, and gave a coy little shrug of her shoulders.

"I love it. I never had a wristwatch before. I might retire the old pocket watch."

"Good. I don't see how you could tell the time with those cracks in the glass."

"I know. I did though for the last fifteen years. Here, open your present." Lana sat at the kitchen table, fondled and turned the little wrapped box, gently fingering the silky red bow. Over and over she felt the wrapper, the bow, the shape of the box.

Her voice quavered. "Franz, if I open it, will Christmas be over? I don't ever want it to end. I have not received a Christmas gift since I was a child. Ah, yes! A homemade dress, cookies, a couple of oranges. I got a bar of chocolate one year. I remember marzipan. Yes, marzipan. I haven't had any of it in a long time either."

"Lana, Christmas won't end. This is our beginning. Open your present."

Slowly, her hands slightly trembling, she opened it. Lana got up from the table, took a few steps toward the window, and then turned to face me. She held the hanging gold necklace to her breast.

"It is beautiful. It's precious." Her eyes sparkled, pearls of tears clung to her cheeks. "Thank you, Love."

A local goldsmith created the necklace. He hammered and carved the pendant combining two daffodils, stems crossed, held together by a rim in the shape of a vase.

We lay on the bed. Two Christmas candles flickered on the nightstand. The traditional heated red wine punch in us added to the glow of the evening.

Suddenly, Lana straightened up and announced, "The last fifteen years? That doesn't add up. You didn't have a watch back at the mine."

"Oh yes, I did!" I grinned. "I had it stashed in my waistband. Wore it while on the train with you. You can imagine how good it felt to have pulled something over on the 'Authorities.'"

"You sly little devil. I love you all the more." She nuzzled her head on my chest.

We stretched the holiday well into the New Year. We giggled and made music together, the Christmas tree a witness. We slept in clouds of bliss. The world danced.

—

A young mother and her three-year-old son arrived at the hospital in the NSU sidecar. She had suffered severe lacerations and a bullet that dangerously lodged in her chest cavity. The child lost sections of his hair when pulled from the spiraled barbed and razor wire fence. I pitied the woman, but respected her immense determination. Lana felt drawn to visit the young mother and spent time sitting close, holding her hand. The doctor removed the bullet, but her fever failed to drop. She drifted in and out of consciousness. While Lana communed with Fania, the mother, I played with her son, an adorable young tyke. Again, the bushy-haired man entered the ward and abruptly turned to walk back to his office. This time I followed him and knocked on his office door.

"Come in," was the sharp answer. The man stood behind his desk, his back to me, as he watched Lana through the mirror glass windows.

"What is that woman doing here?" He snapped in broken German. "I saw you with her."

Trying to calm his alarm, I said, "She is trying to cheer the hurting folks out there."

"I know," he said more harshly, showing a hint of paranoia. "Why does she keep coming here? I saw her several weeks ago. What is she after?"

"We came here to comfort the young mother out there."

"Comfort, huh?" He growled. Expecting an explanation, he spun around to face me.

"Father!" He breathed in shock and sank to his chair.

"Nikolai! My son, I didn't know. . .," I managed to cry out, holding onto the doorknob.

Nikolai sobbed. His head rested on his arms on the desk. I walked to him and placed a reassuring hand on his shoulder.

"It's all right," I whispered. He struggled to get up to meet my hug. An overwhelming joy burned in me.

"Can we sit?"

He waved his arm toward a group of small chairs. "It's, . . . Tatilana Popova out there!" He pointed with gritted teeth. "The Soviet agent. I know she snoops around in Berlin. She constantly hounds me and looks to silence our operations. Why are you with her?"

"Nikolai, calm your fear. Her days of working for the Soviets are over."

"But . . .?"

"I know this is a shock. You must believe me. She is on our side."

Nikolai looked at the floor and then into my eyes. He turned to stare through the window in silence. After sitting again, he mumbled, "On my side. . .?"

"Son," I said, "she and I've started a new life together. She is my wife." Nikolai, still in shock and lost for words, I continued, "Can I ask her in? . . . Or should I leave you alone?"

"Don't leave me . . .. It's, it's all right . . . ask her in," he managed to say as he ran his long fingers through his hair.

35

The hours spent at the hospital were challenging, and at times pleasant. Too often, though, Nikolai rolled in on his motorcycle with a wounded escapee clinging to his back and the sidecar filled with a mate or a friend critically wounded. Contrasting such cruel realities was the three-year-old Anatoly, who cackled and frolicked with the staff, while his mother fought for her life.

"What will happen should the little fellow's mother die?" I asked Nikolai.

"I hate to have to consider that. We have adoption programs." Nikolai turned in his chair and watched the boy play. "We'd first dig to see if a relative may have crossed to the West before him. I'd never recommend sending him back. He may have a grandmother back home, but most often he'd end up in an orphanage. That's not good."

"He sure is a happy boy," I said. "He doesn't know how gravely ill his mamma is."

"You and Lana are worried about that, aren't you?"

"Yes, it's painful to see her wither away. I hope a good family will adopt the curly headed tyke, should she pass," I said. "He is a little younger than my boy Peter when I last saw him."

"Don't be sad, Father." Nikolai whispered. "Your boy and girl in America are doing well, you said in your letter several years ago."

"Yes, I know, but I didn't get to watch them grow up."

—

The postman delivered an oversized envelope from my mother, not the norm.

My dearest Franz,

I know you and Lana are happy. This makes me happy. I must say, though, that I miss you here with me. I'm plugging along as best I can. Zenta, my sister, and I get together and share stories about our ailments. Good thing she is close by. I'm sending you two letters from the Lady in Garmisch. Didn't want to let any more time pass. I pray you two come to visit soon.

Your loving mother

"I think my mother is beginning to fail. She is not as steady with the pen."

"Your mother misses you. It'd be good to chat with her again."

"I'd say so. The last time you two didn't get done," I said. Lana smiled.

"Let's plan to visit soon. And while there, we could check into the requirements for us to travel to see your children in America."

"Hum. A good point. It doesn't hurt to find out," I said, welcoming the idea.

I read both of Marlena's letters out loud. Lana was interested, and in no way showed any jealousy toward the other woman.

"Marlena has a man friend. Well, why not?" I said. "After you dropped off the daffodils, my writing to her became a bit mundane."

"Ah yes, daffodils do their thing," she said smiling.

"I wish Marlena well. She is still young enough to start a new life."

"Looks like we missed a chance to see them both when they came to München to see Benjamin at the university," said Lana.

"I didn't miss anything. I've all I want right here," I said. "She is a remarkable woman, though."

"Kind hearted, from what you've told me."

"That she is."

—

The maimed kept coming, along with death. Fania gave up her fight. I had the privilege of taking her to the morgue. That evening Lana suggested we take little Anatoly home with us.

"We could comfort him when he realizes his mother is no longer around," she said.

Coming home with us became the routine. Anatoly went to the hospital with me in the morning to be among familiar faces. His presence was medicine to all who were recuperating. He also loved coming home with me. Lana researched the boy's possible family connections but found no definite relatives.

Anatoly's favored pastime was looking out the window, watching the traffic below. Apparently, he never lived in an upstairs flat or saw cars before. We chuckled as he stood on a stool and perused the world. He'd have his little feet crossed and wiggle his toes whenever something interesting passed by on the street below. Cars always drew a little chatter and giggles out of him. I bought two little metal race cars. We'd raced them down a cardboard ramp propped from a kitchen chair. He cackled and ran in circles, smacking his bare feet on the terrazzo floor.

When Lana played the piano, he scooted close and snuggled to her side. Mesmerized by the music, he'd reach for the keys to add his own melodies. My violin playing usually put him to sleep. The routine of the days settled rich and deep. The boy slept against the wall next to me.

"Take a look at this," Lana said. "This is a list of children in one orphanage in Bremen. Seventy-two children, ten years old and younger. Many of them of deceased escapees. Is Anatoly ready to be stuck away like that?"

"How long is the adoption process?" I asked.

Lana did not answer.

I continued the rambling and tried to put in perspective the sad and intriguing situation.

"In an orphanage he'd be but a pebble in a gravel pile. How would he grow? How could he blossom?"

"Franz, something better than an orphanage is awaiting the boy. I can feel it."

"He's not a bother. Is he?" I said. "We'll take care of him until the authorities give us other directions."

—

My typewriter repair business grew to include fixing adding machines and cash registers. The space under the bed became my warehouse for parts. A board on a stack of old bricks was my workbench. We had to dance around equipment on our bedroom floor. I know it was an unattractive situation, but Lana never said a word.

When the folks at the infirmary found out I was in the office machine repair business, A new onslaught of work hit the apartment. I stayed so busy, my volunteering shrunk to a few hours a week. I raised the price for my work, hoping it would curtail the flow of new jobs, but that didn't dampen the business either.

I spoke to Nikolai about it. "You know the new business I fell into?" I said.

"Yea, the one of fixing stuff?"

"It has gotten a little out of hand. The money is good, saving toward America you know, but I don't get the time to work here at the clinic as much as I'd like to."

"Well," Nikolai smiled, "looks like you're up to your old love. Tinkering that is." He waited for me to say what was on my mind.

"It feels good I must admit," I said. "I've got a problem, though, "I can't walk around the apartment anymore without falling over typewriters and stuff."

"So, you need space and want more time at the clinic."

"Yup."

"Come to think of it, the back storeroom is full of boxes scattered all over the floor." He stopped and pondered some more. "If I could talk somebody into donating some shelving, and get that stuff off the floor, you could set up shop in there."

"Hey, that sounds good," I said. "It'll take care of both problems. I'll be right here when action breaks out. I like that. Thanks."

—

Anatoly enjoyed playing with the discarded parts. He built imaginary bridges and things. Instead of walking the streets of Berlin, we stayed busy playing with Anatoly in the park or by the river. Snacking at all hours, as we had gotten use to, we set aside in support of a more regimented time for family meals with our dimpled new addition. Love glued us all together.

—

The hospital accepted a donated Jeep. It sprang into action immediately to transport wounded escapees. Nikolai bestowed the motorcycle to me, to an old fellow, a true potion of youth. It didn't change my graying hair, but it sure made me strut a little bowlegged. Feeling a bit cocky, I scooted around the perimeter of West Berlin, connected with our secret checkpoints, and hauled the wounded.

As Lana and I became more privy to Nikolai's plans and schemes. Our hearts and minds were drawn ever closer to his operations, which always added to being more involved.

"Why don't the two of you think about joining me on a deep-sea fishing trip?" Nikolai asked one evening as we headed out the door.

We pondered Nikolai's question while eating supper, Lana asked, "Why would he ask us to go fishing?"

"This hardly sounds like a vacation," I said. "You recall he said, 'to think about it.'"

"Obviously he wants us to discuss it," said Lana. "It is another way of suggesting to spread our range of thinking and learn more of the overall scope of his operations."

"I get what you're saying. It's a test. He wants us to tell him what he is up to. He is testing us to see if we and he are thinking alike. I venture to say his plans are to introduce us to much bigger roles in the human rescue effort."

"That almost sounds illegal," Lana said. "But isn't it exciting."

—

Nikolai kept the fishing trip quiet. No discussions, other than the day of departure.

Our military Jeep, with its three civilian occupants, scooted through the city's free zone to the border checkpoint. Nikolai presented the proper permits to the East German guards, who obviously knew him. We stepped from the vehicle so it could be inspected. Our papers as employees of the British and American occupation forces, although unpaid volunteers, counted as sufficient. The border guards of West Germany stopped the Jeep again, the body count renewed. The allotted time for travel from checkpoint to checkpoint was verified according to the stamped pass.

In Wolfsburg we parked the Jeep and boarded a train to Lübeck, then on to Travemünde, a small fishing town on the Baltic sea. Altogether a long day.

"Nikolai," I said, "on the way here we reminisced a lot. Now that we're looking at the Baltic sea, I want to know who brought the fishing poles?" We had a good laugh.

Lana pressed on. "We're not out to catch fish, are we? Two-legged fish, maybe? We don't know how. We're positive they're not going to wash up on shore."

Nikolai straightened his shoulders, and with confidence he explained. "Now with Lana on my side, I no longer have to watch my back as much. However, there are still plenty of diehard followers of the State trying to impress their superiors. It is not a free border by any stretch." He took a deep breath. "From now on, I would like very much for both of you to take on more challenging roles. I am convinced, with your backgrounds, you're capable of outsmarting the humdrum brains who guard the border."

Our fishing boat, along with others, headed for deep waters when the dark of night took over. For hours the crew labored with precision and skill as they pulled in their nets, with amazing results. Around midnight, however, all engines were silenced. The crew curtailed all fishing activities and stood at the stern, staring. The captain sent repeating yellow blips of light into the darkness. The only sounds intruding the stillness were the waves' gentle kisses against the hull of the ship. Inky black night blended with the deep waters. An intermittent eerie glow streamed from a cigarette the captain sucked. The yellow blips continued. Everyone stood listening and strained to get a glimpse. A glimpse of what I was not sure. My heart raced, stretched by strange expectations. Then the men stirred. I strained the harder to see, but I saw nothing. Two crew members untied the small dinghy. Within seconds the little boat bobbed in the water attached by a rope. I continued to scan the blackness. Nothing.

Lana tugged on my coat, "Listen!"

First a hum, then a low buzz. A boat similar to ours appeared out of the dark. One of the men gave the dinghy a shove toward the other vessel. I heard a slight thud. A life ring from the other boat, attached to a rope, landed in the dinghy. In silence, men dressed in black pulled the dinghy toward the other boat. In no time, four huddling persons were pulled toward us. With practiced ease two men helped the newcomers on board. The sequence repeated. Eight persons soon disappeared into the lower deck of our vessel. The captain removed a small sack attached to the life ring. He then threw the ring back into the water. Not a word broke the silence.

Back in the harbor, before the nights catch of fish was unloaded and weighed, the human cargo stepped on land in a dimly lit inlet. Later, once Nikolai settled with the fishermen, we darted to join the liberated folks in the shadows. All stared, eyes wide open, hair disheveled, obviously frightened. Each of the defectors carried his or her life's belongings in a small satchel. Nikolai distributed tickets for the train ride to Wolfsburg. There, the eight new arrivals would be given an address and directions to receive help in the relocation process.

In Wolfsburg, Lana, Nikolai and I stretched out along a wall at the train station and slept a few hours. As we drove back to Berlin I asked Nikolai, "Tell us, how did the folks manage to get on board the other ship?"

"This is where the gall of the operatives comes in," he said. "At least one if not two of the boat's crew are not fishermen. They travel throughout East Germany, Poland, and even Russia and communicate with other groups in the network to land these high-priced fish."

"You mean you make money trading people?" Lana asked.

"No, no. The fee covers the cost from wherever to Wolfsburg. Both of the boat captains receive a little to make it worth their while. The operation you witnessed we developed for the more affluent. As for how they got on the boat without being spotted is a matter of location, time, and water level. For the venture you've witnessed, we found a fishing village with piers along the backside of a seawall. The base of the wall, its footing, is exposed at low tide, creating a narrow ledge, or walkway, to the boat. The escapees, along with their hired guides, arrive in the village at different intervals. They wait for darkness, then one by one, when the water's ebb is cooperating, they scurry like frightened rats along the footing of the wall to the boat. With the tide out, the boat itself is far below the dock. The pier's lighting only strikes the captain's upper bridge. A rope ladder hangs in the shadow from the side of the boat to help them on board. One of the mates shoos them into the belly of the boat. Simple."

"Nikolai Sakharov, are you the mystery Mr. S?" Lana asked.

"You may believe so," Nikolai said, not taking his eyes off the road.

"Really?" Lana exclaimed. "I'm gonna have to give you a hug. I've been admiring your cunning for quite some time."

"You better wait till we get out of this Jeep." We all had a laugh as we continued on toward Berlin.

The apartment, being shut tight while on the deep-sea mission, took on a musty smell. Soon however, the teakettle whistled and the simmering lentil and ham soup filled the room with its aromas. Lana's curtains flowed in the early summer breeze. The din of the city became our music. We ate in silence, missing little Anatoly.

"Do you think he pined for us?"

"Probably not. Not for one night," I said. "Two nights he may think we shuffled him off."

"Let's get that little tyke. Now! Hurry. We'll finish the soup when we get back."

Anatoly's rosy cheeks glowed. He only spoke of his mother when reminded by some silly thing. Keeping the boy busy and curious made my heart swell. Together we watched a pair of swallows build a nest under the eaves and later observed them feed their eager young. Whenever a new morsel arrived and he heard the chirping, he giggled. Anatoly became the glue in our life. He filled in voids and crevices in our daily routine as well as in our souls. We too had built our nest.

Lana took a folder from her briefcase and spread its contents on the table. "Look at this."

The information plainly stated Anatoly's assignment to an orphanage in Nürnberg, in the American sector. Transportation would be by train. One additional adult roundtrip ticket would be paid for by the agency."

My heart sank. An overwhelming weight dragged me down. We both stared at the boy as he stood on his small stool and happily looked out the window.

"What now?" I asked with a lump in my throat.

"Franz, we knew this was coming."

"I know. Yet it's so unexpected. You're not glad the day has come?" I said.

"No! Can you think of another option?"

"I . . . I can't imagine Anatoly in an orphanage. Can you?"

"Are we picturing a Soviet orphanage?" Lana asked.

"No matter what. An orphanage means he will be gone. . . . Gone! I wish he could be . . . around for a while longer."

"How long?" Lana asked as she retrieved an envelope from the nightstand. "Here sweetheart, I already filled in everything."

"Adoption papers?"

"All you have to do is sign also . . . look," Lana pointed, "his name could be Anatoly Brunner. He'll be four years old in September. You'd have your boy back the way you left him!"

We became a family of four. Nikolai, always eager to join us for Sunday dinner, insisted on taking his little brother to the park afterward. He spent hours playing and teaching Anatoly to kick a soccer ball. I tried my skill in making a kite. *It's a Brunner thing!*

* * * * *

Epilogue

Could my story have taken place? Why not? Many German prisoners, given the chance to live, made new lives for themselves in Russia.

Did this book remove my soul's anxieties and did it satisfy my hope? No. It brings to light, however, the unwavering truth what families endure who have husbands, fathers, sons, or other loved ones missing in action or held prisoner. We must never forget the MIA and POW from all our wars—they may be, or are dreaming of coming home.

Franz X. Beisser, III